Tarantella

Kathy —
Thank you so much
for supporting my
literary dream!
Keep dancing —

A. T. O'Hara

Tarantella

Scot T. O'Hara

OhBoy Books
Chicago, IL

Tarantella by Scot T. O'Hara
Copyright © 2017 Scot T. O'Hara

OhBoy Books
400 East Ohio Street, #1602
Chicago, IL 60611
www.OhBoyBooks.com

ISBN-13: 9780997013436
ISBN: 0997013435

Printed in the United States of America

Other works published by OhBoy Books:
The Dandelion Cloud by Dale Boyer
No Justice! by Judith C. Handschuh

For Angelina and Jerry O'Hara, who always supported my writing dreams.

And for Dolly, who makes my life beautiful.

Death ends a life,
but it does not end a relationship,
which struggles on in the survivor's mind
toward some resolution which it
may never find.

—— ROBERT ANDERSON

The day the child realizes that all adults are
imperfect,
he becomes an adolescent;
the day he forgives them, he becomes an adult;
the day he forgives himself, he becomes wise.

—— ALDEN NOWLAN

CHAPTER 1

Death

Chicago: November 1994

POP DIED IN his bed at Cape Canaveral Hospital in Florida the day after Thanksgiving, 1994. After thirty-five years, the least significant thing separating us that morning was the thousand miles between Cape Canaveral and Chicago. No voice had called out to me in my dreams, and I awoke that morning with no sense of loss—only a satisfied, rested sigh.

The previous night, my younger sister Rosalia cried as she described Pop's precarious condition. It was the first time I ever heard her cry. She begged me to fly down immediately to join the rest of my family at Pop's bedside. Although I promised her I'd think about it, I really had no intention of rushing to Pop's side. I had done that with disastrous results after his first heart attack six months earlier. I convinced myself Pop was too ornery to die after this attack—just as he had been too ornery to die after his first attack. I thought I'd stall a few days to remind him he couldn't just expect me to come running every time he got sick.

That night, after talking to Rosalia, I turned off all the lights in my living room and stood in front of my window looking out across the Chicago skyline from the seventeenth floor. Only the pale, yellowish glow from the city streets below filtered into the room. As I sipped from a glass of wine I'd poured to calm my nerves, I conjured up thoughts of Pop and the rest of my family: Ma, Rosalia, Paddy, and Doughna Mira. Memories of my youth and home in Florida—the scene of so many defining moments in my life—tripped through my head: the kitchen where I had waited until the middle of a hurricane to defiantly declare I was gay; the hall bathroom where Pop had rinsed the blood from Rosalia's hands and feet; the bedroom where Pop slapped the dream out of me; and the rock garden out front with the rattlesnake coiled inside.

I was barely awake when Rosalia, sobbing, called with news of Pop's death and the old, familiar feeling of failure swept over me as it always did where Pop was concerned. After assuring her I would come for Pop's funeral, I hung up the phone and slammed my fist into the sofa cushion, cursing aloud.

"Damn it," I said. "Damn. Damn. Damn." My voice failed, but my jaws kept mouthing the words. I pictured Pop as I remembered him, but in the memories, he seemed somehow less threatening—sadder, older, more fallible. I had screwed up again.

I felt angry and confused. What was I supposed to feel? Could I feel loss for this man I despised? Why should I care if he lived or died? Why, in God's name, should I go back for his funeral when we had barely spoken—except to fight—for over a decade?

Outside my window, flurries drifted skyward in the updraft generated by my apartment building. I considered the significance of the snow falling up. Ma would find all sorts of omens in it and see it as a sign. Perhaps she would be right. Perhaps it was a sign. And yet, I thought, perhaps the snow wasn't really rising. Perhaps I was falling.

I arranged to return the next day to Merritt Island, where Pop would be buried in the hot Florida sand. Long ago, I had convinced myself that I would never—could never—feel anything for Pop again. But I was wrong. As I climbed into bed the night after Pop's death, emotions welled up in me like water from the Florida soil, if you dig down deep enough.

CHAPTER 2

Pop

Chicago: May 1994

POP HAD HIS first heart attack in the spring of 1994. I had arrived at home late from my job as an editor for a small Chicago paper, cursing the Chicago cold that was lingering so late into the season. Even after six years, I had not acclimated to the weather. As I slipped my key in the lock, I heard the muffled ring of my phone. I hastily flung open the door, gashing my knuckle on the jagged key. I winced as I hurried in and snatched the phone from its hook.

"Hello." I said as I put my wounded finger in my mouth to suck.

"Anthony?" I recognized Rosalia's voice. "Is that you?"

"Yes, it's me." I tasted the salty flavor of my blood and held my finger in front of my face, scrutinizing it and trying to disguise the annoyance I felt.

"Anthony, thank God I caught you. I didn't know if anyone called you yet," she paused, hesitating uncertainly. "Pop's had a heart attack." She blurted. "Ma called an ambulance and they took him to the hospital this morning."

Tarantella

My chest tightened. In the foyer mirror, I saw my mouth open and shut in shock, like a man who had been shot in the chest. My hair was plastered to my forehead from the misty rain falling outside. I felt the cold trickle of water dripping down my spine and fumbled for the support of the wall behind me. Although I saw my fingers braced against the wall, I felt as if I were falling into a dark hole. After a moment, I heard the erratic whistle of my own breathing and Rosalia in my ear again asking, "Anthony, are you okay?"

"Okay," I repeated. "Yeah, I'm okay." I slid to the floor with my back against the hard, unyielding wall. My nostrils filled with the pungent aroma of the vanilla potpourri carpet freshener I used. It reminded me of the cookies my grandmother used to bake. How ridiculous, I thought, that I should think I smelled cookies baking while Pop lay dying.

"Anthony, what's wrong? Are you still there?" She sounded like a frightened child.

"I'm here," I said, trying to focus on her words. "Jesus! How is he?"

"I'm not sure. We're still at the hospital waiting for the doctor to talk to us. Ma's a nervous wreck, though. She just went down for a cup of coffee and a smoke, so I thought I'd call you." Rosalia was trying to seem strong, but I knew her voice well enough to recognize her fear. "The doctors don't seem to know much yet. Ma thinks he looks a little better than when he first got here, but maybe that's wishful thinking. I think you should get down here right away."

"What good would it do?" I asked.

"Jesus Christ, Anthony!" Rosalia snapped. "When your father's dying, you don't ask questions, you just come. Don't the two of you *ever* stop? Can't you just put your anger aside for once? If you can't do it for yourself, come for the family."

"I didn't say I wouldn't come," I protested and changed the subject. "Tell me what happened." I pictured Pop as he was the last time I'd seen him—yelling and shaking his fist, his red face framed by his white hair, his blue eyes crackling with rage. It's a miracle he hadn't given himself a heart attack years ago.

"I don't know exactly," she said. "He was working in the yard. You know how he is with his damned palm trees."

I knew. I had once accused Pop of loving his palm trees more than he loved me. Maybe that was because he could control the trees, ensuring his private grove looked perfect. If a palm tree started growing crooked, he'd fasten a rope to it to straighten it out. If that didn't work, he'd lop it down and replace it with a new seedling. Passersby would stop their cars as they drove past Pop's yard, pointing and gaping at the magnificent and unexpected stand of queen palms in our yard. Pop had not been as skilled at controlling his children.

"He'll be okay," I reassured her reflexively. I knew she could tell I was just offering empty words, but she accepted my reassurance nonetheless. "He's too tough to die."

"So, will you come?" Her voice sounded frail.

I hesitated involuntarily. I didn't know what to say. I didn't want to go—didn't know what I'd say to Pop if I did go. I thought again about the last time I'd seen Pop: I had told him and Ma I was moving to Chicago. We had ended up shouting at one another and I had stormed out, yelling that he'd never have to worry about seeing his "fag son" again. How could I go back now? I cradled my head in my hands and wedged the phone between my shoulder and my ear. A small smear of blood streaked the wall where I must have brushed my finger against it.

"Anthony? Did you hear me?" she repeated. "I need you."

"Does *Pop* need me?" I snapped, suddenly angry about being forced to decide. "Has *he* asked for me?"

"Come on, Anthony," she said. "Don't start. He hasn't asked for *anyone*. There aren't any hidden layers of meaning here. He's too out of it for it to mean anything."

It means something. I winced. *It sure as hell means something to me.*

Looking up, I was startled to see Steven, my lover, standing over me in the foyer, toweling his hair dry from a shower. Stripped to the waist, Steven's tan chest, with a sprig of dark hair at its center, drew my eyes. He looked younger than his thirty years, his body firm and muscled, and I had trouble focusing on Rosalia's words in my ear with him looming over me. I hurried to end the call.

"Okay, Rosalia, I give up. I'll be there tomorrow. As soon as I can get a flight out." I handed the receiver to Steven. As he hung it back on its hook and I thought about facing Pop, the sensation of falling into a dark hole swept over me again. Steven shook his strawberry-blond curls and looked away, his gaze lingering on the bloody smear on the wall. The slatted late afternoon light fell across his body in stripes.

"What the hell's going on now?" he demanded. "Did I hear you right? You're going to Florida to see your folks? Can you really be that stupid? Well, don't even think about asking me to come along. I'm not going to see that son of a bitch."

"Give me a break," I said. "Pop had a heart attack. What the hell do you want me to do? He could die."

"You should be so lucky," he said, returning to the living room.

I watched his receding figure, feeling oddly relieved by the increasing distance between us. When he was close, I felt like he sucked all the oxygen from the room.

The taut denim of his blue jeans shifted across his buttocks as he walked away. Even after ten years together, I still found Steven incredibly sexy and he knew it. The light seeping in from the living room window silhouetted his body, making his shoulders look even broader and his waist even smaller, like an idealized male form that Michelangelo might have sculpted. He disappeared into our bedroom, banging the door shut behind him. I felt guilty for thinking about Steven's body while Pop might be dying.

I thought about leaving Steven behind to return to Pop and Merritt Island, back where I had not ventured since Rosalia's wedding a dozen years ago. If the roles were reversed, I had little doubt that I would have accompanied him, and he would have *expected* my support. His refusal was more a rejection of me and my need for him than a desire to avoid Pop. In light of the problems we'd been having lately, how could I have expected him to join me? Yet, I felt something tear deep inside me with his refusal.

I looked at my body—small, hairy, unmuscled. I had inherited Pop's depressingly ordinary body. I noticed the blue ink splotches staining my hands like bruises from the editing markers I used in the newsroom all day and recalled how Pop's hands, too, had been ink-stained from keeping his accounting ledgers. Often, Pop would arrive home from work and head directly for the bathroom to wash his hands. But it wasn't until years later— after we had moved to Florida and Pop had retired—that the ink finally faded and, for the first time, Pop's unblemished hands appeared, pink and ugly, like a pair of small, hairless animals. They seemed emptier without their purplish spots, crueler somehow.

I fingered the spots on my palms, thinking about how they marked me as Pop's son, like an inky birthmark. I thought about Pop lying in a bed at Cape Canaveral Hospital. Was I ready to see him again? Would he want me to come? Or would we end up right where we were before his attack—at each other's throats? I could never please Pop, and he never missed an opportunity to remind me of my failings.

I stood up and started to follow Steven into the bedroom, then stopped, and returned to the kitchen. From the cabinet beside the stove, I retrieved our phone book and found the heading for "Airlines."

Only after I booked a flight for the next morning did I head into the bedroom to confront Steven. He pulled on a powder-blue shirt, then stood spread-eagled in front of the mirror above our black-lacquered dresser, combing his hair and spraying it into place.

"Your hair was already perfect," I said as I closed the door behind me and sat on the edge of the bed. "But then, you knew that."

"So, when are you leaving?" he asked, turning to face me as he nonchalantly undid his pants and tucked in his shirt.

"Tomorrow," I said. "Early. I wish you'd change your mind and join me. It'd make me feel a lot better to have you along." Even *I* wasn't quite sure I believed this.

"I already said no." He zipped his pants, then rechecked his hair in the mirror. "Besides, I think we could use the time apart, if you know what I mean."

"And if Pop dies?" I asked. "Will you come down for his funeral?"

"Then, we'll see," he said noncommittally. "Anyhow, I'm about to head into work. I'll say goodbye to you now, so you don't have to wake me in the morning." He gave me a quick, passionless kiss on the cheek and headed into the adjoining bathroom.

I laid back on the bed and rubbed my eyes with my fingers. I could hear Steven brushing his teeth in the bathroom. After a moment, the water went off and I looked up as the bathroom door opened. He headed directly for the bedroom door, paused briefly, and turned back to face me before exiting.

"Have a good trip. I hope everything turns out okay." He gave a curt wave of his hand, then closed the door behind him. As I listened for the sound of the apartment door closing, I smelled the sweet fragrance of Polo cologne drifting out of the bathroom.

I hope so too, I thought. *And not just in Florida.*

The clock on the dash of the rental car registered 1:45 the following afternoon as I passed the Merritt Island marker at the crest of the Hubert Humphrey Bridge over the Indian River. The island, located between the Indian and Banana rivers, stretches over forty miles from north to south and nearly eight miles across at its widest point. I first glimpsed the island in 1972, at the age of fourteen. Pop had abruptly decided to move the family to Florida after a particularly nasty New York winter. The view from atop this bridge had stunned me then: the dense green of the island beckoned from the east like an oasis. Once again, despite all the pain it represented, I felt a surge of emotion at the sight, a sense that the center of my being somehow drew its life from this island, like a tap root running from Chicago to Florida.

As I crossed the bridge this day, white-capped waves and sailboats zigzagged across the river. I wrinkled my nose in revulsion as the oily smell of rotting fish drifted up from the remains of the old Indian River Bridge, part of which had been left as a fishing pier beneath the towering new structure. A moment later, as I drove off the bridge and onto the island, the sweet fragrance of purple jacaranda replaced the stench of rotting fish. The syrupy scent and the sight of the First Baptist

Church unleashed a burst of memories. I had once been infatuated with a boy named Tommy, who attended this church. He made me a gift of the *King James Bible* and I felt a thrill each time I opened its gilt-edged pages and thought of Tommy's blond hair and wide, earnest green eyes. In his church that day, all I could think about was Tommy. I heard barely a word of the sermon, only savored the hug of greeting he had given me when he saw that I had come. I sat with my head down, stricken again by the familiar sense that I was committing a sin by being here in this alien church where God wasn't Catholic; that I was betraying my faith and my family out of my lust for Tommy; that I was consumed with evil for feeling these feelings for another boy. I hurried out of the church before the service ended, making up some excuse about having to get home, but assuring Tommy that I had enjoyed the sermon and would give serious thought to converting. On my way out, I picked a jacaranda from the church garden. Its blossom smelled sweetly illicit, this flower I had stolen from Tommy and his church. I carried it home with me and hid it between the pages of *King James*.

Crossing the island today, I passed the many shops that bordered State Road 520, the main thoroughfare across the center of the island. A little further on, I passed Sykes Creek, a broad waterway that ran down the middle of the island. Dozens of anhingas perched, as always, on jutting branches that overhung the creek to the north. They dotted the low-hanging branches of the trees and shrubs that lined the water's edge like shimmering purplish eggplants, sunning themselves in the midday heat with their blue-black, glistening wings outstretched and their heads tossed back. Their serpentine necks coiled across their backs like long, poisonous black moccasins, hence the name they were known by locally: snakebirds. I remembered once being told anhingas migrate in "kettles" and I always visualized kettles seething with black snakes. Deep, booming grunts sounded and reverberated from the hiding places of alligators in the marshy fringes of the creek. I felt, as I often had as a child, like I was travelling through some primordial swamp.

Continuing east across the island on the way to the hospital, I passed the bait shop and heard the sharp blast of a barge on the Banana River. I glanced again at the time, 1:53—only eight short minutes to cross the island it had taken me a lifetime to escape. The soft, pink coquina of Cape Canaveral Hospital emerged from the river on my left like a giant conch shell. I swung down the entrance drive and slipped into a parking space, then cut off the engine and leaned back in the seat. Taking a deep breath, I sat for several minutes watching a white-tufted egret wading gingerly just off-shore. The lone, frail-looking creature cocked its head first left, then right. Failing to find what it was looking for, it hopped into the air and flapped off to the north. Somewhere in that direction, I thought, lay Chicago, where, only a little over three-and-a-half hours ago, I had begun this odyssey. Now, here I was about to enter a hospital, about to try to make peace with a man with whom peace seemed impossible. I wanted to feel something for Pop—knew I *should* feel something. But I didn't. Perhaps I couldn't.

What I did feel as I stepped out of the car was a powerful sense of obligation that had compelled me to come here, a world and a lifetime away from the day before. I felt numb as I headed for the entrance. *He's dying*, I told myself. *Just play the dutiful son: make all the right motions and get the hell out of here. Make the rest of the family happy. Then, you can finally put all this behind you and live your own life in peace. But how could a lie bring peace? How could I live with myself if I let Pop think he'd won?*

I paused in front of the hospital entrance, ran a hand through my hair, and stepped inside. Noticing the hospital gift shop across the hall, I cursed as I realized I hadn't brought anything to give Pop when I saw him. I slipped inside and searched hurriedly for a passable offering, a gesture of good faith, but nothing so sincere that I would feel I had surrendered. I skipped by the "World's Greatest Dad" plaques, past the rich Cadbury chocolate bars I knew Pop loved. Near the end of one aisle, I spotted a display of white, men's terry-cloth robes and snatched one off the shelf. Pop had always refused to wear robes, said "only sissies wear robes." My family would see it as a nice gesture, but Pop would recognize my ambivalence. I had the clerk wrap it for me, then tucked it under my arm and headed to the front desk for directions to Pop's room.

The elevator plinked to announce my arrival on Pop's floor. When the doors parted, I glanced down the long, bright hall. A lone nurse in a white uniform sipped coffee and leaned on one elbow across the desk. I fought back a sudden urge to stay on the elevator, to return to the first floor, to flee. However, I stepped into the hallway and headed for Pop's room. I could feel my pulse quickening as I drew closer. *Why, exactly, am I here?* I thought again about turning back, but I forced myself forward to Pop's room and roughly palmed his door—too roughly, I realized, as it flew open and banged against the wall.

My dramatic entry failed to disturb Pop, who looked surprisingly frail and small on the large bed. Beside him, a thick shock of sunlight slipped through his open window and spilled across the foot of his bed. The TV opposite the bed was on low, murmuring softly. My eyes focused on a cluster of gray-white flecks of dust, hovering like mosquitoes in the patch of sun.

Stepping closer, I studied Pop briefly from the bedside. His limp body was curled in a fetal position and his breathing was so shallow I detected no rise or fall in the sheets atop his chest. The skin on his face was tinged by the pallor of death, so ashen and thin it had turned nearly translucent, revealing a delicate web of throbbing blue veins that spidered across his cheeks and temples. The pulsing of these veins revealed that life continued inside Pop's fragile body. He looked not so much like a man as he did like an overripe, bruised fruit—a banana detached from its vine, consuming its own skin to survive. This Pop seemed so unlike the Pop who peopled my memories: vigorous and larger than life, cowing me with only a look or a gesture. The thinness of his skin gave Pop a sheen of alabaster, like royalty. I reached down to touch him, yet held back at the last, afraid both of waking and bruising him. I startled myself, for I had never stopped to consider that I might be capable of bruising Pop. I noticed Pop's left eye, where the surrounding bone had shrunk back after an auto accident in his youth, leaving the socket oversized and imprinting his face with a permanent, raised-eyebrow look of doubt. All my life, I had never known whether Pop trusted me, because of this disapproving countenance.

I turned to examine the equipment stacked beside Pop's bed. A gray box with an oval screen blipped intermittently as a green slash arced across its glassy surface, moving from left to right and angling up from the bottom of the screen for a moment. It rose halfway up the screen, then plummeted back to the bottom again, before blipping and repeating itself. For a moment, I watched, transfixed by Pop's heartbeat pattern flashing on the screen. A bag of clear fluid dangled from a metallic stand near the head of Pop's bed, slowly dripping its contents down a slender tube that snaked and vanished beneath Pop's bed linens. Another bag hung from the bed rails. A bright, yellow liquid dribbled into the bag from a second tube, and I realized, with a start, that this was Pop's urine.

I cleared my throat to announce my presence, as if sounding a warning, so that Pop wouldn't be so startled by my presence.

Pop stirred and turned groggily toward me. He looked flaccid and old and I felt unexpectedly moved by the obvious decline in his vigor. He used to make me tremble by merely raising his hand. The white blanket slid off his bare, freckled shoulders. I could see the gray hairs that sprouted from his saggy chest protruding over the top of the blanket—gray hairs that once were thick and black like my own. Pop's small, wizened face regarded me through listless blue eyes. His oversized left eye seemed to gape at me doubtfully, as if uncertain whether I was real or a specter from his dreams.

"What the hell *you* doing here?" He asked in a voice harsher than I had expected.

"You're sick," I said. "I came to make peace. Don't you think it's time?"

Suddenly aware of the weight in my arms, I remembered his gift and held it out to him. Nodding at the package, I said, "I brought you something."

Pop glanced at the shiny package encircled with a turquoise ribbon and then back at me, staring me in the eye pointedly. He pulled the white blanket snugly up to his neck and folded his pale, fleshy arms over his chest, steepling his fingers without accepting the package I offered.

"So," he said at last, shrugging his shoulders, "the prodigal son's come home to make peace after all these years. I s'pose you expect me to just go along with you?"

"Come on, Pop," I said, reoffering the package. I was taken aback by his immediate distrust. Perhaps my motives *weren't* the purest, but I didn't want to fight. "Let's let bygones be bygones. I know we can't change what's been said and done in the past, but can't we put it behind us and try to start fresh again with each other?"

"That's a nice speech," he said, his voice flat and raspy. He closed his eyes and remained silent for so long I began to think he had drifted back to sleep. "I s'pose we could try," he said at last. His eyelids parted and he stared at me until I had to look away.

I set the package gently on his chest. Pop wrinkled his nose as if he smelled shit. I recalled the same expression on his face when, long ago, I had timidly offered him a sheaf of school papers, saying, "I want to show these to you, Pop. I got an A." I was eight.

"An A on a couple of papers don't mean much," he'd said, and grasped the ends of the newspaper tented across his knees, shaking it into an upright position between us. "Show me your report card when it comes. That's the only thing that means something." He then thrust one hand out from behind his paper and waved me off, dismissively fanning the air. "Don't bug me when I'm reading the paper."

I didn't cry until I got back to my room, out of Pop's sight. Then, I flung myself onto my bed and shredded the papers Pop had rejected, vowing never again to care what Pop thought.

Pop laid his white hand, tagged with the hospital's ID bracelet, atop the package and regarded me with a creased forehead and a dubious pout on his lips. He blinked his oversized eyeball suspiciously and paused a beat, as if resting after exertion.

"What's this?" he asked finally. "Some sort of peace offering? You coulda made your peace without this."

"I know that, Pop," I said. "I just wanted to bring you something since I haven't seen you in so long."

"You didn't have to come, you know," He said, shifting to a more upright position and propping the tiny, flat hospital pillow beneath him. I started to assist him, but he put out his hand to stop me. "No, I can do it. I'm not totally helpless yet. Is that why you're really here? Because you thought you *had* to come?"

"Of course not. I'm here because I *wanted* to come," I said, stepping back indignantly. "What son wouldn't come to see his Pop in the hospital?"

Pop again turned his dead eyes on me until I looked away, searching for a place to sit so I could hide the discomfort of standing there while he stared at me. A painting of blood-red roses in a pale vase hung on the wall beside the door. Beneath the painting was a chair. I dragged it over to Pop's bedside, scraping it noisily across the flecked white floor, and sat down. I turned back toward Pop, who was now staring distrustfully at the package, unsure of what to make of it.

"Aren't you gonna open it?" I motioned to the box.

Pop drummed his bony-knuckled, freckled fingers on the package. My thoughts were suddenly interrupted by the sound of Ma's whiskey-tenor voice in the hallway.

"Where is my husband's doctor? You said he'd stop by over an hour ago." The door burst open and Ma stood in the doorway. I could see her silhouetted by the bright hall lights. Not even five feet tall, she looked like an oversized doll with a too-loud, Bette Davis voice. She faced out into the hallway and shook her fist emphatically, causing her waist-length auburn hair—still without a speck of gray—to cascade over her shoulders and down her back like flames. "Well, let him know we're still waiting. I guess he thinks we've got nothing better to do." As she shut the door behind her, she gathered her hair in her hands and flounced it across her shoulders. She turned and headed towards Pop's bed.

"Those doctors just think they can keep you waiting all day. Now the nurse is saying it'll be another hour—" Her fiery brown eyes lit on me, seated beside Pop's bed. Her expression shifted from a scowl into a broad grin as she flung out her arms and rushed towards me. "Anthony!" she practically shrieked as I stood to meet her. She tipped up on her toes and we kissed and traded hugs. She touched my cheeks with her warm, olive hands that smelled of smoke. She glanced back at Pop. "You came! I knew you would."

"Of course I came, Ma," I said. "Didn't Rosalia tell you I was coming?"

She turned back to face me. "I haven't talked to Rosalia since last night, but she'll probably stop by here later. She's at work now."

Ma turned to Pop and gestured at me. "I told you he'd come."

"Yeah, you did, didn't you?" Pop cocked a bushy white eyebrow. He held up the package I had brought. "He brung this for me. I guess he figures I might croak."

"Come on, honey. Be nice. He came a thousand miles for you." Ma opened the small, black leather purse she held in her left hand. After rifling through its contents briefly, she pulled out a gold-and-white pack of cigarettes, tapped one out, and inserted it into her mouth. She began fumbling through her purse again.

"That's right." Pop agreed in a wry voice, flashing a too-brief smile. "He came a thousand miles for me. To make peace. Isn't that something? Who woulda guessed?"

I felt my smile vanish and my back straighten, but I held my tongue, reminding myself how guilty I'd feel if Pop died and our last words were angry.

"Now, honey." Ma intervened to head off a fight. "Why don'tcha open your gift?" Her cigarette bobbed in her mouth as she spoke. Locating her lighter, she pulled it from her purse. She noticed me frowning. "What's wrong?"

"You can't smoke in here, Ma," I said, and pointed at her cigarettes.

"Oh, shit. I keep forgetting." She yanked the cigarette out of her mouth and rolled it between her fingers, as if trying to decide whether to flout the rules. "I don't know what the hell difference it makes."

Pop ignored us and shifted the package back onto his belly. He tore at the wrapping, peeling it back to reveal a box labeled "Man's Robe: White. One size fits all." He eyed me for a moment, then blinked.

"I already have a robe," he said, finally.

Ma said nothing, only frowned, and returned her cigarette to its package.

I felt Pop's eyes on me; felt my skin burning; felt Pop trying to analyze my guilty reaction. *Why had I even bought him something?*

"You can have more than one," I said, attempting to regain my composure and evade Pop's stare. "Consider this one your hospital robe."

"That's right," Ma agreed brightly. "You can never have too many robes." She picked up the box and examined it, saying, "And this one's real nice and fluffy."

Pop narrowed his eyes and examined the robe more closely, then pointed at the label. "He bought it downstairs," he said, sounding triumphant. "Lookit the label. I recognize it cuz that's where the nurse got that one for me." He pointed to a robe hanging on the back of the door to his room. He looked wounded. This time, I felt his pain—felt guilty because the gift *was* an afterthought, and here he was, maybe dying. *What was I thinking?* Instead of making amends, I already sensed that my visit was reinforcing our separateness. I had never been able to communicate with Pop, and his heart attack had done nothing to change that. Pop hadn't mellowed a bit. Neither had I.

"You shouldn't of wasted your money." Pop pushed the robe aside.

"Now, now," Ma tried to cut the sudden tension filling the room, but my blood pressure had shot up and I wasn't about to let Pop go unanswered.

"Don't start, Pop, okay? I made a mistake, but I *was* trying to make peace with you for God's sake. Look where it gets me." I jerked myself out of the chair and shoved it back against the wall. I was acting childish, but I didn't know how to save face except to defend myself, right or wrong. "Do you always have to tell me how I screwed up?" My words sounded as empty as they were. I reminded myself that I had come to mend fences so I could live with myself if Pop didn't recover. I tried to sidestep the argument I felt coming. "I don't want to fight with you, Pop."

"That's right," Ma said, rubbing her hands together frantically like a praying mantis as she stepped in between us. "I don't want no fighting today." She turned to Pop. "You're here to get better. And *you*," she said turning back to me, "shouldn't yell at him. He's your father."

Tarantella

Not missing a beat, Pop looked past Ma at me. "Why can't you just admit you got it downstairs? Nothin' wrong with that, 'cept you shouldn't be trying to kid yourself. I thought you was the one who insisted on everything being out in the open and honest? Like when you threw the way you live in our faces. If you're gonna sling shit, you better watch out for the splatter."

Pop rarely missed an opportunity to mention how I lived, ever since the day—fourteen years before—I had told him and Ma I was gay. He still insisted I had "chosen" to be gay deliberately and specifically as an attack on his masculinity. Once, in the heat of another argument, Pop had shouted, "I'm ashamed I gave birth to a faggot son! Maybe you shoulda died when you was born." I had spit at him and stormed out of the room. But, I had never been able to stop obsessing over his words—over the realization that Pop was ashamed of me, and wished I hadn't survived; that he thought my life was shit. Even now, years later, I'd never forgotten his words. It doesn't really matter what triggers the poison—there's no drawing it back.

"Why do you always have to dredge this shit up?" I wanted to fling the vase of flowers on the table beside Pop's bed at him. I resisted, saying only, "I told you I came to make peace and, sick as you are, you're all set to dump on me. Haven't we already had this fight? Dozens of times? Why can't we ever get past this goddamned subject?" I turned and took a series of deep breaths to calm myself. When I turned back, Ma stepped into the gulf between me and Pop.

"As a matter of fact, let's change the subject," Ma said, pulling a cigarette back out of the pack and sliding it into her mouth, then pulling it out again. "Did I tell you—"

"Maybe we can't get past this subject because you can't deal with anyone disagreeing with you. And, just maybe, you came back because you thought I was too sick to argue with your bullshit." Pop turned his back to me and addressed Ma. "You can't tell me you're happy about the way he lives either. I know better. But I ain't just gonna lay here and make like I like it."

Ma stepped back and put the unlit cigarette in her mouth and said nothing.

I looked from Ma to Pop. "You know, Pop, you don't pay my bills anymore. I don't live under your roof. I don't even live in the same goddamned state as you anymore. All because I didn't want to deal with you telling me how I should live my life. Frankly, Pop, I can't change 'the way I live,' as you put it. And, even if I could, I wouldn't because I like my life. You've got no right to tell me how to live or who to live with."

"Stop it!" Ma had rediscovered her voice. She clapped her hands at me. "Don't talk to your father that way."

"But it's okay for him to talk to me the way he does, right Ma? Why am I always the bad guy?" I pointed a finger at Pop. "He may be your husband," I said, then touched my own chest as I added, "but I'm your son. You seem to forget that. I don't need your approval to live my life and be who I am."

"I know," she said quietly. "You don't need nothing from us. You say so all the time. You don't care what we think. We gotta accept everything you do no matter what. And we're not *allowed* to say what we think cuz you don't want to hear it."

"I've struggled too hard and too long to accept myself the way I am to allow either of you to tear me back down," I said, shouting and gesticulating in their direction. "As far as I'm concerned, you only *do* have two choices: accept me the way I am, or lose me. I don't have any gray areas left in me, Ma. No half-ways. It's all or nothing, as far as I'm concerned. I won't accept anything less." I felt outraged at having to defend myself. This wasn't why I had come. *Why had I let Rosalia talk me into this? How could we make peace when our wounds were still so raw?* I considered storming out of the room, but I heard Rosalia's voice in my head, saying, "When your father's dying, you don't ask questions, you just come." Why didn't things ever seem so black-and-white to me?

I watched Ma holding Pop's hand and saw her keeping a careful eye on the oscilloscope. Pop looked at me steadily, but said nothing. Rosalia had said I should make peace with Pop for the good of the whole family. I calmed myself down again, took a deep breath, and decided to try a different approach.

"I'm here because I wanted to come, Pop. Rosalia said you almost died yesterday, so I came to see you."

"Yes," Pop agreed, nodding. "I can *see* how much you care." His quiet words cut through me like a knife blade.

I sputtered, enraged. "Well, I ain't here for my health. . .I'm *not* here for my health." I hurriedly corrected myself whenever I heard the echo of Pop's language in my words. The urge to leave nearly overpowered me, yet I stayed, knowing my family would never forgive me if Pop died after fighting with me.

"Yeah, that's right," Pop said, "I nearly forgot—you're here for *my* health." He turned and stared out of the window. I could see the nodules of his vertebrae protruding through the skin on his back, like a bony archipelago. "Well, you've seen me and I'm still kicking. So, why don'tcha just go back to Chicago now? No reason to stay. Sorry you wasted your time since it don't look like I'll be croaking this time." The oscilloscope beeped faster.

"You two just don't ever stop," Ma said. "All you ever have to say to each other is ugly. You're like two roosters in a cockfight—won't neither of you stop till you draw blood. I can't hardly stand either of yous anymore. How can you come in here and fight with your father when he's sick? Let it go, for once!" She glowered at us, as if daring either of us to defy her and continue our argument. She put her hand over Pop's heart as if to shield him. The beeping slowed again.

I looked at her standing in the splash of sunlight streaming through the window. She seemed more frightened and small, I thought, than threatening—like a rabbit bluffing to frighten off a fox. Her dark eyes flashed and shifted back and forth between Pop and me. The sunlight lit her hair like flames.

The accusation in Pop's words echoed in my ears, which burned on the sides of my head. A wave of nausea shook me, and I thought for a moment I might retch. I knew I should listen to Ma and ignore him, but couldn't, so I turned my back to Ma and faced Pop directly, pointing angrily.

"Are you asking me to go?"

"Stop," Ma said, quickly squeezing between me and Pop's bed. "Can't you let him alone? For God's sake, he's just had a heart attack! Do you wanna kill him?"

"That's *exactly* what he wants," Pop said. "But let him alone. It's time we had this out. Besides, it's the first time he's shown any balls in his life." He looked me in the eye and said, "Go or stay. Do whatever you gotta do."

"What do you want from me?" I asked. "Blood? You want me to leave? Just say the word and I'll be outta here." I thrust an accusing finger at him. "But don't ask me to come back again, 'cause I won't."

"You know, Anthony," Pop said, "I guess I just don't give a damn what you do. Isn't that exactly what you want from me? Just agree and go along with every fucking thing you do, whether I like it or not? I'm not supposed to have any goddamned opinions. Just shut up and accept everything without a peep. Well, fuck that shit."

I felt my hands reflexively form fists. *I could leave*, I thought again. *Even Rosalia would understand now.* But, sometimes, when you're falling, you can't walk away until you hit the bottom first.

"You're a selfish son of a bitch," I said and stomped to the window to put some space between us. "You know that?" I looked back at them. Ma had slipped her arm around Pop. It was as if they were braced against me.

"I came here to fix things between us, but you don't give a shit about that. All you want to do is tell me how much you disapprove of the way I live." I glanced out the window at the broad blue expanse of river below. "Well, save your breath, Pop. I already know." I turned back to face them.

"You came outta guilt," Pop said, "not to make peace. We both know it."

That stopped me. I watched the green blips course across the oscilloscope screen beside Pop's bed. We glowered at one another. I wished the fighting and screaming and the insistent beeping would cease; that the room would fall completely silent; that Pop would just disappear. I looked at him. He pulled his bedsheets up under his chin and turned on his side, drawing his arms and legs together in a fetal position. He looked feeble and old, and I felt a twinge of regret at the harshness of my words.

"I guess you want me to play the bad guy, here," Pop said at last in a weak voice that seemed to come from the hallway. "Just remember that it took you thirty-five years to accept the way you are. You gave us about thirty seconds." Ma sat on the edge of the bed and caressed his arm. He seemed like such a little shred of a man. How could he generate such anger in me? Why couldn't I just accept him? I wanted to touch him to see if he was real. But I hung back, unable to connect with him, sure that he would pull away from me if I tried. I remained standing in the window across the room from him and Ma, wishing that maybe—just maybe—Pop would look up at me and say, "Stay." I turned to face the window, letting the sun's heat bore into me.

"I guess our feelings don't matter to you," Pop said after a moment. "Maybe it *would* be better if you left."

I felt stung, afraid I might cry. I shook my head and recomposed myself, then turned to face them.

Tarantella

"So, you finally said it," I snapped. "I came all the way from Chicago to be here with you and you're sending me away. I should have had my head examined for thinking you'd ever change. Don't worry, Pop. You'll be fine. You have to *have* a heart to die from a heart attack."

"Anthony, stop it!" Ma took Pop's freckled hand in hers. "When did you get so cruel?"

"What do you expect after the way you two have always treated me?" I said. "Pop tears into me and you don't say a word. That's the way it's always been with us. Even when I was a little boy. You think you were just handing out advice, but you don't even listen to yourself. By not taking sides, you took sides, Ma. Don't you see?" I pointed at Pop. "You chose him over me."

"I can't believe you came down here to say these things now, when your father's in the hospital. I won't have this. You're tearing this family apart! You stop right now, or you go," she said, standing protectively between me and Pop. "I mean it, Anthony. You forget who you're talking to."

"No, Ma," I said, walking over to the head of Pop's bed. "I know *exactly* who I'm talking to. I'm talking to the man who made me feel worthless my whole life. And to the woman who let him do it and is still defending him."

"Don't," Ma said, putting her arm out in front of her. "Don't say these ugly things."

"Lookit how the palms is wilting." Pop said suddenly, as if he had lapsed into a trance. He was staring out the window almost as if he'd forgotten we were still in the room. "It's hot outside, and muggy. Nothin's moving. Ain't even no birds flying by. Not a one." He waved a white hand toward the window. From the head of his bed, I watched the loose skin on his back ripple over his spine with the motion. "They never seem to fly much when it gets so hot. The sun's out and it looks like a beautiful day, but it's hot and muggy and uncomfortable. It ain't the right time for no one to be doing nothing 'cept sitting in his own space, waiting for things to get back to normal. Ain't the time to fix things when they're at their worst. You ever noticed how that works?"

"Come on, Pop," I said. "If you got something to say, just *say* it." I reached down and gripped his shoulder, rolling him back to face me. "Just tell me if you want me here. That's all I want to know."

Pop swiped a hand across his eyes. He pursed and unpursed his lips. "You're an adult—you do whatever you want, Anthony. I was just saying that I don't know why you bothered to come."

"Fine," I said, abruptly standing. I shoved the robe box roughly off the end of his bed. It skidded onto the floor with a slap. "Remember that you told me to go, Pop, 'cause I won't be back. Ever! Paddy was a lot smarter than me, I guess. At least he had the sense to stay away after he left."

"Stop it." Ma stamped her foot and placed one hand on her forehead like she was taking her temperature. She turned away from me in dismissal and picked up the robe box from the floor. She placed it carefully on the bed and ran a hand over Pop's covers, smoothing the wrinkles out of the fabric.

Pop faced the window again; he had drawn his body up into a small, protective ball. "Ain't the time for fixing things when it's all messed up," he mumbled to himself.

Tarantella

Ma, looking alarmed, cradled Pop in her arms. "Anthony, please, just go. You can come back when you're *really* ready to make peace."

"I'll go, all right," I said, bolting for the door. "But I won't be back." I felt clammy and nauseous, and I had trouble making the door handle work.

"Don't say that, Anthony," Ma said. "Blood's thicker than water. This family's gotta stay together."

I gaped at her incredulously. "Why, Ma?" I asked. "Because we're so close? Because we're so full of love for each other? I don't think so." I flung the door open and stepped into the bright corridor. Holding the door ajar, I glanced back into the room and added, "Our blood is more like venom."

I didn't pause until I reached the elevator bank at the end of the long, white corridor and punched the elevator call button. *Did Ma and Pop love me?* I wondered as I waited. Did I *really* love them? I thought about how we had ended up fighting again, even though I had come here to patch things up and make peace. My stomach churned and sweat prickled my scalp. I couldn't be sure if I was getting sick, or just feeling guilty about how I had behaved with Ma and Pop.

The elevator doors opened with a ping and I stepped inside the dark, empty box. When the doors closed, I felt suddenly trapped—trapped in this descending box and trapped in my life. The elevator stopped abruptly and opened on the first floor. I exited, wishing I could transport myself to another life as easily as the elevator had moved between floors.

I stepped outside the hospital, anticipating the relief I would feel, but instead, experienced a growing sense of discomfort. The air felt heavy on my skin: hot and sticky. I began to worry again that I might vomit. Pop had been right about one thing: the time for fixing things was *not* when things were at a crisis. You can't assess the damage until after the disaster. Only then can you figure out what it'll take to fix things. What would it take to repair this damage? For a second, I looked up, but couldn't distinguish Pop's window from the others on this wing.

I hurried toward the rental car, consumed by a nearly over-whelming urge to flee, to return to Chicago and Steven. But I felt uncertain about my life in Chicago, too. My relationship with Steven offered no guarantees, and I felt a growing sense of un-ease. I found myself daydreaming frequently about leaving every-thing and running away to some place where no one knew me; a place where Ma and Pop and Steven couldn't find me.

I leaned against the steering column, replaying the exchange with Ma and Pop. They were right about one thing, at least: I *had* expected blind support and automatic acceptance. Was that so unreasonable? I was their son. Why should they need time to accept me? Didn't they realize the longer they took, the more rejected I felt?

I started the car's engine, suddenly realizing that, by now, Rosalia would be wondering where I was. I turned out of the parking lot and sped towards her apartment. Perhaps talking to Rosalia would assuage my growing sense of nausea, of panic.

Rosalia had become the bridge between me and my family. When I had considered going my own way and forgetting my family, Rosalia held me fast as an anchor, preventing me from permanently leaving the harbor.

"Pop's just being Pop," she told me, after I recounted my exchange with Pop. "He doesn't know how else to be. Jesus Christ, Anthony, he's going on seventy years old—it's a little late to expect him to change."

"I'm so tired of hearing that," I said. "It's the great cop-out: 'I'm too old to change.' Well, sometimes you've *gotta* change, or else things change around you, and you get caught in the backwash."

"Come on, Anthony," Rosalia said. "It's Pop we're talking about, not some damned computer. You can't treat your father like that. You gotta understand, he doesn't see it like you do. Pop wants you to be the way he imagined you'd be."

"Yeah, straight," I snapped.

"Okay," she said, begrudgingly, "that's part of it. But he also wants you to be happy and healthy and successful. To him, your being gay makes all those other things impossible."

"Oh, come off it, Rose," I said. "I can be gay and still be happy, healthy, and successful."

"*You* know that, and *I* know that," she said, "but Pop doesn't. And Ma doesn't. They grew up in a different time, and maybe they need to open their eyes—"

"And their narrow minds," I interrupted.

"Whatever," she said, frustration plain in her voice. "I *know* you understand what I'm saying, even if you don't want to hear it and don't like it. Things were different for Ma and Pop, and you don't instantly unlearn all the stuff you were raised to believe was true. It takes time and patience, and sticking with them when you don't think they'll ever get it. Jesus, Anthony, they're your parents, for God's sake. You can't just forget about them or pretend they don't exist."

"Why not?" I asked. "They seem happier that way. Besides, Paddy did it. Maybe he had the right idea: running away."

"I know you," she said. "You couldn't have lived with yourself if you'd done that. Besides, we don't even know what happened to Paddy. Maybe he's regretted it all his life. And, believe it or not, Ma and Pop aren't happier without you. They love you even if you can't seem to see it or accept it. Just give them a chance to come around."

"Why *me*? Why can't *they* make the effort this time? I'm tired of always being the one to compromise."

"I know," she said, sighing. "I know. Well then, just try not slamming the door forever. Keep it open—a crack at least. You can't reconnect if you aren't around. Maybe that's the lesson Paddy taught us."

After settling in at Rosalia's, I thought about her words. Had I closed the door for good this time, fighting with Ma and Pop at what might be Pop's deathbed? Even if Pop recovered, how could we ever put this behind us? Was I fooling myself to think things could ever be right between my family and me? Was I so hard to love?

Perhaps the failing was in *me*. Even Steven had changed toward me—grown distant and cooler. Lately, it seemed like we ended up fighting every time we were together, which, with Steven's job, had grown less and less frequent—a fact I think we both had begun to appreciate. But wasn't it wise to close and lock your door if what's on the other side might hurt you? Then, again, was something wrong with me? Was I the one filled with poison?

Surely, I thought as I reflected on it, I'm not too late to save myself. Surely, an antidote existed.

Ma

Rochester, NY: 1958

I'VE HAD A hole in the middle of my chest since the day I was born. My brother Paddy used to say it was a "hole in your soul." At my birth, the doctors folded me in half like a piece of bread, cracking my sternum. Perhaps this hollow where my breastbone should be proves I lack some essential piece that others take for granted— perhaps the piece that would have bonded me to my family.

My older brother, Paddy, told me once, before he ran away, that he never believed Ma was really having a baby when I was born. When Ma's belly had started swelling, she had jokingly told him she was growing a monster inside her, and he believed her. Later, when she and Pop told him it was really a baby growing inside her, he said he didn't believe them. "At night, I'd dream about Ma's belly popping open and a big monster leaping out and swallowing me whole while she and Pop watched and laughed. I began to wish that thing in Ma's belly would just go away. That's why I was so afraid of you being born. I was afraid you would swallow me up." At this point, Paddy had looked up at me with a funny grin on his face, then said, "In a way, I was right."

I have stitched the fabric of my birth story together from snippets shared over the years variously by Paddy, Doughna Mira, and my parents. On the day of my birth, Paddy said Ma and Pop seemed upset. Ma's pains kept getting stronger and more frequent. "This kid's gonna be a heller," Ma said between pains. "They say the way you come into this world is the way you'll live your whole life."

Paddy said he mostly remembered Ma yelling and snow swirling outside the car. "The headlights looked like they were shining on this long, white sheet that was hanging a couple inches in front of the car and moving with us. Pop kept saying he couldn't go no faster and leaning farther and farther over the steering wheel to see better, until his breath started fogging up the windshield."

On the way, they dropped Paddy off at my grandmother's house. We all called my grandmother "Doughna Mira" ever since the day Paddy, just two at the time, mistakenly called her "Doughna" instead of "Nonna," the Italian word for grandmother. The name stuck because Doughna was always speckled with flour from the loaves of bread dough rising on her counter or baking in her oven. Doughna lived with my Aunt Pee, Ma's oldest sister and my godmother. Aunt Pee's real name was Philomena, but everyone had called her Pee since she was a little girl. Their house was on the way to the hospital. Ordinarily, a few-minutes' drive, this trip had taken more than an hour in the snowstorm.

Paddy said Doughna Mira and Aunt Pee rushed outside when Pop's car pulled into the driveway. After Aunt Pee took Paddy by the hand, Doughna squeezed into the back seat and told Ma and

Pop, "I'm going with you to the hospital and no one better try to stop me."

No one tried to stop her.

It took them another two hours to get to the hospital and Dr. Blanca didn't arrive until an hour after that. By then, Ma's labor pains were already long and deep and wrenching. Doughna said the doctor let her stay with Ma in the delivery room, but told Pop, "Men don't have any sense when babies are being born," and chased him out to the waiting room. When Pop left, Dr. Blanca told Doughna Mira he thought Ma might have twins because she was so big; but after examining her, he said she'd hardly dilated.

"This could be a long night," he warned her and headed off for a cup of coffee. "I'll be back in a little while."

Ma's labor dragged on through the night, hour after hour, just as her pregnancy had dragged on for ten months. I have always wondered if, even then, I had sensed the danger that awaited me there in that tunnel between womb and life, and had tried to evade it by delaying my birth.

As Ma's labor pains intensified, Doughna Mira said Ma began shrieking at Dr. Blanca, insisting that something was wrong, that this birth wasn't at all like Paddy's birth. Doughna Mira said she sensed something was wrong, too, although Dr. Blanca told them both to stop worrying. But his face showed his own concern. Dr. Blanca kept checking and rechecking his instruments and sighing. Finally, he shook his head and told Ma her intuition was right.

"I thought you were having twins, but I was wrong. You're having just one baby. A very large baby," he said at last. "Much larger than I expected. Maybe the biggest we've ever seen in this hospital."

"What's that mean?" Ma asked. "Is that a problem?"

"Just how big are we talking?" Doughna Mira asked as she stroked Ma's hair.

"Now, ladies," Dr. Blanca reassured, "don't panic. There's nothing to worry about. We'll take care of you. But we may have to break your pelvis to ensure we can get the baby out safely."

"Can't you do a C-section?" Ma asked, obviously frightened.

"No," Dr. Blanca said, "it's too late for that. We're just going to have to help it along. We'll give you a spinal to ease the pain as soon as we can." He put his arm gently around Doughna Mira. "I'm afraid you're going to have to leave the delivery room now. Why don't you go out with Nurse Ann and tell Seamus what's happening?" He turned his attention back to Ma.

Nurse Ann and Doughna Mira found Pop in the waiting room. Doughna Mira sat down beside him without saying a word while Nurse Ann remained in the doorway. Doughna Mira said Pop looked at them and said, "Something's wrong."

"The nurse didn't even look up," Doughna said. "She just said, 'There's a complication with the delivery.' I didn't say anything, just squeezed your dad's hands to let him know I was with him.

"Then your dad told the nurse, 'Look me in the face, and tell me straight out what's wrong. No bullshit.'" And when the nurse looked up, we both knew it was bad, real bad. Her face looked gray and sad.

"'The baby's much bigger than we expected, and it's already in the birth canal. It's too late for a C-section, or we would have done one.'

"'Whoa, slow down,' your dad said. 'What are you saying? That the baby's too big to come out? How can that be?' And I watched the nurse's reaction because I was scared. Really scared. I knew your Mom might die, but I tried not to let your father see because there was no sense in both of us being scared.

"'It happens,' the nurse said and shook her head. 'We just didn't see this coming.'

"'What *can* you do?' your father asked. I could tell he still didn't understand how serious it was until the nurse answered, 'Pray.' She knelt in front of us and put her hands on ours and said, 'We'll do what we can, but Serena's so tiny. There are limits.'

"'You mean she could die?' your father asked, suddenly grasping the seriousness.

"'They could *both* die,' the nurse said. 'This is a Catholic hospital: we're not allowed to choose. But we're human, as well as Catholic. Dr. Blanca will do whatever you think is best.'

"I started crying then, and your father jumped up and pulled away from us. 'What kinda choice is that?' he shouted back at the nurse. 'How can I choose who lives and who dies?'

"The nurse stayed real calm and said, 'You don't have to, but that baby's coming out—one way or the other. If something goes wrong, we're not allowed to make a choice, even if we could save one of them by letting the other one go. But, the doctor will honor your wishes—if you tell him what they are.'

"I looked up at your father. He was chewing on his knuckles and I saw blood on his lips, but he didn't seem to notice. Then, he came back to the sofa beside me and laid his head on my chest and he cried—the only time I ever saw your father cry. He apologized to the nurse for not acting like a man and said, 'I can't. I can't decide.'

"The nurse said, 'I understand,' and patted your father on his back. 'I've got to get back to Serena now. I'll come back as soon as it's over.' Then she stood up and headed back to the delivery room.

"Your father looked at me, then at Nurse Ann as she walked away and called after her: 'If it comes to it, save my wife.' The nurse paused and nodded without turning around, then hurried from the room. Your father sat back in the sofa and stared into space for a long time. I told him not to be too hard on himself for making a choice because it made no sense to let you both die if one of you could live. He just looked at me, and I saw tears in his eyes. He said only, 'How can I raise these kids alone?'

"If things had turned out different, I'm not sure if he could've handled it. After that, we didn't speak to each other because neither of us knew what to say. We could only wait. Only now, we were waiting for news of death, not birth.

"Hour after hour went by. We thought we were going to lose both of you, but we didn't say a word to each other, just tried to look confident. More time passed, and I began to wish it would just be done with so we could mourn and try to get on with our lives. I wondered what your father would do without Serena.

"The next thing I knew, your father was shaking my arm to wake me and Dr. Blanca was standing there in the waiting room. I remember looking up at him and feeling confused because he was smiling. It seemed obscene. Then he said: 'You have a son. They're both doing as well as can be expected, considering.'

"Your father and I looked at each other, slowly realizing it was finally over. I was still a bit hazy, but it suddenly hit me that you had *both* survived, that I still had a daughter and your father still had a wife and a new son. But, something wasn't right because the doctor still looked troubled.

"'So what's wrong?' your father asked.

"'We had trouble getting the baby out,' the doctor said, watching our faces.

"'What kind of trouble?' I asked, suddenly concerned again.

"We had to compress his shoulders together to get him out. We broke his sternum. That's his breastbone.' He took a deep breath and looked your father square in the eye. 'There's a chance he may be paralyzed permanently. We won't know for sure for a few days. But they're both alive and out of danger. Serena's very weak because we had to cut her extensively. But look on the bright side and be happy—they're both alive.'

"He shook our hands and left the waiting room and I cried again and thanked God and took back all the things I had said the night before. Then, we called the rest of the family to give them the news. The blizzard had lasted all night, so none of them had made it to the hospital. In fact, it was over a week before they got the streets all plowed and things got back to normal, so they all waited to come for a visit until after you and Serena got home. By that time, we knew you weren't paralyzed—you were just a giant fourteen-pound baby. You're still the biggest baby they ever had at St. Mary's Hospital.'"

I have always believed Pop blamed me for putting him through this trauma. This resentment, I believed, explained why Pop always came down so tough on me. I felt tolerated, but unwelcome, my whole life. At the same time, I believe Pop's decision to defy God and church to save her life moved Ma. It touched her so deeply, it welded her to Pop, excused all his other faults and shortcomings, and evoked a powerful defensiveness in her where Pop was concerned.

Despite being born large, by the time I was five, I was the smallest child in kindergarten. I'm convinced I willed myself small, hoping I'd be noticed less by Ma and Pop. The less noticed, the better: drawing their attention was usually a mistake.

I still remember the first time they punished me for disobeying them. Ma had a firm rule about animals in the house—they weren't welcome. I had been playing in our backyard when I stumbled across an injured garter snake. I scooped it up in the jacket I was wearing and hurried inside to show Ma and Pop and ask if I could keep it as a pet. But I stumbled as I entered the kitchen where Ma and Pop were sitting over coffee at the breakfast bar with Rosalia—barely a year old at the time—in a high chair between them, and Paddy on the opposite side. As I thudded to the ground, my jacket slipped out of my hands and fell open on the floor. The snake seized its chance and, as Ma and Pop looked on, two feet of live snake streaked out of my jacket and under the nearby stove.

Ma's eyes widened in fear. She grabbed Rosalia in her arms and leapt onto her stool. Paddy stood up in his chair and Pop jumped to his feet, yelling angrily at me.

"Jesus Christ!" he shouted as he approached me. "What the hell did you bring in here?"

I backed away and rubbed my elbows, which I'd skinned in my fall. Tears were already springing to my eyes—partly from hurt and partly from fear. I looked up at Pop, who now loomed over me, and my voice failed. I only blinked and sniffled.

"Don't ignore me when I ask you a question!" Pop bellowed. "What the hell did you let loose in here?"

"It was a garter snake," Paddy volunteered, jumping down to join us in the kitchen.

"You little shit! You know you're not supposed to bring animals in the house!" Pop bent over and roughly picked me up and swatted me hard on the behind.

I shrieked in pain and surprise.

"Spank him later," Ma shouted at Pop. "Get that snake out of my kitchen first. You know I *hate* snakes." Rosalia started to cry and Ma shushed her, bobbing her up and down in her arms.

"It went under the stove," said Paddy, bending to peer underneath.

Pop dropped me back on the floor abruptly and grabbed a broom from the kitchen closet beside the stove, then squatted on his hands and knees and poked the broom handle into the small space under the stove. The snake suddenly slithered out and ribboned across the linoleum floor under the cupboards on the opposite side of the room.

"Paddy, you get away from there!" Ma yelled. "It's probably poisonous. You're gonna get bit." Paddy reluctantly returned to his chair.

Pop yanked the broom from under the stove and followed the snake to the cupboards. Ma shrieked and climbed up on the countertop with Rosalia. She pulled the hem of her robe over her knees, as if she were afraid the snake might try to slip under it.

"Kill it!" she screamed at Pop. She shifted Rosalia over her shoulder with one arm and flailed her other arm in terror. "Don't let it get away."

"No," I begged. "Don't hurt it, please!" But I needn't have worried because the terrified creature had slipped behind the cupboards and disappeared from Pop's sight and reach. After poking and prodding about with the broom for a few more minutes, Pop shrugged and stood up.

"It got away," he said to Ma. Behind him, Paddy flashed me a victory sign.

"Oh, Jesus," Ma said, nearly in tears. "It's probably got rabies. I'm not getting off this counter until you find it and kill it."

"Then you're gonna be up there a long, long time," Pop said, "because it's behind the wall and I'm not tearing the house down over a stupid garter snake. Besides, snakes don't get rabies. We'll get it when it comes out." Pop leaned the broom against the counter and lifted Ma and Rosalia down. Paddy hopped back down and tried to see behind the stove. Ma put her feet gingerly on the floor, slipped Rosalia back into the high chair, and snatched the broom, holding it in front of her protectively, watching for any movement. Paddy returned to his chair to watch.

Pop picked a wooden spoon from the sink and sat on a stool facing out into the room. He motioned to me with the spoon, and I froze in place. I had watched Pop spank Paddy with the spoon many times before. I would make faces at Paddy while Pop hit him. But Pop had never spanked me.

"Anthony," Pop's voice seemed to boom across the kitchen, "come here."

I didn't move, only looked at Pop and trembled. Behind Pop, Paddy stretched out his lips with his fingers and stuck out his tongue at me. Ma turned towards me and I pleaded for her help with my eyes.

"Do you hear your father talking to you?" she asked. I nodded. She swatted me with the broom. "Get over there. You know the punishment for breaking the rules. No animals in the house—especially not snakes!" She swatted me a couple more times for good measure. She began tugging open cupboard doors and clanging pots and pans, hoping to scare the snake out of hiding. She was panicking and, for the first time, I found myself as terrified of her as I was of Pop. Startled by the noise, Rosalia started screaming in her chair, but no one paid any attention to her.

Tarantella

Pop looked madder than ever. All the noise Ma and Rosalia were making was adding to his anger. I had unleashed something—some poison—in my family by bringing that snake into the house. I knew Paddy sensed it too, because he stopped making faces and ran out of the room. "You're not too small to spank anymore," Pop said. "And you know your mother's afraid of snakes."

"I didn't let it go on purpose," I said. "I fell."

"Don't even start, Anthony. I don't care how it happened because you shouldn't of had that thing in the house in the first place." He held the wooden spoon aloft before him like a sword. Then he motioned with it and said, "Bend over and touch your toes."

"No, Pop," I pleaded and edged away. Ma continued clanging pot lids together behind me and Rosalia continued screaming in her chair at Pop's side.

"Come over here, I said." Pop pointed to the space directly in front of him. "Now you get two. Do you wanna go for three?"

"It was an accident." I whined, but bent my head submissively and inched forward.

"Three!" Pop said angrily. "Goddamn it, Anthony. I'm through playing games with you. If you're old enough to be bad, then you're old enough to get spanked. Keep it up mister and you'll be one sorry little boy." He shook the spoon in the air menacingly and I reluctantly sidled up to him. "Now, turn around. And bend over."

I turned around slowly and gingerly bent forward a few inches, turning my head to watch Pop. He banged the spoon on the countertop behind him with a resounding crack, and Rosalia resumed her screaming anew. Pop ignored her. "I said turn around and bend over. Now you get four."

I turned my head and stared stone-faced at my toes as I bent over. Behind me, Pop growled, "Touch your toes." I dropped my arms so my fingertips brushed my toes. I heard the slice of air as Pop swung the spoon. I involuntarily jumped aside and the spoon struck only air. The force of his swing nearly pulled Pop off his stool. He grabbed my shoulders, roughly hauling me back in front of him and snarled, "Don't you dare move again!" Then he brought the spoon down with five sharp smacks in rapid succession. I winced and cried out after each hit, tears pouring down my cheeks. I recalled how Paddy never made a sound and never cried when Pop spanked him, and wondered how he could manage such a feat. Behind me, Ma had stopped banging the pot lids and was tending to Rosalia. I heard her tell Pop, "Okay, that's enough. He's learned his lesson." Pop told me to go to my room and get out of his sight for a while.

I ran to the room I shared with Paddy, crying and convinced that Ma and Pop hated me. Paddy was lying on his bed. He looked up as I came into the room.

I wiped my eyes and nose and lay on my bed across from him. Paddy and I weren't close. He was seven years older than me and much too grown up to be bothered with a little brother. His frequent battles with Ma and Pop, however, made him a perfect conspirator against them.

"I *hate* them," I said after a moment.

Tarantella

"Me, too," Paddy said, staring up at the ceiling. I watched Paddy's face. He was something of a mystery to me. The gap in our ages prevented us from being truly close. But, at least about this one thing, we were in agreement.

"I wish they'd both die," I said.

"Me, too," Paddy said, still staring at the ceiling, his flame-red hair leaping around his head like wildfire.

"One day, they'll be sorry, cuz I'm gonna run away," I said. "And I'll never come back."

"Not before I do," Paddy said, turning finally to look at me.

A couple days later, while Paddy was at school and Pop was at work, Ma found the garter snake under the sofa, dead. Maybe it had been injured too badly, or maybe it starved, or was scared to death by all the commotion that day. She wrapped it in some newspaper and took it out to the trash can in the garage. Then she scrubbed the floor and sprayed Lysol so thick I could hardly breathe. She yelled at me all the while: "You little shit! Don't you ever bring another snake into the house. I'll beat the shit out of you myself. Jesus Christ, it was probably full of some disease and we're all gonna get it now and die. Now, get outta my sight. You make me sick with how bad you are."

As I headed outside, I heard Rosalia waking from her nap. Rosalia was a vociferous child from birth, demanding and re-ceiving attention from Ma and Pop from the moment of her arrival. She barely slept, and seemed to be crying about something constantly. Ma and Pop devoted themselves to keeping her entertained because she would gurgle and coo under their ministrations; but she sent forth a wail that rattled the kitchen cupboards when ignored.

I leaned against the side of the house and started crying about my dead garter snake being put in the garbage. How could Ma treat a living thing this way? My anger over her and Pop's reaction to the snake returned full force. I noticed forsythia blooming around the periphery of our yard, their tiny yellow blossoms a sure sign of the changing seasons. I remembered that Ma despised the pretty blossoms, once reacting with horrified shock when I'd wandered in from the garden with a handful of the flowers for her. She'd swatted them out of my hand onto the tiled floor and kicked them out the door. "Don't ever bring those flowers into this house again." She shook me by the shoulders, but I could see she was more frightened than angry with me. "They're bad luck! Jesus Christ, I hope we don't have trouble now because of you."

This drab, New York, spring day, I defiantly picked a handful of forsythia and dropped them into the red wagon I used to drag around everywhere with me. I glanced back to check if Ma was watching from the slate gray house, but the windows were all vacant. I extracted the garter snake from the trash and placed it ceremoniously atop the flowers in my wagon. Then, on impulse, I decided to give the snake a burial. I took the wagon handle in my hand and ambled across the backyard into the woods beyond. At the next street, I turned west and trotted toward what I knew only as "the bay."

Tarantella

Irondequoit Bay is a large inlet off the New York side of Lake Ontario. Pop had taken me and Paddy to the overlook at the end of our street a couple of times. The dark bay lapped like a hungry creature at the narrow strip of gravelly shore near the base of a cliff more than a hundred feet high.

I decided I would toss the snake's body and the forsythia blossoms over the cliff into the bay, a sort of make-shift funeral for my would-be pet. I carted them behind me as I rattled along the street, hearing Ma's and Pop's warnings ring in my ears: "Don't go near the bay. It's too dangerous." Despite the fear swirling inside me like the snow on the day I was born, I was determined to conduct a funeral. If I fell off the cliff, it would serve them right: they would find me with the snake clutched in my fist on the shore.

The oak trees grew increasingly dense as I approached the end of the street. Here and there, tucked into tiny, shadowy gaps between the trees, houses peered back at me as I passed. The oaks flung down dark, ominous shadow-figures on the roadside. I glanced back, but my street and house were far behind and out of sight. All I could hear were the sounds of unseen birds chattering in the dark woods around me.

At the end of the street, I pulled my cart through the yard of a house that backed up against the bay. I could feel the coolness of the water, could hear the lap of its waves rolling over the shoreline. At the base of the cliff, behind the house, the glistening bay waters rippled, and the smell of fish engulfed my nostrils. I winced in distaste. The buzz of traffic wafted across the bay from the busy roads on the opposite shore.

I rattled up to the brink of the drop-off, fearlessly leaning over to look down. I scooped a handful of the yellow blossoms from the wagon and flung them up and over the cliff, but a gust of wind seized and scattered them—some sailing over the cliff, some flying back over my head and into the yard behind me. Leaving the wagon at the edge of the cliff, its black handle dangling perilously into empty space, I scrambled after the flowers tumbling across the lawn to collect them. Glancing up, I saw Ma and a neighbor woman in front of the house, climbing out of a car and heading in my direction. I darted quickly into the dense shrubbery along the cliff's edge to hide. Ma would kill me if she saw me here. I could smell the new green growth on the scratchy shrubs around me and the dirt beneath me. I edged my way deep into the undergrowth, until I felt my foot dangling off in empty space over the cliffside, filling me with an exhilarating lightheadedness and sense of dread.

I heard Ma's voice and froze in place, scrunching down and flattening my body atop the cold dirt. This was as far as I could go. Behind me was only a chasm, and in front of me was the wrath of Ma. I was more afraid of Ma finding me than I was of slipping off the cliff. I held my breath as I watched our neighbor, Mrs. Williams and Ma, with Rosalia in her arms, stop in front of me.

"Oh, Jesus Christ!" Ma said suddenly. "That's Anthony's wagon. He never goes anywhere without it. Son of a bitch!"

I panicked and glanced to my left. The handle of my wagon still wobbled squeakily in the breeze atop the cliff. Ma would drag me from my hiding spot and spank me with the wooden spoon. For a moment, I considered throwing myself over the cliff.

Ma and Mrs. Williams ran toward the wagon and I heard Ma gasp.

"Jesus Christ!" She said. "It's full of forsythia. He's dead: I know it!" In her arms, Rosalia started to cry and Ma shushed her harshly. "I told him never to come down here."

"Calm down, Serena," Mrs. Williams said. "We don't know anything yet."

"*I* know. Those flowers bring death," Ma said. "I always tell him, 'Anthony, don't go near the bay. Anthony, stay in your own yard.' I can't look." She started crying and Rosalia began to wail. Ma rocked her in her arms, but Rosalia only wailed louder and Ma became impatient, saying, "Goddamn it, Rosalia. Don't do this now. I have enough to handle already."

"You take care of Rosalia and I'll look," Mrs. Williams said.

Ma pointed an accusing finger in my direction and I closed my eyes, certain I had been discovered in the underbrush. "Look at the forsythia all over the ground," she said. "I can feel death here. Oh, Jesus, it's like a funeral."

I saw Mrs. Williams look down at the bay, slowly scanning the shoreline in both directions. Then she looked up at the sky briefly before dropping her face in her hands and weeping. I remember the scent of pine needles from the shrubs around me and Ma's strangled scream from the yard behind Mrs. Williams.

"God, no!" she cried, and with her free hand, she tore at her blouse and shrieked Sicilian words in a voice I didn't recognize.

Rosalia resumed her wailing at Ma's reaction. I clung desperately to the ground, terrified by these strange sounds coming out of Ma's mouth.

"Oh, God," she said when her English came back. "I told him never to come here. Now, see what he's done? Oh, shit! Better he'd never been born than this. Oh, Jesus. Why?"

My body felt as cold as the ground. Ma wished I'd never been born! I felt alone and unwanted. Again, I felt the urge to fling myself over the cliff.

"Serena!" Mrs. Williams spun around to face Ma. "Serena. It's okay. He's not there! He's *not* there."

"He's *not* there?" Ma said, confused. "Are you sure?"

"Yes. I'm sure," Mrs. Williams grasped Ma's arms. "He's *not* there. I was just so relieved . . . I'm sorry. I didn't mean to scare you. I wasn't thinking."

"Oh, God!" Ma shouted. "Oh, thank God." She hefted Rosalia to her other shoulder. "I swear I'm gonna beat the shit out of him when we find him. Where the hell can he be?"

"Maybe he went back home," Mrs. Williams said. "We should go back now." She grabbed my wagon and started to bring it back with her, but Ma stopped her.

"No," Ma said. "Empty it first." Mrs. Williams dumped the rest of the forsythia and the garter snake over the cliff and they headed back to the car to continue their search of the neighborhood. I heard the engine start and the crunch of gravel as they drove away.

I cowered in the garden most of the afternoon, shivering from the cold ground, petrified they would return. When I finally got up, my body felt sore, and I was filthy with dirt. I didn't know where to go—not home because Ma would beat me; Pop, too. So I wandered up the street, keeping out of sight. Soon, the sun set, and the light began to dwindle. As the light faded, the air began growing colder, and I was shivering in my light jacket. Car headlights swept down the streets beside me, creating terrifying shapes and shadows in the woods. A dog leapt against a fence behind me, growling fiercely. In my panic to escape, I stumbled and fell into a patch of bushes that scraped and scratched at me. I started crying, imagining sounds, remembering Paddy's stories about bogeymen and ghosts that attacked children in the dark.

At last, I found myself quivering in front of the door of my house, trying to work up the courage to knock or go in. The door opened suddenly and Ma stepped into the doorway. I was so startled I began crying—a panicked, terrified bawling that I couldn't control. It seemed to scare Ma, who threw her arms around me and dropped to her knees. Pushing back my hair, she cursed me in Sicilian, "Oh, Antonio! *Mi precioso bambino! Jesù e Mari!*" She hollered for Pop to call the police and let them know I'd come home, so they could stop searching. Then, she reached out to touch my cheek and I flinched, expecting a slap. After giving me a bath, Ma gave me a bowl of ice cream and made me sit in her lap all night, and I remember thinking she was just making certain I didn't run off again.

All Pop said was that he'd "bust my ass" if I ever pulled a stunt like this again. I kept waiting for a spanking, but it never came. All I could think about was Pop making me touch my toes while he paddled me, and Ma tossing my pet in the trash can.

I thought about Ma cursing me. I thought how they both hated me. I daydreamed about running away or dying—anything that would make Ma and Pop miss me. I wanted them to feel sorry for treating me this way.

I wondered if Paddy felt the same way. We never discussed it. At the time, I was really too young for him to confide in me. It must have been tough for Paddy—an only child for seven years until I showed up, followed by Rosalia a couple years later. I guess Paddy never felt connected to me and Rosalia—he was already a teenager by the mid-60s when I was just entering the first grade. The age gap that separated our lives left him no siblings to go to for understanding and sympathy. Paddy must have felt terribly alone and isolated in our midst.

By the time 1968 rolled around with its infamous summer of love at Woodstock and riots during the Democratic Convention in Chicago, Paddy was nearly seventeen years old, and I was still too young to comprehend the significance of current events. Paddy was looking a tour of Vietnam square in the face. He grew belligerent and contrary, arguing constantly with Ma and Pop, privately telling Rosalia and me that we didn't have to do what Ma and Pop said.

While I was trying to become less visible, Paddy seemed to be making himself impossible to ignore. One day, he told Ma and Pop they were stupid if they voted for Nixon. "You'll regret it one day," he warned them. "He'll ruin this country and I'll tell you right now I ain't going over to 'Nam to get killed for some asshole warmonger like Nixon."

"Don't you talk like that about someone who's running for President," Pop shouted back at him. "You don't know how lucky you are to live in America. Anywhere else, and you and your hippie, draft-dodger friends'd be in jail. You're ruining this country. I'm sick to death of hearing you complain. If everything's so goddamned bad, why don't you just leave? You're nothing but a bunch of troublemakers, that's why."

"Didja ever think, just maybe, we're *saving* this country?" Paddy shouted as he jumped up. He flung open the door and slammed it after him.

"The two of you are gonna be the death of me," Ma called from the kitchen. "The way you two go at it drives me crazy. Why can't you two talk about anything else except war and politics? You know you'll never agree, so why not drop it?"

"I ain't never gonna have no kidduh mine disrespectin' this country," Pop sputtered. "Not while he's living in my house and I'm paying the bills. I'll kick his ass out before I allow that, and don't you think I won't neither, cuz I will. I didn't risk my ass in Korea so punks like him could wreck this country."

I remember looking at Pop when he said that. His face was red and he was shaking his fist angrily to punctuate each syllable.

I'll never forget the day Paddy really *did* run away from home. In retrospect, it seems a thunderclap should have marked his going. Hailstones should have dropped. A tornado should have spun down out of the sky. Rain should have streamed down in torrents. But, it was an unremarkable day—neither hot nor cold, neither cloudy nor sunny—just an ordinary, lukewarm, cotton-on-blue day near to sunset. No purples or reds streaked the sky, just a gradual easing from azure to deepening black—like my life after that day.

I hadn't even realized Paddy was at home that day, down in his basement bedroom with the door shut and his radio turned off, until he tramped up the checkerboard tile stairs slowly, quietly. I caught up with him in the door of the breezeway. Beyond him, the blue-black Eastern sky hung like a dark oil cloth over the earth. The air was hushed and still, and I heard a katydid singing somewhere in the front yard. Paddy seemed to sense me watching him from the kitchen entrance and snapped erect, turning to see who was there.

When he saw me, he set the suitcase in his hands on the floor and his shoulders softened like butter melting. His face relaxed and he sort of grinned—a foolish grin, like when you get caught in the middle of a white lie.

Paddy glanced across the yard and back at me, and I followed his eyes. The dense stand of dark, green oaks that lined the back yard cast black shadows in the dusk. Dark, empty spaces encircled their thick, grey-brown trunks like holes in the night, hiding places where danger surely lurked. I remembered how I had been frightened of these same gnarled trees when I hid there, five years before, contemplating whether I should return home.

Tarantella

The light beside the breezeway door was glowing, and tiny insects swarmed around it. Paddy watched them for a minute, then reached up and plucked a ladybug off the illuminated globe and held it in his palm in front of my face.

"Ladybug, Ladybug," he chanted in the childhood rhyme, "fly away home." He blew the bug off his palm and it disappeared into the night. He grinned at me and said, "More like, fly away *from* home," and laughed so his red hair shook. He hefted a sack up onto his shoulder. He paused for a minute, perhaps thinking what he would say, what excuse he could make up that a nine-year-old would accept. It had to contain at least enough truth to hold me off for a little while to give him a chance to get away from here. I looked up at him wondering what he was up to.

"Don't say nothing to Ma or Pop, Anthony," he said at last. "Don't tell them nothing 'bout seeing me go, okay?"

"Why not?" I swung from the doorframe like a door flapping in a breeze.

"Cause I don't wanna be found," Paddy said quietly. "Ever." He watched my reaction curiously. His eyebrows coalesced around the bridge of his nose and two creases ridged his forehead. His nostrils flared like an animal testing the air, and he drew erect, motionless, while he considered his next words. He must have felt guilty, like he had shocked me, so he added, "Maybe I'll see *you* again sometime, though."

I tried to make sense of Paddy's words. "Did Pop kick you out?"

Paddy laughed again. "No," he said, "Pop didn't kick me out. I'm kicking myself out."

"Where will you go?" I asked. When I had considered running away I could never figure out where I'd go. I understood *wanting* to go. But go where?

"None uh your business. 'Sides, I don't want Ma and Pop to know. At least, not right away. They'd try to stop me and make me come back here. And I ain't staying here."

"Ma will cry if you go."

"Maybe," Paddy considered. "I hope so. But I doubt it. Not for me."

"Course she will."

"Maybe if *you* ran away, Anthony. But not me. She don't love me like she loves you."

I considered his words. How could Paddy think Ma loved me when it was so obvious she didn't? Paddy turned away from me and I felt a sense of panic and doom at the prospect of his leaving. He had always been there since the day I was born. I covered the hole in my chest with my hand like I was swearing an oath and, to convince Paddy to stay, I lied to him, "Ma loves us all the same."

Paddy glanced around the yard. "Then I'm sorry for us all." The sun was below the horizon and night plunged the outside into a bluish darkness. "Gotta go, Anthony. See you someday, okay?"

"Take me with you," I pleaded as he started to leave.

He stopped and walked back to where I was standing and took my face in his warm hands. "I can't," he said, shaking his head regretfully so his hair shook like red flames. "You're too young."

"*Please*," I begged.

"I wish I could," he said. "But I can't. They'd never let me go if I took you with me." He turned back toward the woods. "Bye, Anthony." Paddy walked down the three concrete steps to the grassy lawn and darted across the backyard, disappearing finally into the black oaks, tall shadowy outlines against the night sky. I watched the place where Paddy vanished into the wood for a long time after he was gone, half expecting him to reappear and laugh and say I was "gullible" for believing his story. But he was gone.

I went back inside and dropped into the gold-colored sofa and watched television after Paddy left. Later that night, Ma asked if anyone had seen Paddy and I said, no. I never told anyone about seeing Paddy disappear into the oaks. Maybe I'd run away one day, too; I needed to believe it was possible to escape. I checked the trees every day for a long time, to see if Paddy would reemerge from them. He never did.

Paddy was right about one thing—I never saw Ma or Pop cry about him leaving. Not once. They only seemed mad. Just like they were mad about Paddy's grades in school; mad about Paddy's bad attitude; mad that Paddy wasn't perfect. After he left, Ma and Pop seemed mad only that Paddy had done this to them. They even celebrated with a special dinner that night. Ma made all the things that me and Rosalia liked best: spaghetti and meatballs, and creampuffs with chocolate icing for dessert. Later that night, she even cooked up a batch of Italian fritters and let us dip them in sugar.

"I'm glad if that little son-of-a-bitch ran away," Pop said to Ma as he sliced a dark bruise from the banana he was eating. "He was just trouble anyhow, and a bad influence on the rest of the kids." He wrapped the bruise in a paper towel and dropped it into the trash.

"Still, he's just sixteen," Ma said as she poured herself a beer. "Maybe we should try to find him and have them bring him back."

"He can stay right where he is as far as I'm concerned. He'd only run away again. We can't tie him down, you know. Sides, why go bringing trouble back?"

The day after Paddy ran away, my teacher asked my class to write a story about a fish. I tried to write the best story I could to please Ma and Pop. It was all about Lost Fish, who swims off on an adventure by himself and gets swallowed by a shark, but lives on inside the shark's belly. Lost Fish's family think he's dead, and they cry and cry and holler so loud that Lost Fish hears them from inside the shark. He feels happy to know they miss him and, after he hears them, wishes he could return home. Finally, he swims up out of the shark's belly and right out of a gap in the shark's teeth. His family throws him a party because they're so relieved he's alive and home again. Lost Fish becomes a hero and lives happily ever after.

My teacher read my story to the class and told me that I should try to write more because it was a very valuable gift that I had—I shouldn't let it go to waste. She sent a note home to Ma and Pop with my story, but Pop said he wouldn't look at it and didn't see why she was making such a fuss over a "kiddie story." Ma said she didn't want to read a story about a fish. Crushed, I vowed to prove them wrong. Besides, I liked the attention and praise my writing brought me from my teacher and my classmates. To spite Ma and Pop, I started writing all the time. My grades turned into mostly As. Then, even Ma and Pop noticed. Pop told Rosalia these were the kind of grades he expected out of her, too. He warned me, though, not to let my grades go to my head because he *expected* me to get all As, all the time.

"I'll pound you with the wooden spoon again if your grades go down," he threatened. "And it'll be for your own good."

Ma also warned me: "I better not see you acting like no Mr. Smarty Pants, or *I'll* beat the shit out of you."

So, I wrote and studied more, partly because I liked to, partly out of fear, and partly to please Ma and Pop—to be the good little boy they wanted me to be. Pretty soon, I stopped watching for Paddy; stopped expecting him to come back; stopped thinking about whether he was right to feel sorry for all of us.

But, Paddy had taken a part of me with him into the woods the night he ran away. I would sometimes touch the hole in my chest and wonder if I was missing some vital organ. I felt Paddy's absence there in that empty space. Sometimes, I would dream about Paddy and me. In my dreams, we were trapped in a dark cave with no air to breath, struggling to find an exit. After a while, we would get separated, and I would suddenly realize I was alone in the cave and didn't know how to get out. I would awaken then and feel terribly sad. Sometimes, I could swear I heard Paddy breathing in the next bed, swallowed up by the darkness, like an unseen ghost.

CHAPTER 4

———— ❧ ————

Funerals

Merritt Island, FL: May 1994

MY RUN-IN WITH Pop at the hospital had left a dark depression I felt powerless to shake off. To make matters worse, an early heat-wave had settled in oppressively. Even after night fell, the air remained stifling and humid. The hands on the clock on Rosalia's bone-white living room wall pointed to the 12 and the 4—12:20. Rosalia had gone to bed hours ago, but I couldn't sleep.

I loved Rosalia's apartment nearly as much as I loved Rosalia herself. Her personality inhabited every inch of the place with a warmth, a gentle strength, and a constant cheerfulness. It was the landscape paintings on her walls; the soft glow cast by her amber table lamps; the family photos on her coffee table; the comfortable-yet-sensible furniture in her living room; the collection of colorful glass birds scattered all throughout her apartment.

Standing at the open second floor window sipping a Dr. Pepper, I wrinkled my nose at the fetid scent of dead fish from the dark marshes just behind Rosalia's apartment complex. From the window, I could see the black swath the marsh sliced through the island's yellow streetlights, sickly yellow lights that reminded me again of Pop's illness. The fight in his room had tarred me with a residue of remorse and more than a little anger. But the real possibility of Pop's death—something impossible to imagine only a few brief days before—left me rattled and filled with ambiguous feelings. On the one hand, I felt lonely and orphaned at the thought of Pop dying; on the other hand, I felt strangely relieved and liberated, as if some huge barrier were being lifted.

I tried to picture Pop in a casket, still and cold as he was in life, only with his eyes closed. In my mind, Pop's glasses perched atop his long, broad nose, their dark frames casting shadows over his face. His big, cold hands—still and white—would be criss-crossed on his chest. Ma would stand beside the casket smoking in the musty funeral parlor with dim, amber lights. Only a single wreath of yellow roses would rest beside the casket. My relatives would look dour, like they were sucking on lemons. Their murmuring voices would be the only sound in the room.

I would stand back, watching it all unfold, fighting to keep that contented smile off my face, happy that the man who had always made me feel insignificant was gone. Perhaps I would feel liberated by Pop's death. I always imagined that I would. Yet, somehow, I doubted it. Like everything where Pop and I were concerned, clear, simple feelings rarely played a part. Perhaps I'd be pissed—pissed that he had died and left me behind to deal with the baggage he'd handed to me; pissed that I'd never really felt like he wanted me or loved me; pissed that I could never live up to his expectations; pissed especially that I never felt the love I wanted and expected to feel for my father. He had always been Pop to me—never Dad—and that bothered me a great deal. I wanted to talk about my "old man" the way I heard other sons speak of their fathers—fondly, nostalgically, like they were talking about a friend. I had never considered Pop my friend. He was Pop, a fact I could not change. He was a part of my life, despite wishing I could leave him behind in Florida.

But Pop was not dead, I remembered as I set the can of Dr. Pepper on the polished teak chest Rosalia used as a coffee table. I settled on Rosalia's sofa and ran my hand over the rich, lustrous wood. I remembered my first funeral: Grandpa's wooden casket had resembled this chest. Bigger, of course, but just as cold and grainy to the touch. When Grandpa died, we spent most of the next three days with Ma's family. The same thing happened whenever a relative passed away. After a while, I came to associate family with funerals because funerals brought the entire family together.

I remembered Grandpa's funeral vividly, although I didn't recall Grandpa as a person at all. I recalled Grandpa simply as a dark brown box, surrounded by flowers. To me, Grandpa was a casket: hard and cold.

At the funeral, I remember Ma was seated between Pop and my Uncle Joe. Shortly after we arrived, Ma leaned into my Uncle Joe's jacket lapel.

"I thought the old bastard would never die." Her whiskey-tenor stage whisper raked the musty air in the somber room. "He was a mean old cuss. Remember that day he slapped us and said, 'That's for not doing nothing. Think what I'll give you if you do something.'?"

"This isn't the time, Serena," Pop said, trying to pull Ma back toward him. But Ma resisted Pop's pull.

"I remember," my Uncle Joe chimed in, nodding and plunging a long finger deep into his dark, bristly beard. The sound of his scratching seemed to echo in the room. "That was the day he pulled me out of school. I was only fifteen, but he said he'd managed fine without school and so would I."

"I think he was afraid we would turn out smarter than him," Ma said, pulling her cigarette from between tight lips and expelling a thick stream of smoke into the air, as if she was exhaling the history of her life with her father. "He yanked me out of school when I was seventeen, remember? I was just six months short of graduating, and even had my graduation outfit all picked out. But he said Mama needed my help, and that was that."

"Serena, come on now. Quiet down," Pop said. "You're disturbing everyone. Besides, even you said your father always put food on the table."

"Besides, nothing," Ma said. "Did you know he spit in my face when I told him I was going to marry you? Of course not, I never told you because I was too embarrassed. He spit right in my face and said I couldn't be his daughter if I was going to marry a Mick—only a whore would do that. He was wicked, mean inside and out. I hated him from as far back as I can remember. I still do, and his dying don't change nothing on that score. I only wonder why it is the wicked ones live so long."

"Come on, Serena," Pop soothed, putting an arm around her. "That was a long time ago. Forget about it. He was your *father*, after all, and you've gotta respect him."

"Bullshit!" Ma shouted, pulling out of Pop's arms and leaping to her feet as everyone turned to stare. Her voice was shrill and loud when she continued. "He was a bastard to all of us." She swept her arm around the room and looked at the faces of her many brothers and sisters. "I hated him and I know the rest of you did, too. I can't sit here and pretend I'm sorry he's gone. I'm not."

"Hush now, Serena," Pop tried again, pulling her back down to the bench. "Don't talk like that about your father. It's not right. Honor thy father, no matter what."

I remember watching Ma's reaction. Her dark eyes stared evenly ahead and she rose again, shrugging out of Pop's grasp.

"I don't care who he was. Respect goes both ways and he never respected me." She looked around at her family. "Maybe the rest of you can pretend you're sorry he's gone," Ma shrilled. "I'm not sorry, though, and I won't sit here and cry about that bastard."

"Serena, stop!" Pop snapped. "You're upsetting your mother."

Ma looked over to where Doughna Mira was sitting a few rows ahead. Doughna Mira glanced back toward the commotion with a defiant look on her face. Pop tugged on Ma's hand to draw her back into her seat, but she pulled free and ran out into the aisle.

"Watch your sister," Pop hurriedly told me, gesturing at Rosalia; then, he squeezed out into the aisle after Ma. Uncle Joe followed Pop.

Ma watched Pop coming toward her and puffed vigorously on her cigarette for a moment. Then, she pursed her lips tightly, dropped her cigarette to the floor, and crushed it out deliberately with the toe of her high-heeled shoe. She marched purposefully up to the big, dark box encircled by flowers, then spun around to face the crowd, as if daring someone to challenge her. A smile settled on her olive face and her dark eyes blazed. As Pop shouted and loped toward her, Ma wheeled around to face Grandpa's box, and her auburn hair flashed gold in the amber of the room. I saw Doughna Mira, calm as ever, without a wrinkle of concern and only an inscrutable little smile pasted on her creaseless face, watching Ma. Then, a chorus of raucous voices and shrill screams erupted behind me.

Ma commanded the attention of the whole room and she knew it. I could tell because her shoulders squared off when the shouting began. As tiny as she was, she seemed big.

Pop looked puny and helpless—too far away to prevent what was about to happen. Ma bent over Grandpa's box, leaned forward—lower, lower—dipping down as if she were about to kiss him farewell. The shouting hushed abruptly.

In the uncomfortable silence, I heard the splat as Ma spat vehemently, then turned toward the room. The room itself and everyone in it seemed to gasp collectively and hold their breath for a long beat. Pop pulled up short and I felt a sickly twist in my stomach. Then, Ma's shoulders sagged and her head slumped to her chest. If Pop hadn't rushed to catch her, she would have flopped on the floor. I heard Ma weeping as Pop scooped her up in his arms. Only Ma's weeping and the hush in the room kept me from laughing at the whole, absurd episode. As Pop carried Ma out of the hall, Uncle Joe dabbed the spit from Grandpa's waxy face with a handkerchief. Doughna Mira never moved from her seat or changed expressions. After a moment, the silence broke and I could hear all of my relatives talking about Ma.

"Poor thing," said my Aunt Lucinda. "Lord knows we all hated the old man, but this just isn't the time for a scene like that."

Ma never apologized for spitting on Grandpa in his casket. She said it was just a thing she had to do. Pop would always shake his head and say he didn't understand how Ma could hate her father so much. But I understood. Over the years, I thought often about how I would do the same thing someday when Pop died. Only I wouldn't cry afterwards.

I jumped when Rosalia padded into the nearly dark living room behind me and touched my shoulder. She was small: barely five feet tall, with auburn hair and olive skin. She looked like a softer version of Ma. She was the youngest, and, as kids, got Ma's special attention, which I always resented. But as we got older, we really grew to rely on and confide in each other. We kept each other's confidences, and we were there for each other in a way that Ma and Pop never were. As we grew up and lived our separate adult lives, we remained close spiritually, if not physically.

"You scared the hell out of me, you spook." I said. I looked up at her ghostly reflection in the dark window pane; then, I turned to face her. She pushed a small, thin hand through her rumpled hair and squinted at me through bloodshot eyes still sticky with sleep. Rosalia's eyes were her single most striking characteristic: one was deep cobalt blue, and the other was cow-eye brown. To me, it was the outward reflection of the duality of her nature:

firm and sensible, like Pop, and yet, emotional and passionate, like Ma. I had Ma's eyes.

"Whatcha thinking about, Anthony?" She raised a curious eye toward me as she plopped, hands first, to the sofa. Whiskers, her cat, glided onto her lap like smoke, and she ran her hand absent-mindedly over his fur. I could hear the low rumble of Whisker's purring.

"About Grandpa's funeral." Turning back to the window, I scrutinized my own reflection in the glass. My dark hair and eyes seemed part of the night, barely visible. My skin looked near-ly green, and my torso merged into the image of the wooden chest, as if I were rising out of it. I turned back to look directly at Rosalia. "And how I'll feel if Pop dies."

Rosalia continued petting Whiskers while my words settled in the room. It seemed to me the thought was nearly palpable in the quiet—as if it had body and force. I could almost see it slip onto Rosalia's lap beside Whiskers. She, too, seemed to caress the thought, to scrutinize and consider it. She noticed me watch-ing her and smiled, an odd smile that quivered uncertainly on her lips.

"I've thought about it, too." She lowered her voice to a near-whisper. "I've even wished it. More times than I care to admit." She paused and ruffled the fur on Whiskers' haunches; the cat arched sinuously. "Sometimes I think I can hardly wait for the day. Is that awful for me to say?"

"Probably. But I've felt it, too." I looked down at the wooden chest. "What happened to us, Rose? Why can't we love him like other kids love their fathers?" I noticed the photo of Ma and Pop on top of the chest and nodded toward it. "Why can't he be more like *other* fathers? And why can't we give him what he wants from us?"

"Let me tell you something, Anthony. Something I haven't told anyone else. About the way Ma and Pop reacted when I told them Trap and I were getting a divorce." She looked at her reflection in the window and I looked too. Her long, undulating hair seemed darker than I knew it was, and she looked even smaller and younger than usual. She pulled her frilly white robe around her like a comforter and crossed her legs on the couch. She jostled Whiskers, who looked up at her, licked her arm, then readjusted himself in her lap.

"I made them sit at the kitchen table. But when they sat down and looked at me, I didn't know how to begin. So, I just blurted it out: 'Ma, Pop: Trap and I are getting a divorce.' Ma didn't even react, just looked at Pop and waited. Pop's face never changed. He just stared at me with those ice eyes of his for a couple of minutes. Then, he stood up, pushed his chair in, and took a step back. "'Well,' he says, 'I guess you want us to say something now?'

"'That would be nice,' I said to him, and smiled just as sweet as you please." She smiled a forced, artificial smile.

"'Well, I'm not sure what to say to that,' Pop says with a shrug. 'Just what exactly does a father say to his little girl when she tells him she's going to break her oath to God? Do you realize you'll be excommunicated? Marriage takes work, but then you kids have always been a bunch of quitters...from Paddy to

Anthony, and right on down to you. When the going gets tough, you're all very good at running away.'"

"That's Pop for you," I said. "Always ready to label you a failure right when you could use a little support." I felt behind me for the arm of the sofa and sat down on it.

"You know I didn't sit tight for that. I jumped right up outta my chair. But before I could get up in Pop's face, Ma was there between us. I never even noticed her get up. She put out her hands between us like a boxing referee separating two boxers.

"'Calm down, both of you,' she tells us. Then she looks straight at me and says, 'Why do you always have to upset him?'"

"Oh, Christ," I said, "I swear, if Pop had shot you, she'd tell the cops it wasn't his fault because you upset him. Everything upsets Pop. What the hell are we supposed to do? Stop living? Or just not tell him anything? Then, he'd be upset that we didn't tell him anything. Face it, it's always a lose-lose proposition where Pop's concerned."

Rosalia scratched Whiskers under the chin and the cat's head lolled back in ecstasy.

"I really wanted to tell them both to get fucked and run the hell out of there," Rosalia said.

"Why didn't you?" I asked.

"What good would that have done?" She picked Whiskers up off her lap and set him on the sofa beside her. "I literally counted to ten—I'd never really done that before—and thought about it from Pop's point of view: How he doesn't know what's become of Paddy; how you've moved way up to Chicago and don't talk to him anymore; how his daughter was getting a divorce that he felt would ruin her life and make her a pariah. I'm sure they had high hopes of having a grandchild by now, and it looks like that might never happen at the rate the three of us are going. I decided that Pop was just afraid of what would happen to me and so he was lashing out. So, I sat back down and sipped my cup of coffee. Ma came back to the table a minute later, and Pop—well, he just continued standing there. And we all waited."

"I don't know how you did it. I would've been so pissed off I'd've just called him an asshole and stormed out. I don't know how you could be so reasonable when he was being such a jerk," I said.

"I was still pissed, but my voice was very calm. I looked them both square in the face, then said, 'I know you don't mean that, and I understand how upsetting this news is. Believe me, it's upsetting to me too. But there's no point in fighting or calling each other names. You know I've been trying, and that I've been with Trap for a long time now. It just isn't working, and I don't want to be miserable. Or make Trap miserable just to prove something. And I really don't care what the Pope thinks about it because he's not the one who has to live with my decision: I do.'

"And Pop says, 'Thank God you never had any children. This would make them all bastards.' I must've looked totally shocked, because Pop walked right up to the table, sort of loomed over me, and asked: 'What are you going to do without a husband? How will you live?'"

"As if you've ever had a problem taking care of yourself," I said. "How can he ask such stupid shit? Honestly, you'd think we lived in the Dark Ages! You know, he barely goes to church himself, but it's the first crap he throws in your face whenever you tell him something he doesn't want to hear."

"I think I've finally realized that's his crutch when he's scared and doesn't know what to say. It's easy, you know?" she said, looking over at me. "I just reminded him that I had lived on my own and supported myself just fine before I married Trap, and I would again. And I told him I knew he was just worried about me, but that he didn't need to be because I knew what I was doing, and this was the right decision for me.

"'So whadaya want from us?' Pop said, 'Nothing, Pop,' I said. 'I just wanted you to know so you weren't surprised. And I don't want you to worry because I'm fine.' I looked him square in the eye, and I could see him relax a bit. Then, I turned to face Ma.

"'Ma,' I said, 'anything you want to say?'" Rosalia addressed the question to the empty space beside her on the sofa. I turned, almost expecting to see Ma sitting there.

"And do you know what Ma says? She says, 'Oh, don't get me involved in this.' Can you believe it? Like she isn't involved! Then she lit up a cigarette, big as you please, and sat there blowing smoke around the room."

"Jesus, that's just like Ma. She lets Pop talk for her like she can't have an opinion of her own. What's her problem? Sometimes, I feel more pissed off at her than at him. At least with Pop, you know where you stand and what he's thinking. With Ma, I feel like you never know what she thinks. All she wants is for everyone to make nicey-nice all the time, even if we really don't agree. That's more frustrating to me than fighting it out with Pop. How do you put up with it?"

"I just decided I can't let it bother me. If Ma doesn't want to offer an opinion, then fine. I can't make her talk if she doesn't want to. It sort of just came over me that I'm tired of fighting with both of them about what I'm supposed to do, or what I should do, or why I'm making the wrong choice, or whatever. I figured we couldn't fight about it if I didn't fight back. If I stayed reasoned and calm, eventually, they would calm down, too. And it seemed to work."

"Yeah, but don't you worry that maybe you've given up your soul in the process?" I said, thinking about Pop in the hospital bed this morning. How could he look so helpless and still have such power over us?

"I didn't give up anything. I just refused to argue with him, is all." She sunk her thin fingers deep into her hair and pulled it back. "Arguing wouldn't have changed anything. And this way, I avoid getting myself upset. Who knows? Maybe they'll come around eventually."

"Or maybe not," I said. "I just hate letting Pop win when I know he's wrong."

"That's the problem, Anthony," she said, sitting forward again. "The way it's always been with all of us fighting all the time, *none* of us wins: we all get pissed off. None of us listens to the others. But we're always fighting about everything. Maybe Ma's been right all along. Maybe all the shit we fight about doesn't really matter in the long run. Maybe making nicey-nice *is* what's important, after all."

"What's this, Rose? Some new Buddhist philosophy you've picked up? I just don't know how to turn off my feelings that way. When I get pissed off, I'm pissed off and I can't pretend I'm not. I can't believe that you, who's always been the biggest no-bullshit member of the family, is saying this. What happened? Did you dream about walking toward a white light or something?"

"Go ahead and joke about it, if you like, Mr. Smarty Pants," she said. "I actually did see the light, metaphorically, when Trap and I decided to split up. When something like that happens, you examine the kind of life you've been leading. You start questioning the shit you always took for truth because, obviously, all those stories about happily-ever-after are bullshit. Either that, or you're not the good person you thought you were because, if you were, how come this bad thing is happening to you?" She eased Whiskers onto the ground, then got up and walked over to me. Taking my hand in hers, she sat down beside me.

"You start to realize," she said, stopping to correct herself, "*I* started to realize that being right all the time is boring. And that insisting that everyone understand *my* point of view is selfish. I had to own at least some of the responsibility for what has happened to me in my life."

"Well, you know I agree with you there," I admitted. "Blaming everything that happens to you on others seems so weak. Once you're an adult, it seems to me, you're responsible for what happens from that point on."

"Exactly," she said, slapping my hand and sitting forward to look me in the eye. "And that's true of your problems with Pop, too."

"Are they *my* problems, Rose?" I asked. "Or *Pop's* problems?"

"Probably both," she said. "That's the point. That's the revelation."

"I keep thinking—hoping—he'll change," I said, shaking my head dismissively. "I keep hoping that one day, I'll answer the phone or the door and Pop'll be standing there telling me how wrong he's been; how sorry he is for the hell he's put me through; how he really *does* love me, and how he's going to turn over a new leaf from now on." I looked at her and laughed out loud. "Kind of pitiful, isn't it? Sort of like waiting for a snake to change into a butterfly."

"I don't think it's as impossible as you make it out to be," she said with sudden seriousness. "You've got to give him a chance, Anthony; but you've got to try yourself."

"You can't be serious, Rose," I said, pulling my hands free of hers and leaning against the back of the sofa. "How do I try when he calls me a faggot? What should I say when he says I'm sick and perverted? Or better yet, why should I make the effort when he's not? He's never going to change, Rose. Never."

"He already has—a little bit. He's let the whole divorce thing pass by, and he treats me as if it never happened." Whiskers hopped up in her lap again, walking a small circle before settling down. Rosalia stroked him between his ears. "Don't get me wrong: his words still sting. I just refuse to let him goad me into behaving like him. It feels very powerful and liberating to let it go and to be the adult. I'm not saying it's the perfect solution, but it's helped me, and it might help you. And, I swear to God, I think he's starting to change."

"Oh, please, Rose," I scoffed. "Pop doesn't know what 'change' means. Let me tell you, it was the same old Pop at the hospital this morning. He hasn't changed a bit, near as I can tell."

"I'm serious, Anthony," she said. "I realized I could hate Pop forever, or I could try to understand where he's coming from, and not accept the things he says and does, but to sort of separate that from how I feel about him. I've gotten to a place where I can love him in spite of that. He does love us, Anthony; but he doesn't understand us, and he doesn't know how to communicate with us." She eased Whiskers off her lap, then stood up, arched her back, and stretched her arms full out. One of her knees creaked from the strain of this new position.

"I don't know if I can do that, Rosie," I said, also standing up. "I have a hard time ignoring the hateful things he does. Jesus, I think sometimes he's just a downright mean son-of-a-bitch. Why does he always have to ride my ass?"

"Why does anyone behave the way they do? I just think you need to look past that surface behavior, or you'll never get past this." She walked over to the window and pulled shut the drapes. "Anyhow, it's late. I'm going back to bed, brother of mine."

"Yeah, I think I'll turn in too." I followed her down the hallway. At the doorway to my room, she turned and gave me a kiss on the cheek. "I'll see you in the morning."

I wanted to tell her I loved her, but, strangely, couldn't find the words: another of Pop's failings I had inherited.

Inside the room, I took a pair of shorts out of the dresser drawer Rosalia had emptied for my use. I remembered the dresser, a light oak model with numerous scratches and nicks. Rosalia had used it as a little girl over 20 years ago. Holding the shorts out in front of me, I thought about the day of Rosalia's accident when I had been wearing a pair of shorts much like these.

"Let's all go swimming." Pop had said, checking his watch and clapping his hands together. "But only if you're all ready in the next five minutes." We all raced to our rooms to change because we knew that when Pop said five minutes, he *meant* five minutes. Pop had once returned home from the drive-in before the opening credits finished rolling. He had given us one minute to settle down. When we failed to comply, he said, "I warned you and you didn't listen," and drove us back home—not even stopping to get his money back.

Ma had looked up in surprise and touched her hand to his chest. "Aw, honey." We protested, cried, and pleaded but Pop never responded and Ma finally shushed us, saying, "You're just making it worse." When we arrived home, Ma told us to get ready for bed.

So, when Pop gave us five minutes to get ready, we moved. In fact, we were ready before Ma and Pop. While we waited, we began playing in the living room, chasing each other in an impromptu game of tag. Rosalia tossed a crumpled piece of paper at me and darted toward the Florida Room in escape.

But Ma had closed the sliding glass door between the living room and Florida Room before going in to change. Rosalia smashed into the door with such force that the glass shattered.

She passed through the door and landed on her feet in the Florida Room with a bewildered look on her face. Long, jagged shards of glass surrounded a narrow and elongated oval space in the sliding glass door. A dull red smear coated the jagged glass on the lower section of the door.

Rosalia stood motionless and silent, a red pool spreading quickly at her feet. She looked out at me and grew visibly pale. Suddenly, I was aware of the sound of my voice, my screaming voice. I screamed and screamed without even meaning to and I winced at the shrieking and my inability to stop.

Ma, in her bathing suit, dashed into the room with Pop trailing a few feet behind her. "What's going on?"

I pointed a shaky hand toward the Florida Room. Rosalia was standing barefoot in her fluorescent pink bathing suit, amidst a sea of glass on the Florida Room floor. Blood dripped from her left arm and puddled around her feet. She still hadn't made a sound.

"Oh, God!" Ma stopped in midstride, immobilized. "Oh, Jesus!"

Pop slipped into the Florida Room, first stopping to open the glass door. Then, stepping quickly, but carefully, on the broken glass in his sandals, Pop scooped Rosalia up in his arms, lifted her gingerly, and carried her to the bathroom. Looking back at me, he warned menacingly, "Don't you go into the Florida Room." His voice trailed after him from the hallway. "Glass is everywhere!" Ma followed him and I heard their voices from the bathroom.

"Jesus, she's cut up pretty bad."

"My God. Look at her arm."

"Christ! Put that towel around it. We need to get her to a hospital quick." The bathroom door opened and Pop dashed down the hall with Rosalia still cradled in his arms. "Anthony, get in the car. Now. Move!"

I moved.

Inside the car, the stifling air became saturated with the musty scent of blood, but no one said a word. Rosalia leaned on Ma's shoulder, immobile. Ma cupped a hand around the back of her head and caressed her hair with her fingers. I never saw Ma and Pop look so concerned. When I had broken my arm a few years back, Pop had told me to quit my belly-aching and act like a man.

Ma had wrapped my beach towel around Rosalia's arm and it now glistened with red wetness. Aunt Philomena, my godmother, had given the towel to me when we moved to Florida. "Anthony," she had said after I unwrapped and unfurled it. "Remember your Godmother whenever you use this." The towel bore a picture of a little house encircled by the words, "Home is where your heart is."

I looked at Ma, her arms around Rosalia, who was nestled in between her and Pop. She kept inspecting the towel wrapped around Rosalia's arm and looking worriedly out of the car window. I remember thinking, at first, how angry she and Pop would be at Rosalia for breaking the glass door, but this heightened attention and worry was a surprise. Somehow, Rosalia had succeeded in getting Ma and Pop's full attention—something I had never managed. As we pulled to a stop in front of the hospital's emergency room, I erupted.

Tarantella

"That's *my* towel."

"Anthony, please." Ma shook a fist in my direction as she helped Rosalia from the car.

"She's ruined my towel." I stamped a foot on the hot hospital pavement. "Why didn't you use *her* towel instead of *my* towel?"

Ma slammed the car door. "Your sister's hurt and all you can think about is a goddamned towel? You make me sick." She waved me away with her free hand. "Get out of my sight."

I skulked into the emergency room several paces behind my family. I watched from the far corner of the waiting room as Pop carried Rosalia up to the window. Ma unceremoniously rushed me into the waiting room and said, "Sit here and behave, or I'll beat yer ass when I get back." Then, she turned and hurried back to rejoin Pop at the counter.

I felt rejected and excluded, as if I were no longer part of the events around me; as if this were some kind of television show, and not real. I heard Pop say, "screw the paperwork!" and saw him push his way into the ER. Ma and several nurses rushed after him.

Except for me, the waiting room was empty and cold, despite the oppressive heat outside. Feeling abandoned, I looked down and kicked my naked white legs back and forth in front of me. Reminded of my state of dress, I felt suddenly ashamed, like it was somehow indecent to be wearing a bathing suit in a hospital. Hospitals were like churches in my mind: solemn, sad, boring, and invariably white inside and out. I feared God might strike me down for my petulant outburst in the parking lot.

I glanced around me, feeling very small and alone in the big, sterile waiting room and ER entrance. Across the hall, nurses and doctors scurried back and forth and chatted with each other, seemingly oblivious to me and my family. Every now and then, the large double doors split apart as someone entered or exited the ER, and the muffled noise of distant traffic or the buzz of a cicada seeped in.

The fluorescent lights in the ceiling and the white walls and floors gave the waiting room and entire ER a sort of ethereal glow, and it occurred to me that this might be what death looked like. I had heard stories about people who had nearly died, and they all seemed to describe a long, white hallway and white lights. I wondered if Rosalia might die and why I didn't feel sorry for her. I felt only bored and vaguely annoyed that no one was paying any attention to me. I was also frustrated that our day at the beach was over before it began, and angry that Rosalia had ruined my beach towel.

The automated doors whisked apart and a red-faced, middle-aged man in a ragged tee-shirt rushed in, towing a small girl with curly blonde hair who held a pink washcloth against her left eye.

"Daddy, go slower." The girl's squeaky voice sounded like a hinge. "I can't see you."

"I'm sorry, Becky," the man replied, turning and scooping her up in his arms. "Let's go get your eye taken care of." He carried her to the desk, setting her down beside him, then he rang a bell on the counter.

A nurse appeared quickly and said something I couldn't hear and waved her arms like a bird flapping its wings in a stiff wind.

"Can the doctor check my daughter right away?" the man asked, concern visible on his face. He pointed down at the little girl. "I want to be sure there's no permanent damage to her vision."

The nurse leaned back on her heels, surveyed the man and the little girl, who whimpered but continued pressing the pink cloth to her eye. Moving her hands to the girl's shoulders, the nurse gently guided her into a cubicle. The man followed a few steps behind.

I heard a commotion down the hall and slipped from the waiting room to see what was happening. I could hear voices coming from behind the ER door. "Get him on the bed. Good. Now, get a monitor on him." I cracked the door open a few inches, enough to see several nurses rushing around someone on a hospital bed. When one of them moved to make an adjustment, I recognized Pop in the bed and was about to enter the room when I heard Ma's voice and stayed put. "Oh, Jesus! He's had a heart attack. Oh, my God."

"Oh, no, Mrs. McMurphy," one of the nurses replied calmly. "He just fainted from the blood. Why don't you sit with him?"

Ma stumbled into view. The nurse took her elbow and helped her into the bed beside Pop's, then pulled the curtains closed and headed toward the ER door. As I frantically raced back to the waiting room, I wondered if they all might die: Rosalia and Ma and Pop.

Except for the soft voices coming from the television on the wall, the room was completely silent. I felt bewildered, alone, blinking like someone who had just stepped out of a dark cave into the full sun. I stared at the dark ER door, wondering what I'd see when it opened; wondering if my life might change; wondering why I felt so calm. I turned my attention to the TV, where a new-born chicken was trying to figure out who his mother was. I felt strangely at peace as I watched darkness descend. And waited. And waited.

The smell of sea spray lingered in the air, detectable even over the ammonia scent that seemed to emanate at once from everywhere in the room. I pictured the beach, where we were headed before this interruption: its crisp, sea spray scenting my hair and my skin. I recalled our very first expedition to Cocoa Beach shortly after our move to Florida. I had expected to find Jeannie from the *I Dream of Jeannie* show, which was set here. Instead, Rosalia and I found a lifeguard waving at us from shore. At first, we'd ignored his flapping arms and insistent whistle, sure he was calling some other bather. After a couple of minutes, however, we realized he was motioning to us. We headed for shore, bewildered about what rule we had violated.

"Don't you *ever* ignore a lifeguard when he calls you!" He shook a long, bronzed finger in our direction. "You think I'm out here for my health?" We shook our heads timidly. He pointed into the water beyond us. "There's a shark out there. Everyone has to get outta the water till he's gone."

We wheeled around to look where he pointed. A fin cut through the water, barely fifty yards offshore. Ahead of the fin, like corn kernels in a popcorn popper, tiny silver fish leaped and skittered.

"That shark followed those fish in to shore," the lifeguard snapped. "Go stay with your folks till I give the all clear." He motioned us off and spoke into a walkie-talkie.

My eyes flashed to the gray fin, slashing back and forth in the surf. I inhaled the sea air and closed my eyes. That was the first time I understood that death was always lurking somewhere. Now, here at the hospital, I wondered if I was about to encounter it again.

Gradually, after so long on my own, I fell asleep.

When I reopened my eyes, the sun was down outside. I looked down the hallway. The ER door was open wide and the beds, where Ma and Pop had been, were empty. I panicked. My breath caught in my throat and I hiccoughed. My eyes swept over the hallway and the part of the ER I could see from my seat. No Ma. No Pop. No Rosalia. No doctor. Not even a nurse in sight.

I remained silent, impassive. If Ma and Pop were dead, where would I go? Would I be put in an orphanage? Would Doughna Mira take me to live with her? Would Paddy have to come back for me?

Movement on the other side of the window caught my eye. The ER doors opened and closed, and another rush of sea spray filled my nostrils. I imagined a shark swimming into the hospital ER and swallowing Ma, Pop, and Rosalia without leaving a trace. I remembered the blood on the shattered glass door. The television droned behind me, interrupted occasionally by the sounds of the laughtrack. Outside, it was dark.

At the sound of voices down the corridor between the ER and the waiting room, I got up to investigate. I found Ma and Pop, still alive, in the hallway. I felt oddly disappointed to see them looking as if nothing unusual had occurred. I felt the frightening, yet exciting, prospect of change recede into normality. Pop held Ma around the waist with his arm. The doctor, a large, red-faced man with short, blond hair, spoke to them slowly, deliberately.

"The cut on her arm was extremely deep." He indicated on his own arm where Rosalia had been gashed. "It needed over 150 stitches to close. We can't be certain she won't lose the use of her arm: the glass severed a lot of nerves and muscle tissue."

"You sayin' she's gonna have a paralyzed arm?" Pop moved his hands to Ma's shoulders. Ma clasped her fingers over her chest and shook her head weakly.

"It's possible. We weren't even sure we could save it. It's still too soon to tell, but we're hopeful."

"How long before you'll know for sure?" Pop pulled Ma against him protectively.

"Not long—a few days at most. She lost a lot of blood. In fact, we thought we might lose her there for a minute, but she's a tough kid." The doctor poked his head into the ER, then leaned back out. "She's doing fine now. We'll have her all stitched up in a minute and you should be able to take her home."

"I better go check on Anthony," Ma said as she stepped out of Pop's grip. "He'll be wondering what's happened to us."

Tarantella

I darted back into the waiting room before Ma saw me in the hallway. But, when Ma didn't appear after several long seconds, I poked my head back into the hallway again and saw her standing outside the entrance smoking a cigarette. Obviously, I thought, Ma loved her cigarettes more than she loved me. I returned to the waiting room and Ma walked in just before Pop and Rosalia appeared in the doorway. Rosalia's arm was in a sling and she seemed unnaturally quiet, like a zombie. As if taking our cue from Rosalia, we were all quiet and reflective for the rest of that day.

I never used my towel again, even though the blood came out in the wash. Ma put stickers all over the sliding glass door and on every window in the house to make sure we didn't crash through any more glass. And I remember Rosalia's blood on the driveway pavement and in the Florida Room and down the hallway in the house. In the heat of the day, it had dried and curled up from the floor like maroon wood shavings, hardly resembling blood anymore.

At the time, I hadn't realized how close to death Rosalia had come. She had lost a great deal of blood and had sliced through many nerves, muscles, ligaments, and tendons in her arm. But she regained full use of her arm, and the only residual evidence of the accident was the jagged, curving scar on the inside of her arm, which she turned to her favor with the other kids in school.

She would show them her scar and claim a shark had bitten her. The vaguely mouth-shaped scar and residual paranoia from "Jaws" made her into something of a legend in the schoolyard.

After it became clear that Rosalia was fine, I felt resentful of all the attention showered on her for being stupid. Why hadn't Ma and Pop spanked her, or at least yelled at her, for breaking the sliding glass door? Rosalia had wrecked the day for all of us and had ended up being the center of attention for weeks. I, on the other hand, followed the rules and worked hard in school and got noticed by no one.

CHAPTER 5

Poison

Rochester: 1972

IN THE SPRING of 1972, my life and my view of the world changed suddenly and dramatically in dual ways: one self-induced and another imposed on me. It felt like a reckoning of my former life and a transition to a new life in which I had the opportunity to start fresh and become a new, good Anthony.

The first lilacs scented the air as I headed into our backyard. The far corner of our backyard in New York was cluttered with dozens of home-made rabbit coops. What had begun with two pet rabbits—one mine and one Rosalia's—had grown into dozens. I loved them, even though they didn't do much. They just hopped around in their cages. They ate, they shat, and they made baby bunnies. To control the baby boom, Ma and Pop forbid us to put two pets together in a single cage; they also threatened to sell our rabbits to a local farmer for food, if we disobeyed. We cried and carried on and promised we wouldn't put them together; but periodically, another litter of baby bunnies would appear.

One evening, while I was alone at the pens, with my favorite bunny, a six-month-old Dutch rabbit I called Nitbit, because he was a little bit of a thing, and he acted like a nitwit, I decided to put him into the cage with his mother, Forsythia (whom I had named to spite Ma).

Forsythia came out of the back of her pen and sniffed at Nitbit, who seemed more interested in the green ceramic food bowl nearby. I could hear the other rabbits stamping their feet impatiently around me as they waited to be fed. As Nitbit wandered toward the food dish, Forsythia reared back slightly on her haunches and bared her teeth. She lunged forward, tearing wildly at Nitbit and knocking him onto his back. She lunged again, before Nitbit could recover, and ripped at his exposed underside, tearing open his belly like you would open a bag of instant oatmeal to pour it into your cereal bowl. Everything came spilling out as I stood riveted in place, unable to respond.

As Forsythia savaged him, Nitbit's mouth opened wide in terror, and he screamed. His horrifying, compelling, almost human-sounding scream—long and plaintive and panicked—seared through my own belly. I winced and grabbed at my middle with open palms, as if to protect myself. The other rabbits darted into the enclosed portion of their cages to hide.

I looked at Forsythia, now standing over Nitbit with blood on her mouth, her teeth still snapping. I was so stunned, I felt immobilized. Why would a mother attack her own child?

After a long, shocked interval, I flung open the cage and Forsythia retreated to the back. I carefully, gingerly, lifted Nitbit out of the cage and set him on the ground beneath it. He was still alive, but staggering, occasionally toppling onto his side. I left him staggering under the cage, dragging his innards behind him through the straw and droppings beneath the pens.

I found Ma in the kitchen. The aroma of coffee filled the room. She looked up as I rushed in.

"Ma! Ma! Come quick, one of the rabbits is hurt bad." I pulled on her hand, trying to drag her outside.

"I ain't got time for that now, Anthony." She pulled her hand free and grabbed her pack of cigarettes from the counter beside her, tapped out a cigarette, and lit it with her lighter.

"But, Ma," I pleaded, "you have to come *now*."

She took another deep drag from her cigarette before saying, finally, "Okay, let's go see what mischief you've gotten into."

I led her into the backyard and pointed at Nitbit under the pens.

"What's wrong with him?" Ma looked puzzled. I started sobbing without expecting to and Ma told me to bring Nitbit over to her so she could look at him. I didn't want to touch him, but I gingerly scooped him up and showed him to Ma. "Where's he hurt? I don't see a thing." Ma took a puff on her cigarette and exhaled white smoke over Nitbit and me. I turned Nitbit slightly to expose his belly. Blood stained my shirt. Ma leaned forward to look at his injury. Her eyes widened just for second, and her hand shook a little so the ash tumbled off the end of her cigarette.

"Jesus Christ! What did you do?" she said.

"I don't know," I stammered. "I put him in the cage with Forsythia and she attacked him. I didn't mean to do it."

"You never mean to do nothing," she said. "Put that thing down and go get some old newspaper from the trash."

I carefully set Nitbit on the ground. He hobbled a couple steps and caught a paw in his own intestines and toppled on his side. I sobbed and Ma waved her hand in my direction. "I said go get some newspaper, Anthony. Now!"

I darted to the garage and returned with several sections of the prior day's paper. I handed them to Ma, but she pointed to Nitbit and said, "Now wrap him up in the newspaper."

"But Ma, he's still alive." I looked at her, not comprehending.

"I can see that, Anthony. Now, do what I said. Wrap him up." She inhaled on her cigarette and the tip glowed blood red. "Wrap it up tight." I gingerly obeyed her, looking up when I had finished. "Now, go put it in the trash can by the road. The trash men will be here in the morning." She pointed in the direction of the front yard.

"But Ma, he's still alive. Can't we take him to the veterinarian?" I looked up at her without moving. My own insides felt like they, too, were slipping out of my belly.

"We can't, Anthony. He's hurt too bad and, besides, you know we can't afford it. Now, go put him in the trash."

I felt helpless, unable to make Ma understand and knowing, somewhere in the back of my own mind, that Ma was right: Nitbit could never survive. I felt him squirming inside the wrapped paper. I carried him to the trash cans lining the road in front of our house and carefully set him atop a sealed bag in one of the cans. Ma followed at a distance, smoking and watching. The newspaper twitched and turned. Suddenly, Nitbit's head poked out, followed by his body. He struggled out of the trash can, toppling to the curb. I ran back to Ma and hugged her around the waist, sobbing. Ma pulled away from me and walked purposefully to the garage. A moment later, she reappeared. Pop's axe was in her hand.

"You caused this Anthony," she said as she soberly placed the axe in my hands. "Now it's time for you to be a man. Take this axe and put that rabbit out of its misery."

I looked at her—incredulous—and took a step back in disbelief. "Cut off his head?"

"No, no. Hit it on the head with the flat side of the axe." She motioned me over. "It's time for you to grow up, Anthony; men clean up the messes they make. You did this; now, you have to handle it."

I walked back to the curb. My legs felt like springs, wobbly and unsteady. I knelt down and gently cradled Nitbit's head in my hands, folding his ears forward. I swung back on the axe and brought it forward and down against Nitbit's exposed head with a gentle tap. Then, I dropped the axe on the curb with a clang and dropped back on my haunches.

Ma was watching me, telling me to try again, waving her arms at me, but I couldn't move. I watched Ma's mouth snap open and shut as she cussed at me. Her white teeth flashed. I turned away at the sound of a car pulling into our driveway. Pop was home.

Ma rushed to the car as Pop emerged, and I could hear her telling him what happened. I wanted to run away, but Nitbit was struggling to right himself again and I couldn't leave until it was over because I had caused it all, and I knew I had to pay for what I'd done. Surely, I was the most evil little boy ever born and deserved whatever I got. I wondered if Ma would ask Pop to hit me on the back of my head with the axe, too. At the time, I hoped he would because I felt so much pain in my chest I wanted it to end. All of this was my fault: no one could undo what I had done.

After a few seconds, Pop strode to the curb beside me and took the axe in his hands. Big hands. Big, ink-stained hands. I watched his hands grip the dark wood handle, drawing it back over his shoulder and forward again and down, down. The axe banged resoundingly on the pavement, missing Nitbit's head by several inches. Pop let the axe tumble out of his hands in the dirt.

I looked up at him. He looked at the ground like he was ashamed of himself and said, so quietly I wasn't sure whether I heard or imagined it, "I can't do it, neither." That surprised me. Why wouldn't Pop be able to do it? Surely, Pop was a man, and yet, he couldn't hit Nitbit either. Suddenly, the difference between Pop and me, which had always seemed so vast, felt a little smaller.

"Jesus Christ," Ma said. "Can't either of you be men about this? Never mind, I'll take care of it." She stomped into the house and called my Uncle Joe who lived a few blocks away and asked him to come over. He arrived a few minutes later and unhesitatingly clubbed Nitbit on the crown of his head, between his silky ears. Nitbit crumpled to his side and stopped moving without ever uttering a sound. But his eyes remained open, and I imagined they were staring at me: accusing me; damning me for my disobedience; condemning me for killing him.

Tarantella

Uncle Joe nudged Nitbit onto his back with the toe of his boot. "Jesus Christ, it looks like a fucking tiger got him. What in the hell did you do to him, Anthony?"

"One of the other rabbits attacked it," Ma said.

"It's all my fault," I said, and started shaking uncontrollably.

But Uncle Joe shrugged and wrapped Nitbit back in the newspaper and put him back into the trash can. Pop carried the axe back to the garage. Ma called to me, but I couldn't seem to move, like I was frozen in place, so she lit another cigarette and went inside trailing white smoke after her.

Uncle Joe followed Ma inside, glancing back at me leaning against the trunk of a silver maple—braced against it, really, so I wouldn't fall over. Pop reemerged from the garage, stopped with his hands on his hips, looking at me. I looked back at him without reacting or thinking. My mind felt empty, as if everything had leaked out onto the ground like Nitbit's blood. The shaking passed and I felt nothing at all—almost like I wasn't really there; like I had witnessed everything from a great distance and hadn't been a part of it at all. I think I knew, even then, that something had changed inside me. I felt pain because what had happened to Nitbit was my fault. Mine. I was stunned that Nitbit's own *mother* had done this to him. I was shocked that Ma thought I should end Nitbit's suffering by killing him. But I had failed again and so, Nitbit had suffered even more because of me.

I was staring at the blood on the curb when Pop came up behind me and set his hand on my shoulder. "Let's head inside. I think you've learned your lesson today. When we tell you something, it's for your own good. Bad things happen when you don't listen." He steered me inside. I went straight to my room, climbed into bed, and pulled the sheets over my head.

The second big change in my life began, coincidentally, right after Nitbit's death.

When I awoke the next day, I went out to the front curb and found the trashcans empty and Nitbit gone. Only a blood-stain bore witness to the previous day's events. Nitbit's blood had turned dark, almost black, under the New York morning sun. Even after the stain eventually faded, I was sure I could see its dark, accusing outline in the gutter. I began to pray that I could escape, get far away from all this blood.

I had recently read the story of Tom Sawyer. When Tom and Huck ran away, I thought about Paddy and wondered what had become of him. The dense stand of oak trees at the farthest edge of the yard, where Paddy had disappeared, were alive again—after a particularly brutal winter—with brilliant green leaves. Time and again, I thought about running away like Tom and Paddy, but I always froze in place—the same way I had frozen with Nitbit. Paddy had been gone four years already. I could no longer recall what he looked like or remember the time when we shared a bedroom. I imagined all kinds of evils had befallen him and that he was sorry he had run away.

I let my gaze wander over our enormous yard where the mowing season would begin soon enough. I dreaded it. Every year, I had more trees to dodge as Pop continued to plant more and more in what was already the most tree-covered yard on our block. I glanced at the dozens of maple trees—all planted by Pop—pregnant with reddish-green nubs of spring growth. The lilacs behind the house had already begun blooming, but the main bloom was still a week or two away. I hardly noticed the stranger when he drove up and went inside to talk to Ma and Pop.

After the man left, Ma and Pop called me and Rosalia inside and shared the surprising news: we were selling our house and moving to Florida. I hardly paid attention to the specifics: something about Pop quitting his job, taking a risk moving the family without a definite job, being glad to leave this "Goddamned cold, snow machine," —about leaving everything behind.

Rosalia complained bitterly about the prospect of moving.

"I hate Florida," she announced. "I won't go."

"You'll love Florida," Pop countered. "It's sunny and warm and you'll be able to go to the beach all year long."

Pop walked over to Rosalia and swung her up onto his shoulders. "You'll be the prettiest, most popular girl in Florida," he said, setting her down on the sofa and tickling her sides until her squeals of laughter turned into shrieks. She squirmed out of his reach, only to come right back for more, despite her protests.

Rosalia had commanded Pop's attention for as long as I could recall. She was pretty and outgoing and Pop doted on her. I couldn't understand why, because she misbehaved all the time and her grades were mostly Bs and Cs.

When I showed Pop my last report card, he pointed his inky index finger to the lone B.

"Why is *this* here?" he asked, scrutinizing my face as if he might find the cause of my failing there.

"It's only one B, Pop," I said. "I'll still get an A for the semester. I promise."

"That don't excuse it," he said sternly. "You just don't concentrate, Anthony. You can do better; I know it. This don't mean nothing until you can get all As and keep getting them. *Every time.* Here, take this back, and don't disappoint me next time." He tossed the card back to me like it was a report of some criminal activity I'd been a part of.

"Why don't you yell at Rosalia?" I complained. "My grades are way better than hers."

"Girls don't need good grades," Pop said. "She'll have a husband someday, but you're going to have to work for a living and, without good grades, you'll end up digging ditches."

Rosalia sidled up behind Pop and embraced him, while sticking her tongue out at me. "You're gonna be a ditch digger," she jibed.

"Well, it's better than being a brat, like you," I shot back.

"You apologize to your sister this instant," Pop said. "You're not too big for me to spank, smart-ass."

"It's not fair," I protested. "I get better grades and I still get in trouble. I don't care if she is a girl; she's still stupid. And a brat."

I felt the sting before I ever saw Pop move. He smacked his big, ink-stained hand across my bottom with a resounding thwack.

"Don't you ever call your sister stupid again, mister," Pop said. "Now, apologize before I give you another one."

I felt humiliated, and knew my face was flushing bright crimson from the heat I felt emanating off it. I hated Rosalia at that moment and, if Pop weren't around, I would have slapped the fat grin right off her face. But Pop *was* around.

"I'm sorry," I said grudgingly and headed toward my room.

"I want to see straight As next time, Anthony," Pop called after me. "You'll thank me someday. You'll see."

I stomped into my room and slammed the door behind me. I resented Rosalia for being a girl and pretty and having it easy. When I broke a rule, I got spanked or yelled at or both, but Rosalia would give Pop a look and he'd forgive her and tell her not to do it again. Every time Pop let Rosalia off easy or took her side, I resented her more, until we barely spoke to each other. By the time of our move, Rosalia and I were almost like strangers to each other.

Rosalia was also Ma's baby. Ma catered to her constantly, which bred further resentment in me. I avoided Rosalia as much as possible. Only a few months after Rosalia's birth, Ma was diagnosed with cancer of the cervix and had to go to the hospital for an operation that meant she couldn't have any more children and, I suppose, that made Rosalia extra special, since she was the last. Pop said Ma got cancer because I was so big that I messed up Ma's insides when I was born and she never was right after that. I started thinking of myself as a kind of cancer that caused bad things to happen wherever I went: I gave Ma cancer by being born. I killed Nitbit. I couldn't ever get my report card the way Pop wanted it. And, I wasn't pretty, like Rosalia. Or brave, like Paddy. Or anything that marked me as special and worthwhile.

It was like I didn't exist at all, except when I messed up; then, they'd all laugh at me. So, I stopped trying to learn new things and gave up on the things I couldn't do well, like sports and telling jokes and practically everything that wasn't somehow connected with writing stories or studying. I read everything I could lay my hands on, and studied constantly to ensure I knew more than anyone else in my classes did. The other kids at school made fun by calling me "Brain" and "Mr. Wizard," but I liked it because it made me special. I could see they were jealous. My teachers told me to ignore them because I'd "show them what's what one day." I looked forward to that day.

By the end of June, our house had been sold and we headed for Florida in a big truck that Pop drove, and our station wagon, which Ma drove. We alternated riding with Pop in the truck— every time we stopped, Rosalia and I argued over the privilege, and shifted positions like musical chairs. I was engrossed in reading *Rosemary's Baby* as we motored down the coast, barely noticing as we slipped from one state to another. I felt a special connection to the baby. Bad things seemed to happen when I was around too, and I was convinced that my whole family hated me.

Yet, our move to Florida filled me with hope: This was my chance to restart my life. I vowed things would be different—I would make friends in Florida and I'd forget about everything that happened in New York. I'd do everything right from now on. In Florida, I would follow every rule, obey Ma and Pop blindly, never argue or disagree. Rosalia never fought with them openly, but behind their backs, did all the things Ma and Pop forbade. But I began following every rule. If I always did as I was told, I would never get into trouble. At least, that's the way I saw it at the time. I was convinced bad things happened because I was bad. From now on, I would only be good. Maybe then, Ma wouldn't turn on me the way Forsythia had turned on Nitbit.

Even as I anticipated the changes, I worried about the past: How would Paddy find us again? How could I undo the things I had already done? How could I change *my* life if Ma and Pop were still the same?

On the second night of our move to Florida, we stopped at a motel in South Carolina. After checking in, we headed to the restaurant next door for dinner. We sat at the table and I felt like an adult with a menu in front of me, trying to decide what I wanted to order. For the first time, I felt grown up and, with New York behind me, I began to believe things would be different in Florida. Rosalia was sneaking sugar cubes out of the bowl on the table and slipping them into her mouth when Ma and Pop weren't watching.

When the waitress came to the table, Ma ordered for Rosalia and herself, Pop ordered next. Finally, the waitress looked my way.

"Just a minute, Anthony," Ma said before I could order, concern creasing her face. "What's that over your lip?" All eyes turned in my direction.

Puzzled, I reached up with my hand, but I felt nothing unusual. "What?" I asked.

"That." Ma pointed at me and I felt my lip again. "Right there. Is that a caterpillar over your lip? Or is it dirt?" And she and Pop and the waitress hooted with laughter as it dawned on me that she meant the tentative beginnings of a moustache that recently had sprouted on my face. I blushed and looked down at the table.

"I wonder if he's got another caterpillar in his pants," Pop said, between guffaws. And he and Ma and the waitress and even Rosalia burst into still louder laughter, causing the people seated at the neighboring tables to glance over and smirk.

I watched them all laughing at me. The waitress seemed embarrassed, too, and said, "They're just funning with you, honey. It's okay. Why don'tcha give me yer order?"

But I couldn't speak. I was afraid if I opened my mouth I might croak like a frog or start crying. I felt like I was back in New York. How could I leave New York behind if they brought my shame along with us? Once again, I felt like a freak in their eyes, with hair sprouting from unfamiliar places. I saw them all looking at me, and I felt utterly and completely ashamed.

"Oh, come on now, Anthony," Ma said. "It was just a joke. Give the waitress your order and stop being a baby." I blinked in response, but said nothing. Ma turned to the waitress and told her to bring me a hamburger and fries. I didn't speak during the entire meal and went straight to bed as soon as we got back to our room.

I lay in bed awake for a long time after Ma and Pop turned the lights out. I thought about slipping out of the room during the night and running away where they would never find me. Perhaps this was what Paddy had felt—what had driven him away. But I wasn't Paddy, wasn't nearly as brave as Paddy. I was afraid of being alone, so I gaped into the darkness until I drifted asleep finally and dreamed about swimming in the warm ocean when we reached Florida.

Shadowy, yellow morning light glowed behind the curtains when I awoke to the sound of Ma's shrill voice.

"Oh, Jesus Christ. Who pissed the bed?" She loomed over the bed and drew back the covers.

I became aware of how cold and wet my pajamas felt. Rosalia and I looked at one another trying to figure out which one of us was the guilty party. Ma reached down to feel Rosalia's pajamas, but found them dry. Surprised, she looked over at me in disgust. I felt the stiff pressure of her fingers on my thighs as Ma touched her fingers to my pajamas, and realized with horror, that I had wet the bed for the first time in years.

"Aw, shit, Anthony. I should of known it was you!" Ma wrenched her hand away and hurried into the bathroom to wash it. "Thirteen years old and still pissing the goddamned bed. Why don't you grow up? You make me ashamed of you."

"I didn't know." I felt betrayed by my body, betrayed and humiliated. I loathed my body—I was sprouting hair from all sorts of unexpected and embarrassing places—above my lip, under my arms, on my chest, between my legs. So much hair that even the other boys in gym class had noticed, pointing and laughing. No one else had the dense growth of hair I boasted, except David Eddings, who was about a foot taller than me so, of course, no one kidded him. I felt like a freak, and dreaded the end of each gym class, when Mr. Thomas would clap his hands together and say, "Okay, men. Hit the showers." I would stall as long as possible in the vain hope that the other boys would be finished before I got undressed, so they wouldn't see me naked.

Pop climbed out of his bed and pulled on his pants. "Son-of-a-bitch," he said, shaking his head. "You pissed on your sister? I can't believe what a little pig you are. When will you ever grow up? Get over here and touch your toes."

"No, Pop. I didn't do it on purpose. I swear."

"Did I ask if you did it on purpose? No, I didn't ask. Now, get your wet, little piss-ass over here. You're up to two. You want three?"

I slid from the bed and eased over toward Pop, turned, and touched my fingers to my toes.

"On the count of three," Pop said. "Are you ready? One... two...three."

I jumped to a standing position and flinched in anticipation of the blow. I heard Pop snort and laugh; he hadn't moved his hand at all. "I told you to touch your toes. Now you get three, Mr. Piggy. Bend over."

I bent over again, and Pop administered three sharp smacks with the flat of his hand. It sounded like he was slapping his hand in a puddle.

"Aw, shit," he complained. "I feel like I just put my hand in the toilet." Then, he went to the bathroom and washed his hand. Tears rolled down my face from the throbbing pain. Rosalia giggled at me and made faces while I waited for my turn to use the bathroom to clean up and get out of my cold, wet pajamas. Ma and Pop made me wait until last since I had caused the commotion. When, at last, it was my turn, I could barely move out of pain and embarrassment. Nothing was going as I had hoped. By the time we left the hotel, I could hardly concentrate on anything, except how humiliated I felt. Pop told me to get into the truck with him.

"How come he gets to ride in the truck after he peed the bed?" Rosalia protested.

"Because I said so," Pop replied, and motioned in my direction. "I said get in the truck." I grabbed *Rosemary's Baby* and climbed into the passenger seat, partly pleased at the privilege and partly wishing to avoid the attention. Although it was still early, the temperature had already soared into the nineties. The truck had no air conditioning, unlike the station wagon, and heat poured through the windows in a sweltering, 60-mile-per-hour stream. The sweat dripped down Pop's stubbled face and his shirt darkened with wet spots as we drove.

I shifted uncomfortably, repeatedly wiping the sweat from my face and neck with the towel that was draped over the seat to keep it from getting too hot in the sun. I couldn't stop thinking about the scene in the restaurant the night before and the one in the hotel earlier that morning. I felt like the whole world was against me, which only upset me more. When I looked up, we were already into central Georgia. Interstate 95 stretched far into the distance, where it seemed to melt in rivulets of shimmering heat. On either side of the roadway stretched a dense, swampy marsh. I opened my book and tried to concentrate, but the bouncing forced my eyes to focus and refocus continually.

Suddenly, I felt a twinge of nausea, and I glanced up from my reading in surprise. I shut my book and set it beside me on the seat. A second, stronger wave of nausea clutched me, and my head drooped down between my legs. The sweat on my back felt like a clammy river.

"What in hell are you up to now, Anthony? Sit up in that god-damned seat, mister." Pop reached out with one hand and yanked me up by the collar of my shirt. I moaned.

"I don't feel so good." I leaned back against the seat as another bout of nausea swept down on me, and the bright sun vanished behind roiling waves of black. Between reading in the moving truck and the anxiety of the last two days, I had upset my stomach. My breakfast rose into my mouth. I leaned my head out the window and vomited until my stomach felt better, the darkness lifted, and I could raise my head off the doorframe. I looked over at Pop.

I had vomited directly into the seventy-miles-per-hour wind and it had blown everything straight back inside the window, coating Pop from head to toe. He was wiping his eyes and cussing in a continuous stream, without appearing to take a breath.

"Oh, Jesus H. Christ! It's a goddamned hundred degrees out and we're in the middle of a fucking swamp in the middle of nowhere. Aw, Christ almighty! I don't fucking believe this, Anthony. I don't believe it. Whadaya, stay up nights thinking up this shit? Jesus Christ."

At the first gas station, Pop squealed off the road and raced for the bathroom to clean up. When he came out, he smacked the back of my head and told me to go in and wash off and put on a change of clothes. By the time I got back out, he had cleaned up the truck. He told me that I wasn't allowed in it anymore and asked Rosalia to come with him. Rosalia stuck her tongue out at me as she climbed up into the truck.

I headed to the car and, as I approached, Ma leaned her head out.

"How are you feeling?" she asked.

"Okay," I said.

"Well, don't try that little stunt with me, mister," she warned. "I won't put up with it."

I slid into the back seat of the car and opened my book. Ma snatched the book from my hands. "That's probably what made you sick in the first place," she said. "No more reading until we get to Florida."

I knew that was only part of what made me sick. I had been thinking about David Eddings, from school, and had gotten aroused. To hide my arousal, I had placed my book over my lap and continued reading. My eyes had to keep focusing and refocusing as we bumped along, and I had suddenly begun to feel nauseous. I was thirteen, and my body seemed to have developed a mind of its own. But, I couldn't explain that to my parents, so I lay down on the back seat and fell asleep.

When I woke, my stomach had settled and the car's air conditioner felt cool on my skin. I sat up and peered out the side window. A sign welcomed us to Florida while another encouraged us to stop for orange juice at the Welcome Station ahead. Pop, ahead of us in the truck, turned in at the Welcome Station and Ma followed him into the parking lot. She stopped the car and grabbed her cigarettes from the dash. "Come on," she said. "I guess your crazy father wants orange juice."

I looked around me as I took my first steps in Florida. Except for the area right around the Welcome Center, Florida looked a lot like New York, but the oaks and maples had been replaced with pines and a smattering of scruffy palms. It didn't seem the least bit like the tropical jungle I was expecting. And the only birds I saw were sparrows that could have followed us from New York.

Inside the center, an elderly woman with white hair poured us each a small paper cup of orange juice. It tasted a lot like the orange juice Ma made us in New York, only a lot more pulp, which I hated. After a couple of minutes, Pop crumpled his cup and tossed it in the trash and said, "Let's go."

So, Ma stubbed out her cigarette and pulled her purse over her shoulder. Pop looked at us and asked, "Who wants to ride in the truck?" We both said we did. Pop looked at me and said, "No pukers allowed," then turned to Rosalia and said, "Come on, Rosie. You're not a puker, are you?"

Rosalia made a face at me and stuck out her tongue again as she followed Pop to the truck. I told myself that I didn't like riding in the hot truck anyhow, but I wanted to cry, even though I knew it was ridiculous. I wished I were different so Pop would love me the way he loved Rosalia.

As we continued driving, I wondered if Pop felt *he* needed a new start, too. Hadn't I overheard him telling Ma about being unappreciated at work? Hadn't Ma suggested getting away from everything and going somewhere new and warm? What were *they* running away from?

We stayed on Interstate 95 for several more hours until we passed a sign that said "Cocoa Beach." Then, we headed east. After a minute or so, we came to a stoplight at the base of the biggest and most beautiful bridge I could remember seeing. A sign announced that this was the Hubert Humphrey Bridge and identified the river it spanned as the Indian River. The bridge arched elegantly into the air, rising perhaps a hundred feet over the water. From where I sat, it looked as if the bridge simply ended at the top of its arch, when we would plummet into the river. After this morning, I almost wished we would.

"Oh, Jesus Christ," Ma gasped, leaning forward to see the top. Ma hated to drive over bridges—any bridge—because she was afraid of heights. In New York, she would drive miles out of her way to avoid crossing one. But on this journey, she had no choice, crossing many bridges because she had to. Pop would have told her to stop her belly-aching if she had objected, so she never said a word to him, only cussed each time we came up to one, lit a cigarette, popped it into her mouth, and crossed herself like she was entering a church.

While waiting for the light to change, Ma lit her cigarette. "Anthony, you cross yourself and don't move until we're off this goddamned bridge," she said. I watched in the rearview mirror as her cigarette bobbed up and down with each word. Defiantly, I only moved my hands and pretended. Ever since that day, I have refused to cross myself in fear. Perhaps that's why I've always had such trouble getting from one place to another.

The light flashed green, and Ma crossed herself and followed Pop up the steep incline. The sound of the car engine seemed to double its volume with the extra effort of the climb.

At the exact center of the span, a simple green road sign with white lettering announced, "Merritt Island." We could see the island—below and ahead of us—densely covered by trees. The highway sliced through the foliage like a belt cinched around a waist. The intensity of color—blue river, green island, black pavement, yellow sun—stung my eyes, and I gasped in amazement. Neither of us spoke a word after that, until we touched down on the island. I felt like I was looking at the Garden of Eden.

We continued east across the island until we saw a second river—the Banana River—before us. This time, however, a causeway led to the other side with only a short, squat bridge in the center. Ma pulled the cigarette from her mouth, heaved out a great white smoke cloud, crossed herself yet again, and said, "Oh, Jesus, this whole state is covered with goddamned bridges. I'll be lucky if I can leave the house when we buy one."

The Banana River stretched nearly a mile from shore to shore and glistened under the late afternoon sun. This water seemed more black than blue. A little over halfway to the other side, a building rose on the north side of the causeway on its own little island. A sign identified the pinkish structure as Cape Canaveral Hospital. Another sign identified the city ahead of us as Cocoa Beach. At A1A, we turned south and pulled into the Satellite

Tarantella

Motel a few blocks ahead. Beyond the motel, we could see and hear the ocean. Waves rolled up to shore at an angle, and the smell of salt hung in the air. As Pop went into the motel office, we asked Ma if we could swim in the ocean; she said we'd have to see about that. Pop returned from the office and drove a little further down the parking lot. When he stopped, we pulled into the space beside him and climbed out.

"We're here. Anyone for a dip in the ocean?" Pop looked over at us as we all shouted our enthusiastic replies. We hurried into our motel room to change and raced down the path to the beach. Dropping our towels and shoes and shirts in the sand, we followed Pop as he ran into the water and dove into an oncoming wave. The water felt cold at first, and I felt my stomach muscles tighten in response. Pop and Rosalia chased each other a few feet ahead of me; behind me, Ma waded only a few feet from shore in ankle-deep water. She held a cigarette in the air between puffs to keep it dry.

A wave splashed against my chest, sending plumes of salty water cascading over my head and into my mouth. I swiped a hand across my face to clear my eyes and tried to take in everything around me. This ocean was a lot bigger than Irondequoit Bay in New York. I could see across the bay, but the ocean seemed to reach forever. And this water was salty, yet it didn't sting my eyes. I felt something rough under my feet, reached down and pulled up a sand dollar: a round, disk-shaped creature that lived on the ocean floor. As I held the delicate shell in my hand, I could feel its cilia-like "legs" moving against my palm. Suddenly, my world seemed full of new and exciting things, and endless possibilities. Holding the sand dollar before me, I crossed myself with it, then let it go. This was the start of my new life.

The first two weeks in Florida were magical, like a vacation that would never end because, after all, we had moved to the land of vacations. During the day, Pop would go job-hunting and we would go down to the beach with Ma. We learned to beachcomb for shells, and how to locate and dig sand fleas and ghost crabs out of the beach sand. We bodysurfed, built sandcastles, and spent the entire time playing. In the evening, after Pop returned, we would go out for dinner, and afterwards, we would stop by Carvel's for an ice cream. In New York, I ate only chocolate ice cream but, in Florida, I discovered vanilla and ordered it every day. It tasted exotic and exciting, perfect for this new life of mine.

One day, Pop came home and announced that he had found a new job and bought a house on Merritt Island. I felt thrilled at the thought of living on an island, and remembered how beautiful it had looked that day from atop the Hubert Humphrey Bridge. The next morning, we left the motel, and Pop led the way to our new house. He pulled into the carport of an aquamarine coquina house with a backyard canal. No one moved until Pop hopped onto the driveway, clapped his hands together, and said, "Look alive. Everybody out. We've got work to do."

Hours later, with the truck unloaded, I sat in my new bedroom. I looked at myself in the new bathroom mirror: tan skin, sun-lightened hair. But I still felt the same. I was like an animal that had shed its old skin for a shiny new one—but my insides hadn't changed. I had expected to feel completely different in Florida, but here we were and I still felt like me. I wandered into the living room: the house was new, but it was filled with the same furniture. Nothing seemed very different to me. I didn't know what to do or where to go. I had no friends to visit, so I pulled a book from an as-yet-unpacked box, and plopped on the sofa to read.

I read a lot after arriving in Florida and felt oddly and intensely alone, even though I hadn't exactly had an abundance of friends back in New York. The new yard was so small compared to the two acres we had in New York. There were no trees to climb—only a couple of big palms out front. So, I would wander to our back yard and sit on the seawall, dangling my feet over the canal. Every afternoon, around four, the sky would darken, the air would start blowing, lightning would flash, and thunder boom as rain beat the ground with a fury I never realized rain could possess. In minutes, the ground outside ran with water, and the street looked like a river. The lights would blink on and the air would cool. But, in twenty minutes, it was over as abruptly as it began. The sun would come out before the rain ended, and the wind would vanish. In a few minutes, the heat would return, and the water would disappear into the ground, evaporating in ripples of heat that made the air look like it was moving. Not a sign would remain of the recent fury except downed tree limbs and palm fronds, or patio furniture lying upside-down in the middle of front yards.

About a month after we moved into our new house, the school year began. I was entering the ninth grade, my final year of junior high school. The name of the school was Edgewood Jr. High and, as I awaited the school bus that first day, I wondered what it would be like.

The school was hot, hotter than I ever dreamed. When I complained, another student called me a Yankee.

"Why don't you go back to New York, Yankee?" he asked.

"Yankee! Yankee!" the other students chanted.

"Maybe you should go to Jefferson. That's where all the rich Yankees who can't take the heat go, because it's air conditioned," the first student said.

Later that day, in gym class, the coach sent us out to run a few laps on the track behind the school. On the far side of the track, a few of the other boys gathered and I ran over to join them. They were watching a bunch of birds skittering up and down in the field a few feet away.

"What is it?" I asked.

"A snake," another boy said. "You can spot them because the birds like to chase them."

Another boy ran out to where the birds were playing, causing them to fly away. He chased something in the grass and suddenly lifted a triumphant hand in the air. A dark, two-foot snake writhed and squirmed in his grasp and he ran back towards the group.

"What kind of snake is it?" I asked.

"It's a rattler," said the boy, thrusting the snake into my face. I jumped back instinctively. "Looka the little scaredy cat," the boy chided. "He's afraid of a little glass snake."

Tarantella

"What's a glass snake?" I asked, taking a cautious step forward to examine the wriggling creature.

"It's a snake that breaks. Watch." He grasped the snake in the middle and snapped it in two with a sharp crack. Then, he tossed both pieces into the grass and he and the other boys laughed and resumed their laps. I walked over to where he had tossed the pieces. The tail end writhed and whipped back and forth, but the front end was nowhere to be found.

One Saturday about a week later, Pop got home early from work and decided to take us to the beach. I finished changing into my bathing suit first and let myself out to wait for the rest of the family on the driveway.

As I clicked the screen door closed behind me, I noticed a dozen or more sparrows flocked along the sidewalk, chattering raucously. Like big, brown dandelion spurs, they floated up and down along the walkway. Remembering my classmate's comment, I approached the swirling commotion of birds and noticed a snake—a very big snake, with gray-brown and white markings—slipping silently and purposefully along the walkway. At first, I thought it was a glass snake, but the coloring differed and it was larger. Much larger. I decided it must be a rattlesnake, even though I had never seen a rattler before—except in a book.

The insistent whine of a power saw from somewhere down the street buzzed in my ears as I gaped at the sparrows performing an intricate-but-erratic dance like playful children. All the while, they chittered noisily, like an audience awaiting the start of a movie. Meanwhile, the snake, seemingly oblivious to the hubbub around it, slipped off the sidewalk into the coarse Bermuda grass.

From the house behind me, I heard Ma yelling. "Goddamn it, Rosalia. We don't have all day. Now, get finished changing or we'll just leave your ass at home."

"Good. Leave me home," came the equally tart reply. "I don't want to go anyhow."

"Get ready, you little shit! You're going. You can't stay here by yourself."

A smirk creased my lips. Rosalia had become quite rebellious of late. I admired her resistance—even wished I could be more like her—but knew I lacked her gumption. She awed me with her strong-willed disregard for Ma's threats, and Ma didn't seem to know how to respond. Rosalia had mastered indifference. She exasperated everyone she encountered, including me. But I knew Rosalia possessed a powerful weapon—a weapon I had not yet learned. At that time, I couldn't shut things out; I heard and reacted to everything, no matter how hard I tried to ignore them.

As I edged up toward the flighty sparrows, they flitted into the palms lining the grassy span between the road and the walkway. There they continued chattering, watching me from above. I glanced up at them, wondering what they were saying. Perhaps they were brothers and sisters discussing their mutual predicament; perhaps they all resented my intrusion for different reasons. They eyed me suspiciously, but didn't flee.

Worried about the snake, I hurriedly glanced back to gauge its current position. It had slithered across the spongy lawn, moving toward me in a slow zigzag. I took a startled step back and stood stock-still a moment, enthralled by its dangerous proximity. Deep down, my belly tingled with an involuntary shudder.

The soaker hose in the front lawn sprayed sulfur-laden artesian well water with a soft hiss on the sun-browned grass. The water's foul odor, like decaying fish, tugged at my stomach.

The sparrows flitted anxiously back to the sidewalk, just beyond the snake's reach, taunting it, fluttering away as soon as it moved in their direction. I watched the tiny birds tease the snake as if they were dancing some kind of death-defying, exhilarating ballet—a ballet that could, at any moment, come to a swift and fatal conclusion. I scarcely dared to breathe, only gaped and raised my hands, palms up, to my face, lacing my fingers protectively over my mouth to keep from crying out. I wanted to scream, but something snatched my voice away.

"Whatcha doin' there, Anthony?" Rosalia's voice asked from somewhere behind me.

I backed a few steps from the walkway before turning around and running toward my smaller sister. I latched onto her arm and hauled her roughly toward the screen door, so that she wouldn't see and scare off the birds and the snake. Rosalia, startled, resisted my grip and wrenched away.

"You crazy, Anthony? Leave me 'lone. I don't have to go in."

"Yes, you do. Get in the house, goddamn it, or I'll drag you in." I shook my head at the unintentional curse and glanced back toward the walkway for the tell-tale birds to gauge the snake's location. Rosalia's eyes followed mine.

"Whatcha lookin' at? What are those birds doing?"

"None of your business." I grabbed her shoulders and propelled her toward the door. "Get in." I yanked the door open, shoved Rosalia inside and followed her in, letting the door snap shut behind me with a sudden whoosh.

Pop was just inside the door, sitting at the dining room table. He looked up at our sudden struggle in the doorway. "What the hell's going on?"

"Anthony's pushing me," Rosalia protested, "and he swore."

"Shut up!" I snapped. I saw anger flash across Pop's face and hurriedly added, "There's a rattlesnake in our front yard." I pointed out the door. "A big one."

"What the hell you talkin' 'bout, Anthony? What the hell would a rattlesnake be doing in our yard?" Pop rose from the table and strode to the door; I stepped quickly aside to let him pass.

"I wanna see the rattlesnake, too," Rosalia whined after him.

"You stay inside," Pop snapped, pointing down at Rosalia's sneakered feet. "Anthony, you show me what you're talkin' about. It's probably just a goddamned garter snake."

Pop clumped out the door with me right behind, pointing at the smattering of sparrows, still fluttering near the sidewalk. "There," I said. "By those birds."

Pop marched down the curving driveway toward the sidewalk and I watched him take an abrupt step back when he realized the snake was longer than he was tall. He bent at the knees and hunched over for a closer examination. "Look here," he called back to me and pointed at the motionless serpent. "It's all gray and brown—just like the garter snakes I used to play with when I was a kid. It's just a big goddamned garter snake, like I said." He moved towards the elongated creature and began reaching out a hand to catch it.

"It's a rattlesnake," I insisted. Even though I wasn't sure myself, I felt indignant at his dismissive attitude. "You ever see a garter snake that big?"

"We're in Florida. Everything is bigger down here. Even the goddamned roaches are 'most as big as my hand." But he hesitated, withdrawing his hand and eyeing the serpent uncertainly. "Go next door and get one of the neighbors. Maybe they'll know what kinda snake it is."

"It's a rattler!" I repeated stubbornly.

"Go, I said!"

I dashed across the yard as Ma burst out of the screen door. I heard Rosalia's voice bleating from inside the house. "There's a rattlesnake outside. There's a rattlesnake outside."

"What's going on?" Ma hissed at me without looking. I pointed at Pop and darted the opposite direction across the lawn toward a thickset black man with yellow-orange hair, who had appeared from inside the garage next door.

"Come quick," I hollered to the man. "There's a big snake in our yard."

The man looked up, puzzled, and then followed me across the yard. As we approached, Pop waved his hand toward the skittish birds and asked the man, "Know what kinda snake that is?"

The man pulled up short and gaped at the snake. His eyes bulged momentarily. He took a quick step back and blurted, "That's a gall-danged rattler, that's what it is. Hoo-whee, I'll be gall-danged!" He motioned toward Ma and instructed, "Call the cops. They'll send a dep'ty right over to kill it."

Ma scooted nervously back inside the house, the door snapping shut behind her. I felt elated and vindicated as I slipped between the car and the front door. Pop hovered over the rattler, near the end of the driveway.

"Git away from that thing," the man hollered at Pop. "They's dangerous. I seen one coil up and jump ten feet once, may God strike me dead if'n I ain't tellin' you true. And last year, this guy over in Cocoa got bit by a rattler and died. It was in the paper, I swear."

The birds flitted suddenly back into the palm tree in an impromptu migration.

"Oh, shit!" Pop blurted and dashed toward the driveway, leaping onto the rear bumper of our station wagon. A gray-brown streak passed harmlessly underneath the car and slithered up against the far wall of the house. The neighbor darted back toward his house, disappearing inside with a slam of a door.

"I'm going to get something to move that thing," Pop hollered as he jumped down off the bumper and darted through the screen door. His disembodied voice called from inside the house: "You keep an eye on it and don't let it out of your sight."

Soon after Pop went inside, the snake glided along the wall, stopping just below the lower lip of the screen door. A moment later, I noticed Pop approaching from inside the house, but I couldn't find my voice. For an instant, I visualized Pop opening the door and the snake biting him, sinking long, curved, white fangs deep into the tender flesh of his legs—legs that would give way beneath him as the poison raced to his heart, terminating its contractions, constricting his lungs, paralyzing his entire body, and leaving him to die in twitching, convulsing agony. All I could think was how sorry he'd be that he hadn't listened to me because I was right. At the last moment, I tried to call out a warning, but froze—only a strange, croaking squeak came out.

Pop pushed open the creaky door and stepped onto the hot concrete of the driveway. I winced with expectation, but the snake didn't strike; it remained frozen in a tiny indentation beneath the lip of the door. Pop ran toward me, asking, "Where's the snake?" I pointed at the base of the door.

"Jesus Christ! Why didn't you warn me?" he snapped. "I never saw it and I practically stepped on the damned thing! I coulda been killed." He eyed me suspiciously. Then, he hollered for Ma and Rosalia to stay inside the house, warning them that the rattlesnake was under the door. A moment later, I could see the two of them behind the screen door, straining to see the snake.

"The police are on their way," Ma hollered to us.

Almost before the words were out of her mouth, a black and white police car marked "Brevard County Sheriff's Deputy" squealed into the driveway. A fat man in a gray-brown uniform stepped out. I stared at the gun suspended from his waist, a gun he removed as he approached the two of us, standing about fifteen feet from the snake, still immobile beneath the door stoop. "Where's the son-of-a-bitch at?"

"It's right in front of the door to the house," Pop said, pointing.

"Damn! Can't shoot it there; the shot could ricochet off the wall." He returned to his car, opened the trunk, and pulled out a square-topped shovel. "I'm a' have to cut off its head with this. That's okay. I hate goddamn snakes. It's more fun this way anyhows."

He walked toward the house, stopping a few feet from the front door. "Stay still, darlin'. Papa's comin'." He eased another step forward. The snake remained motionless. Pop and I followed close behind like twin shadows, moving as the deputy moved. Rosalia watched with Ma from inside the screen door. The deputy took another step. No response. Another. Another. He poised the shovel in the air about six inches from the snake's head and paused briefly. "That's it, darlin'. Don'tcha move." Bending from the waist, he brought the shovel down with a sharp clank on the cement drive. The shovel cut into the snake just below its head and its long torso began thrashing back and forth wildly, coiling and uncoiling, its blood seeping along the concrete, its rattle sounding like dry leaves scratching against each other. "Take that, you son-of-a-bitch. I'm'a cutcher head off." He pressed the shovel against the ground firmly with both hands and slowly eased one foot onto its hilt to bring more weight to bear. Noticing our approach, the deputy warned, "Stay back. This bugger's a tough old broad—like cutting through rope made uh' gristle." We backed away. The snake's mouth gaped open and the fangs slashed the air, its body whipped back and forth, and the deputy cackled and spit. The shovel suddenly scraped sharply against the pavement as the snake wriggled free and darted along the edge of the house toward the front yard.

Tarantella

"Sum bitch!" The deputy cursed, angrily banging the shovel against the concrete. "I'll be danged. That's one tough mother. Ain't no snake ever got out from under my shovel b'fore! Don't worry none; I'll get her yet."

The snake slithered along the edge of the house, pausing a moment before streaking across the blue-green Bermuda grass and into the stone garden. It disappeared under one of the boulders stacked around the garden. Yucca plants sprung from gaps between the boulders, and drab pittosporums cloaked the ground in shadows, completely hiding the snake's mottled form.

"Shit!" the deputy shouted. "I was a-feared of that. These danged rock gardens is home to these buggers. They can stay underneath for days and not come up fer air. We'll never get her now."

"Aw, shit!" Ma called from the doorway. "Now whadda we do? It'll probably come out and get one of us as soon as you leave."

"No, ma'am. These buggers is more a-feared of you than you are o' them. She'll probably hide out till you leave; then, she'll slink back down towards the swamp." He pointed to the wildlife preserve that bordered the neighborhood. "Just stay away from that garden for a little while, 'cause you don't wanna take no chances with a pissed-off rattler, of course. But she'll be off, by and by."

I stared at the splotch of bright maroon blood on the driveway, marking the site of snake's encounter with the shovel. The deputy walked back to the door and scraped his boot across the blood and warned, "Better hose this down right away or it'll dry on the pavement. Then, you might never get it off. Snake blood turns black in the heat." He looked at Pop and grinned, "I hate to leave without my souvenir. I keep 'em so's I can keep track o' how many o' these buggers I kill."

"What souvenir?" Pop asked, dropping his arms to his sides and walking to the edge of the driveway for a brief, bended-knee inspection of the rock garden.

"Hell, the rattle, o' course! You never kills a rattler and leaves its rattle on. They make a good souvenir or a baby rattle for the kids."

"Not in my house," Ma said as she stepped gingerly out of the house. She looked at the bloodstain and then at the rock garden. The lines on her forehead betrayed her fear and incredulity that the snake had escaped.

"Why, sure. They makes good rattles for kids. They sounds like a bunch of old teeth in a paper cup. You should get one and try it. Hell, my kids love 'em. I got a shitload of them at home. All sizes. My kids played with them when they were little. Saved me money from buying baby rattles." He chuckled, hefted the shovel onto his shoulder, and glanced down at the red-smeared pavement. "Damned things bleed like a sieve," he said. He shook his head and snickered. Heading back to his car, he climbed in and started the engine. Then, he paused to lean his head out the window, and said, "Give me a call if you need me again." He backed out of the driveway and sped down the street.

As soon as the deputy left, Pop told me to hose down the driveway. Then, he looked over at Ma, who continued to gape at the rock garden.

Tarantella

"Honey," Pop called to her, "we might as well head for the beach. Maybe by the time we get back it'll be gone." He jerked his head towards the rock garden. Ma looked uncertain, but nodded her agreement.

After Ma went inside, Pop inspected the yard quickly while I turned on the hose and unwound it from the wall reel. Warm water surged from the nozzle, and I sprayed it on the splotch of blood, turning it from red to magenta and to a series of increasingly pale pinks. I directed the spray to wash the snake's blood into the grass.

Satisfied that no other snakes lurked in the yard, Pop told me to finish up and change into my bathing suit, then went inside. I washed the blood from the driveway and watched it soak into the grass without a trace. I smiled as I shut off the water and recoiled the hose. Maybe now Pop and Ma would pay attention to me; I had been right, after all, about the snake. It *had* been a rattlesnake. Maybe they would begin treating me the way they treated Rosalia.

I looked around the yard; the birds had disappeared too. It all seemed so peaceful, so harmless. The sun was shining; the sky was blue and cloudless, and the air was motionless and hot. I thought about this place where I now lived. It suddenly felt very different from New York: full of strange things you didn't notice at first glance; beautiful and hot and exotic; full of life and danger. I eyed the rock garden, staring at all the dark places and shadows—at the blood streak that disappeared under the rocks and at the crevices, knowing one of them harbored a rattlesnake.

I finished coiling the hose. The intense heat had already evaporated the water from the driveway and lawn. Only a faint, dark stain, like a shadow, remained of our encounter a few moments before. I felt strangely exhilarated by the excitement and danger of it all. New York seemed a lifetime ago. I could feel the blood beating like a pulse in my ears, a rhythm calling to me; a rhythm that wasn't yet complete, made up of all the blood and the poison, all the hurt, and things I couldn't seem to understand, things that I was both a part of and apart from, things I knew I must someday face, like the rattlesnake lying in wait in the rock garden.

CHAPTER 6

Fires

Merritt Island: May 1994

I WOKE EARLY the day after my fight with Pop in the hospital and booked an early evening flight back to Chicago, where Steven was waiting. Then, I went out for a drive around the island to restore my equilibrium—my contact—with this place I once called home. Each time I returned, the island seemed changed— increasingly remote, increasingly alien, definitely not home. The sky was hazy, the air intensely hot, and the strong smell of fire pervasive. The Everglades, stricken by intense drought, were burning and choking the entire state with dense, acrid smoke.

Heading north on Courtenay Parkway along the western edge of the island, dozens of memories flashed through my head as I passed first, my old high school and then, Divine Mercy Catholic Church, where I had briefly attended mass. In spite of Pop's vehement disdain for the church because the local priest insisted on "telling me how to cast my goddamned vote" and Ma's refusal to attend without Pop at her side, they both seemed tremendously pleased each time I went to mass.

I pulled into the church parking lot and stopped the car. Before me towered the new church—an enormous gold pyramid, supposedly the largest pyramid in North America—glinting in the bright, hot sun. Dwarfed beside it stood the dimpled, gold dome that had served as the main church during my childhood. It looked small and tacky now, but I remembered how impressed I had been as a child.

I recalled the last time I had attended mass in the pyramid: when Steven had come to visit, more than ten years ago. Steven had insisted on going to mass at Divine Mercy and, against my better judgement, I had agreed.

As we'd pulled into the church lot, Steven whistled.

"Jesus Christ! You go to church in a fucking pyramid!" He scrambled out of the car.

"Yeah, so?" I'd winced, but he put his hands on his hips and gawked at the church, appraising it closely.

"I can't believe it. That fucker would hold three of the churches I went to as a kid." He headed for the door, where streams of people were entering, and I followed him. "They say pyramids have all kinds of mystical properties. Like, they can slow the aging process, and stop your beard from growing, and ward off evil, and illness, and shit like that."

"Steven," I flinched, "please, you're in church. Watch the mouth."

"Yeah, right. Sorry." He glanced around to see if anyone was listening.

I dipped my fingers in the holy water and crossed myself before entering the sanctuary. Steven watched me and grinned, then sidled up alongside.

"It's so bizarre to see you like this. In a church. It's like watching voodoo shit on TV."

"Shush. Haven't you ever been in a church before?"

"It's different in Baptist churches. We don't cross ourselves and use finger bowls and shit." He grinned at me and I shook my head.

"Well, then, just be quiet and watch." I strolled down the aisle and spotted two empty spaces in a pew toward the front of the church. "Follow me." I motioned with my hand. Before sliding into the pew, I genuflected.

"Why'd you do that?" Steve's breath tickled my ear and I rubbed it with my hand.

"Do what?"

"Bend down before you took your seat."

"It's called genuflecting. It shows respect for God." I wasn't sure that was why Catholics genuflected. I'm sure I knew once, but I hadn't the vaguest notion just then of the reason I did anything in church. In fact, I wasn't sure why I had agreed to come here with Steven. He had insisted that we go, said he wanted to "see what Catholics did. Up close and personal." I felt vaguely disturbed by his comment, as though he only wanted to criticize and belittle. Although it had been a long time since I'd gone to services, in spite of my differences with Catholic teachings, I still considered myself spiritual, and felt keenly offended by Steven's lack of respect.

"Just be quiet and watch, since you wanted to come here so bad." I turned to the altar. The priest was just entering.

"Did you go to church much when you were a kid?" Steven leaned against me and stage-whispered.

"For a while," I said, "but I stopped going a long time ago." Steven looked handsome and sweet there in the gold pyramid. Behind us, I recognized many familiar faces of neighbors and school acquaintances. Some recognized me and nodded, and I nodded back. Most didn't seem to notice me.

The service began. Steven slid a hand under my thigh and squeezed playfully. Startled, I shifted away, glancing quickly around to make sure no one had noticed. "Stop that! We're in church." I felt hot in the face and annoyed at his indiscretion.

"What's the big deal? Lots of other couples are holding hands." He gestured around the church.

"There aren't any other couples like *us*. Please, quit it. You're embarrassing me." I looked straight ahead. On the altar, the priest motioned for everyone to rise. We stood.

"Embarrassing you? Did I hear you right? You said I'm embarrassing you?" I could feel the anger in his voice, which had grown louder and rose an octave.

"Come on, Steven. Don't make a scene here. We're in a church." The congregation pulled out their kneelers and knelt. I felt Steven glaring at me as I knelt.

"I know we're in a goddamned church. Does that automatically mean we're also back in the closet?"

"I didn't say that," I said in a hushed tone, embarrassed by the attention we were drawing. "I just don't think this is the time or the place to make a big scene." I glanced around to see if anyone I knew was seated close enough to overhear our conversation.

"I wasn't making a scene. All I did was touch you. You're the one getting all bent out of shape about it." Steven leaned forward in the pew. "We've been at your parent's house all day and I haven't been allowed to touch you because, God forbid, one of your parents should see us. That would be the end of the world. Now, I can't touch you here because we're in a fucking church and, God forbid, the Pope might see us and send us straight to hell."

"Oh, come on, Steven. You're blowing this way out of proportion. I just don't feel comfortable doing it in church."

"That's the problem, Anthony," he said. "We aren't doing anything *wrong*. Don't you get it? You're not straight. No matter how hard you pretend to be when you're at home and in church, you're still gay." A couple of people in the pew in front of us turned around to look at us.

"Ssh," I said. "Do you have to be so loud? That's what I mean about making a scene."

"Do you have to be so fucking ashamed of who you are? There's nothing wrong with us, but you're acting like there is, and I won't sit here and pretend I'm straight."

"I'm not ashamed," I protested. "I just don't see the need to flaunt it all the time. Do you always have to be gay? Every minute of every day?"

"Yes. I do." Steven was practically shouting, and I immediately regretted my words because they had pissed him off. There'd be no calming him down now. "I can't turn it on and off like you can. I'm gay all day long—365 days a year. Last night you fucked me and now that we're in a church, you want everyone to think you're straight!" He stood up and squeezed past the people seated beside us. At the end of the pew, he shouted—loud enough for nearly everyone in the church to hear him, even over the strains of organ music that filled the church—"You're just another fucking faggot, Anthony. Just like me. Why are you so ashamed of yourself?"

He ran up the aisle. The parishioners nearby gaped at me as I squeezed down the pew after him. Before running up the aisle, I turned toward the altar again and genuflected.

I caught up with Steven in the foyer. He looked so hurt and vulnerable that I burst into tears. After watching me cry for a while, Steven hugged me and said he was sorry. I was the one who *should* have been sorry, but at the time, I was too frightened. I thought I had accepted myself and, suddenly, in the middle of church, among the people I had grown up with, Steven had forced me to see that I hadn't. I needed Steven to help me get through this, to help me accept myself. As we hugged and cried and kissed together in the foyer, I heard the priest say, "I am the Lamb of God. I take away the sins of the world."

As I sat in my car, in the shadow of the Pyramid, on the day after my fight with Pop, I noticed a dense cloud of black smoke to the north and smelled fire. It had been a hot, dry spring and brush fires were consuming the land of the wildlife refuge that surrounded the Space Center on the north end of the island. This was a semi-regular spring event.

For a moment, I flashed back on my childhood in New York, to the time I, myself, had started a fire: I couldn't have been much more than ten at the time. Ma and Pop were out in the yard with Rosalia. The stove caught my eye when I slipped into the kitchen to sneak a cookie from the cabinet. I turned on the burners and heard the hiss of gas and the poof of flames igniting, and watched the blue ring of fire for a few minutes. Fire has always fascinated me.

I don't know what possessed me, but I pulled a tissue—a pink tissue, I remember—from the Kleenex box beside the sink and touched one end to the flame. As the flame began consuming the tissue, I caught a strong whiff of the lilacs outside.

I looked out the window over the sink and into the backyard. Pop was digging in the garden and Ma was sitting near him in a lounge chair. She was dangling a cigarette between her fingers over the edge of the chair. I could see the cigarette rise to her face every now and then before dropping again as a cloud of white smoke swirled out of her nostrils. The only sound was a lawn mower buzzing down the street.

I touched another tissue to the burner on the stove. It burst into flames, and I let it drop on the burner when the flames got near my fingers. I can still remember the way it smelled: dry and woody. When it went out, I grabbed another tissue and tossed it over the fire. It burst into flame and burned, and feathery ashes floated up over the stove.

I snatched a handful of Kleenex and dipped one edge into the flame. They burned so fast I panicked. I saw the trash can nearby and flicked the tissues into the can just before the flames burned my fingers.

I can still see it, like a movie in slow motion: the tissues hung in the air for an instant before sort of floating from side-to-side like a pendulum until, finally, they dropped into the trash can. I was so relieved and scared that I shut off all the burners. But, when I looked back at the trash can, orange flames were leaping out of it. They kept getting higher and higher, like long, hot, yellow fingers. Suddenly, the whole trash can was on fire. I panicked and screamed out the window.

Pop jumped up in the garden and chucked the shovel into the soft dirt; it stayed upright. He looked toward the kitchen. The flames were leaping high enough for him to see them through the window by now. Pop's whole face darkened, and I just stood in the window looking out.

"Christ. He's set the house on fire!" Pop yelled, and pointed at me in the window.

Ma leaped right out of her lounge chair and looked at the window. "Oh, my God. Get him out of there!"

I saw the breezeway door fly open, and Pop dash in. He left the door ajar, and I could see blue sky streaming in behind him.

I wanted to run and hide, but I couldn't move—not an inch. I stood in the doorway between the kitchen and the breezeway gaping at the flames. They were over my head by now, and the trashcan seemed to be shrinking. I saw Pop coming toward me from the corner of my eye and I remember ducking because I thought he was going to hit me.

Instead, he ran right past me and snatched the trash can. It was melting, and the flames were practically spilling out across the kitchen. He held the trash can at arm's length in front of him, turned back to the breezeway, and carried it out the door and into the driveway. I followed him. As soon as it hit the pavement, the flames swallowed the can and it melted into a yellow puddle.

When Pop turned around and saw me, his hands snapped into fists and his face turned white as ash. He came at me. I started to run, but he grabbed my shirt. His voice sounded more like hissing than words.

"You stupid shit. I should have let you burn! How come you never listen to what I tell you, Anthony?" His teeth were clenched. Then I started to cry, and he shook me.

"You're starting to act just like Paddy, and I won't have it, Anthony. Not again. Not for one goddamned minute. We put up with his shit for 17 years, and I'm not gonna put up with it from you for even one minute. I'm warning you right now."

"I'm sorry, Pop. I didn't mean to do that."

"You never *mean* to do anything, Anthony. I'm sick to death of all the shit you don't *mean* to do." He swatted me on the butt, over and over again, and then he told me, "Get out of my goddamned sight. You make me sick! Sometimes you make me wonder why we even had you—any of you. Not a goddamned one of you appreciates what you got. You know what happens to bad kids, like Paddy." He shook that big square finger of his at me.

I don't blame him for spanking me. I guess I deserved that. But I *do* blame him for making me believe he might send me away at any second. After that, every time I got into trouble, I thought he'd make me disappear, just like Paddy. Even after I was old enough to know better, I found myself immobilized by the prospect of doing something that might be perceived negatively, for fear of the potential consequences. Being liked ensured survival; being disliked or failing meant possible banishment.

I decided to continue my tour of the island, now heading north toward the smoke, passing the Brevard County Courthouse, where I had once spent many hours as a reporter on the county government beat. My stomach lurched as I went by—the tension of that job still haunting me. With each new assignment, I'd worried that I couldn't get past my shyness again, that this time they would see through my act, and recognize my panic for what it was: inwardly, I feared Pop was right about me—that I really didn't measure up.

As I crossed under the Beeline Expressway and over the Barge Canal, I glanced to the west. The Volkman's Fish Camp sign still hung at the edge of the highway. I knew from Ma that the property had been sold recently. This had been where I worked my first summer after college. Mr. Volkman had hired me because of my friendship with his daughter, Elsa. I had taken Elsa to the Valentine's Day "Sweetie Banquet" during my senior year. We'd had fun at the dance, but I panicked as I drove her home, the way I always panicked whenever I took a girl home after a date. How would I get away this time? Always, I was afraid, they would recognize my panic for what it was: recognition that I had no sexual interest in girls, only a strong sense that I *should*, if I ever expected to have a "normal" life. When I'd dropped Elsa at her home that night, she asked me if I had ever French-kissed before.

"No, I don't think so." I squirmed uncomfortably behind the steering wheel, leaning against the car door and staring through the windshield.

"Wanna try it with me?" Her voice was matter-of-fact, almost clinical. I turned toward her. Her brown hair haloed around her head in the moonlight. I could hear cicadas buzzing in the distance. We had our windows down and, by now, the omnipresent mosquitoes had discovered our presence among them. I swatted as a sharp twinge pinched my neck, and felt the splat of blood from the too-slow insect.

"Okay." I felt the sweat on my forehead and the back of my neck. Struck dumb, I sat there motionless as she slid toward me. I heard the sucking sound of her thighs as they peeled away from the vinyl seats, smelled the sulfur air scented by the water drawn up from the artesian wells in every backyard, and something akin to terror as Elsa reached an arm around my neck to pull my face to hers. We kissed, and I was suddenly aware that Elsa's mouth was open and her tongue was probing between my lips. Instinctively, I opened my mouth and Elsa's tongue slithered inside like an inquisitive snake, darting behind my teeth and pressing against my own tongue. I felt both repulsed and excited: I was

French-kissing a girl! I closed my eyes, discovering the sensation was rather pleasant. I was surprised to feel my body reacting, coming to life in ways I never expected to experience with a girl. I responded by pushing my tongue into Elsa's mouth, tasting her lips, and searching in her mouth. After a moment, Elsa pulled back and straightened her dress.

"Well, I guess I should go in. I can see Momma watching us." But I wasn't listening. I knew I could never go on another date with Elsa. Now that we had French-kissed, what would she expect next?

Further north, I passed Policicchio Groves and inhaled deeply the intoxicating scent of orange blossoms that perfumed the air. Beyond that, I came upon the guardhouse at the entrance to the Kennedy Space Center, where I turned around and headed back south. I hadn't been far from here when the Challenger exploded. Standing at the press site on Space Center grounds, I covered the launch as I had all the previous launches, watching the silver ship rise on its finger of flame and, feeling the rumbling beneath my feet, in my chest and head, as always. Grinning in sheer amazement at the spectacle before me, I was amazed, yet again, to bear witness to it, report on it, like I was an important journalist, and not just a writer for the local weekly rag. The cloud of vapors swelled and encircled the shuttle, as always. And, as always, the gulls on the ground and in the lagoon between the shuttle and the press site leaped into the air *en masse*, beating a panicked retreat.

But, this time, the finger of flame widened, instead of flaring and receding, as the first stage separated and fell away. It widened and widened, engulfing the glistening craft. A plume of smoke spread out from, and swallowed, the shuttle, which disappeared and failed to reemerge. I stared in mute realization. I had seen satellites blown up by NASA in the past because they had veered off course and threatened populated areas. I never once considered a shuttle might explode, that astronauts—whose hands I had shaken, whose voices I had heard, whose words I had recorded in my articles—might die on a warm summer day over Merritt Island. Thinking back, I wondered: *Had I veered off the course of my life? And, in doing so, might I explode like that Shuttle, the pieces of my life cascading over everyone around me?*

I pulled onto Tropical Trail so I could look at the Indian River as I drove back to Rosalia's. Across the river, I could see the buildings in Cocoa. The river's edge always held a certain beauty for me: trees lined the shore, and tiny islands dotted the river, which was quite shallow everywhere except the channel used by boats. From here, the river looked deep blue and nearly glass-smooth on the surface. This close to the water, the air contained a fishiness that never quite seemed to dissipate. I glanced at the clock on the dash—2:10. I thought about driving to the southern tip of the island, but that was over twenty miles away, and I wouldn't want Rosalia angry with me for being late. After all, I didn't have much time to spend with her as it was. I would have liked to see if the dragon still guarded the southern tip of the island, but then I remembered the dragon was visible only from the water; maybe Rosalia would know if it was still there. I remember being frightened when we first moved to the island and heard about the dragon. I had believed it was real. When I saw it for the first time, years later, from Pop's boat, and discovered it was a wooden icon, I felt disappointed. Yet, afterwards, I felt glad it was there, guarding the south end of the island the way the Space Center guarded the north. I felt protected and safe as a child.

Now, however, I understood the danger wasn't *beyond* the island. It had been living right there the whole time, with us on the island, lurking in our homes and rock gardens. The danger *was* us and, sometimes, those we most trusted.

When I walked back into the apartment, Rosalia was still in the kitchen. The spicy, herbal scent of pasta and marinara sauce seasoned the air inside. I stood in the doorway to the kitchen and watched her, a tiny dervish of activity, before clearing my throat to signal my return. Rosalia glanced up and smiled, pulling a wisp of dark hair back out of her face.

"I'm glad you're back," she said brightly. "I have a job for you."

"Do I need my ears cleaned out? I thought I heard you say you've got something you want me to do."

"Don't get smart. I just thought you could make some salad while I finish the rest." She waved her hand over the counter, cluttered with food. "Do you think you can manage it?"

"Oh, I *think* so." I jabbed a finger at my chest. "You're talking to the world's best salad maker, in case you hadn't heard."

"We'll see. Just don't make a big mess is all I care about." She pointed to the refrigerator. "Everything you need should be in there. And the salad bowl is on the shelf over the sink." She pointed again.

I rolled up my sleeves dramatically. "Stand back and let a genius work."

"Oh, God, I'm already sorry I asked." She laughed and turned back to one of the bowls on the counter and began stirring vigorously.

I held the head of the iceberg lettuce aloft, examining it like poor Yoric's skull. "You know, I've been thinking about what you said about Pop last night."

"Uh-huh." Rosalia continued stirring without looking up.

"I *do* feel sort of bad. Like I failed with Pop yesterday." I banged the lettuce head firmly on the counter top to loosen the stem, which easily broke away. I tossed it aside. "I really hate failing at things." I took a sharp knife, cut the head in half and then, in half again. Taking a quarter at a time, I broke the lettuce into pieces in my hands, tearing the green leaves into ragged shreds and dropping them into a large bowl that Rosalia, who suddenly materialized at my side, handed to me.

"Pop *does* have his good points, you know." Rosalia stopped, remembering, and pointed at me with her fork. "Remember how he was when I went through those glass doors and got all cut up? He's the only one who kept his head. Hell, he probably saved my life that day."

"Yeah, I suppose," I said. "But what was he gonna do? Let you die? That wouldn't look too great now would it? The way I remember it, he did what he should've done. That's all. He took you to the hospital."

"No," Rosalia said, still pausing from her dinner preparations. "It was more than that. He was genuinely frightened. I saw it in his eyes. And, I'll never forget that he passed out. He's always trying to act tough, but he's not really. I think he gets a lot more frightened than he lets on. I don't think we really understand him at all."

"And I don't think he understands *any* of us." I added. "You might be right about the tough-guy act—I've thought the same thing, too. What I don't get—what I'll *never* get—is why he thinks he needs to be a tough guy."

"I don't know," Rosalia said, opening the sauce pot and stirring. "Maybe it's generational. You know, men were *supposed* to be tough in Pop's generation. Besides, I think he can't figure out why we act the way we do, either."

"And the funny thing is, *he* made us the way we are."

"Oh, come on, Anthony. No one can *make* you anything you're not. You're the first one to argue that, once we turn eighteen, the way we act is our own choice. We can't put the blame on Pop for what we don't like in ourselves. We should be able to change ourselves, right?"

"I suppose. It's just that, sometimes, I feel like we're starting at a disadvantage because Pop was a lousy example of how to behave. I just hope to God I don't turn out like him."

"I hate to be the one to break this to you, but you're *exactly* like him in a lot of ways." Rosalia covered the marinara pot and looked at me. "And that's not all bad, you know."

"Now you're just being mean," I said, feeling as if my worst fears had been realized. "How are Pop and I alike? That's a scary thought, you know."

"In a lot of ways," she continued. "You look like Pop looked at your age. You sound like him. You have the same sense of humor. You're just as stubborn as he is. You absolutely refuse to back down from anything when you think you're right."

"Yikes," I said. "And what happened to the good qualities you mentioned?"

"You're both intelligent. You're hardest on yourself. You're both pretty driven. Neither of you understands the other. And, deep down, I think you love each other."

I fell silent, cutting small wedges of tomato and slivers of green and yellow peppers, then pouring them and handfuls of chickpeas, raisins, sourdough croutons, and peanuts over the top of the lettuce. "*Voila—la salade c'est finis,*" I announced finally. Rosalia looked up at the ceiling and spread her arms like a supplicant.

"Jesus Christ, Anthony. Do you always have to show off your education?" She shook her head and her hair bobbed up and down as if it were on springs. She shoved a pan into the oven and leaned forward to check the temperature.

"I can't help it. Must be one of those things I inherited from my father," I said. "Seriously, Rose, I hear what you're saying. You're probably right—I catch myself saying something and I can hear the same words coming straight outta Pop's mouth. There's more of him in me—in both of us—than I care to admit. And it's part of what makes us who we are, I suppose. But there are things about Pop that I really hate. Things I wish I never had to deal with again. And don't tell me you don't know what I'm talking about, because I know you do."

"I know what you're talking about. I won't deny it," she said, then walked over to her wine rack and pulled out a bottle of red wine. "Why don't we have a drink?" She poured each of us a glass of wine, and handed one glass to me. "You may need this. I invited Ma for dinner tonight."

"Oh, Jesus!" I reacted. "Don't you think it might be too soon after our fight yesterday?"

"Maybe," Rosalia admitted. "But if we wait until you go back to Chicago, it may be too late. I thought we should take the chance. Is that okay?"

"I'm not sure," I said.

"I think you have to try," she urged. "Will you?"

I looked at her face, her eyes pleading with me. "Okay, Rose," I said. For once, I would trust in her instincts. *Hell, why not?* I thought. *My instincts were obviously useless.* Holding up the wine glass, I said, "I'm going to need this!"

"I'll drink to that." She replied, and we both drank deeply.

"So, why don't you tell me about what's been going on in your life, Rosalia," I said, changing the subject, after we had each downed our first glass of wine.

"So much has happened this year that it doesn't even seem real. It's like someone else's dream that I'm part of," she sipped from her wine glass, then ran her tongue over her blood-red lips. "The actual divorce is just the final step, you know. It wasn't Trap's fault. We were so different. I suppose that's what attracted me to him. Trap was so un-Irish. You know, sort of lanky and cheerful with big, glittery dark eyes. He was everything Pop wasn't. That should have been my first warning—I was running away from Pop instead of finding someone who suited me." She rested her head on her hand and twirled a strand of her dark hair between her fingers as she continued. "Even the first words Trap spoke to me were a warning: 'You look like you need someone like me to keep you company.'"

"Sounds dreamy," I said. We both laughed out loud. I poured myself the remainder from our first bottle of wine; then, opened a second bottle and poured another glass for Rosalia. We were getting smashed; I figured it might make dinner with Ma easier to handle.

"Trap hates people who dance around the truth. He says what he thinks. And he always claimed to be afraid of our family. He insisted that everyone knew all Sicilians were part of the Mafia. But, since we're half Irish, he called us the 'McMafia.'" She turned to face me, and we both burst into laughter again.

"The McMafia?" I repeated. "That makes it sound almost cute. But maybe he was right to be afraid of us. *I* am."

"Oh, hush," Rosalia said, chuckling. "He always claimed that I was 'larger than life.' I told him I didn't know what he meant and he said, 'You sort of fill up a room—you've got presence.' I suppose I liked the way that sounded. He made me feel important."

"Well, he was right." I saluted her with my wine glass. "You are. So what changed? After the wedding, I thought you were hitched for life."

"Trap was sort of a dreamer. I mean, he was always thinking." Rosalia's eyes looked wistful, shiny. "He had an idea every minute, all right, but he never seemed to follow through on any of them. He was always telling me about all the things we'd do one day—stuff like buying a big house or having kids or traveling around the world. And, even though I knew we'd never do any of these things, I always believed him because he was that kind of guy. The kind you believe without questioning because he's just so damned sincere about everything.

"But, after a while, I realized he was only dreaming aloud. I mean, I dream at night while I'm asleep; Trap did it in the middle of the day while he was wide awake. And he really believed it, too—all of it. At first, so did I: it all sounded so real, so possible."

"So, when did that change? What's wrong with having dreams?"

"I guess it started a couple years ago when I turned thirty. I started thinking about all the things I had expected to do by then, but hadn't. And all the things I'd probably never do if things kept on as they were." She finished her third glass of wine. I offered to pour her a fourth, but she shook her head. "Last year, we celebrated our sixth anniversary, and I started to think about having kids. We had agreed to postpone kids until we were ready. But I began to realize that we'd never be ready. Trap was floating from job to job. He didn't stick with anything and he had no real career goals—at least, none that he seemed interested in pursuing. Finally, I told him that we needed to decide what we wanted out of life, and work toward it. He seemed shocked. 'What's wrong with our life?' he asked me. I told him that it wasn't leading to anything, and he didn't seem to understand why our life needed to *lead* to anything: he was happy with it the way it was."

"But you needed more than that," I concluded for her. "You needed to feel like you were doing more than treading water, year after year; like you had a partner, not a child."

"Yeah," Rosalia nodded and looked closely at me. "Sounds like you understand."

"Yeah. Maybe," I stuttered. "I don't know. I mean, I love Steven, but sometimes I feel like I'm living someone else's life. Like things are just happening around me and I have no control over them."

"But you *do* have control," Rosalia said. "I guess that's what I had to realize. I couldn't force Trap to live the life *I* wanted to live, and I couldn't live *his* life anymore. I suppose, from that perspective, *I'm* the one who changed and screwed things up. Trap never changed and never pretended to offer more than he had to give. But, I could never be happy just coasting through life, never trying to be more than I already was."

"How did you tell him? That must have been awful. I don't know if I could do it." I took another swig of wine.

"Actually, that was the *easy* part," she said quietly. "We were sitting in bed one night and I just blurted it out. I told him our relationship had stopped working, and he agreed. We both cried and told each other how much we loved one another. And it was true, you know?" Rosalia's eyes were glistening now.

"I felt like my heart was breaking and I kept hoping he wouldn't argue with me because I knew I might give in, and that would be a mistake. But he saw it, too. And so, we filed for divorce."

"Wow, you've got more strength than I do, Rose," I said. "I don't know if I could do it."

"You could if you *had* to, Anthony," she said. "There just comes a point when you wake up and say to yourself, 'What am

I doing with my life?' If you can't answer that question, it's time to make a change."

"But if you still loved each other, why didn't you try to work it out?" I asked.

"There wasn't anything to fix. I wanted one thing and he wanted another. And we were both right in wanting what we wanted, but we could never have what we both wanted together." She poured herself another glass of wine.

"Oh, God, I remember how soft his cheeks felt that night. His eyes seemed like big black mirrors, and I could practically see my own reflection in them when I told him I didn't think I could go on like that any longer. He was hurt, genuinely hurt, because he really wanted us to stay together. We both did. We cried a lot, but we both knew it was over. I hated letting go, but I think I woulda hated hanging on even more." Her face relaxed and she glanced up.

I took her hands in mine and she smiled at me. Her dark eyes glistened in the semi-darkness. The sun had dimmed noticeably while we had been talking. The window behind Rosalia was orange, like a fiery painted square.

"You did the right thing, Rose," I assured her. "You'll find someone else—someone with the same dreams as you."

Rosalia walked to the window and pulled the shade aside to look outside. The orange sun blazed into the kitchen, silhouetting her.

"Doesn't it amaze you that Ma and Pop have been together for nearly fifty years? Fifty years! Something must be working, right?"

"Maybe not. Maybe they're not as brave as you—maybe they were just afraid to make a change."

I stood up and joined Rosalia in the window.

"Sometimes, I wonder if we might've been better off if they *had* split up. What would we be like if Pop hadn't been around?"

"Don't say that, Anthony," Rosalia said, picking up our wine glasses from the table and carrying them to the sink. She washed and rinsed them, folded the dishrag and dropped it over the spicket, then leaned back against the counter. "Pop's a pain in the ass, but I'm glad he was there. I can't imagine life without him. He did his best, which, I know, wasn't always good enough, but he *did* try."

"I'm not so sure," I said. "I feel like he suffocated us. We weren't allowed to be who we were. We had to obey, to be what he wanted us to be. I feel like I spent my whole childhood pretending to be someone I'm not. And, the minute I stopped pretending, he cut me out of his life. Ma must have seen it, too, but she didn't say or do anything. You seem to have forgiven them, or at least gotten past it, but I haven't yet. And they still haven't accepted Steven, which means they haven't accepted me, either."

"I'm not sure we see our childhood in the same way. You have a pretty strong personality, Anthony. Pop certainly didn't suffocate that out of you. And you got your strength from someone, don't you think? Don't forget: Ma is a product of her generation. Women didn't fight with their husbands. But I've never seen Ma as a shrinking violet. She battled with Pop plenty of times, but you didn't seem to notice that. And I think they *have* accepted your relationship and the fact that you're gay. They've probably also noticed that you don't seem real happy in your relationship—same way I'm sure they noticed I wasn't happy. Give them some credit, Anthony. Sometimes you're too suspicious of their motives."

"Such as?" I asked.

"Such as, did you know that you were Pop's measuring stick? God, I think if he asked me, 'Why can't you be more like Anthony?' one more time, I would've screamed."

"No way! He said that?" I looked at her face, thinking she was pulling my leg.

"Oh, come on, Anthony. Ma said it, too. You must have heard them. They both said it all the time. Why do you think I resented you so much as a kid?"

"I just figured you were jealous," I said, grinning.

"I *was* jealous, I guess. You were always the 'perfect' one. You never did anything wrong. And Ma and Pop never let me forget it."

"Jesus," I blurted. "I could never do anything *right*. If I never did anything wrong, it was because I thought Pop would send me away if I did. After Paddy ran away and they didn't go after him, I was always terrified they'd just turn their backs on me if I wasn't perfect—if I didn't do everything they said."

A knock at the door startled both of us. "Oh, shit!" Rosalia said. "That'll be Ma. She's always early. Would you mind letting her in so I can finish up in here? You talk to her for a few minutes while I put everything on the table."

"She might turn right around if I answer the door," I said. "Or slap me."

"Oh, come on, Anthony. She won't do either. And it'll give the two of you some time to talk privately. You probably need it after yesterday."

"Just a few minutes, you promise? After that, either you rescue me or I'll have to kill you." I headed for the door, wondering how Ma would react to me after yesterday's shouting match at the hospital.

"Hello, Anthony," Ma said evenly, looking beyond me into Rosalia's living room.

I leaned down to kiss her cheek, which she accepted without response.

"Hi, Ma," I said, stepping back to let her into the apartment. "Rosalia says she'll join us after she finishes up in the kitchen."

Ma marched in and took a seat on the sofa, only then looking up to scrutinize me. Her auburn hair seemed limp, and she was rubbing the fingers of her left hand with her right. Uncomfortable in her gaze, I asked, "How's Pop today?"

She eyed me for a moment longer, then reached into her small brown purse and pulled out a pack of cigarettes and a pastel pink lighter. She closed the purse clasp with a click and shook a cigarette out of the pack, rolling it in her fingers while she considered her response.

"He seems a little better today," she said at last, slipping the cigarette between her lips and lighting it with the lighter. She inhaled deeply from the cigarette and held the smoke inside for a long moment before she exhaled. "You know, Anthony, whether you believe it or not, your father loves you. It hurts him when the two of you fight. And it hurts me, too."

"I'm sorry, Ma," I said. "I didn't plan to fight with him, you know. Sometimes, he just gets me so upset. Why can't he ever just talk to me? He's always gotta take a shot. Even when he's sick."

"He's not good at just talking, Anthony. You should realize that by now. He's 69 years old and he doesn't know how to change. You know, he may not be around much longer, so you may not got many more chances." She took a long drag on her cigarette and, without seeming to notice, exhaled the white cloud of smoke directly in my face. My eyes stung and teared up. "Why don't you go see him again tomorrow, Anthony? Maybe you'll both be in better moods by then."

I shook my head and frowned. "I can't, Ma. I'm heading back to Chicago tonight."

"Tonight?" Ma looked incredulous and angry; her brows formed peaks on her forehead. She stood up, punctuating each syllable with her cigarette. "Why would you come all the way from Chicago and stay for barely twenty-four hours?" As she took a drag on her cigarette, she walked over to Rosalia's picture window, then turned to face me, exhaling another white cloud of smoke. As the smoke swirled and dissipated around her, she said, "One little disagreement and you're packed and ready to run back to Chicago? Why did you come down here, Anthony? Was your father right, after all? Was it just the guilt that brought you?"

"I don't know, Ma. The last thing I wanted to do was fight with him. After the scene yesterday at the hospital, I'm thinking maybe it would've been better if I hadn't come. I'm just not up to this."

"Not up to what?" she asked, eyeing me fiercely. "Not up to your father? Or me? Or not up to *not* fighting?"

"I didn't mean that," I said, wondering where Rosalia was. Surely, it had been more than two minutes. "I just think it'd be better if I went back to Chicago."

"Better for who, Anthony? For me? For Rosalia? For your father?" She returned to the sofa and sat down, facing away from me. "Better for *you*, maybe. That way, you don't have to deal with any of this—not with your father's heart attack, or your fighting, or anything. You can go back to Chicago, where you won't have to think about any of this."

I looked at this small, feisty woman on the sofa. *How could this be my mother? The same mother who let so many bad things happen to me as a child? The same mother who let my father treat me like shit? Where was her feistiness then? Why was she so fucking loyal to Pop? What had he ever done to earn it, except be a bastard?*

"Come on, Ma," I said. "Let's not fight tonight. I was hoping we could have a nice dinner and talk before I leave. Maybe it is selfish of me to leave, but what good would it do to stay? There's nothing I can do for Pop here. All we do is fight, and he doesn't need that right now. I'll come back when he gets better."

"Dinner's ready," Rosalia called out as she entered the living room. She furrowed her brows at me as she leaned down to hug and kiss Ma. "Come on, you two. Let's go in the dining room. You can argue while we eat."

"We're done arguing," I said. "Aren't we, Ma?"

Ma eyed me without budging for a moment. "We haven't even begun yet," she said. "But we can eat." Then, she rose abruptly and headed into the dining room. Rosalia and I looked at each other and I shrugged my shoulders. Then, we followed Ma into the dining room.

"How is your friend?" Ma asked as we entered the room and sat down.

"Steven, Ma. And he's not my 'friend'—he's my lover." I said. "Anyhow, he's fine."

"How come Steven didn't come down with you?" Rosalia asked, hurriedly heading off a reaction from Ma as she dished pasta into our bowls. "Is he feeling alright?"

"He's feeling fine," I said. "Too good, in fact." Noticing both of them looking at me strangely, I added quickly, "I mean, he's back at work, so he couldn't get the time off on such short notice."

"Does that mean he's getting better?" Ma asked.

"No, Ma. He'll *never* get better. It just has its ups and downs, and Steven's on an 'up' right now. But his T-cell count keeps going down—and that's definitely not good."

"So, how are *you* dealing with it?" Rosalia asked. Ma looked at Rosalia and then, back at me, the look on her face telegraphing her fear.

"Don't worry, Ma. I'm still negative," I said. Turning back to look at Rosalia, I added, "I just don't want to feel sorry for myself, or for you to feel sorry for me. And I especially don't want to feel like you're afraid of me. Or of Steven."

"We're not afraid of you, silly." Rosalia said. "We love you. Both of you."

But the fear I had seen on Ma's face said otherwise. I wasn't sure how Ma and Pop might react if I contracted the disease. Sometimes I felt like they were waiting for me to say I had sero-converted; so they could say triumphantly, "We *knew* this would happen," so that Pop could show me one more time how wrong I had been.

"Thanks, Rosalia," I said. "That helps. And don't worry about me, I'm hanging in there. I'm just a little afraid, you know? I don't know what I'll do after...after Steven's gone. Sometimes I feel useless by myself. I wonder why anyone would want to be with me. I don't want to be with myself, sometimes."

"Now you sound foolish," Ma said. "You always had a million friends. Always."

"Not so much anymore, Ma," I said. "We keep pretty much to ourselves most of the time. I still don't have many friends in Chicago."

"How's your job going?" Rosalia asked.

"It's going fine," I said. "But, you know, it's only a job. With all the stuff we've been going through with Steven, you start to realize how unimportant your work is in the scheme of things. When you're talking life and death, having perfect grammar in your news article doesn't seem quite so important anymore."

"But your writing was always important to you," Ma said.

"Don't get me wrong, Ma, I still work hard at my job, and sometimes it feels like the only sanity in my life. But it's not the focus it used to be. There are too many other things going on to be able to focus on my writing. At least, not at the moment."

"Are you happy, Anthony?" Rosalia asked suddenly. "Don't take this wrong, but I'm sitting here listening to you, and you sound so sad and worn out. What's happened to the nobody-can-stop-me-Anthony I grew up with?"

"I haven't seen that guy around for a while," I said. "But it's not all grim. Do you realize Steven and I will be celebrating our ninth anniversary soon? I guess that's something I can be happy about."

"Of course," Rosalia said. "I hadn't realized it had been so long already."

"I've never understood what the two of you have in common," Ma said. "You two are like night and day. What do you possibly find to talk about?"

"Let's not go there tonight, Ma. I know Steven's not your favorite person." I said. "I just thought that, after all these years, you and Pop would have accepted him."

"We *have* accepted him," Ma said flatly. "You never let us forget about him. Or his illness."

"He has HIV, Ma."

Yes, I know, Anthony." She fell silent, twirling pasta onto her fork. "Sometimes I feel like we can't talk about anything else anymore. And when we try, we always end up back on this subject, somehow."

"It's a big part of my life right now, Ma. Can't you understand that?"

"And your father is in the hospital with a heart attack. Doesn't he deserve some attention, too?"

"I don't think that's what Anthony was saying, Ma." Rosalia tried to rescue me, but Ma would have none of it.

"I know what Anthony was saying," Ma said. "And what he wasn't saying."

"So tell us, Ma," I said. "How is Pop *really* doing?"

Ma watched me for a moment as she continued eating, then put her fork down and smoothed the napkin in her lap. "The doctor decided the heart attack was caused by a blockage. His neck veins were so clogged up, the doctor says he's lucky he didn't have a stroke, too. They cleared the blockages, and he seemed a little better. But then, you'd know that, if you had gone to visit him today."

"It's hard to get over there every day," Rosalia offered, running interference between me and Ma.

Ma said nothing, but ran a slice of garlic bread through the marinara sauce on her plate. I stayed silent, deciding it best to avoid this issue completely.

No one spoke for a minute. Rosalia stood up and gathered some dishes off the table and carried them into the kitchen. She returned to the dining room and opened the window. Along with sound of crickets and spring peepers in the distance, the strong smell of smoke poured into the room.

"Smells like the Everglades are burning up again," Rosalia commented, shutting the window again. "I hate that smell. Makes me sick."

"It's the smell of death," Ma said eerily. "It's a smell I'll never forget. Never."

Rosalia and I looked at each other, then back at Ma, who stood, cigarette in hand, and walked over to the window. She continued talking with her back to us both.

"That smell brings back everything about the night my family's house burned down. All the nightmares. All the things I've tried to forget." Her voice trailed off as a swirl of white smoke encircled her head.

Rosalia and I knew the story. How, when Ma was just seven years old, she had awakened to find the room she shared with Aunt Pee filled with smoke and the entire family home in flames. How they had raced out into the hallway, where they could hear their parents and siblings crying and shouting and choking. How she and Aunt Pee had to run down the burning stairs, dodging the flames and feeling the heat. How she was sure they were going to die.

There were 18 in the house that night. Once outside, Doughna Mira, Ma's mother, frantically counted and tried to run back inside to find the ones who were missing. Grandpa had to hold her back, telling her it was too dangerous to go back inside. So, they had to wait there, watching the flames consume their home and waiting as, one by one, each of Ma's brothers and sisters emerged from the house and ran to join the family in the street.

That night, Ma's house burned to the ground, taking her brother, Carmine, with it. Her family waited and waited, but he never came out. Carmine's bedroom was directly across the hall from Ma's. In their panic, she and Aunt Pee hadn't thought to check on Carmine, and they still blamed themselves for his death.

"Remember when you started that fire in the kitchen?" Ma asked, turning to face me.

I nodded.

"That day, I froze again." She was almost whispering. "When I looked up and saw the flames, I thought, 'Not again.' But I couldn't move—it was like my feet were stuck in cement. All I could think about was Carmine, and how it was happening all over again. But your father ran in and rescued you. Pulled you right out of there and put out the fire."

"I remember him running in, Ma," I said. "But I think I remember it a little differently than you do."

"What do you think it takes to run into a burning building, Anthony? When you think your father doesn't love you, you should think about that. He ran into a fire to save you. And he'd do it again if it happened today. You should think about that."

I hadn't considered that day in those terms before; hadn't thought about the episode from Pop's perspective. Ma's words made me doubt my own memories for the first time. But I wasn't quite ready to place a crown on Pop's head, yet. Too much other baggage stood in between us.

"I haven't forgotten, Ma," I said, at last. "I never said I don't love Pop. I just don't understand him very well. And we don't seem to talk the same language sometimes."

"Then you should learn how to speak his language, Anthony," Ma said. "The same way you'd try to understand someone you didn't know; you'd figure out a way. You wouldn't just run away."

"Ma," I said. "I don't think going back to Chicago is running away. I live there, for God's sake. And I'll come back. This just isn't the right time. Pop could try to learn *my* language, too, you know. The road goes two ways."

"When you're older, you'll understand. The road starts to go only one way. And it doesn't go very far—not far at all. It's a pretty short road ahead, and it's a long, long way back—farther than you can manage, sometimes. You'll understand that some-day." She walked over to the table and gathered up her purse and cigarettes. "Have a safe flight home, Anthony."

Not knowing what to say, I leaned down to kiss the cheek she offered me.

"Thank you for dinner, Rosalia," Ma said as Rosalia walked her to the door and kissed her goodbye. "I'll see you tomorrow. I'll tell your father you're coming to visit him."

As I drove away from Rosalia's apartment a little while later, the sun was already slipping into the margins of a white sky drawn open like a picture screen, fading into darkening varia-tions of light: golden-white to bone, to beige, to drab, to gray, and finally—to nothing. The dense smoke of brush fires seemed to consume visibility mere yards beyond the reach of the tallest trees. My headlights were two fingers into the hazy night as I headed for the airport.

Tree frogs crick-cricked from the nearby marshes and insects buzzed like machinery humming in the distance. Staccato bleatings of crickets and occasional yawlings of a dog or cat, nearly indistinguishable, one from the other, pooled together in the dark. The margins of the island thrummed with life, life that was immense and overwhelming in its vastness and variety.

As I crossed the Indian River Bridge, I felt the pull of the island, an allure I had despised and fought against ever since I'd left home. *Why had I even come back?* I wanted to snap my fingers and stop feeling anything. Stop all this buzzing and humming and cricking. I longed for a single, identifiable sound. Anything but this amalgam of activity, this blur of life, my past: these memories of the island; of home; of Ma and Pop and Paddy and Rosalia; of myself as a child; of Doughna Mira; and of Steven. Suddenly, everything in my life seemed false and painful and jumbled together like the life on this island—the good and the bad melded together. But, just now, all of it felt hurtful, humiliating. It was all part of my life— unavoidable and permanent.

As a child, I had felt invisible in my own home, always believing Ma and Pop wished I were something I was not—someone I never would be. Now, Rosalia was insisting that my own memories were false, as distorted and hazy as the smoky island air. By trying to be who Ma and Pop wanted me to be, I had failed to become who I really wanted to be.

I felt so confused, so lost. Had I really come home because I thought I should? A *pro forma* appearance to prove what a good son I was? I felt the truth of the accusation; I felt the shame of it, too. I didn't want to be here. I certainly wasn't here out of love or concern for Pop. The surprising thing was that Pop had seen through me, through my good son act. Maybe he always had. Maybe everyone saw through me. Except me.

I thought about Steven. Steven, whom I was running back to in Chicago. He, too, had accused me of doing things because I thought I should, not because I felt them. His accusation had enraged me, and yet, thinking about it now, I felt the truth of it. I knew, too, that the wonderful relationship I had bragged about to Rosalia and Ma was a fiction, a story I *wanted* to be true, a life I *wished* I was living. But I wasn't. And now, I suddenly realized, I had to accept the blame. Steven had been the honest one, saying what he really felt—good or bad.

I had buried my true feelings, set them aside, as I had always done. But the buried hurt and pain from my relationship with Steven—from my entire life—had been accumulating. Much as I hated to admit it, it had all begun to seep out of me like water from the Florida sand, unstoppable.

As I sped across the island, I knew I needed to confess these things to Steven. Perhaps confession would make me feel safe with him again. Perhaps I just needed to hold him, and let him know how much I really *did* love him.

I wondered what Pop was thinking about at this moment. Did he understand all these things that I was just beginning to understand tonight? How could I accept such awareness from a man I had always considered selfish and insensitive? Was Rosalia right? Had I misread him? Then, too, how could I have understood so little about my own life? Was the anger I felt towards Pop unjustified? Had I caused the hostility between us? Too many painful and vividly clear memories argued against it. Ma and Pop had never been there for me. They still weren't. Even tonight, Ma's slight of my relationship with Steven was evidence of how they *still* didn't accept me. Why did they always make me feel so insignificant? Why did I feel Pop's disappointment so clearly, so viscerally, each time I saw him? If Pop and Ma really loved and accepted me, why had they never said so?

No, I thought: *Rosalia must be wrong. Hadn't she been wrong before when she advised me to tell them I was gay?* "They'll accept you as you are, Tony," she had assured me. "They're our parents and they love you. If you have secrets this big between you, how can you ever hope for an honest relationship? They don't really even know who you are."

What a disaster that had been! Surely, Rosalia was mistaken again; but I *wished* she was right because, despite myself, I needed to hear Ma and Pop say they were proud of me, say they accepted me, say they loved me. Even after all these years—after moving 1,500 miles away from them, after carving out a new life for myself that didn't include them—after all these things, Ma and Pop were still at the center of everything. In fact, in taking all these deliberate steps to exclude them from my life, I had only increased their power over me.

From atop the Humphrey Bridge, the orange glow of dozens of brush fires across the island flickered in my rearview mirror.

Scot T. O'Hara

Everything seemed to be on fire—the island, my home, my family, my past, my present, my future—as if my resentment had set it all ablaze. Even as I sped away, my emotions seemed to increase with each mile I put between us. The distance, the secrets, all the steps I had taken to separate them from my new life—none of it had done anything to quell the flames.

CHAPTER 7

Awakenings

Merritt Island: 1976

By the time I turned eighteen, I reached the conclusion—both confusing and horrifying at the time—that I had no interest in girls. None. Despite the constant barrage of heterosexual messages from television, movies, books, friends, and family, I felt none of the female-induced excitement expressed by other boys my age. Publicly, I disdained their comments as vulgar; inside, however, their vulgarities stirred me. I imagined my classmates' arousal, imagined them having sex. After gym, I avoided looking at the other boys as they showered, fearful that I might become aroused. At night, I would masturbate while visualizing my classmates naked, touching me, me touching them. Beyond touching, I wasn't sure what boys did together, but I wanted to find out. As my thoughts became increasingly dominated by sex, I tried to distract myself with activities and studying. If I stayed busy, I thought, I wouldn't have time for these abnormal thoughts.

I knew the world judged thoughts like mine to be sick and evil. At home and in school, from family, friends, and strangers, from movies, television, and books—everywhere I turned—the message was clear: *Boys who like boys are bad*. Even the Bible labeled people like me sinners, doomed to hell. The first time I read or heard the word, "homosexual," I knew instinctively that it described people like me. The terms "faggot" and "queer," which my schoolmates and I had called each other all these years without understanding their full cruelty, took on new and acutely painful meaning. When a classmate called me a faggot one day near the end of my senior year, my heart seized and I wanted to die. I was certain I had somehow given myself away, certain my darkest secret had been discovered. My face turned red and I stammered some childish rejoinder, like "takes one to know one," and scuttled away like a cockroach. I understood the boy was using faggot in place of "jerk," but the term evoked an immediate, visceral, and panicked response that I found myself terrified by and unable to control.

In spite of my terror, I desperately wanted to experience sex, but the distance between wanting and doing seemed insurmountable. I found myself sympathizing with dogs in heat, wishing I could simply rub myself against the objects of my desire. My situation seemed so hopeless. How could I meet someone like me when I was too afraid to let anyone in on my secret? Even if I met him, how could I let go of my inhibitions when all the voices in my head kept repeating: "Good boys don't do dirty things like that. Boys who touch other boys go to hell."

The day Pop decided to tell me about sex, I wanted to die. His words were decidedly unhelpful, his message wholly pointless.

Shortly after my seventeenth birthday, Pop came into my room one evening just before I went to bed.

"Whaddaya know 'bout sex, Anthony?" he asked as matter-of-factly as if he were asking what I knew about vegetables.

"Nothing," I said nervously. "I dunno." I tried to avoid his eyes hoping he'd let it drop. But Pop was bent on having "the talk" with me.

"Well, then, I guess it's about time we talk about this." He sat on the edge of my bed and took off his glasses, then paused for a moment. "Probably shoulda had this talk a few years back, but you didn't seem interested in girls yet, so I figured it could wait a bit. Now, it seems past due. You got a girlfriend, yet?"

"No, Pop," I said quietly. I felt trapped, miserable. I waited for Pop to reply, but he just kept watching me and rubbing his chin. He looked as uncomfortable as I felt.

"Well, what would you like to know?" he asked finally.

"I dunno," I said, turning red in the face. My ears burned. Pop watched me carefully.

"Don't be such a sissy, Anthony," he said, shaking his head in disgust. "Jasus, you'll be lucky if you lose your cherry before you turn thirty." He paused for a minute, as if deciding what to say next. "Sex is nothing to be ashamed of. The man puts his penis inside the woman's vagina. That's really all there is to it. You do know what penises and vaginas are, don't you?"

"Yes." I cringed at the words coming out of Pop's mouth. Vagina—it sounded like a disease. I could picture some doctor saying, "You've contracted vagina. Take these pills three times a day and stay away from girls." How could I tell Pop that what I really wanted to know was what happens when there were two penises involved? I knew I couldn't ask him for the kind of guidance I really wanted, so I decided my best option was to play along and hope it would all be over soon. "I know what they are, Pop."

"Good. Just don't go getting a girl pregnant," he said, sliding his glasses back in place. "You come to me if you have any questions about it. But that's really about all there is to it. No big deal, and nothing to be ashamed of." He stood and walked back out of my room, closing the door behind him. I flopped face down on my bed, mortified. My heart pounded after he was gone, and I hoped it would burst so I could die. Instinctively, I knew sex would never be easy for me. Pop had it all wrong: sex *was* a big deal. A *very* big deal. And there seemed to be a whole lot to be ashamed of.

I thought about sex from the moment I awakened until I went to sleep—and then, I dreamed about sex. I thought about sex when I watched television, when I was in school, when I was driving or at the mall, when I was in bed, alone, at night. It frightened me, how much I thought about sex.

I even thought about sex when I was at church after Father James arrived. He was young and blond and very handsome. When he preached the sermon, I never heard a word he said. Just the sight of him aroused me, and I would spend the entire mass thinking about what he would feel like to touch or kiss, what he would look like naked. I imagined how it would feel to graze my fingers across the tufts of blond hair on his flat chest and down his belly. To stop these thoughts, I avoided looking at him, staring up at the high, vaulted ceilings with gold-painted rafters and wondering if God sensed my shame. After mass, I would melt into the exiting crowd, fearful that Father James would detect the desire on my face. I felt such revulsion at my impurity that I believed I deserved to die or disappear. Finally, I stopped going to church and buried my secret even deeper.

At the end of my senior year, I was named class salutatorian. I hurried home to tell my good fortune to Ma and Pop.

"What the hell's a salutorian?" Pop asked.

"Salutatorian," I said. "It's the person with the second highest grade-point average in the entire class."

"Second place is second rate," Pop said. "I hate graduations anyhow, long and boring. I didn't even go to my own."

"But I'll be giving a speech. Don't you want to see me?" I couldn't believe he wouldn't come. He was just being obstinate, as always. Nothing was ever easy with Pop.

"Nope. Maybe if you came in first. Besides, I hate speeches. I got better ways to spend my time than listening to some asshole speechify. Even if yer that asshole. You can show me what yer gonna say and I'll read it." He turned to Ma and asked, "Any coffee left?"

"On the counter beside the sink. Right where it always is," Ma said.

I felt stunned by Pop's indifference, shocked at his refusal to attend my graduation. Surely, he would reconsider if Ma came. After Pop left to get his coffee, I asked Ma, "You're gonna come see me graduate, at least, aren't you?"

"We'll see," she said. "I'll talk to him. But if I can't convince him, you know how I hate to go anywhere without him."

I remember heading out into our yard, tears stinging my eyes. Clearly, they didn't care about me, I told myself. Why else would they treat me like this? I sat in the front yard on the prickly Bermuda grass, letting the hot Florida sun engulf my body, bake into my scalp, into my arms and legs, into my chest. It felt like a living force, enfolding and comforting me with a powerful warmth. I would be alone at my graduation, no family member to witness my speech or watch me cross the stage. Damn them for abandoning me! Damn them for their lack of support. But, why had I expected anything different, when this same pattern had been played out again and again? Why did I feel so keenly hurt this time? When would I ever learn? *To hell with them*, I thought. I was going to give that speech—with them or without them. I refused to let them spoil my graduation.

When the day arrived, as I knew he would, Pop dug in his heels, stubbornly refusing to attend, and Ma said she "didn't feel right" about going without him, which meant Rosalia couldn't go either. So, I went on my own and gave my speech. I walked across the stage, got my diploma, and flipped my tassel with my classmates. But I felt strangely unmoved by it all. When my friends asked me to join them at a classmate's house to celebrate, I declined, saying I had to get home. I drove down to the beach and sat in my car, watching the ocean from the parking lot, and cried for all the hurt and pain and shame. What should have been a crowning moment seemed pointless and insignificant. Ma and Pop had ruined my graduation after all, in spite of my best efforts.

Waves angled in to shore and little shore birds darted alongside, jabbing at something only they could see in the foam. Voices of children rang from the distance. I could see them, parents in tow, frolicking at the water's edge, shrieking at every wave splashing into them. The sun drooped below the treetops along the narrow spit of land to the west. Long pink-and-white streaks striped the sky. I could smell the salt in the air and a faint odor of fish. The rush of waves rose and fell again and again, almost hypnotically. I watched them develop from a bump on the distant surface, growing larger as they neared shore, until they curled over and toppled down in white foam on the sandy beach. *Why do they always move at an angle?* I wondered. My life was like these waves: never proceeding in a direct line, always following a circuitous path around a series of detours and roadblocks. Maybe there was an easier way, but I sure as hell didn't know what it was.

I looked at the horizon, where the blue-grey ocean met the magenta sky. I considered marching into the water, deeper and deeper, until the water closed over me and I could see the fishermen's hooks dangling beside me; until my breath burst out of me in a final, gurgling bubble; until the sun faded from magenta to purple to black, and—finally—disappeared. Then, I'd disappear, too. They'd find me later, like some waterlogged Ophelia, still in my graduation robe. But I doubted they'd understand why. I'm not sure I understood myself—I just wanted to stop the pressure in my head. Stop the rushing, rushing. Stop dancing around everything that mattered. The world was moving around me, and I was afraid, so terribly afraid, that I wouldn't be able to keep pace much longer. I felt tired. I'd been hurrying for seventeen years, and I still hadn't gotten anywhere.

As the sun set and the sky purpled, I pushed aside the self-pity and dried my tears. I would start over at Northwestern University, the college that had accepted me, in Chicago. Only this time, Ma and Pop would be far away, and I would control my own destiny.

When Ma and Pop drove me to McCoy Jetport in Orlando to catch my plane to Chicago and college, and Merritt Island vanished behind me, I felt different from the way I had the day we arrived in Florida. The island was not the Eden I had first believed it to be. Knowing I was leaving—maybe for good—aroused unexpectedly strong emotions. I felt a powerful sense of being adrift, like Ulysses, only I was not heading to a place I knew and missed, but searching for a home I had never known, uncertain whether it even existed.

I think when we choose to leave behind the people and the places we've known, we are admitting—even though we probably don't realize it at the time—that something is missing from our lives. I know, for me, this was certainly true. I didn't know what I was seeking at the time; I only knew I hadn't found it on the island.

As we headed for Orlando, where I would begin my journey to college, the afternoon clouds rolled up from the west and the sky turned purple and black as a dark, roiling storm line advanced to meet us. We reached the jetport just as the storm struck. Boarding pass in hand, I waited at the gate with Ma and Pop as rain battered the runway, blowing in swirling gusts that resembled the angled waves on Cocoa Beach. Lightning stabbed directly earthward, and thunder boomed before the lightning faded. The silver chariot that would carry me to my new life cowered on the runway just outside our window.

"Jasus," Pop said. "I sure as hell hope they don't cancel yer flight, cuz I ain't making this trip two days in a row. I don't know why you'd book an afternoon flight when you know it storms like this every goddamned day. You just don't use yer head, Anthony. You may be headed fer college, but you still ain't so smart as you think." I bit my tongue, as I had all summer. Ever since I had been accepted to Northwestern, Pop had complained about everything related to college. I had chosen the wrong school—why not attend a "man's school," like West Point or Annapolis? My major, journalism, would leave me "poor as piss." Why not study "something worthwhile, like medicine or law?" School expenses would steal bread from my family's mouths. Never mind that I had won a nearly full scholarship, he protested: "I still have to pay for your transportation and food, don't I? Why do you have to go all the way to God-forsaken Chicago when there are perfectly good schools in Florida?"

"That lightning could come right through the window," Ma worried out loud, but Pop ignored her. "Seamus! Don't stand so close to it, please." Ma only used Pop's given name when he upset her. It sounded alien and strange to my ears. It was an Irish name, and Pop had always hated it. I remember Paddy once saying, "Seamus. That's a good name for the old bastard, 'cause he's always shaming us." Although Paddy had run away almost ten years ago now, his words still rang fresh in my head whenever I heard Pop's name.

"Ah, Jasus, Serena," Pop complained, "you and yer superstitions'll be the death of me." He returned to his seat, forgetting his grumblings for a few moments.

When the storm suddenly diminished to a drizzle, the flight attendants seized the opportunity, quickly handing each passenger an umbrella and sending us skittering across the tarmac with a warning to watch for puddles. Before picking up my carry-on bag, I bent down to hug and kiss Ma. As I slung my carry-on over my shoulder, Pop stood and faced me. I didn't know what to do for a minute, but then he stuck out his big, white hand. I took it in mine, and shook it, hurriedly and uncomfortably. It felt hard and hot, and he looked as uneasy as I felt.

At the doorway, the attendant handed me a black umbrella. I thought I heard Pop say something to Ma about "that dumb boy" as I opened it and started to pick my way across the wet pavement. I felt angry that he couldn't even let me leave in peace before he began his sniping. I wondered why they hadn't just dropped me off instead of waiting with me.

On board, my window seat faced the gate. Still fuming as the plane backed away, I saw Ma and Pop framed in the window, uncharacteristically arm in arm, smiling and waving at me. This image of them stayed with me, even after all the intervening years and events. They looked pleased to be getting me out of their hair, and I felt more determined than ever to carve out a new life without them. What Pop didn't know was that I had selected Northwestern *because* it was so far from home. Sure, it was a great school, and I had been lucky enough to get a scholarship. But, mostly, it was far from Merritt Island and Florida. And Ma and Pop.

By the time the plane taxied to the runway and took off, the storm returned. We were barely off the ground before the rain began pelting us and, as my chariot sprinted for the clouds, lightning began to flash around us. I feared that we would be struck, but moments later we broke through and emerged in sunlight above the clouds. I felt transformed.

Three hours later, we descended through the clouds at the last moment and landed quickly. Exiting the plane, I marveled at the enormity of O'Hare Airport. Vast and intimidating and thronged with people, the airport was nothing like the tiny jetport I had left behind in Orlando. I worked my way to the ground transportation center where the school promised a welcome van would be waiting to whisk me and my fellow freshman arrivees to our new home. On the bus, the greeting committee talked about how special we were, and how happy they were to have us there, but I hardly heard a word as I stared out the window at the passing scenery.

The campus in Evanston, just north of Chicago on Lake Michigan, was stunning, populated by statuesque, granite-and-limestone buildings, and magnificent old trees. The welcome van dropped me at my new dorm, the Northwestern University Apartments, and I gathered my belongings and headed inside to register. Inside my room—my home for the next nine months—I felt sad, yet a bit relieved to discover that my new roommate, Jim, was not in. I ran to the window and looked out; we had a commanding view of the courtyard from the seventh and top floor. I had never imagined living so far above ground and, already, I loved it.

As I unpacked my belongings, I wondered what Jim would be like, and whether we'd be friends. I worried, as I had all summer long, that he'd somehow be able to tell I was gay. When he finally showed up, I found him pleasant enough; but he pledged a fraternity and moved out three weeks later, leaving me on my own for the rest of the year. I had worried needlessly.

I spent most of my time that first year studying and at my work-study job in the journalism library. Sounds were muffled in the one-room, basement library by the books and thick, brick walls. The dim lighting gave the illusion of night or, more accurately, of dusk at all hours, and the faint odor of mildew permeated everything. The library was small and rarely used in the evenings, so I found myself alone with lots of time to study or just contemplate life. I could practically feel the pages of the books and newspapers in the room yellowing and fading all around me while I sat at the front desk, near the entrance door, working every weeknight between six and eleven; the same way I felt my own life was passing me by.

It was there, after nearly six months on campus, at about half-past-ten on a Tuesday night in March, I encountered my first openly gay student—the first unquestionably gay man (other than myself) that I had ever seen. He had a pink sticker on his book bag that read: "Manpleaser." I noticed it the second he came into the library. The blatant sexual nature of the slogan jarred and thrilled me. I couldn't stop staring at him, and wondered if he could sense my fascination and nervousness. He was so unremarkable that I was a little disappointed, despite my excitement. I had expected the first gay man I saw to be exotic and overtly sexual, but here he was: smallish and thin, and rather nondescript. He picked up a newspaper off the shelf and sat at one of the study tables to read. I glanced over at him about every other second, and kept hoping he'd approach me. I'm sure I would have panicked and made a complete ass of myself if he had, but still, I was nearly breathless with desire. I felt desperate to make contact with him, yet panic-stricken by the very thought of it. Finally, about ten minutes before closing, he looked straight at me and approached the counter.

"Yes?" I asked, standing as my heart clanged against my rib cage. "Can I help you with something?" I struggled to maintain my calm, but inside, my head reeled. Perhaps we would go to his place and talk before we made love. Or perhaps we'd go out for a drink.

"Is there a rest room around here?" he asked.

"Um, yes," I managed, startled by his mundane request. Perhaps he wanted to have sex in the rest room. Certainly, I had heard of such things, but I never imagined partaking myself. Yet, this was college, after all, where I was supposed to try new things.

He blinked and looked vaguely annoyed as he waved a hand in front of my face, "Well? Where is it?"

"Oh," I said, suddenly aware that he wasn't at all interested in me. I frantically pointed and said, "It's just down the hall on the right."

He shook his head and rolled his eyes at my odd behavior and headed out the door. I dropped back into my chair and cursed myself for being such an idiot. I felt my face burn with embarrassment, and was suddenly seized with panic that he had read my filthy thoughts and been offended. After a few minutes, he returned, picked up his backpack, and left without a word. I wanted to apologize to him, but decided that would only make things worse. When the door swung shut after him, I cursed myself again for not being bold enough to even ask his name or strike up some sort of conversation that might have led to something more. But I couldn't. I froze, as usual, and the opportunity was lost. I vowed to speak to him the next time he came in, but he never did.

Tarantella

I spent my first two years at college longing and frustrated; so, by my third year, in spite of my commitment to change my life, I still had no close friends, only acquaintances and classmates. I had moved into a single room and lived my life like a hermit. I attended class, studied, and worked at the journalism library— no time for friends or having fun or just hanging out. I never let anyone get close to me for fear they'd figure out who I *really* was, and I was too terrified to admit it to myself most of the time. In order to avoid painful admissions about my sexuality, I distanced myself from everyone. On occasion, I'd see flyers for Gay And Lesbian Alliance (GALA) events that I'd dream about, but never attend. And, I wrote occasional letters home, telling Ma and Pop and Rosalia how much I missed them, which wasn't true either.

In October of my junior year, the leaves turned scarlet and swirled to the ground in a final frenzy of color, dancing on lawns and streets before the snow fell. Summer was turning into autumn and, unexpectedly, my life was about to change with the season. One Friday afternoon, I accompanied a classmate to dinner at the local Burger King. Jeff and I had met over a year ago in our first reporting class. Occasionally, we'd grab a bite and visit, and once, we even went to a movie on campus. He was a nice guy with wheat-gold hair and beautifully clear skin. I found him witty and fun to be around, and he seemed to like me, too.

After we finished our burgers, Jeff asked me to come over to see his off-campus apartment and catch a little TV. For once, I was caught up with my homework and I didn't have to work at the library that night. Besides, I wasn't looking forward to going back to my lonely dorm room and feeling sorry for myself.

When we got to Jeff's place, we tossed our book bags on his dining table and Jeff showed me around the place, which was small, but cozy. He had a minuscule kitchen with a dining area, his living room doubled as his bedroom, and he had a small, old-fashioned bathroom with a tub on claw legs. Posters of Broadway shows, Linda Ronstadt, and Stevie Nicks decked his walls. Jeff asked if I wanted a beer. I said I didn't like beer, so he asked if I wanted to share a bottle of wine he'd just bought. I rarely drank wine either, but I didn't want to seem like I was too weird, so I agreed. He told me to turn on the TV and sit somewhere, so I switched on the set, took off my shoes, and reclined on one side of the bed—the only piece of furniture in the room, other than a desk. I was aware of the twinge of excitement I felt at the thought of sitting on Jeff's bed, but pushed it aside when Jeff returned with two wine glasses, smiled at the sight of me on his bed, and handed one glass to me.

"To another fucking year of school," he said, and held out his glass.

I delighted in his vulgarity, clinking my glass against his and saying, "Amen." He sat on the opposite side of the bed, we watched some inane comedy, and chatted about school. After a couple more glasses of wine, I became aware of Jeff's arm hairs brushing again my own, and the air seemed suddenly charged with electricity. My head was spinning when Jeff asked if I was seeing anyone.

"Not really," I said. "How about you? Are you dating anyone?"

"Nah," he said. "I don't know if I'm ready for that."

"I know what you mean," I said, pleased by his response. "I never have time and, besides, I feel like no one wants to touch me with a ten-foot pole."

Jeff plucked a ruler off the desk beside his bed. He tapped it against my arm and said, "Maybe you're right. But at least now you've been touched with a one-foot ruler." He laughed and we both downed another glass of wine.

I scanned the room and spotted a spatula on the kitchen table. I leaped up, grabbed it, and dashed over to Jeff. "*En garde*," I said, brandishing the spatula before me like a dueling sword, feeling electricity spark invisibly between us.

Jeff grinned and leapt to his feet on the bed, accepting my challenge. He adopted a spread-eagle stance, whipped the ruler through the air a couple of times, and said, "*En garde*, yourself."

I jumped onto the bed and slapped my spatula against Jeff's ruler. "Take that, knave," I said. "This is a duel to the death."

We whirled about, parried and sortied with our "swords," shouting "Hah" and "Take that," and laughing, until we finally fell back on the bed, begging for a time-out and more wine. I lost track of how much wine I'd had, but eagerly gulped down the glass that Jeff was offering. My head and the rest of my body buzzed with energy. I jabbed Jeff in the chest with the spatula and said, "I wouldn't touch you *here* with a ten-foot pole."

Jeff grabbed his ruler again and pressed it gently into my side. "And I wouldn't touch you *here* with a ten-foot pole."

Feeling suddenly daring, I poked the spatula into his belly. "I wouldn't touch you *here*." I felt a thrill run through my belly, and my pulse quickened.

Jeff touched my hip with the ruler. "I wouldn't touch you *here*." Jeff's eyes glittered with energy. I imagined it was his fingers, not a ruler, against my hip.

Emboldened by the wine, I said, "I wouldn't touch you *here*," and touched the spatula to Jeff's groin. I felt supercharged with sexual energy and excitement and nearly overpowering terror as I watched for Jeff's reaction. I couldn't breathe, my heart was leaping against my rib cage, and my penis surged powerfully erect.

Jeff looked up at me, eyes wide in surprise, and touched his ruler to my crotch. "I wouldn't touch *you* here either." For a moment, neither of us moved.

I felt the blood rush from my face, like I was draining out of myself, and I gaped at Jeff without moving. I experienced a sudden, intense fear and arousal as Jeff's glistening, green eyes widened and he looked like he was frightened of me. I hesitated, not knowing what to do: proceed and expose my true sexual feelings, or stop and pretend it was all a game? Before I could move, Jeff dropped his ruler and pulled the spatula out of my hand and dropped it on the floor as well. He touched his fingers tentatively to my cheek, as if he were trying to determine what I was made of. A charge raced from the point of contact on my cheek straight to my groin. I wanted to fling myself against him, but I held back and followed his lead. I touched his cheek. How remarkable, I thought: it felt warm and soft against my fingertips. I'd expected a man to feel rougher, like a leather strap. But he felt as fragile as the robin's egg I had found in a nest one spring long ago, smooth and warm and incredibly delicate. I was holding my breath, afraid if I breathed, the shell might break.

Jeff moved up against me, pressing his cheek on mine, encircling me with his arms, hugging me against him. I pressed into him and clasped my arms around him. We fell back into a reclining position. Then, Jeff was on top of me, and I was so excited I could feel the pounding of my heart, until I thought it would burst right out of my chest. I was shaking like I was cold, but I felt hot and flushed. I couldn't stop shaking. I realized it was fear and desire, and that Jeff was shaking, too.

Suddenly, I was holding his face in my hands and touching his golden hair. He pulled off my shirt and I removed his. His naked chest gleamed in the flicker of the television, the only light in the room, and I could smell the scent of sandalwood on his skin. Jeff shut off the volume, twisting his arm to reach the control knob from the bed, then turned back to look into my face, and I at his, for what seemed like hours before running his hand over my chest. I felt a charge from every follicle. I thought suddenly to myself: *Oh, God, it's happening at last* and touched his chest and both nipples, which felt softer than the rest of him until they hardened under my fingers. He shivered in response and moaned, "Oh, God. Oh, God." I shivered, goose flesh puckered my skin, and I reached lower to touch his groin. He stopped short, looked me square in the face and said, "I can't believe you're touching me there." I froze in sheer panic at the thought that this was all some terrible mistake, that I had misjudged him and he would leap up any second now and run screaming from the room, shouting, "Faggot! Faggot!"

But he didn't run away, only rolled over, removed his shoes and pants and unbuckled my pants, shucking them while I lifted my hips aloft so he could draw them down and off. The air in the room felt cool on my bare skin, but Jeff felt warm when he rolled back on top of me. He felt so good there, I wished we could stay like this forever. We pressed ourselves against one another, clad only in our underwear, and he kissed me. His tongue slipped into my mouth and I remembered that night in the car with Elsa and wondered if this was how it had felt for her. I kissed him back, twisting my tongue around his, wrapping my arms and legs through his, rolling him onto his back. I reached down between us and removed his underwear, and then my own, and looked at our two penises, red and straining, and wondered if it felt as good to him as it did to me I. I let my body drop down on top of his, pressed my hips into him, and felt his hips under me, pressing up to meet mine.

We ground against each other frantically, wildly, like two animals fighting for turf, and our mouths were over one another. Our hands roved up and down each other's flesh and suddenly, it was over as I felt the explosion rising up out of my belly, rising and bursting forth. I cried out in pleasure, threw back my head and heaved a great breath, then realized Jeff was gasping beneath me and had come, too.

I dropped down over him and listened as our two hearts and our breathing slowly returned to normal. I couldn't stop thinking: *At last, at last, at last,* and wondered if Jeff was thinking the same thing. I hoped we would do it soon again, then again, and never stop, even to eat or sleep or go to class—but we both fell asleep. When I awoke, Jeff was in his bathroom showering.

When he came out, towel belted around his waist, he noticed I was awake and said, "It's almost noon." He rummaged through his dresser and pulled on a fresh pair of underwear without removing the towel around his waist.

"Is it?" I asked, wondering if it had only been one night. "Too late to be shy," I said, laughing.

"Yeah, right," he said, pulling on a shirt. He seemed subdued, not at all like last night. "We should get going, don't you think?"

"I suppose," I said, climbing out of his bed. "Can I use your shower?"

"Uh, sure, I guess," he said, turning quickly towards his kitchen as I climbed naked out of the bed. "I'll pull out some cereal or something while you wash up."

I wanted to kiss him or touch him or say something about the night before, but he was already digging in the refrigerator, so I let it go and headed into the bathroom to wash. When I finished and dressed in my clothes from the night before, I joined Jeff in the kitchen.

"How do you feel?" I asked as I walked up behind him.

"Huh? Oh, okay," he said. "I'm not sure, really. You want cereal?"

"Sure," I said, and he handed me a box of Corn Flakes. I sat at the small dining table, a folding table with two wicker chairs, and poured the cereal into the bowl he handed me. Jeff sat in the chair opposite me, poured himself a bowl, and began crunching into them. He looked beautiful, all golden and fresh.

"What aren't you sure about?" I asked, starting to feel unsure myself. Maybe I was imagining it, but Jeff seemed suddenly nervous and uncomfortable.

"I dunno," he said between bites. "I mean, I liked it but, you know." He stopped eating for a moment and looked at me. "That your first time?"

"Uh-huh," I nodded. "Yours, too?"

"Yeah. I didn't really expect that, either. So, I don't know where to go from here, you know?"

"Me either," I said. "We can just sort of play it by ear, if you want."

"Yeah," he nodded eagerly. "Play it by ear. Let's just see how it goes."

I finished my cereal, grabbed my book bag, and Jeff walked me to the door. "Well, I'll call you later, okay?" he said.

"Yeah, okay." I hefted the book bag over my shoulder and turned toward him. He took an uncertain step backward. I wanted to kiss him goodbye, but he seemed too nervous, so I said, "Well, call me," pulled open the door, and slipped out. I hurried home to my dorm room.

I dropped my book bag on the sofa and went into the bathroom. I turned on the hot water and felt the steam on my face. I wondered when Jeff would call and how soon we would do that again.

Jeff never called over the weekend, so I stopped him after class on Monday. We talked outside as other students rushed around us on their way to class. The sun was out, although dark, gray clouds covered most of the sky. The cool, gusty wind periodically kicked up little eddies of swirling leaves. I asked Jeff why he hadn't called.

"I don't know what to say, man." He looked fearful, continually glancing around us to see if anyone was listening.

"Well," I said, "would you like to get together again? Maybe this weekend?"

"I can't," he answered quickly. "I mean, I don't know. What can I say, Anthony? I didn't mean for that to happen."

"Well, it happened. Now what?" I could see he was terrified. I was, too, but it had happened, at last, and I wanted more.

"Now, nothing," he said. "I mean, I can't. I'm not, well, I don't wanna be gay, Anthony, so I can't do that again. Can't we just go back to being friends like before?"

I felt my stomach twist, felt the sweat prickling my back and arms, but somehow I managed to keep my composure enough to answer Jeff. Of course, we'd stay friends like before. Of course, I could understand how he felt about this. Jeff seemed relieved as he walked away, but I sagged against a leaf-bare tree after he was out of sight. I couldn't understand because, for me, it was like a door had been opened and a whole new world revealed. Now that I'd seen it, I couldn't just forget about it. I couldn't pretend that it didn't exist, that I didn't hear its siren call. I couldn't believe that Jeff could either, or would want to. But he was clearly panicked by what had happened and was running the other way—something I could understand. In fact, my own reaction surprised me. Why wasn't I feeling panicked, too? Why wasn't I feeling guilt and remorse? I felt only relief, like I had been unburdened of a great weight. I didn't know where I was headed next, only that I wasn't going backwards.

After that, Jeff and I said our uncomfortable hellos in class, but we never got together again. After my junior year ended, I never saw him again. But, even now, I can still replay everything that happened that night. I can see his golden hair, feel his warm, soft skin, and smell his sandalwood scent.

I felt like the world had opened to me after my experience with Jeff. In spite of the fact that he had panicked and run from it, I wanted more. Only I didn't know what to do to make it happen. A few months later, in the spring of my junior year, I ran into a boy named Cliff in the main library's poetry section. I had seen him before and we had nodded and smiled, but we'd never spoken to each other. My radar beeped and buzzed, sensing a kindred spirit in Cliff, but I was too frightened to approach him, much as I wanted to. Then, one day, Cliff asked if I would maybe like to go over to the student center for some coffee or tea. I felt a rush of excitement and arousal surge through me. I wanted to jump up and say: yes, yes, yes, I'll go anywhere with you! Instead, as usual, I froze.

"I'm safe," Cliff said, holding out his hands. "See? No weapons."

"Okay," I managed, grinning nervously. I set the book I was reading back on the shelf and followed him over. We both ordered tea and sat at a table in the corner by a window. We went through all the preliminaries—Where you from? What's your major?—before Cliff finally took a chance.

Tarantella

"I noticed you were reading Ginsberg," he said, looking closely at my reaction. "Isn't he great?"

"Yeah," I said, not quite sure how to respond. I decided to take the opening. "He seems so comfortable about stuff that I still struggle with." I gulped at my presumptuousness, then panicked about how he might react. I suspected Cliff was gay, but I was far from certain. Was this some sort of elaborate trick to uncover my secret? Cliff noticed my discomfort and jumped in.

"I still struggle with that stuff, too," he said. "Maybe we could struggle with it together sometime?" My scalp immediately flushed with heat and pin-prickles of sweat, mostly from the excitement and the shock of his blunt directness. "I'm sorry. I've embarrassed you," he said, then added with a wink, "but, I must say, you blush beautifully."

"Um, thanks," I stammered, feeling the scarlet heat in my face and ears. "I don't know why I do that. I wish I could turn it off."

"I like it," he said. "It's very sweet." He looked down at his hands. "I think you're very sweet and I'd like to see you, if you wanted to." He stirred his nearly empty cup of tea, and the spoon clanked noisily against the sides of the ceramic mug.

Sunlight poured in through the window, glinting off the gold in his hair. I flashed briefly on Jeff. Only Cliff—all solid and tan and decidedly not shy—looked nothing like Jeff. I marveled that he could be so honest, so daring. I could never have managed to be so direct. I watched him fidget nervously, and wondered how he could be so fearless about asking me out, and so nervous about my reply. It helped relax me a little.

"I'd like that," I said. I didn't want to miss the opportunity he had presented to me. He looked up immediately and exhaled deeply. He smiled, and we sat there, grinning foolishly at one another.

"Would you like to get together for dinner and a movie this weekend?" he asked.

"That sounds great," I said, leaning forward across the table. "I love movies."

"I hope you love other things, too," he flirted.

We exchanged numbers and addresses and agreed to call each other the following day. I practically floated home—I couldn't recall a single step of the way afterward.

We saw each other that weekend and nearly every day the following week. Cliff asked me to spend the night with him after taking me out to a romantic dinner for our third date. My heart thumped, and I felt a flush of excitement and fear even as I heard myself accepting his invitation.

"Now, don't expect the Taj Mahal," Cliff said as he opened the apartment door. "It's not much, but it's home."

Cliff's personality pervaded the tiny efficiency. Beside his bed hung large posters of Richard Gere and Richard Hatch. The kitchen was filled with brightly colored drinking glasses and matching plates, neatly stacked beside the sink. A painting of a cityscape, with the Eiffel Tower beside a flowing river, hung above the TV. The bed was neatly made up with a gray-and-maroon blanket and matching sheets. Moonlight streamed through the kitchen and living/bedroom windows, casting a warm glow over the entire apartment.

Tarantella

"It's wonderful," I enthused. "I love it."

Cliff scooped me around my waist and pulled me over to his bed. "I'm glad," he said. "Now, let's get naked." We stripped off our clothes and climbed under the cool sheets on his bed, turning toward one another expectantly. Cliff reached out his hand and traced it down my face and over my throat, and I let the sensations flood over and through my body, closing my eyes to submit myself completely. Pulling me toward him, Cliff pressed his lips against mine and kissed me firmly, passionately. I slid one arm under the crook of his neck and the other around his side, running my hand over the small of his back.

"You feel wonderful," I said, sighing with pleasure.

"No talking," Cliff said, pressing a finger against my lips. "Just enjoy."

He rolled on top of me and I could feel his erection against my belly, pressing into me as I pressed up to meet him. His hands and tongue danced over my flesh and I felt sensations I never dreamed of. By the time we both climaxed, I felt completely satisfied and happy; I never wanted to leave his bed. Cliff kissed me and wrapped his arms around me. Before long, we were both aroused and we made love a second time, only more slowly and deliberately.

In the morning, Cliff waited in bed until I awoke and we made love a third time, luxuriously, as beautiful yellow sunlight streamed through his windows and lit up his entire apartment in a golden, sexual glow. I felt immersed in Cliff, and I never wanted the moment to pass. Nothing rushed and inebriated, like with

Jeff—just tender and purposeful and loving. Loving, the way I understood, at last, two men could be.

In the month we had before summer break, Cliff and I were practically inseparable, spending every minute outside of class or work together. We studied together, ate together, and slept together nearly every night in his apartment. Before I knew it, I was dreaming of our life together after school.

Cliff refused to hide who he was, refused to accept life in the closet. It was one of the things I found so attractive about him. He had no doubt about who and what he was or what he wanted. I envied his certainty and his strength and he coaxed me along the path to accepting myself.

"You've got to open up, Anthony," he'd say. "You'll never be happy if you can't accept yourself and stop hiding who you are."

Intellectually, I agreed with him and longed to be as open as he was. But the door that had opened my first time with Jeff, had only opened so far and, even after spending time with Cliff, it was still only open a crack. Somewhere inside, I still believed what I'd been taught as a child: homosexuality was sinful and immoral. Getting beyond this mindset was like running through Florida sawgrass—you ended up bloodied and scarred. It was easier to avoid than run through it.

"I do accept myself," I'd insist to Cliff, "but, unlike you, I don't feel the need to brag about it." But Cliff saw through me. The evidence that I hadn't accepted my sexuality mounted, as did the tension in our relationship. By June, we were regularly hashing and rehashing the issue. Cliff insisted I needed to come out to Ma and Pop and I insisted they didn't need to know; in fact, had no right to know.

The night before the start of summer break, Cliff took me to dinner at a romantic restaurant just off campus. He would be spending three months at home in North Carolina, while I remained on campus for a summer job, only heading home for a brief two-week visit around Labor Day.

After placing our orders, he caressed my arm affectionately and I flinched, glancing around instinctively to see if anyone had noticed. Cliff slid stiffly and purposefully back in his seat, regarding me as if I had physically pushed him.

"What's that about?" he asked.

"I'm sorry," I said, shrugging my shoulders apologetically. "It's just—people were watching and I was afraid they'd see us."

"So, what if they did?" He leaned forward, placing his elbows on the table.

"I just feel funny about it, that's all." I glanced around to see if anyone was eavesdropping on our conversation. "You've got to remember, Cliff, you've been out for over two years, so you're more comfortable about things than I am. It's only been a month for me."

"So," he said slowly, "how long do you suppose you'll need, Anthony? How long do we have to pretend we're straight—you know, just pals? You know how I hate that. I want to be with you, and I don't care who knows. You don't seem ready, and it's spoiling everything, Anthony."

"I'm not doing it consciously," I said nervously. "Honestly, I *am* trying."

"I don't get it, Anthony." He leaned toward me and whispered into my ear. "You like the sex part, right? You don't seem to have to pretend about that."

"That's different," I said. "That's just the two of us."

"Our relationship is just the two of us, too," he said. "And who *you* are is just you. You can't spend the rest of your life trying to make everyone think you're straight. At least, you can't do that and have a relationship with me."

I hurriedly glanced around the dining room again.

"Quit worrying about who's listening to us! Does it really matter a damn what a bunch of people you don't even know think?" He gestured toward the other diners.

"Well, no," I said, flustered. "I'm just not as comfortable as you are yet, Cliff. You've been out for years. I'm still adjusting. You have lots of gay friends. I don't."

"And you never will, Anthony," he said. "Not if you can't accept who you are. Either you're gay or you're not. And, if you're not, what the hell are you doing here with me? I'll tell you right now, I'm not going to hide out with you forever. I don't want to go backwards, and I won't let you make me feel guilty or dirty about who I am."

"I don't want that either," I said. "Can't you be patient a little while longer? I'm working on it, but it's not easy for me. I think this summer will really help—it'll give me time to adjust. By the time you come back, I'm sure I'll feel more comfortable. It's a big adjustment for me."

Tarantella

"Remember, I grew up in North Carolina," Cliff said. "If you think it was easy coming out down there, you're wrong. But I did it, and I'm glad. If you're not ready to come out in college with me at your side, when will you ever be?"

"I'm trying," I said. "It's hard, though. Sometimes I don't even realize when I'm being ridiculous. It's not like I'm not trying."

"I know," he said, relenting a bit. "I went through it, too. Everyone does. But you've got to stop now. You're so down on yourself, and I can't handle it because you're really a great guy. You shouldn't feel bad about being gay, and you've got to stop worrying about what everyone else thinks. It's 1979—things have changed."

"I can't help it sometimes," I said. "It's like second nature to me. What if someone told my parents? They'd die."

"You can't worry about that. They're a thousand miles away," he said. "Besides, *you* should tell your folks."

"They'd be upset." Cliff just didn't understand about Ma and Pop, I thought, or he wouldn't be saying this. "Jeez, they'd explode if I told them. They'd not only throw me out of the house, they'd also refuse to pay for my last year of college. Then, where would I be?"

"If they get upset, so be it," he said, stabbing at the asparagus in his appetizer. "At least it would be over with. Until then, you'll always be second-guessing yourself, and you'll never be able to get past this and become whoever it is you're supposed to be."

"I'll work on it over the summer," I promised. "I'm not ready, yet. Soon, though."

"You're too busy being this incredible figment of other peoples' imaginations. It's not fair to you. Or your parents. Or me."

Cliff pushed his appetizer away and looked intently at me. He was so beautiful, and I didn't want to do anything to lose him. Of course, he was right. I knew it then; I had known for a long time: I just didn't know how to make myself trust it.

"Okay, okay," I said. "I'll try. I promise. Now, lower your voice—you're making a scene." I picked up my wine glass before he could respond. "Let's toast to it. I promise to try harder if you promise to be patient with me. I do love you, you know."

"I know," Cliff said, touching his glass to mine with a resonant clink. He smiled mischievously and took my hand in his. "It won't be as hard as you think. You'll see. Once you start, it gets easier to be yourself—automatic almost."

"I hope so," I said, fighting the urge to pull my hand back, squirming inwardly with the awareness that the wait staff and several guests had noticed and were flashing looks of disgust our way.

"It will. I promise." He took another sip of his wine and smiled broadly, creases rippling across his forehead. "Besides, I love you, too. That should help."

"It does," I said. "And I'm glad you're around to help me."

"Well, it's a good thing I am," he said, pointing at me. "You'd still be hiding in the library dreaming about doing things instead of enjoying them."

"You're right," I said, without much conviction. I thought how much easier it was to keep silent. At least then I didn't have to face the prospect of telling my parents I was gay. But staying silent had ensured I was also on my own most of the time. Cliff was right: I should stop worrying about what strangers thought. But, how could I not worry about what my family thought? Other than Cliff, they were all I had. Why tell them something they really didn't need to know? They were a thousand miles away. What possible good could come from telling them?

Over the summer, after Cliff left, I filled most of the time I wasn't working with reading to avoid thinking about facing Ma and Pop at the end of the season. At the beginning of the summer, Cliff and I spoke on the phone about our plans for the next school year. During every call, he asked if I had talked to Ma and Pop yet. And, each time, I had to confess that I hadn't. By midsummer, the calls had grown increasingly awkward and then, ceased completely.

Our dinner conversation reverberated in my head, especially the part about it not being fair to him and his unwillingness to live with my secret much longer. I knew this had become a wedge between us. I had to accept myself if I wanted to share my life with him—or with anyone—and I had to come out to my family before I could really accept myself.

Returning to campus that fall for my senior year, after a brief visit to Merritt Island, I knew I had to talk to Cliff right away. I hadn't heard from him for a while, so I decided to stop by his dorm room the next afternoon.

Cliff opened the door and seemed surprised to find me standing there. I leaned in to kiss him, but he pulled away.

"Can we talk?" I asked, tentatively, unsure how to read his changed demeanor toward me.

"I don't really think we have anything left to talk about," he said, turning icily away from me, and starting to pull the door closed behind him. "You gave me your answer over the summer every time we talked."

"Did I?" I asked rhetorically. I was taken aback by the hard edge in his voice. Before I could continue, Cliff interrupted.

"You did," he snapped. "How long did you think I would wait for you to get up the nerve to come out to your parents, Anthony?" He shook his head sadly. "After the second and third and fourth calls with no progress, I had to rethink things."

"Really," I said. "What exactly did you rethink?" I asked, my pulse quickening.

"I rethought *us*," he said. "I just didn't see how I could stay in a relationship with someone who was so deeply closeted."

"But——" I started.

"But nothing," he interrupted. "I couldn't keep waiting on you, Anthony. I'm sorry, but I've moved on."

His words struck me like fists. I felt numb, unable to respond, barely able to comprehend.

"I'm really sorry, Anthony," he said, waiting briefly for a response before nervously adding: "I mean, it's really for the best, don't you think? It's good we realized this before we got too involved, you know?"

Tarantella

"Sure, Cliff," I managed. "If you say so. I actually came over here to let you know that I *did* tell my parents. Just before the summer ended. Like I promised I would. Stupidly, I thought I'd surprise you with the news. But now, I think I need to go."

My head was spinning. Cliff looked stunned. I was definitely *not* okay: I wanted to run down the hallway and out of the dorm, and just keep running. I wanted to quit school, there and then. Maybe I'd hop on a plane and just fly away to a place where no one knew me, or knew what a loser I was—somewhere I didn't have to feel so worthless all the time. But, of course, I didn't do any of these things. I turned to leave.

"Anthony, wait," Cliff murmured.

I turned back. He was standing in his doorway, looking startled.

"Why?" I asked. "It's not like *you* were willing to wait for *me*."

I turned away and headed down the hall.

As I walked across the campus, I thought about how many things I had left behind out of fear or anger. The people in my life had been like Ma's smoke—there for a minute, and then, gone. Pushed away by emotions that remained submerged, until something stirred them back to life. Then, malarial, like mosquitoes rejuvenated by rain, springing suddenly to life and buzzing about; with each feeding, depositing a blood-borne contagion. Like a mosquito, I carried Ma's and Pop's contagion inside me; I seemed to infect everyone I met. How could I ever hope to build a relationship when I carried such a powerful poison inside me?

Cliff had expected me to fail. And why not? Hadn't I failed time and time again? It was clear I understood nothing about relationships. I felt completely inadequate. But then, look at the example I had been given by Ma and Pop.

After the disaster with Cliff, I decided to ignore my sexuality during my senior year and focus on graduating. I kept to myself most of the time and shut down all attempts to befriend me. I couldn't wait to graduate, so I could start fresh again. I didn't know how many more chances I'd get to start over, so I was determined to do a better job next time.

I met Steven the day I turned twenty-one. After so long ignoring my desires, the occasion seemed like a good excuse to lose my gay bar "virginity" by making my first pilgrimage to a Downtown Chicago bar. Why shouldn't one disaster beget another, I figured? Besides, I wanted to console myself with drink. Bad decisions and poor judgment seem to travel in packs.

Tarantella

I took a taxi to a gay nightclub in the city I had heard about. When I arrived, I stared at the neon sign from the cab, unsure whether to go in or to ask the cabbie to drive me back to my lonely-but-safe dorm room. I wondered if the cabbie knew it was a gay bar and what he thought about taking me here.

"Hey, buddy," the cabbie interrupted my thoughts. "Is this the place or not?"

"Uh, yeah," I managed. "Sorry." I paid him and stepped onto the curb.

The sign flashed pink on my skin and I felt like I wanted to run away, like I was doing something illicit, like I'd get in trouble if someone caught me here. It was the way I felt the first time I bought a copy of *Playgirl* and looked at the pictures of naked men inside. I was swept by the same incredible surge of sexual excitement and terror—the very sensations I felt Ma and Pop had bred in me, to ensure I would never do what I was about to do. Finally, deciding it was better to be inside than stand on the curb for all the world to see, I paid the cover charge and stumbled through the dark doorway.

Inside, the music throbbed, and dozens of men danced together on a crowded dance floor to my left. On my right was the bar. I picked my way through the men watching the dancers and sat on one of the barstools. A bartender in form-fitting shorts took my order for an amaretto sour, which I remembered Cliff used to drink. I sipped on my drink and watched the hubbub around me. It was a Wednesday night and I had an 8:00 class the next morning, so I promised myself I'd head home within the hour.

"Hey, guy," a voice beside me called out loudly. "Anyone sitting here?"

I looked up and saw a young, red-haired man gesturing at the empty barstool beside me. He was tall—maybe six feet—and had green eyes that reminded me of a cat. He was dressed in tight jeans with cowboy boots and a white dress shirt, and he cupped a beer in one palm.

"Okay if I sit here?" he repeated when I didn't respond.

"Yeah, sure," I said, stammering and nodding. My heart started beating faster, and I felt my panic rising. *Shit*, I thought to myself: *don't have a heart attack. All he asked was to sit down. Relax already.*

"My name's Steven," he said, reaching out to me with his hand and grinning broadly as he sat down.

I shook his hand, which was warm and broad, and said, "I'm Anthony. Hi." I was trying to think of something else to say, but he spoke first and rescued me.

"Mind if I call you Tony?" he asked. "I love that name—so sexy!" Before I could respond, he continued, "So, where you from, Tony? I don't remember seeing you around here before." He jiggered his chair around so he could watch the dance floor and still talk to me.

"Evanston. Well, I go to school there, anyhow." He nodded, waiting for me to explain the "anyhow" part of my response. "I was born in Upstate New York, but I really grew up on Merritt Island, by the Space Center, in Florida." Few people had ever heard of Merritt Island, so I always added the "by the Space Center" part so they would know approximately where it was.

Tarantella

"Oh, man, you're a Southern belle." He shook his head in mock-sympathy and took a swig of his beer. "I was born and raised right here, in Chicago." He looked me up and down, then said, "Florida, huh? Guess that makes you a true Dixie Queen."

"I guess," I said, and gulped down the rest of my drink. I didn't know what to make of my bar mate. He seemed more than a little juiced, but pleasant enough. Besides, we were only sharing neighboring bar stools and he was sort of cute, in a redneck way. He had broad, heavy features—strong and masculine—and a thick, red-brown moustache. Red-brown hair covered his head in flowing waves that caught little glints of light even in the mostly dark room. He pulled out a pack of cigarettes.

"Mind if I smoke?" he asked.

"No, it's okay," I said, despite my distaste. "I'm used to it. My folks smoke."

"Your folks live in Florida?" he asked as he lit a match and touched the flame to the end of his cigarette. He inhaled, and the flame tilted inward, toward his cigarette. I could hear the paper and tobacco crackle as they burned, even in the din of the room. The pungent bite of sulfur filled my nostrils as he shook out the match and dropped it into an ashtray that he snatched off the counter behind us. He inhaled again, deeply, and again, I heard the tobacco crackle, and saw the cigarette tip glow. He didn't exhale for what seemed like minutes, and when he did, he closed his eyes, and a look of complete satisfaction filled the features of his face.

"Yeah," I finally answered his question. "My folks still live on Merritt Island."

"Cool," he said, opening his eyes suddenly.

I was staring at his face. I hurriedly and self-consciously glanced away.

"It's getting kinda late," I said nervously, looking at the watch on my wrist.

"Right," he said, brazenly looking me up and down like he was appraising a horse. I spread my legs wider and sat up straighter. "You sure are nervous as a fish on a hook."

"I'm sorry," I said. "I'm not very good at this."

"Not very good at what?" he asked, raising one eyebrow suggestively.

"Not *that*," I said quickly, realizing he had misconstrued my meaning. "I'm not very good at making small talk. You know, at meeting people."

"Oh," he said. "Maybe you're better at *other* things?"

I felt my mouth drop open and my eyes blink twice. If the lights were brighter, my red face would have matched his hair. When he started laughing, I felt like a foolish, little boy.

"I'm sorry," he said after a minute. "Let me get you a refill." He motioned to the bartender to bring him another beer and refill my drink, then turned back to face me. "I didn't mean to embarrass you. I'm really not laughing at you. I just haven't seen anyone blush like that since high school. You sure you're not still in high school, Tony?"

"I'm in college," I replied, before I caught the mischievous glint in his eye and added, "but I already told you that."

"So," he asked, as the bartender delivered our drinks, "what makes a college boy like you blush?"

"I can't help it," I said, nervously sipping my second amaretto sour. "It just happens. I was hoping it was dark enough to hide it."

"Not very likely," he said, taking a gulp of his beer. "You're practically glowing in the dark. I think it's kind of a turn-on to see a man blush." He wiped his mouth with the back of his hand and banged his beer down on the counter. Cliff had also liked men who blushed. "So, what're you studying, college boy?"

"I'm taking journalism. I'd like to write for a newspaper after I graduate," I said, taking another sip of my drink. "What do you do?"

"I wait tables."

The music suddenly blared from the dance floor. He tipped his beer bottle at me and shifted to watch for a moment. I turned toward the dance floor, too, but continued to study him from the corners of my eyes. Although I was sure he spotted me looking at him at least a couple of times, he never reacted or let on that he had noticed. As the song ended, I saw how late it was getting.

"I think I've got to get going," I said.

"Why? Do you turn into a pumpkin at midnight or something?"

"No, but I've got to be up early for class tomorrow."

"Well, then, I enjoyed talking to you tonight, Tony," he said. Then, looking up and winking, he added, "And making you blush."

"Me too," I said. "I mean, nice meeting you, Steven. Bye." I reached out my hand to shake his, but he stepped forward and grabbed me around the hips, pulling me against him. I could feel his erection pressing into me, and I knew he could feel mine against him. He looked up directly into my eyes and winked, grinned devilishly, then bent me back at the waist and kissed me hard on the lips. Finally, he let me up and stepped back, bowed at the waist, and swept his arm dramatically before him.

"Good night," he said. "Don't let the bedbugs bite." Then, he chuckled, turned, and strode onto the dance floor.

I watched him go before I could catch my breath. Slowly, I became aware of people around me, watching the entire episode. I blushed again, but felt charged with electricity, energized and pleased to think that I had given him an erection, as he had me. I contemplated following him and telling him I'd changed my mind and decided to stay. But I knew what that would look like, and I didn't want to look like a slut, despite my temptation.

I caught a taxi home and masturbated as soon as I got inside while thinking about how good Steven had felt pressed up against me—how strong and good and hard he had felt, and how much I had wanted him. I didn't even feel ashamed of my feelings and desire until after I had masturbated a second time. Only then did I think about how I hardly knew this man, about how it would look if I went to bed with a man the first night I met him—about how I was supposed to love someone before sleeping with him. But, I already felt like I could love Steven—if given the opportunity. As I dozed off, I cursed myself for not thinking to get his phone number or even his last name before I left the bar. How would I ever find him again? I was such an idiot! I lacked all common sense when it came to relationships and meeting people. It was like the situation with the boy in the journalism library all over again; my timidity had probably cost me another chance to meet a potential lover.

The next weekend, I went back to the bar hoping I'd encounter Steven again. I left after barely an hour, depressed and disappointed. The following weekend, I tried again with the same result. I told myself I'd missed my chance and to forget about him.

But I couldn't forget. I thought about him all the time; and every time I thought about him, I got an erection and had to force myself to think about something else to regain my composure. By spring, I despaired of ever finding Steven again, after at least a dozen unsuccessful trips to the bar. Yet, after attending a school play one Friday night a few weeks before graduation, I decided to try one last time.

At the bar, I checked my appearance as I passed through the mirrored entranceway. Inside, the dance music blared, and the room was crowded with mostly young, attractive men. The dance floor was packed with sweaty dancers, many of whom had removed their shirts: their sweat and body heat permeated the room like a sauna. I scanned the dark, moving mass around me. I watched as men greeted one another with hugs and kisses on the cheek. I felt strangely ill-at-ease with the casual and almost feminine affection displayed by these gay men.

"Wanna dance?" asked a man to my right.

Before I could reply, someone reached around me from behind and wrapped broad, warm hands over my eyes, whispering with hot breath in my right ear, "Guess who?" I could feel the heat of his body behind me, pressing against me lightly. It excited me wildly. I could feel my pulse quicken along with my heartbeat and a stirring in my groin.

"I'm not sure," I said, trying to turn my head.

"Well, I'll be danged," the voice said. "You're blushing again. I guess this is getting to be a regular thing with us."

"Steven!" I said with enthusiasm and spun around to face him.

"You remembered my name," he said grinning. "What do you suppose that could mean?"

"It means I was hoping to run into you again," I said, more boldly than I had intended. I felt my cheeks blush, and wondered why blushing around Steven seemed to have become a regular pattern. I looked at Steven, and suddenly realized I hadn't the slightest idea of what to say to him. He seemed to sense my nervousness.

"This is a great song," he said, glancing out across the dance floor. "'Play That Funky Music.' It's one of my favorites. You wanna dance, Tony? See, I remembered your name, too. I guess it *does* mean something."

I felt a charge run through me at the thought that perhaps he was interested in me, too. I nodded, followed him onto the floor, and danced for the first time with another man. Steven danced with abandon, and I followed his lead and let myself go as well. We danced for another couple of songs before Steven suggested we stop for a drink. He asked me to save us seats while he went to bar.

I sat down on a bench seat along the far wall. I watched Steven at the bar chatting and laughing with the bartender, who glanced over in my direction briefly and gave Steven a thumbs-up sign. I felt like I had just passed some sort of test, and the butterflies I felt in my stomach all fluttered their wings briefly in response. At last, Steven joined me with a beer for him and an amaretto sour for me.

"How'd you remember what I drink?" I asked.

"I never forget a drink. I'm a waiter, remember? It's what you were drinking when we met."

He grinned at me and hoisted his beer as if to salute me before taking a swig. He wiped his lips with the back of his hand and pulled out a cigarette. He lit it and put the matches and the cigarette pack into his shirt pocket. He was wearing tight jeans and a body-hugging black tee-shirt, beneath which his nipples protruded prominently. His hair swept back from his face in dangerous, red-gold cascades.

I felt like I was caught in the undertow on Cocoa Beach.

He saw me looking at him and grinned, then stood and pulled his stool up so close beside mine that his left leg pressed against my right.

I felt his body heat, and a series of electrical charges shot through me.

"What're you looking at?" he asked.

"I'm sorry," I said blushing again at my lack of discretion. "I was just looking at your face."

"And what do you see?" he asked, leaning in so close I could feel his breath on my face.

I looked at him again. His hair seemed to sparkle under the colored bar lights and his thick moustache looked masculine and inviting. Even in the dim flickering light, I could see he sported an incredible bronze tan.

"I see auburn hair that looks like it's full of gold dust the way it sparkles," I said. "And I like how thick your moustache looks. You've got cat eyes—you know, big and green. And you look like you lay out in the sun a lot."

He grinned and took a drag off his cigarette. "I like that. It sounds good the way you say it. But you're wrong about one thing—I hardly ever lay out in the sun. I'm just part Sioux. That's just my natural Injun color, girl." He grinned at his campiness and took another long drag off his cigarette while he stared me up and down. "Now, it's my turn to describe you," he said at last. "I see someone who's got his shit together and who's smart and good looking. And nice."

"I like the way you describe me, too," I said, smiling at him.

"Let me see your palm," Steven said suddenly, butting out his cigarette in the ashtray and holding out his own hand. I put my hand in his, looking inquisitively at him.

"Do you read palms?" I asked.

"Not very well, but a friend of mine does, and he's showed me a few things." He traced his finger along the line running up from my wrist and I felt the tingle run directly to my groin.

"This here's your life line," he said. "See how long it is?" I nodded. "That means you'll live a long time. And this," he touched his finger to an intersecting line. I closed my eyes with pleasure, listening to his craggy voice. I enjoyed how warm his hand felt holding mine and how gentle his touch was. "This is your love line. Looks like you recently met someone who could end up as your lover." I opened my eyes at that, and he glanced up at me and grinned. He cupped my hand between both of his and continued looking at me for a long moment.

After a while, I felt a little self-conscious, so I took his hand and opened it palm up and said, "Now, it's my turn to read your palm."

"Oh, you read palms, too, eh?" he asked, winking at me, but spreading his fingers wide.

"As well as you, I think," I said. "Now, hush up. You're disturbing the psychic vibrations." I looked at his wide, strong palm resting in my hand. I wanted to lift his hand to my lips and kiss it, lick each finger, press it to my cheek, press it against my chest and groin. I traced my index finger along his life line, beginning at his wrist. Only a quarter of its path up, the line broke where it was crossed by a jagged gash, then reemerged a little further up, where it continued its arc toward the span between his index finger and his thumb. Disregarding the break, I said, "Your line runs all the way to the other side of your hand. I guess that means you're going to live forever."

Steven grinned at me.

"Now, let's check out your love life," I said.

"That's love *line*," he said, correcting me.

"Oh, right," I said. I looked back at his palm, but found no intersecting lines at all. "Well, I don't see any love lines at all. I guess that either means you won't ever fall in love with anyone; or, you fall in love so often, all the lines have blended into one another."

He slid his hand out of mine and up my arm to my shoulder and neck; then, he ran it across my face. His touch was gentle and warm. As he traced a finger over my lips, I closed my eyes and pressed back in my seat. He ran his hand up to my hairline and pushed my bangs away from my face. Cupping my head with both of his hands, he pulled it firmly toward his. I kept my eyes closed until I felt his lips make contact with my own, and his tongue slipped between my lips and glided over my teeth. I pushed my tongue in his mouth and he sucked on it like a piece of candy. I opened my eyes to look at him and found his eyes closed and the skin taut on his face. He ran his hand inside the neck of my shirt and brushed his fingertips over my nipples, rolling them gently between his fingers. Then, he pulled back and pressed his lips to my ear.

"I'd really like to go home with you," he whispered hoarsely. His hand slid from my belly to my groin, and pressed firmly against my erection. I felt the instant wave of pleasure wash over my body, and didn't hesitate more than a second.

"Are you sure?" I asked. "Remember, I live all the way up in Evanston. Do you have a car?"

"No car," he said, breathing the words into my ear.

"That's okay," I said, "we can take a taxi. That's how I got down here."

"Sounds good, but I may need cab fare to get home afterwards," he said, running his tongue along my ear. "Do you mind? I didn't know I'd meet you again."

"That's okay," I said. "I don't mind."

"Great," he said pulling away and sitting back in his seat. "Just let me finish my beer and piss first." He chugged the last of his beer in one gulp and headed to the restroom. He returned a few moments later and said, "Well, that's a load off. Let's go."

We headed straight for my bed when we got to my dorm room, and made love without speaking a word. Afterwards, I made us some tea while he watched me from my sofa.

"I like this place," he said. "I feel really comfortable here."

"I'm glad," I said, pouring the hot water into pink ceramic cups that said "His" and "His." "I hope that means you'll stay all night."

"No problem," he said. He lifted the cup I handed him to his lips and blew gently across its rim. "I don't have to work till Monday afternoon."

He stayed that night and all the following day and night. Before I left for class on Monday morning, I gave him cab fare to get back to the place he said he was staying temporarily. We met for dinner that evening, and he came back to my place for the night. Every night that week, he was with me, and every morning, I gave him cab fare so he could get back to his place again.

On Saturday morning, I woke up and looked at him in my bed with the sunlight streaming through the shears. He cradled his head in his arms, and his red locks spilled over the white sheets. His breath came in long, heavy bursts and his legs were splayed out—one over me and the other reaching off the opposite side of the bed. He looked like he couldn't decide whether to stay or flee. His body looked as inviting as warm bread, and I reached over to touch him with my fingertips. He inhaled sharply and his eyes flickered open. He leaned up on one elbow when he saw me watching him and grinned.

"What?" he asked.

"You're really beautiful in the morning," I said, brushing my fingers lightly across his chest.

"Well, so are you."

"I wish I lived in Chicago, so we could stay together forever," I sighed.

"What do you mean?" he asked, sitting upright. "Aren't you planning to stay in Chicago?"

"I can't," I said, shaking my head. "I graduate next week. Then, I've got to go back to Florida."

"What are you going back there for?" He asked, sounding surprised. He climbed out of bed and pulled on his underwear. "I just assumed you'd be staying in Chicago; otherwise, what're we wasting our time for?"

"I've got to go back," I said, watching him dress and feeling panic growing inside me. "It's where I live. I wish I could stay up here, but where would I live? What would I do?"

"You'd get a job. That's what you'd do," he said, looking at me and waving his arms. "We got jobs in Chicago, too, you know. And they probably pay a lot better than Florida. I didn't think you were just having fun with me. I thought you wanted a *real* relationship—not a trick for a few weeks."

"I *do* want a relationship," I said, sounding like a little boy, "but I also have to go back home. Why don't you come down to Florida?"

"And do what?" he asked, pulling his shirt over his head. "I'm not a college graduate like you. You'll be going home to Mommy and Daddy and what'll I do? No. You need to make up your mind what you want, Tony. If you want me, you gotta stay put. It's your decision: go back to Mommy and Daddy in Florida. Or make your *own* life with me in Chicago." He pulled his still-tied sneakers from under the bed, where he had kicked them off the night before, and slipped them on his feet. Then, he stood and walked to the door. "You call me when you decide, College Boy. It's been fun, but I didn't know you were just playing house with me."

"Wait, Steven," I begged. "Don't go."

"What am I waiting for?" he asked. "You're going back to Florida and I'll be stuck in Chicago waiting tables. I don't plan to do that all my life." He opened the door, then paused and turned around. "You got ten bucks I can borrow for cab fare?"

"Oh, sorry," I said, and pulled ten dollars from my wallet and handed it to him. "I understand what you're saying, Steven, but I really wish you wouldn't leave like this. I didn't mean to mislead you."

"Don't worry about it," he said, taking the bill from my hand. "I'm not mad. Hell, it's been fun. If you decide to come back to Chicago, look me up. But don't take too long, College Boy, ya' hear? I ain't gonna wait around forever."

A week after Steven walked out my door, I graduated from college and headed back to Florida—another potential relationship down the drain. I had a college degree in my suitcase, and Ma and Pop waiting at the airport to take me back home. I felt like my life was directing itself, and I was just along for the ride. I couldn't help thinking about what might have been if I had stayed in Chicago with Steven. Who knows? Maybe it would've worked out. But I was too frightened to do something that spontaneous

and indefinite; so, I found myself back on Merritt Island, back
in my old life, alone once again, regretting my inability to take
a risk, and suddenly, afraid that my four years of college had accomplished nothing.

CHAPTER 8

Discovery

Chicago: May 1994

ON THE PLANE back to Chicago after my fight with Pop, I mulled over the dualities of my life. Was it a coincidence that my astrological sign, Pisces, consisted of two fish swimming in opposite directions? Or was it my destiny to struggle constantly between opposite inclinations? I insisted that Ma and Pop leave my lifestyle alone, yet constantly confronted them with it to ensure they didn't ignore it either. I rushed to Pop's bedside to show my concern, only to fight with him and storm out. And I wanted a strong, masculine lover whom—somewhat illogically—I could take care of.

I had Steven. Steven gave the appearance of masculine strength and insisted fiercely on his independence—yet, he couldn't keep a job, drank too much, and seemed overly comfortable letting me pay his way. I had bragged to Ma and Pop about my wonderful relationship, even as I wondered how much longer it could last. I loved Steven and wanted to make things work, yet he seemed bent on hurting me. He constantly lashed out at me, accusing me of being controlling, telling me I was suffocating him emotionally, assuring me he could find someone else in a minute if we ever broke up. He warned me no one would want me or put up with me the way he did, and insisted, all the while, he loved and needed me. At times, he could be so endearing, I would tear up just thinking about him.

Steven and I had been on the verge of breaking up from the moment we got together. Inside, I think I knew from the start that our relationship was all wrong for both of us, yet our mutual desire to be in a relationship kept us together. That, and the fact that we really did love one another, in our own ways.

As the plane approached O'Hare, I thought about taking a few days off to make up with Steven after our recent problems. Maybe if we could just get away and talk, we could get things sorted out between us and start fresh again. It seemed like a lifetime ago when I had decided to return to Chicago to begin a relationship with Steven. I remembered getting off the plane that day and seeing Steven waiting for me at the gate. How he had scooped me up in his arms causing me to drop my carry-on bag. How we had discussed our plans for finding an apartment together. How exciting it had all been and how happy I was to have someone in my life. Nothing else seemed to matter. So much had changed since then, I thought.

As I hopped in the taxi home, I again thought about how nice it would be to surprise Steven by arriving early. I wanted to feel his arms around me and hear him say he loved me.

I opened the apartment door and Shibah, our cat, rushed to greet me by rubbing her body against my legs. "Hi, Shibah," I whispered, noticing the red digits on the bookshelf clock read 11:56—nearly midnight. Shutting the door silently behind me, I eased my suitcase to the floor and slipped my coat and shoes off. Shibah wandered into the kitchen to my right.

The apartment was dark and silent, except for a soft glow from the doorway to our bedroom. Steven must have gone to bed early, which was odd. He usually stayed up late, with all the lights and both the television and stereo on "for company." Maybe he was sick, although it wasn't like him to keep that from me. Maybe he didn't want to worry me: he knew how stressed I was about the whole situation with Pop.

I crept down the dark hallway. The glow from the bedroom flickered—Steven was a sucker for candle light, although I worried about fire. A draft blew into the hallway. Steven must have the window cracked open. If he was sick again, he'd catch his death of cold.

I paused at the doorway, containing a giggle as I considered leaping onto the bed and jouncing him awake. I decided against it, in case he was sick. I slid noiselessly into the room. Moonlight streamed through the open window and a candle flickered on the dresser. The muffled sounds of traffic gurgled up from the street.

Steven lay sprawled across his side of the bed, naked and enticing, his hair masking his angelic face. His breathing was slow, deep with sleep—a sound I had become so accustomed to that, even standing here, I felt it soothing me, making me feel drowsy myself. I began unbuttoning my shirt, as my eyes adjusted to blue-grey half-light. I would undress and slip into the bed beside him, wake him gently, and we'd make love to celebrate my return. Slipping off my shirt, I looked at him sleeping before me. Only then did I notice the second arm resting on his chest, and the dark, naked shape of a man sleeping beside him on *my* side of the bed.

Instantly, I felt light-headed and cold. I could hardly believe my eyes, but there it was. I took a step backward, towards the hall, as a powerful wave of nausea swept over me. For a moment, I thought I might black out, but the dizziness passed, and I hurriedly pulled my shirt back on. *Who was this interloper in my bed?* I strained my eyes to recognize him, but his dark hair and large, masculine features defied recognition. Where had Steven met him? Why had he brought this stranger into our home? Into our bed?

What a fool I had been! Thinking I'd come home and surprise Steven. Thinking I could save our relationship. What a stupid fool I was! The surprise was on me. I was seized by a powerful desire to escape, to run out of our apartment and just keep running. *Jesus! How long had Steven been cheating on me? Why didn't he just break up with me if he didn't love me?* I wanted to hit him or choke him while he slept. I wanted to chase the stranger from the room. From *our* room.

Instead, I slipped out as quietly as I had entered. Out of the room. Down the dark hall to the front door. I stepped back into my shoes and coat, snatched up my luggage, and eased open the door. As I slipped out of the apartment, I noticed the flashing red digits—12:00. Midnight. It had only been four minutes. Four minutes and my whole life had changed. *Jesus!* Where was I going to go at midnight? I flashed on my childhood, when I believed the boogeyman walked at midnight. But a child believes the boogey-man stays *under* the bed.

I hesitated in the doorway of the apartment. Shibah appeared and began to mew. Afraid she might awaken Steven, I hurriedly closed the door behind me. I hefted the suitcase over my shoulder and punched the down button, then sagged against the wall as I waited for the elevator to arrive. I wanted to get away, to run and run and never stop. My mouth tasted salty, and I realized I was crying. *Damn*, I thought, wiping my eyes, *I've got to compose myself. I don't want the whole world to know my business.* My chest felt tight, like a balloon stretched to its limit—like it might burst open right here. I wondered if Steven would feel guilty if he found me dead of heartbreak in the morning. Probably not, I thought. He'd only feel bad about having to find some new sap to take advantage of.

The elevator bell dinged and I stepped inside. I felt angry that I'd been such a dupe. Fuck Steven for betraying me and destroy-ing our relationship. Fuck Pop for refusing to accept me. Fuck Ma for defending Pop. I felt like my whole world was made of Tinker Toys that had just collapsed around me in a heap.

I stumbled from the apartment building onto Michigan Avenue and the cold air engulfed me. With the back of my hand, I wiped unintended tears from my face and glanced up and down the block. It was nearly empty—not unusual for midnight on a cold Sunday in May.

Where could I go at this hour? I'd been in Chicago for almost a dozen years now, yet had no real friends here: my life revolved almost entirely around Steven. I had a few work acquaintances, but no one really close. And most of our social acquaintances were more connected to Steven than to me. Without realizing it, I had allowed myself to become insulated and isolated. There was no doorstep to dump myself on, no shoulder to cry on, no one to unburden myself to, not one person who really cared about *me*. Without Steven, I felt alone in the world.

Why had I left our apartment? I should have screamed the two of them awake and demanded that *they* leave. But I knew I didn't have the energy for that kind of scene right now. No, I needed some rest first, to clear my head. I wasn't capable of decisions just now. A hotel seemed the logical solution; I had my luggage, after all, and I could decide what to do in the morning. I pulled the luggage strap snug over my shoulder and walked south to the Congress Hotel, taking a room on the seventh floor.

Once in the room, without even turning on the light, I dropped my suitcase beside the bed, walked over and opened the window to let the cool air wash over me. The room faced east over Grant Park and Lake Michigan. To the north, I could see my apartment building, where Steven was probably still sound asleep with his—I didn't even know what to call him—his trick. A whole litany of venomous terms to call a woman who broke up a relationship sprang to mind, but I couldn't think of one for a man. Trick didn't seem strong enough to express my outrage, my frustration, my hurt, and anguish. Slut and whore were words you could spit out. But trick sounded so innocent, so playful. And maybe that was accurate, because Steven behaved like an oversexed teenager: always looking, always pointing out this "hottie" or that "stud," always reminding me that he was "married, not dead," never satisfied with just me.

After a moment, I pulled the curtains closed and walked over to sit on the bed, suddenly aware of my exhaustion. I slid off my shoes and socks and tossed my jacket on the night stand, then slumped back on the big, empty bed and curled onto my side. Only then did I let myself replay the scene in my apartment, and let the hot tears stream across my face as sobs shook my frame.

What if I had actually fainted when I saw the two of them? I imagined them, startled from their careless sleep, snapping awake with a start. Then, spying me on the floor, leaping out of the bed and into their heaped clothes in a frenzy. Maybe they would have panicked, thinking I'd killed myself like some tragic Greek. Perhaps they would have been seized with terror at the prospect of police, suspicion, and humiliation. When they finally realized I had only fainted, they might have tried to conceal their tryst. The interloper would have slipped away with a hurried kiss, and Steven would have roused and tried to convince me that I had only imagined it.

But I hadn't imagined it. I had seen Steven—*my* Steven— sleeping peacefully in the arms of a stranger. *My* Steven, whom I had boasted about to Ma and Rosalia, had brought another man into our bed. I suddenly felt my muscles tense and my jaws clench as I imagined the two of them making love under our sheets, crying out in our bedroom, cleaning up in our bathroom, and— sated—falling asleep. Ironically, I was aware then of how much I wanted to be with Steven right then, to prove to him that it was *me* he really wanted, *me* that he really loved; that this episode was an aberration, *my* fault for not having been there. I couldn't bear to think Steven didn't love me. That Ma didn't love me. That Pop didn't love me. I wanted—needed—all of them to love me the way I believed I loved them. Hurt as I felt, I wanted Steven's arms around me. I wanted Steven's lips kissing mine. I cursed myself for my weakness; for still wanting Steven; for realizing I would probably take him back; for the involuntary erection brought on by just thinking about him now.

Before I dozed off, I thought about the day in 1981 when Steven and I moved in together. A year after graduation, after nearly a year apart—and to Ma and Pop's dismay—I had finally decided to leave Florida to be with Steven in Chicago. I took a chance applying for a staff position at *The Daily Herald*, a suburban Chicago newspaper that a former college classmate had mentioned to me. To my surprise, they hired me. So, I headed to Chicago, renting a second-story walkup apartment I discovered on the North Side, near Wrigley Field. It was a small, one bedroom with beautiful hardwood floors not far from the "gay ghetto," known as Boy's Town. It wasn't much, but it was quaint and cozy and the best I could do on my salary as an entry-level reporter.

When I first returned to Chicago, Steven was living temporarily with friends on the Northwest Side of the city and picking up a few hours as a waiter at a Bennigan's restaurant on Michigan Avenue. He said he was embarrassed about how dumpy his place was and refused to let me see it. So, I called and asked him to come to see my new apartment after his lunch shift ended.

"So, what do you think?" I asked eagerly after giving him a brief walkthrough. I plopped down in the middle of the living room on the hardwood floor and sprawled out on my back, waving my arms around me. "Don't you love it? I do!"

"It's very nice," Steven said flatly from across the room. "I'm sure you'll like it here."

"What about you?" I asked. "Won't you like it here, too?"

"It's not my apartment," he said, walking over to the bare window.

"What are you talking about?" I asked, incredulous. "I rented it for both of us. I moved to Chicago so we could be together. Don't you want to live with me?"

"Of course I want to live with you," he said without looking at me. "But you haven't asked. And I would've liked to help pick out our apartment."

"I'm sorry," I said. "You were working and I thought I'd surprise you. Besides, I needed to find a place right away, so I could get out of the hotel. It's too expensive." Steven continued staring out the window. "Aw, come on, Steven. Don't be difficult." I got up and joined him, placing my hand on his warm shoulder and gently turning him around to face me. "Would you *please* move in with me?"

"I don't know," he said noncommittally, then burst into a grin and took my hands in his. "I'd love to, but are you sure? *I'm* sure, but are *you* sure you're ready for that? You just got back up here yesterday."

"Positive," I said, smiling broadly and nodding. I felt as happy as I'd ever felt. "It's what I wanted from the moment I decided to move back to Chicago. When can you move in?"

"Right now," he said, putting his hands on either side of my face and kissing me. "Why wait any longer? I'll just move in today."

"What about your stuff?" I asked, ecstatic at the prospect of beginning my first, real adult relationship.

"I don't have much," he said. "Just a couple of suitcases, is all. I'll swing by my place after work and get them. I'll be all moved in by tonight." He scooped me in his arms. We made love on the hardwood floor with the sunlight streaming over us, and I hardly worried about what our new neighbors might see or think.

At first, I would meet Steven after he finished work so we could grab a bite together before going home. But, after a few weeks, Steven asked me to stop, saying it made him feel like a child who had to be walked home from school. Even though I knew I couldn't have kept up the hectic pace and long hours much longer anyhow, I agreed reluctantly because it meant that we hardly saw each other. I left for work before Steven awoke, and Steven was at work before I got home. By the time Steven got home at night, I was long asleep. It was a pattern that still continued.

Steven made decent tips at the restaurant on weekends, but during the week, his tally fell considerably—some nights he was lucky to bring home ten dollars. And his paychecks were a joke. He earned only two bucks an hour—less taxes—for about twenty-five or thirty hours of work a week. He often brought home paychecks totaling only slightly more than fifty bucks for a week's work. His cash tips comprised the bulk of his income, but that money never seemed to make it home. Cash was like smoke in Steven's fingers: it seemed to vanish into thin air.

Steven owned little to speak of beyond the clothes on his back. When he arrived that first night, he carried a single tote bag with some underwear, socks, and a few articles of clothing. Although I earned barely enough to scrape by at the newspaper, I frequently picked him up a new shirt or some knick-knack to surprise him. His eyes would light up and he'd beam like a kid at Christmas as he tore off the giftwrap enthusiastically. He was easy to buy for because he seemed to want nearly everything he saw.

"You know, you don't *have* to buy me gifts," he said the first time I surprised him with something.

"I know," I said. "I just felt like it, okay?"

"Yeah, it's okay," he said, holding aloft the denim shirt I had bought for him. "I love it. I love getting gifts, and I've never had a denim shirt before." He immediately peeled his tee-shirt over his head and opened the denim shirt, carefully removing the pins and labels. I watched the muscles of his chest ripple under his skin with each movement of his hand and arm. Then, he pulled the shirt over his head and smoothed back his hair. He unbuckled his pants and unzipped his fly, tucked in his new shirt, and redid his pants. After buttoning the shirt, he looked up at me, stretched his arms, and spun around.

"So, whaddaya think of my new shirt?"

"I think it looks good," I said, nodding with satisfaction, amazed at how sexy he looked. "Looks *real* good."

"It *feels* real good," Steven said, as he checked his reflection in our bedroom mirror. "Why don't we go out for dinner tonight? Then, I can show off my new shirt."

"I thought you didn't have any money?"

"Oh, shit," he said, crestfallen. "I don't. Well, forget it. I just hate to sit home in my new shirt, is all. Feels like a shirt that needs to go out."

"No," I said. "Tell you what: I'll treat you to dinner tonight."

"Would you do that for me?"

"Of course," I said. "I love you."

"I know," he said giving me a quick kiss on the cheek. "And you sure know how to show it."

"I'm glad you approve."

"I love it," he said grinning at me. "Now, it's my turn to give you your gift." He crooked his finger at me as he walked over to the futon we were using as our bed. He undid the top button on his new shirt and said," Why don't you come here and unwrap the rest of your gift now?"

We unwrapped a lot of gifts during our first years together. I felt happier than I ever dreamed I could. I was promoted to Copy Editor at *The Daily Herald*, and received a nice increase in salary. We moved to a larger apartment in a Downtown high rise, where Steven said he had always dreamed about living one day. I hardly thought about Ma and Pop during that time, never visiting, and, only occasionally, calling them. More often than not, we ended up arguing. I was convinced they didn't care about me, complaining that I always had to initiate our phone calls. Once, to prove my point, I decided to wait for them to call me; but after six months, I gave in and called them up to complain that they never called. But with Steven in my life, my issues with Ma and Pop didn't seem to hurt quite so much.

The night I discovered Steven's infidelity, I slept so soundly that not even a dream dared to disturb me. A black, depthless unconsciousness engulfed me and, when I awoke, I understood what people meant when they claimed they "slept like the dead." But my sleep brought no revitalization, no energy for the day ahead: only an exhaustion so absolute that, the next morning, I found myself lying motionless, between consciousness and sleep, for what must have been hours.

I awoke only after sunlight poured through the windows and lit the room like yellow flames. I felt befuddled, groggy. When I remembered where I was and why, my chest tightened as I reviewed the events of the night before.

I was still fully dressed, with my suitcase beside me on the bed. I stripped off my clothes in a rush, seized by a sudden, urgent desire to shower, to cleanse myself of the previous day's detritus. My clothing left creases on my skin, which I rubbed as I padded to the bathroom. I pissed, and my urine smelled acrid. I recoiled from it, flushed, and watched the yellow liquid swirl and vanish from the bowl, replaced by fresh, clear water.

I slid open the shower door and turned on the water, adjusting the hot and cold spigots until it felt comfortable. Then, I stepped back for a moment to peer at myself in the mirror.

My face looked old, weather-worn and taut, like my facial bones might burst through my skin. My hair—grown longer than I usually kept it—tumbled unkempt about my face. It looked almost black, darker than its normal russet brown—the brown of a potato, I reminded myself: Pop's Irish heritage. I pressed my hands against my cheeks, squeezing them together and causing my lips to bulge out in an exaggerated pout. God, how I hated this body I had been born with. I was neither short nor tall, neither fat nor thin, neither attractive nor ugly. I fell somewhere in between, in that awful zone that people called "average." I hated being average, I had struggled my whole life against it. But my looks were my looks. And I was painfully, unequivocally average. Guys like me, with average looks, don't find attractive boyfriends without some kind of sacrifice. Maybe I was lucky to have Steven. Maybe the baggage he brought with him was my penance for taking more than I deserved. The veins in my brown eyes were streaked red from exhaustion, tears, and strain. I wanted to shut them and sleep forever, to close my eyes and drift off until all my problems vanished, until I finally felt rested. I doubted that could ever happen—all I had to do was open my eyes and all the shit would still be there and I would feel exhausted all over again.

I looked over the rest of my naked torso, hairy and square-framed. I had Pop's shape and the same pink, hairy body. Despite my efforts to avoid being like Pop, I looked just like he had at my age. Was I like him in other ways, too? Steven accused me of being controlling; of being selfish; of being too wrapped up in myself—the same accusations I frequently thrust at Pop. Had I inherited my behaviors, my instincts, my personality— everything—from Pop, along with this Leprechaun's body? I prided myself on staying relatively trim all these years: nearly 33 and still no beer-gut like other men my age. Even this I had to concede to heredity; Pop never developed a beer-gut either. Was there nothing I could claim of my own? Was there nothing original in me? Above my dark-haired legs, at my center, my penis sprouted pink from a thick jungle of black hair. Like an ugly, hairless snake embedded deep in my gut. I gaped at it dully, like I was looking at some anatomical illustration in biology class—a clinical, asexual look. I drew back my lips and spat at the reflection.

"Goddamn you." My cock, it seemed to me then, was the root of my problems. Couldn't I trace all of the problems in my life back to my cock? Perhaps, if I wasn't gay, everything would've been different with Ma and Pop. Perhaps if my dick hadn't taken over, I would have made better relationship choices. Perhaps if I had been better in bed, Steven would have been satisfied with me. Perhaps his complaints about me were on target. Perhaps I was blind to my shortcomings—the same way Pop seemed blind to his. Perhaps it was *my* fault that Steven strayed.

I burst out laughing, like a crazy man, for no reason at all. I should be crying, I thought, not laughing, but the thought only made me laugh harder. Maybe I was losing my mind—having an honest-to-God breakdown of some sort. Could anyone blame me? What the hell was I going to do? I sure couldn't stay holed up in this room much longer. I had to go home and face things—face

Steven—and make some decisions about my life. That would be something new for me. I was the Dean of Denial, avoiding painful decisions as long as possible, usually until the decision was made for me. Then, I didn't have to take responsibility for it, only live with it and whine about how unfair it was. I knew it was time to take charge of my own life. I had known it for a long time. But I felt so damned tired, so inept, so abandoned, and so emasculated.

I turned up the hot water and pulled the knob to switch the stream to the shower. Steam rose quickly in the small room as I stepped under the spray. Its heat scorched my body like a flame burning away the outer layers and revealing new flesh underneath. I felt like a snake after it sloughs off its old, dried scales. I could feel my legs tingling—and also my back, shoulders, and scalp. My entire body tingled under the hot spray. But, deep in my bones, below it all, I felt weary. And so alone.

I scrubbed my skin raw. I wanted to scrape away my life upto now, be born anew, forget my past and start fresh. I felt like I'd worn shackles all my life, but I didn't know how to unfasten and leave them behind. While trying to get me to take control of my life, Cliff had once told me, "After you turn eighteen, you're on your own. You can't blame your parents anymore. You're an adult and you've got to acting like one. Blame is just an excuse to avoid making hard decisions." Even when he said it, I felt its truth. I adopted it as my mantra. But the words were hollow because I didn't know how to live by them myself.

I thought about yesterday's (was it only yesterday?) conversation with Rosalia. How did we both grow up in the same house, yet turn out so different? Rosalia had discovered a way to accept Ma and Pop. She remained steady even when they infuriated her. She had developed a positive relationship with them while keeping her dignity and independence. Paddy simply had had enough and took off. He couldn't accept Ma and Pop, so he created a life without them. Rosalia and Paddy had both made decisions about living their lives, while I had not. I wasn't strong enough to create a life without them or with them. I had moved away to escape the day-to-day stuff while keeping in touch just enough to keep them in my life. How could anyone respect my life choices when I really hadn't made any? I wanted it both ways. Afraid to choose, I waffled every time.

I thought about the way Ma silently accepted everything Pop said, never arguing with or contradicting him, even when I knew she didn't agree. Yet, sometimes, apropos of nothing, she would threaten to leave him. I remember praying that she would do it—take us away from Pop; take us somewhere so we could all start over again, somewhere we could make things better. Why had she stayed with Pop?

"I ought to take the kids and get the hell outta here when you go to work," Ma used to tell Pop, and he'd just laugh at her. "You think I'm kidding?" she'd rant. "Don't press your luck 'cause one of these days, you'll push things too far." When he didn't respond, she'd grow silent.

"Don't do me any favors," he'd say matter-of-factly, as he rustled his newspaper. Pop barely acknowledged her threats. He seemed to understand Ma's need to threaten, but knew she'd never follow through. It was a part of their relationship that frightened and confused me.

Ma would puff furiously on her cigarette and crush it in the beanbag ashtray. Then, suddenly, she'd notice us kids, like we'd just materialized out of the air, and she'd yell, "What the hell are you watching? Get the hell outta my sight! You're half of my problem. If you weren't around, I wouldn't have no problems. You're a bunch of ungrateful little shits."

We'd dart out of the room, each attending to our own hurts. Paddy ran away to relieve Ma of one of her problems. Rosalia—hardly seeming to notice Ma's harsh words—would go outside to play with the little girl next door. But me, I heard the words. I would heave myself on my bed and try to invent ways to prove I wasn't a little shit. I didn't know how to prove it back then. I still didn't.

In junior high, I noticed that an acquaintance of mine always stuck close to the class bully. When I asked him why, he told me, "Cuz maybe he won't hurt me if he gets used to me. But I know he'll beat the shit outta me for sure if I try to get away. I'd rather stay and take my chances."

Had I learned the same tactic?

I dressed and checked out of the hotel, heading for the McDonald's across the street from our apartment. It was nearly noon already. I ordered a Diet Coke and sat at a table by the window while I considered how to react. I could confront Steven and demand that he move out. Or I could just continue living with him and forget about what I had seen. Or I could run away from Chicago and make a fresh start somewhere new. Maybe I wouldn't even tell Steven I was leaving—I'd just pack my things while he was out and be gone without a trace before he got home. It felt so tempting, so satisfying.

Suddenly, it dawned on me that running away was the tried-and-true McMurphy solution to everything. The solution to all of our problems. Hadn't Doughna Mira's family run away to America? Hadn't Paddy run away after fighting with Ma and Pop? Hadn't Ma and Pop run away to Florida? Hadn't I run away to Chicago? And now, wasn't I ready to run away again? But what good had running away done for any of us? All those fresh starts, yet nothing ever seemed to change. Moving distracted us from the problems, but after a while they reemerged and confronted us all over again. I knew running away wasn't the solution this time. I would be better off doing nothing at all than running away again.

I wasn't ready to deal with it, however; so, I decided I wouldn't do anything until I could sort things out in my head at my own pace. I wouldn't tell Steven what I had seen because I didn't want to hear any absurd or meaningless denials or promises. How much was I hurt? How shocked, really? I knew Steven had been very promiscuous before we got together. I had known for a long time that Steven and I had problems. Perhaps I had even been aware, down deep inside, that he was unfaithful. All the time we spent apart. All the nights he'd get home late with liquor on his breath. All the excuses he had: the restaurant closed late, a bunch of us stopped out for a drink after work. All the righteous indignation whenever I asked a question about where he'd been. Why would I think he'd suddenly change? Hadn't I always been suspicious in the back of my mind? Why would I think his HIV status would change his behavior?

Why didn't I feel angry? Or outraged? Or sad? I felt nothing. Nothing at all. Only dead inside. Incapable of responding normally—the way other people did without even thinking about it. Like a piece of my emotional machinery had been omitted at my conception. Like I was incomplete, unfinished. Where others reacted spontaneously, emotionally, I needed time to think, time to decide how I felt. *Life shouldn't be so difficult*, I thought.

Perhaps it was my pride that Steven had hurt more than anything. Could I ever trust him again? Everything seemed overwhelming and complicated now that I could no longer deny the evidence. I knew I needed to make a decision—to act—but I felt comatose: I could sense life going on around me, but I was unable to react or speak.

In spite of it all, I still loved Steven. The thought of leaving him terrified me. I felt completely isolated and alone. My whole life revolved around Steven, and I couldn't imagine life without him. I had attempted to start over so many times before without success. But I never really left anything behind. Eventually, the same issues caught up with me again and again. It was time, at last, to deal with them. I was so tired of running.

How could I face Steven again? Hadn't he betrayed me? How could I pretend nothing had happened when everything seemed changed? I thought about calling Rosalia, but knew I wasn't ready to talk about this with anyone. I needed to figure things out for myself first.

I decided to call Steven and tell him I would be home today. No more surprises. I went to the pay phone and dropped in thirty cents. I dialed the restaurant down the block where Steven worked and asked for him. He'd probably be on his lunch shift by now.

"Hello." He sounded out of breath and expectant when he finally came to the phone.

"Steven. It's Tony." I waited for his response to give me time to decide what to say next.

"Tony?" He sounded startled. "What are you calling me here for? Is something wrong? Is your dad okay?"

"Fine, yes. We argued as usual, so I'm coming home early."

"You're coming home? When?" Laughter swallowed his voice on the phone. I could hear the sound of two or three voices singing in the background.

"Is there a party going on?"

"No, just a bunch of guys drinking beer and acting like idiots over their lunch. They're pretty cute, though."

"Of course they are." I snapped. "I'll be home today. Soon, in fact. I'm already at the airport. I can't wait to see you. I've missed you."

"You're at O'Hare? Already?" He sounded almost frightened.

"Yes, already. What's the matter—don't you want me back?" I hadn't meant to say that: I was afraid he'd detect the bitterness in my voice; but it felt good to hear him squirm. "I should be home within the hour."

"I just didn't expect you home so soon, that's all." I heard the muffled, underwater sound of him cupping a hand over the receiver. After a moment, he shouted, "I'll be right there." The muffled sound ceased, and I heard a cough as he cleared his throat. "Look, Tony, I've gotta go. I'll see you tonight." I heard a click, followed by a dial tone.

I returned to my table to gather my luggage and finish my soda before heading over to the apartment. I needed to steel myself before going into our apartment again. I let my mind wander as I stared out the window at the hustle-bustle of Michigan Avenue. Our apartment building across the street suddenly seemed alien and cold, like some anonymous hotel you'd use for a tryst.

I felt frozen in time, and flashed on my high school Physics teacher describing inertia: "A body in motion tends to stay in motion, and a body at rest tends to stay at rest." Perhaps inertia applied to people, too. People in motion were overachievers, while people like me accomplished nothing. I was one of the bodies at rest: inert. But how do you kick-start yourself when you've come to a complete stopping point in life?

I glanced across the street and snapped upright—Steven was running toward our apartment building. A thousand butterflies fluttered in my stomach as I watched him race into the building. Part of me wanted to storm across the street and confront him, and part of me wanted to run away and never see him again. I stayed put, telling myself to relax and to decide what I wanted to do next.

Pop and his illness seemed a lifetime ago, now that I suddenly found myself in the midst of my own crisis. I tried to clear my mind and forget—to gather the courage to cross the street and pretend I was happy to be home. I started erasing the humiliation and anger from my demeanor, my voice, my face, my brain. *Home. Could it ever feel like home to me again? Shit, I should win an Academy Award if I pulled this off*, I thought.

I left my Coke on the table, grabbed my suitcase, and pulled on my jacket. Steven was still in the apartment and it was time to face him. *Jesus! How could I pretend last night hadn't happened? Was I crazy? How could I still love him? How? When I should have kicked his ass?* I should just hate him and confront him and be done with it. Instead, I felt broken. Why couldn't any of my relationships be what I hoped they'd be? Why was I so terrified of being alone?

CHAPTER 9

Tempests

Merritt Island: September 1979

HAVING PROMISED CLIFF that I would come out to Ma and Pop, I had arrived on Merritt Island the week before Labor Day with an enormous sense of dread and foreboding. Would Ma and Pop throw me out of the house? Would they refuse to pay for my plane ticket back to college? At the time, I was mostly worried about my relationship with Cliff. I knew he didn't believe I'd do it. I wasn't sure I could do it myself.

The news stories about Tropical Storm David began almost as soon as I had arrived and, somehow I knew—just as certainly as I knew I was gay—David was coming for me. Every day, both the winds and the news stories intensified, and David drew nearer. The storm amassed menacing strength as it roared into the Caribbean on a trajectory aimed directly at Florida. By the Thursday before Labor Day, David struck the Eastern Caribbean with ferocious, 150-mile-per-hour winds, leaving thousands homeless and dead in his wake.

I had spent my first days at home reading, going to the beach, and trying to figure out how to break my news to Ma and Pop. Although David was near, the air over the island barely moved.

Tarantella

The humidity hung so heavy I felt like I couldn't quite catch my breath. The sweltering heat turned the sky as white as the sun-blasted Florida sand. Outside, the cicadas buzzed, and their thrumming seemed to increase the intensity of the sun by the hour. Energy seeped from me, and I couldn't muster the strength or the courage to discuss my secret, so I put it off, promising myself I'd tell them later. Later, when it had cooled off. Later, when I had more energy. Later, when I wouldn't have to deal with the aftermath for so long.

Ma, Pop, and I watched television Friday evening as we waited for Rosalia to return home from a day at the beach with some friends. The electricity seemed to crackle in the still air, and a newscaster said that David had begun regrouping and growing again over the warm waters of the Atlantic. With winds already back over 100 miles per hour, the National Weather Service warned that David showed the potential to turn into a monster—perhaps the strongest hurricane to strike Florida in one hundred years.

Ma was frantic. She smoked incessantly and roamed from room to room, worrying. "We should pack our bags and board up the windows," she said.

"Don't be ridiculous," Pop replied. "That storm is a thousand miles away. We ain't had one since we been here, and this one's no different. Miami might need to worry, but it'll blow itself out long before it gets up here."

Ma looked unconvinced, but said nothing, only puffed a little harder on her cigarette and paced into the other room, peering out of each window as she passed it.

I said nothing, only felt a sickening tightness in my belly as I watched the satellite images of the storm, which was so large, it looked like it could easily swallow the whole state of Florida. I thought about the story of Sodom and Gomorrah and how God swept them from the earth. I thought about my secret, and wondered which God found worse: The fact that I was gay? Or the fact that I was deceiving my parents about being gay? Perhaps David was coming because of me.

I went outside and sat on the scratchy Bermuda grass to think. Although the sun had already set, the air was still oppressively hot and humid, and so still that not even a leaf moved in the night. The clear sky belied the threat brewing to the southeast. I stared at the stars, trying to pick out Orion, the Hunter, like an old friend looking down on me from above. I marveled at how Orion was also looking down on David as he churned toward us; at how Orion would be there if David struck us—would be there afterwards, too, even if we weren't. Orion would be there, just the same, whether Ma and Pop knew I was gay or not. The thought steadied me. Somehow, it reassured me to realize how inconsequential my secret was.

The next day, hurricane warnings were posted for the Southeast Coast of Florida. Pop said, "I told you so" to Ma, and they relaxed and waited to hear about the fate of Miami. But David lurked stubbornly offshore, slowly skirting the coast, lumbering northward, toward the island: toward me.

Tarantella

That night, the Weather Service posted hurricane warnings for Central Florida, and Pop grudgingly began preparing, "just in case." Pop and I boarded the windows with bits of wood from our shed, and stored our barbecue grill and yard furniture. The scent of David was in the air, like the cleansing scent of a spring rain in the distance. By the time we finished, my clothes were sweat-soaked and clinging to my skin. I felt so hot and uncomfortable I just wanted to strip everything off and jump in the canal behind our house. I sat on the dock, dipped my foot in the water, and grimaced. The canal felt hot—like bath water. The whole world seemed to be steaming. I looked up and searched the still-clear sky. Perhaps it was the wrong time of night, but Orion was no-where to be seen. I wondered if Cliff could see Orion from South Carolina.

Back inside, Pop waved a dismissive hand at Ma when she suggested we should evacuate to Orlando, in the center of the state, where we'd be safer.

"No way. Those weather idiots don't know their asses from a hole in the ground. I ain't going nowheres. We already board-ed up the windas cuz you was scared. But that's it. No damned storm's gonna run me outta my house." He looked at Ma and me and Rosalia like traitors. "If you wanna leave, go ahead: no one's stopping you."

Ma backed down, and we watched the news together—even Pop. The news speculated that David's winds could restrengthen to 150 miles per hour or more. Such winds would raise a deadly wall of water twenty feet high ahead of them and send it surging up to twenty miles inland, engulfing the island, which would revert to the lagoon it had been before men had drained it to build houses. If we were still on the island when David came, we would be washed away. My life felt strangely connected to the island; we would either survive or die together, our fates and our secrets inseparably intertwined.

The next morning, clouds gathered and slowly engulfed us, although the air remained eerily still. Pop covered the inside of the windows with tape and wood, all the while asserting the storm would never strike the island. Sweat rolled down our backs, and the air in the house felt feverish and sickly. A little after dinner, the wind started blowing. Pop pointed to the gentle but insistent wind, and said that would be the extent of this hurricane: a little breeze from the south. The air remained febrile, the breeze merely moving the heat around without providing any relief.

When we awakened the following morning, the sky bubbled and swirled with roiling gray clouds, and the breeze had stiffened to a gale. Birds that dared fly battled to remain aloft, beating their wings furiously against the storm. Palm fronds and tree branches tumbled across lawns and down the street.

Around noon, the news reported that funnel clouds had been spotted in Melbourne, in Rockledge, in Cocoa, and less than two miles away from where we were on Merritt Island. Ma forbid us from going outside anymore, and told Pop that included him. Pop grumbled about her being a "scaredy cat," but stayed inside. The television was our only connection to what was happening outside. With the windows covered, we could only imagine the origin of the sounds we heard.

The eye of David drew inexorably closer and then, around midday, with winds just over 100 miles per hour, abruptly roared ashore near the southern tip of Merritt Island, about twenty miles away. The weatherman reported the eye was now sweeping north: David was coming.

I imagined my family as the intended target. David wanted to destroy us all, blow away our poison with his fury, drown us under his storm surge. Ma, Pop, Rosalia, and I listened attentively to the windows and doors groaning under the weight of the wind. Ma lit and smoked cigarette after cigarette and again tried to convince Pop that we should get the hell out of here. Pop adamantly refused.

"I ain't going nowhere. This ain't nothing. I seen worse thunderstorms than this."

Ma herded us all into the kitchen after the weatherman advised listeners to ride out the storm in the most central room in their house because it offered the greatest protection. We sat claustrophobically around the small kitchen table playing cards and nervously speculating about the source of the sounds we could hear outside. The storm continued to intensify, groaning and roaring as if the earth itself had been wounded. Early in the evening, the power failed, flickering on and off several times before finally ceasing altogether. An eerie, yellowish-gray light seeped in through the boarded up windows. We switched on a battery-operated radio to keep abreast of the weather reports. The reporter announced that the Hurricane Center had ordered the evacuation of Merritt Island, but warned anyone still on the island to stay there because it was now more dangerous to go outside in the hundred-mile-an-hour winds than to stay put. Ma looked at Pop and he glared back at her, as if daring her to comment.

We could hear objects skittering across the roof above us, and every now and then, a gust of wind blew so hard the curtains on the windows would flutter up and down as if invisible fingers moved them. Rosalia started crying. Pop told her to quit acting like a baby and she ran to her bedroom and locked the door. Ma chased after her and pounded on her door, commanding her to come back out with the rest of us, but Rosalia refused. Pop threatened to get a screwdriver to unhinge her door and haul her out—a toothless threat with his toolbox outside and inaccessible in the shed.

I could feel a breeze blowing through the house as the storm whipped the wind through invisible crevices and gaps in the structure. It felt as if the air itself was alive. We heard a roar followed by a thunderous crash in the backyard. Rosalia screamed and burst out of her room, racing back into the kitchen. Pop rushed over to the window nearest the sound and leaned up against it, scanning it to find a gap in the boards so he could see outside.

"Can't see a goddamned thing," he said. "That sounded like the shed blew down."

"The radio says they spotted a bunch of funnel clouds near the mall," I called out, and everyone rushed back to the kitchen table to hear the report. I looked at their nervous faces. "They think a tornado hit the bank over there and tore its roof off. Maybe that was a tornado out back."

"Oh, Jesus Christ," Ma said. "Why the hell didn't we leave last night? Too late now. The house is probably gonna blow down. And us with it."

"That wind's only a hundred miles an hour," Pop sneered. "Hell, that hardly even qualifies as a hurricane. It's just a big windstorm." He put his big hands on Ma's shoulders to steady her. "Relax. We'll be fine."

"The hurricane won't matter if we get killed by a tornado," Rosalia said.

"No one's gonna get killed," Pop said, as Ma lit another cigarette.

"They say if a really big hurricane hits the island, everything would wash away, and there won't even be a trace of anything left," I said, recalling one of my high school lessons.

"Jesus Christ, Anthony," Pop said, shaking his finger at me. "Quit with the morbid shit or I'll bust your ass. You're not too old to pound, you know."

"I'm twenty-one years old, Pop," I said, standing up. "I *am* too old for you to pound. I'm not a little kid anymore who you can hit with a wooden spoon. I'm a grown man, in case you haven't noticed."

"What the hell are you carrying on about, Anthony? Have you lost your goddamned mind?" he said, looking up at me angrily. "I don't need your bullshit now. We're in the middle of a goddamn hurricane. You're a big kid who *thinks* he's a man." He pointed at my chair. "Now, sit your ass back down and shut the hell up."

A loud crash sounded from the yard, and a boom of thunder peeled around us. The air felt charged and heavy, and my heart thrummed in my chest. I felt humiliated and outraged by Pop's words. Without thinking, I took an angry step toward him.

"You've always got all the answers, Pop," I snarled. "I'm so tired of your goddamned self-righteousness. If it weren't for you, we'd be safe in Orlando right now, instead of risking our lives here in Merritt Island. We all wanted to leave, and now we're stuck here. I almost wish something bad *would* happen, so you'd have to admit you were wrong for once. You put *all* of our lives in danger."

"I said shut the hell up!" Pop's face was scarlet, like a boil that needed lancing. "You're a little boy with a big mouth who doesn't know when to shut up."

"I'm *not* a little boy." I shouted at him, but backed a step away.

"You're a damned sissy, that's what you are," Pop shouted back at me. "Still sucking on your Mama's tit at twenty-one. Still thinking you know everything when you don't know jack shit. Still hiding out in school like a little sissy. Why can't you act like a real man?"

I felt like he had slugged me in the chest. For a moment, the air went out of me. Then, I started laughing. I laughed and laughed, the wind screamed outside, and thunder boomed again and again.

"What the hell are you laughing at?" Pop asked. "Have you completely lost your mind?"

"No, Pop," I said, composing myself. "I haven't lost my mind. I just think it's funny. You don't know how right you are."

"What the hell are you talking about?"

"I'm talking about being a sissy," I said, walking up to him and breathing my words into his face so I could feel my breath bounce back at me. "I wasn't going to tell you now, but since you brought it up, I think maybe you deserve to hear it."

"Well, spit it out then if you got something to say," Pop said, licking his tongue across his lips. Rosalia watched us silently from the kitchen table with Ma, who hadn't moved since Pop and I had started yelling. The kitchen window rattled furiously in its frame.

"Don't worry, I will," I said. I grinned at him and took a step back. "What would you say if I said I'm in love?" Pop cocked his head to the left and looked me up and down as if my body were some kind of lie detector. He looked at Ma and pointed a fat, white finger in my direction.

"What the hell's he talkin' 'bout?" he asked. "You know anything about this shit?"

Ma shook her head, reached for her cigarette pack, tapped out a cigarette, and put it between her lips to light it. She inhaled deeply and said as she exhaled, "This is the first I've heard about this." A cloud of smoke accompanied her words. Pop looked back at me, and I watched his shadow shift on the wall behind us as he turned.

"What's this shit you talkin', Anthony? You ain't never mentioned a girlfriend."

I smiled at that. He looked so smug sitting there, watching me like a spider eyeing an insect tangled in its web. Only this time, that insect was a wasp: full of venom and poised to sting. I watched his face and chose my words carefully, calculating how to inflict the most damage.

"That's because there ain't no girlfriend, Pop," I said. Something big slammed against the roof and we both looked up.

Pop looked back at me contemptuously. "I knew you was lying. You never change," he said. Ma looked puzzled and took another drag on her cigarette.

"There ain't no girlfriend," I repeated and braced my hands on the kitchen table. "But there is a *boy*friend." I stood back and waited, watching them both.

Pop felt for a chair and sat down suddenly. He blinked and shook his head like he had water in his ear. I imagined the wasp-stung spider taking a surprised step back in its web, wobbling and uncertain, not realizing yet the wound is mortal. Suddenly, sickeningly, it occurred to me that, even if the spider died, the wasp remained nonetheless trapped in the web.

"What are you saying, Anthony?" Ma asked at last. I looked at her, realizing I had stung not just Pop, but her as well. She stubbed out her nearly new cigarette and lit a second, the lighter shaking in her hand so she had to make several attempts to touch the flame to the cigarette in her mouth.

"Stop! All of you, stop, please," Rosalia shouted above the wind. She looked frightened, glancing from Ma to Pop to me and back again. I knew it was too late to stop what was already in motion. I felt like I was caught in a rock slide that I had triggered. And now I was unable to break my fall.

"I mean I'm dating a man. A man—not a woman," I said flatly, watching their faces as I took a seat at the kitchen table. They looked bewildered, as if they were unable to comprehend my words. They were reeling. I faced the three of them, spelling it out for them: "I'm gay. I've known it for a long time now."

I expected Pop to start yelling, to storm angrily from the room, to curse me, to pretend I was no longer part of the family the way he had with Paddy. My gut felt tight and there was a lightness in my head, as if I'd been drinking and might faint. I struggled against the sensations, bracing myself heavily against the table, and slowly leaned back in my chair, keeping my eyes on them. Suddenly, I felt insecure, like they were all united against me.

Pop sagged in his chair like he had been deflated, and Ma crossed herself several times, her cigarette leaving a smoky sign of the cross floating in the air between us. Rosalia said nothing, instinctively remaining on the sidelines. In one of the bedrooms down the hall, glass shattered and a door blew open with a crash. No one moved.

"You're queer?" Pop asked finally.

"Gay, Pop," I said. Queer was what they called you in school when they meant to hurt you: I hated the word. "I'm gay."

"Well, that's a helluva thing to spring on us like this. A helluva thing," Pop said irritably. He vigorously rubbed his hands together, then held them out in front of him like he didn't recognize them. "Can't never get that damned ink outta my skin neither. Guess I should just accept it cuz it ain't never gonna change." He turned his hands over and back again. "It's just so damned ugly."

I looked away, and glanced briefly at my own hands. I felt chastened, ashamed. Pop's words infuriated me, even though he unexpectedly seemed to be holding back, almost accepting my announcement. But I felt his disapproval, his disappointment. I felt diminished in his eyes.

A sudden quiet outside sucked all sound from the room. I could hear the cicadas buzzing outside and the static buzz of radio, which had been knocked off the air at some point during our argument. Somewhere in the back of my head, I knew David's eye was now over us. Although the storm continued to swirl on all sides of us, we were in the center, where it seemed as quiet as a funeral. It would last only a few minutes, I knew, before the storm returned from the opposite direction, stronger than ever.

I turned back to face Ma and Pop. "I'm sorry," I said, tears unexpectedly running down my cheeks. "I didn't plan on telling you like this."

Pop looked at me, his eyebrows arching up into peaks. "Sure you did. You said it just how you wanted to say it: to hurt us. You wanted to hurt us, and now yer feeling guilty 'bout doing such a good job of it." He stood and pushed his chair up to the table. "I hope yer pleased with yerself. It's a helluva thing to tell us like this."

"I'm sorry," I said, cursing myself inwardly for apologizing again. "Maybe I could have been nicer about it, but it's still true. I'm gay, and nothing's gonna change that."

"I 'spect we gotta live with it, then," Pop said. "I don't like it. I think it's sick. But it's yer life, not mine, and if you wanna live like that just so's you can hurt us, well go ahead. But I ain't gotta like it. And I sure as hell ain't gotta talk about it anymore."

"Not talking about it won't change it, Pop. It won't go away."

"Maybe not, but I don't have to know about it. You keep the dirty little details to yerself, and don't think you can bring yer fairy boyfriend here: I don't want nothing to do with him. If that's how you wanna live, fine. But don't go throwing it in my face." He looked at the front door. "I'm gonna go outside and check on the house now. This subject is closed."

He turned and strode into the laundry room around the corner and pulled open the outside door. The sound of cicadas increased. He stepped through the door and closed it behind him.

I looked over at Ma, still sitting in her seat directly opposite me. She said nothing, just smoked her cigarette, sighing with each exhalation. I watched her until she stubbed out the cigarette.

"Well?" I asked.

She looked up at me. Her face was slack and expressionless. She shook her head and her auburn hair glinted under the light. She looked even smaller than her five feet. Like a little girl who had just been scolded.

"Whaddaya want me to say, Anthony?" she asked. "There's nothing to say."

"Do I make you sick, too?"

"You make me sad," she said. "You make your father sad." She lit another cigarette, then walked to the laundry room, and followed Pop out the door.

Only Rosalia was left at the table.

"I suppose you're mad at me, too?" I asked.

"I don't know what I am right now," she said. "You know it doesn't matter to me if you're gay, of course. I just can't believe you picked the middle of a hurricane to tell us." She looked up at me. "I thought gays had impeccable timing?"

"No," I said, looking at her with surprise and pleasure. "We have impeccable taste, but lousy timing."

We both burst out laughing. Rosalia came over and hugged me.

"Jesus, Rose," I said. "He just pissed me off and it spilled out of me. I've been trying to figure out all week how to tell them, how to break it to them easy. Then, I do it like this. What's wrong with me?"

"Well, one thing's for sure," Rosalia said. "They know *now*. No sense worrying about it. Now that you've told them, you just have to take it from here."

"Mmmm," I nodded. "And just where do I take it, Rose?"

"Wherever it leads you," she said. She kissed my cheek, then headed for her bedroom.

I walked into the laundry room and opened the door a crack. Ma and Pop were standing on the patio outside the door surveying the damage.

"Give it some time," Ma said.

"I don't wanna give it time," Pop replied. "It's his life and it's got nothing to do with us. If he wants to live that lifestyle, no one can stop him. But I don't have to like it. And I don't have to approve of it. And I don't want to know about it."

"Do you want to chase him away, too?" Ma asked. "Isn't one son enough? You stood up to Paddy and he ran away. Now, we haven't seen him in over ten years. Do you want to lose Anthony, too?"

"Paddy made his own choice to leave," Pop said. "I didn't kick him out."

"You didn't ask him to stay, either."

"I ain't gonna beg my children to stay. They gotta do what they gotta do. And I ain't gonna pussy-foot around and pretend I like what I don't like. Anthony can do whatever he wants when he's not around us. But I don't need to know about his sex life."

"Well, don't argue about it with him any more tonight," Ma said, as usual, more concerned about us making nicey-nice with each other than actually resolving the real issues.

What the hell gave Pop the right to judge my life? I hadn't asked for his approval. I'd be heading back to college in two days, but I knew now I couldn't live with Ma and Pop again. I would get a place of my own as soon as I could after graduation. Then I wouldn't have to deal with either of them anymore, and it wouldn't matter what they thought.

I closed the door quietly and slipped back into the kitchen. Moments later, the storm raged anew from the opposite direction, rattling the windows and sending objects banging into the walls outside. Ma and Pop ran back inside, slamming the door shut behind them. They joined me at the kitchen table and Rosalia joined us as we listened for a weather update on the radio, which was working again. No one spoke. Evening had come on, and we gradually dozed off in our seats, the continuous blowing of the wind lulling us to sleep.

When we awoke in the morning, it was still raining outside, but the wind was gone. Our shed had disappeared in the storm, along with everything that had been inside it. The window in my old bedroom had shattered when the storm drove a branch through the boards nailed over it. So many shingles and boards had been ripped from our roof that Pop had to hire roofers to come in and replace the entire roof.

Two days later, without another word about my announcement, Ma and Pop drove me to the airport. I felt confused and upset. I had thrown my homosexuality in their faces to hurt them because I felt hurt. I felt ashamed of myself—not so much because I was gay, but mostly because of the way I used my being gay to bludgeon them, to exact revenge. I thought about their reactions, about the hurricane, about the island, about Orion still watching in the sky.

How ironic that when I returned to college, I lost Cliff anyhow. I had waited to give him the news face-to-face, but I never got the chance. Cliff had moved on before I ever broke the news to Ma and Pop. I had lost him months earlier with all my vacillating.

Nearly one year later, arriving back on the island as a college graduate at the end of June 1980, I knew I couldn't live with Ma and Pop for more than a few days. After tearfully leaving Steven back in Illinois, and thinking I'd never see him again, I felt a new determination to begin anew. The job I had lined up at a weekly newspaper nearby was a long way from *The New York Times*, but it paid a real salary and I felt like I was on my way.

The day after I arrived, I went apartment hunting, and by that evening, I signed a lease on a small, affordable place on the other side of the island from Ma and Pop. That weekend, I would move into my first real apartment to begin my new post-college life.

The island seemed changed—smaller, less fun, less exciting, less everything. Rosalia was seldom around. Trap had asked her to marry him, and they were busily planning a spring wedding. Ma and Pop seemed distant from me, coolly welcoming me back home, asking few questions about my plans; they were almost unresponsive when I told them I had located an apartment and would be moving out in a few days.

Pop shrugged his shoulders at the news. "You're twenty-two. I suppose it's time." He and I had barely spoken since I came home. He seemed aloof and uninterested in me or my plans. He hadn't even mentioned my less-than-stellar final report card of three Bs and a solo A. Pop had never accepted anything less than straight As from me. Did he figure it didn't matter anymore since I had graduated? Or had he given up on me after I told him I was gay? It pissed me off. After busting my ass and graduating in the top fifth of my class, the least he could do was acknowledge the accomplishment. I felt vindicated for not having invited them to my graduation—after all, they had skipped my high school graduation and Northwestern was a thousand miles away. Why put myself through that aggravation again? Pop didn't think I measured up: not in school, not in college, and not in life.

Well, I'd show his ass, I thought. Once I was on my own, I wouldn't have to see him judging me all the time. I could do what I wanted without Pop needing to know about it. And just wait till Pop saw my byline on the front page, I thought. He wouldn't be able to dismiss my success so easily then.

The night before I moved out, after Pop and Rosalia had gone to bed, I fixed myself a cup of tea and joined Ma at the dining table. The only smells were Ma's coffee and her cigarette, its red tip glowing every time she inhaled, a white-gray cloud engulfing her every time she exhaled, and my tea, steaming and sweet with sugar. Suddenly, I felt a closeness we had never shared before, and asked if she ever thought about what she was going to do once she and Pop had the house to themselves.

She poured herself another cup of coffee while she considered my question. The only sound in the room was the glugging of the coffee from the pot to her cup. I watched the steam rise off the cup, obscuring her face momentarily before vanishing into the half-light of the dining room. The warm, sticky night felt close around us, as if the light above us was struggling to keep the darkness at bay. Ma took a deep drag on her cigarette, then she exhaled slowly, from between rounded lips, and the cloud of smoke streamed from her mouth like the body of a serpent.

"Maybe I'll go back to school and get my diploma," she said. "I might like that."

Tarantella

I was surprised. Ma had told me how she had quit high school just months short of graduation to help on the family farm. Then, she met and married Pop right after she turned eighteen, so she had never graduated. I thought she never would. I was surprised a high school diploma still mattered to her.

"How come you quit school before graduation in the first place?" I asked.

"I didn't quit," she said icily. "My bastard father pulled me out. I begged the bastard to let me finish. I only had three months to go, but he didn't care." She fidgeted with her cigarette, picking it up and looking at it for a moment. "He told my principal he needed me on the farm. I screamed at him and argued with the principal, but it didn't help. All my friends graduated, but not me." She exhaled another long stream of grey smoke between us, then waved it away before continuing. "He was a jealous sonuvabitch. He didn't let any of his kids get a diploma. Pulled each of us outta school just before graduation, supposedly to help on that piece-of-shit farm. But he didn't need our help: he just didn't want to see one of his kids get a diploma, 'cause he didn't have one, and he'd be damned if one of his kids was gonna have something he didn't have. He didn't care if he ruined our lives. He just wanted to show us that he was the big cheese." She stubbed out her cigarette, adding, "Now he's burning in hell."

Ma took a sip of coffee, then lit another cigarette and took a long drag. I didn't know how to respond. Why had she never shared this story before?

"What do you need a diploma for now?" I asked, finally. Ma was in her fifties: what difference did it make?

"To prove I'm as good as everyone else," she said, shaking her cigarette fiercely to underscore her words. "I feel like everyone thinks I'm stupid."

"No one thinks you're stupid, Ma," I said. "Besides, a diploma doesn't make you smart."

"I know that, of course." She blew on her coffee. "But if you don't have one, other people treat you like you're dumb. And don't say they don't, 'cause I know different from experience: I've never felt equal. Maybe it's a little late, but I'll have a diploma one-uh these days—mark my words." She sipped her coffee and followed it with a drag from her cigarette like a drinker downing a shot and following it with a bite on a lemon wedge.

"If it makes you feel better about yourself, you should go for it, Ma," I said. "Besides, I think it would be a great experience for you."

"I'm glad you went to college," she said quietly. "And that you're about to start a good job and move into your own place. You're really growing up. I can't believe you're already twenty years old."

"Twenty-two, Ma," I corrected.

"Twenty-two," she nodded, tapping the ash from her cigarette. "Where's the time gone? I remember when we first brought you home. Seems like only yesterday. Your father had to take care of you at first while I recovered. He fed you and bathed you and worried about whether the broken bone in your chest would heal. You were his little miracle boy because the doctors had told him you might not survive after such a difficult birth. But he made sure that you did. He took time off from his job to help me. That was pretty unusual back in those days, you know." Ma stubbed out her cigarette, picked up her coffee cup, and announced she was going to bed.

I watched her walk away and wondered if she had seen my incredulity. Could she really be talking about Pop? Pop, who barely gave me the time of day? Pop, who never missed an opportunity to make me feel bad? Pop, who had consigned me to die before I was even born? He must have felt guilt-ridden—it was the only logical explanation.

In bewilderment, I sat at the table late into the night, my hands around the warm tea cup. How could I still be learning new things about Ma and Pop after twenty-two years? Who were they really? Would I ever understand them? The concept of a diaper-changing, doting-father Pop seemed totally incompatible with the Pop I knew.

I moved into my first, post-graduation apartment over the weekend and began my new job on Monday. My initial assignment—man-on-the-street interviews about the rising price of oranges—ended up on the first page of the Local section. It wasn't Pulitzer material, but I opened and reopened the section, each time feeling a surge of pride at the sight of my byline.

I loved going home to my cozy, if sparsely furnished, apartment at the end of the day. I would read or watch television when I was home, basking in an unfamiliar sense of adulthood. On Sundays, I had pasta dinner with Ma, Pop, and Rosalia at home. We avoided controversial subjects—mostly talking about Rosalia's upcoming wedding plans, my latest article, or some piece of news from the relatives in New York. On occasion, Doughna Mira would join us and she would always tell me how proud she was each time she opened her newspaper and saw my name. Ma and Pop never mentioned my articles.

The months flew by and, before I knew it, the holidays were upon us. The novelty of my apartment and job had begun to wear off, and I had begun to experience the loneliness of solitary life. I would walk around my apartment at night, wishing I had someone to talk to, someone to share my life with. I remembered Steven in Chicago, wondered what he was doing now and if he missed me. I hadn't contacted him since I returned to Florida. But, shortly after Christmas, I decided to take a chance and call him. I dialed his number and another man answered the phone. He told me Steven had moved and gave me his new number. I called the new number and bit my fingernail as I waited for him to answer, uncertain about what I would say to him.

"Hello," came Steven's voice on the third ring.

"Steven? It's Anthony," I stammered. "From Florida. Remember me?"

"Yo, Tony," he said enthusiastically. "Course I remember. Long time no hear. How's it hanging, man?"

"I'm fine," I said. "I was thinking about you and thought I'd just call to say Happy New Year."

"Back atcha, man," he said amiably. "So, how's life in Florida?"

"Fine," I said. "I've got my own place now. And a job. But I miss you. I hope you're not still mad at me."

"Shit, no, I ain't mad," he said. "Shit happens. Hell, maybe I could come visit you sometime. It'd sure be nice to get away from this cold for a little while."

"That would be great," I enthused. "I'd love to see you, and you're welcome to stay with me."

"That'd be cool," he said. "You were pretty hot as I recall. But who am I kidding? I couldn't afford the plane ticket to get down there."

"It's really not that expensive," I said, pleased to hear he found me hot.

"Maybe not for you," he said. "But it's too expensive for me, no matter what it costs."

"Maybe I could buy your ticket?" I offered. I really wanted to see him, touch him, sleep with him, and see if we could get back together again somehow.

"Nah, man. I'd really like to come, but I don't want you paying for me," he said. "I don't want you thinking I'm some charity case or something."

"I wouldn't think that," I protested. "Consider it a late Christmas gift. I feel bad I haven't spoken to you in so long. It would make me feel good and, besides, I really would like to see you."

"Are you serious, man?" He sounded excited. "That would be awesome! I'd love to come down there. I ain't never been to Florida. Fact, I've never been outta Chicago before."

In late February, Steven came for his visit. To avoid missing a weekend shift at the restaurant (those were his big-money nights), he stayed only from Monday evening until Friday morning. I cleaned and straightened my apartment and made all kinds of plans for things we could do each evening after I got home from work. His last full day in town was also my twenty-third birthday. Ma and Pop had invited me over for dinner to celebrate, and I decided I would surprise them by bringing Steven with me. It was perfect. Steven was so beautiful and so full of life, I convinced myself they'd love him; maybe meeting him would make them more accepting.

I spotted Steven the moment he stepped through the gate at the airport. He was wearing the denim shirt I had given him last spring with tight, sexy black jeans and cowboy boots. He came over and gave me a bear hug, pressing his body firmly against mine.

"Yer a sight fer sore eyes," he said enthusiastically. "I can't believe I'm in Florida."

"I'm so glad you're here at last," I said, hugging him back. He had only one carry-on bag—a beaten-up, black-and-brown tote—with him, so we headed directly out to my car. We climbed into the car, and Steven slid his bag on the floor between his legs. Then, he leaned toward me and kissed me hard, slipping his tongue into my mouth. Despite the instant concern about who might see us, I kissed him back.

"Whooh!" Steven said after he leaned back in his seat. "That's just a taste of what you got coming, girl. After all, I gotta pay you back for that ticket somehow!" He winked at me and adjusted himself in his pants. "Guess I better wait till we get home, though."

He looked even better than I remembered, and I couldn't wait to get him back to my apartment. As we drove back to Merritt Island, I pointed out what few sites there were along the Beeline Expressway, and filled him in on what I'd done since graduation.

When we walked into my apartment, Steven asked me to give him my key so he could open the door. He stepped inside and whistled. "This is a fucking great place," he said, scanning the apartment from the entrance. His eyes wandered from the cathedral ceilings to the small living/dining room and kitchen, and settled on the doorway to my bedroom. I closed the door behind me and he took my hand in his. "Follow me," he said, and led the way to my bedroom. We made love and fell asleep in each other's arms.

In the morning, my alarm clock went off and I looked at Steven beside me as I got up for work. Would I someday have a lover to wake up beside every day? I gathered my clothes and went into the bathroom to shower. A few moments later, I heard the shower door open and turned around to find Steven in the shower beside me.

"Mmmm. Good morning, Sunshine," he said, wrapping his arms around me and pressing his naked body against mine. He kissed me as the hot, steamy water sprayed over us and his hands massaged my back. "Let me soap you up," he said, taking the soap from the dish and rubbing it across my back and shoulders. I luxuriated under his touch.

"You don't have to wash me," I said, almost shyly, as he soaped my belly and groin and ass.

"I want to," he said. "I'm enjoying it. And, from the looks of things, you are too."

We made love again in the shower and afterwards, I had to hurry to make it to work on time. Steven insisted on dropping me off so that he could have the car for the day to go to the beach. I felt distracted all day, thinking about making love with Steven.

Steven was waiting outside when I left the newsroom. He was wearing dark sunglasses and red walking shorts with no shirt, and his body was already golden brown—no doubt his Indian heritage. He insisted on driving, and we stopped for some fast food at a restaurant down the street.

"So, what're we doin' tonight?" he asked.

"I was thinking we could drive around the island and I could show you where I went to school and everything," I said.

"Hmm. That sounds nice, but are there any gay bars in town?" he asked. "Maybe I'd let you take me on a date, like to a movie and dancing or something?"

"I've never been to the bar in town," I said, "but we could check it out together if you want. And I love movies. We can sightsee another day, I guess."

Tarantella

We got home late that night and went straight to sleep. Steven had had a bit too much to drink and conked out the minute his head hit the bed. I slipped off his shoes and socks, then undressed myself and slipped into the bed beside him. His breath was sweet with alcohol, and whenever he rolled onto his back, he snored loudly. I loved having him here, and I draped my leg across his body so I could feel him against me, pillowing my head on his shoulder.

I needed the car on Wednesday, so Steven had me drop him off at the beach on my way to work. He said he'd be fine, and that he'd call me at work to figure out how to hook up with each other. I never heard from him, but when I left the building, he was sitting on the steps outside.

"How'd you get here?" I asked, surprised and pleased to see him.

"I met this guy at the beach and he offered to give me a lift, so I figured I'd surprise you, and here I am," he said.

"You mean, you just got in the car with a total stranger?" I asked. I couldn't imagine doing something like that. I'd probably never have even spoken with a stranger, let alone gotten into a car with one.

"Sure," he said. "His name's Peter, and he's lived on Cocoa Beach his whole life. I told him you worked at the paper and he said he knew where it was, and offered to drop me off. I figured I'd save you the trip."

"Thanks," I said. "Did you stay at the beach all day?"

"Um, yeah," he said. "I mostly laid in the sun. I hunted for shells for a while, but I didn't find anything good. Peter showed up in the afternoon—he works construction and goes to the beach after work. And then, he dropped me here. Nothing exciting, but a whole lot better 'n being in the snow in Chicago."

After dinner, Steven said he wanted to check out this bar in Orlando that Peter had told him about. It was called the Parliament House and, according to Peter, it was the biggest gay bar for 500 miles, and lots of fun. I agreed reluctantly because I had to work the next day, but Steven insisted we'd leave early.

The Parliament House was actually a gay resort with a hotel and dance bar. After paying your cover charge, you headed down a mirrored, neon-lit walkway into the bar itself. The music was booming, and lights strobed across dozens of men dancing inside. I had never seen so many gay men at one time, and I marveled how I could have grown up only a short drive away, thinking I was the only one around. Just inside the door, Steven waved at a very attractive, blond and mustached man. He grabbed my hand and headed toward the man, towing me behind.

"Peter!" he said, kissing the man on the lips and hugging him. "This is Tony."

"Nice to meet you," Peter said, shaking my hand. He turned back to Steven and said, "I was hoping you'd make it here. I told you it's always hopping on Wednesday nights. Let me show you around the place."

"Hey, Tony," Steven said, turning to me, "would you mind getting me a beer while Peter shows me around this place? I'll catch up with you in here in a few minutes. Okay?"

Before I could respond, he and Peter headed into the next room. I stood for a moment, feeling awkward and alone in this huge place full of gay men. The music throbbed around me, the lights flashed and strobed, and I felt like I was somewhere illicit, doing something naughty. I went over to the bar and got a beer for Steven, and an amaretto sour for me, then walked back to where Steven had left me, waiting for him to return.

Nearly an hour passed before Steven reappeared. He snuck up behind me without me seeing him, slipped his warm hands over my eyes, and whispered in my ear, "Guess who?"

"Steven," I said, relaxing at last. "Your beer's probably warm by now, you've been gone so long. Where's Peter?"

"Did you miss me?" he asked, wrapping his arms around me and pressing his body against mine. His breath was alcohol-sweet. "Mmmm, I missed *you*." He kissed me firmly on the mouth. I felt pleased that he was back, and felt my body reacting. "Let's dance," he said, breaking our embrace and leading me to the dance floor.

We danced for hours, and I was pleased that Peter never re-appeared. It was late when we finally left, and I knew I'd be tired the next day: my twenty-third birthday. I hadn't told Steven it was my birthday or that we'd be dining with Ma and Pop and Rosalia. I figured I'd surprise him in the morning.

Sunlight was streaming through the window when the alarm went off the next morning. I awoke and thought sleepily about how it was my birthday, yet it felt no different to me than any other day. I rolled over, kissed Steven, and ran my hand down his naked chest: he felt so good. He woke and looked at me through squinted eyes.

"What time is it?" he asked.

"It's after nine," I said. "My alarm just went off, sleepy head."

"Oh," he said, shutting his eyes drowsily.

I kissed him and said, "Guess what?"

"What?" he asked sleepily.

"Today's my birthday," I said.

"Huh?" he asked, his eyes fluttering open. "Today's what?"

"My birthday," I repeated.

"And you're just telling me now?" he asked.

"I didn't want you to feel like you had to get me something," I explained. "After all, you being here is gift enough."

"Still," he said, sitting upright and pulling out a cigarette, "I'd like to do *something* for you. Maybe we could do something special tonight?"

"Well, maybe later," I said. "First, we're supposed to go over to my parents' for dinner and cake."

"Your parents invited me over for dinner and cake?" he asked. "I didn't think they even knew about me. Or that I was here."

"They don't," I admitted. "It'll be a surprise, but I really want them to meet you. I know they'll love you. Because I do."

"You what?"

"Love you," I repeated, feeling dry mouthed. I didn't know how Steven would react. It was stupid and too soon for me to say something like that. We had known each other for nearly a year, yet had only seen each other for less than a week last spring and again for less than a week now. Yet, I wanted to continue feeling what I had felt this week: to continue waking up next to Steven; to continue making love to him; to continue being with him. And I didn't know how to make that happen when he lived a thousand miles away in Chicago.

"I love you, too," Steven replied, pulling me back down into the bed and kissing me deeply. I felt drugged and numb. I had expected him to object to my admission, to tell me it was too soon. Instead, he had responded with the words I had been waiting all my life to hear. I felt like my heart might burst as we made love on the morning of my twenty-third birthday, and I knew that, somehow, we would figure out a way to stay together.

We arrived for my birthday dinner with Ma, Pop, and Rosalia at about six o'clock. I was so excited about introducing Steven to Ma and Pop and Rosalia, so eager for them to see I had someone in my life. As we went inside, my stomach felt inexplicably fluttery. I looked over at the rock garden and wondered if the snake was still hiding inside after all these years.

"Hello," I called out as I poked my head in the door. "Anyone home?"

"Well, hello, birthday boy," Rosalia said, looking up from the living room sofa where she was reading a magazine. As Steven followed me inside, she stood up and frowned briefly, quickly catching herself and asking, "Who's this?"

"This is Steven," I said as I walked up and kissed Rosalia on the cheek. "Steven, this is my favorite sister Rosalia."

"Hmmm," Rosalia shrugged. "I'm also his *only* sister." Then, smiling and shaking Steven's hand, she said, "Pleased to meet you, Steven."

"Steven's visiting from Chicago," I explained in response to the confused look on her face. "I met him while I was in college."

"Aaah," Rosalia nodded. "Did you get a journalism degree, too?"

"Nah," Steven said. "I ain't really the college type. I leave the book-learning to Tony."

"I see," Rosalia said, and I could see her registering the fact that Steven wasn't a classmate of mine; also that he had called me Tony—something I had never allowed anyone to call me before. "Well, have a seat, Steven. Can I get you something to drink?"

"I'd love a beer," Steven said, taking a seat on the sofa.

"Coming right up," she said. "Uh, would you mind helping me...Tony?"

I followed her into the kitchen. Once we were out of earshot, she turned and stage-whispered, "Did you tell Ma and Pop you were bringing Steven with you?"

"No," I said. "I figured I'd surprise them."

"Oh, it'll surprise them, alright," she said. "I just hope you know what you're doing."

"I never know what I'm doing," I admitted. "It's looking like Steven could be a part of my life, so I guess I thought you all should meet. I'm hoping they like him." I looked at her as she pulled a beer from the refrigerator and turned back to face me. "So, what do you think? Cute, eh?"

"Honestly, Anthony," she sighed, then smiled conspiratorially, "Yes, he's cute. But I don't know what Ma and Pop will say. You could be asking for trouble."

"Don't worry," I reassured her. "Where are they anyhow?"

"Out back, barbecuing on the new grill. I'm supposed to come out with you when you get here. So, are you ready to face the music, birthday boy?"

"Let's do it," I said, suddenly nervous as we went back to the living room. I gave Steven his beer, and we headed for the back patio.

"Ma. Pop," I said as we approached them on the patio. Ma was setting the picnic table while Pop cooked on the grill. "This is Steven. He's a friend from college, and he's visiting me from Chicago this week. I hope you don't mind that I brought him along."

"Nice to meet you, Steven," Pop said amiably, stepping away from the grill to shake Steven's hand. "I'll bet it's a lot warmer here than in Chicago?"

"I'll say," Steven agreed. "It's nice to be out of the snow and shit for a while. Pardon my French."

"What do you do up in Chicago?" Ma asked.

"Wait tables, mostly," Steven said, taking a swig of his beer.

Ma looked at me suspiciously, but turned her attention back to the table settings.

"Dinner should be ready in just a minute," Pop called from the grill. "Steven, would you prefer a hamburger or a hotdog?"

"I'll have a dog," he said. Winking at me lasciviously, he added, "I like a nice wiener when I can get one." I winced and hoped Ma and Pop missed the reference.

"I got a big article about the school board coming up in the paper tomorrow," I announced, changing the subject. "It might even make page one."

"That's great," Ma said, placing a napkin beside each paper plate. Steven joined Pop at the grill. I looked over nervously and heard them chatting about football, which was sort of hilarious, since Steven had told me hated the sport. But he seemed to be holding his own, asserting that football was next to God in his book.

Ma finished setting the picnic table and suggested Rosalia, Steven, and I sit down. Steven excused himself to wash his hands as Pop put the meat on a platter and carried it to the table.

"So, what do you think of Steven?" I asked looking at Pop expectantly.

"I dunno," Pop said shrugging his shoulders. "Seems fine. He's a real talker."

"Yeah," I said, nodding. "That he is." I looked at them both and couldn't help wondering if they hadn't already guessed who Steven was. "There's something I need to tell you," I said as Rosalia shot a glance in my direction.

"What's that?" Ma asked as she dished a hotdog onto Steven's plate and a hamburger onto mine. "You getting a raise?"

"No, not a raise," I said, taking a deep breath and watching her move on to Rosalia's plate. "It's about Steven and me. We're not just old college chums. He's much more than that to me."

Ma finished serving the meat and set the platter on the table as if she hadn't heard what I'd said. Then she sat down on the bench and turned to look at Pop. So did Rosalia and me.

Pop didn't look up at us. He stared down at his plate and braced his hands on either side of the picnic table. He inhaled and then exhaled deeply and extravagantly. Ma tapped a cigarette out of a pack that materialized suddenly in her hand. She lit it and rolled it between her lips while she waited for Pop to speak. I decided not to wait.

"You must have guessed," I said. "It must have occurred to you."

"No!" Pop said emphatically, at last. "No, it did not occur to us. It never occurs to us, Anthony. I thought I made that clear the last time you brought this up. We don't want it to occur to us."

"Oh, come on, Pop," I said. "That was over a year ago. You've got to face facts sometime. I'm gay. And Steven is a part of my life."

"We don't have to face anything we don't want to," Pop said.

"Now, honey," Ma said, resting her cigarette on the outer ring of the ashtray in front of her and touching Pop's arm tentatively.

Pop tugged his arm back, pushed his catsup-bloody hamburger away from him, and stood up. "I don't want to discuss this anymore. I'm going inside to read the paper."

"Oh, come on, Pop," I said. "What does that solve? It won't make me straight, for God's sake. It won't make Steven disappear. It won't change anything."

"No," Pop agreed, turning to look at me for the first time. "But, at least, I won't have to have it thrown in my face again. If this is the way you want to live, fine. But I don't have to like it and I don't have to accept such sickness."

"I'm not sick, Pop." I snapped. "There's nothing wrong with me. Can't you understand that?"

"No," Pop said, shaking his head and putting his hands in front of his face as if he was warding off a blow. "I can't understand anything, except that you'll do anything to hurt me. If this is the way you choose to be, fine. Just don't try to shove it down my throat because I won't have it. Did you think I would accept the unacceptable just because it's your birthday? Let's just drop it now."

"No, Pop. Let's not drop it," I said. "This is my life we're talking about. Or not talking about. It's the way I am—not something I chose to hurt you."

"I don't want to hear it, Anthony," Pop said, tossing his napkin on his chair. He turned away and stormed into the house, passing Steven in the doorway. They looked warily at each other.

"Ma," I said, turning to face her as Steven walked up and sat down beside me with a quizzical look on his face. "Is that the way you feel, too?"

Ma stubbed out her cigarette and watched the smoke rise, gray and lifeless, from the stub. "He's my husband, Anthony," she said, finally. "And he's your father, for Christ's sake. Can't you let him alone on this? Why must you keep pushing him all the time?"

"I haven't said boo since I got home, Ma," I said. "But I can't stay silent forever. I won't. How would you feel if someone told you not to mention Pop or bring him around? It's ridiculous. Pop wants me to pretend to be something I'm not and that makes me feel like there's something wrong with me. God knows, I'll never feel better about myself as long as I can't be myself. If you two can't deal with me being gay, then I'm not sure where that leaves us." Steven put his arm around me and nodded supportively.

"Ma," Rosalia spoke for the first time, "Anthony's right. It's not right to ask him to hide who he is. Can't you get Pop to lighten up a little? He doesn't have to like it, but it's Anthony's life, after all."

"I can't go against him," Ma said, lighting another cigarette. "I have to live with him, you know. You're on your own now, Anthony, and living your own life. Does it really matter what he thinks? Why is it so important to you? Why can't you just drop it before you hurt everyone? You're tearing this family apart, for God's sake."

"I'm not trying to hurt anyone, Ma," I said. "I just want to feel good about myself, Ma; same reason getting a diploma still matters to you. Can't you see that? If my own parents can't accept me, who can?"

"Ma," said Rosalia. "For God's sake, you don't want to lose another son, do you?"

Ma fidgeted nervously with her cigarette. She looked at Steven. "You seem like a nice young man. Can't you help explain this to him?"

"Maybe we should go now," said Steven, rising and looking at me imperatively.

"It's not that he doesn't accept you, Anthony," Ma said, turning back to me. "He just accepts you in his own way."

"Yeah," I said. "Pop accepts me—as long as he never has to see or hear who I really am."

"He's not asking you to stop being who you are, Anthony," Ma said. "He understands. But it's hard to change your beliefs when you're nearly sixty. He's only asking that you respect his beliefs when you come home. Is that so bad?"

"Yes, Ma," I said. "That's so bad. Never talking about your husband, never bringing him to see your family, always pretending to be something you're not, never saying what you really feel—just to keep peace in the family. Could you live like that?"

She set her cigarette in the ashtray and exhaled a long, snaking stream of gray smoke that slowly moved across the table toward me. Then, she ran her hand over her lips.

"Actually, I *could* live like that," she said. "In fact, I've lived like that for the last thirty years."

I pushed away from the smoke snake moving toward me. I felt like she had struck me physically. "What are you saying, Ma?"

"I'm just saying you should do what you've gotta do, Anthony. That's all." She picked her cigarette back up and inhaled. Then, she held it in front of her and considered its red tip. "If that means you keep your family together by pretending everything's nicey-nice, then that's what you do. If that means you forget about doing all the things you thought you'd do one day, then that's what you do. You gotta stop being so selfish, Anthony. All I ever hear you say is 'Me. Me. Me.' What about the rest of the family?"

"I can't believe what you're saying, Ma," I said. "Is keeping the family together more important than your own happiness? More important than the happiness of anyone in the family? What good does it do to keep the family together if everyone's unhappy?"

Tarantella

"There are five of us in this family, Anthony, don't forget." She looked fierce. Her hair seemed dark and ominous. "It's something I've never forgotten."

"Maybe you *should* forget about it sometimes, Ma. Maybe you need to think about yourself sometimes," I said. "You know, there's nothing wrong with thinking about yourself now and then. There's nothing wrong with being happy. Maybe if you'd been happier, the rest of us would've been happier, too."

"Happiness isn't everything, you know, Anthony," she said. "You seem to forget that. You hurt a lot of people when you get selfish and only think about your own happiness."

"I can't believe this!" I felt like I was gagging, like I couldn't breathe. I needed air. "I won't live a lie any longer." Suddenly, Steven was at my side, helping me up.

At the doorway, I turned to look at Ma. She was still seated at the table, five paper plates stained red in the center in front of her, smoking furiously. The smoke coiled around and engulfed her, slowly drifting across the table. Rosalia looked dazed beside her, glancing pleadingly up at me, as if begging me to stay. But I couldn't.

I felt numb. Steven led me to the car and drove back to my apartment, telling me to relax; but I couldn't stop thinking about Ma spending thirty years keeping the family together, thirty years without being the person she had hoped to be, without doing the things she dreamed she'd do. Despite her efforts, Pop had driven Paddy away. Now he was driving me away. I thought about Pop pulling all our strings like Geppetto. I felt like a broken marionette, unable to function on my own.

Scot T. O'Hara

When we arrived at my apartment, Steven led me to my bed, undressing me and holding me, pressing his warm, inviting body against mine, whispering in my ear about love and pushing himself inside of me. He made love to me and said I should move away from here, back to Chicago: back to him. He told me I could find another job and how he'd like to live with me. He told me I needed to get away from Pop, to be on my own. I remembered I was twenty-three years old today, and it was time to make my own life. I sensed that I would end up like Ma if I didn't get away—far away—from them both.

I wasn't sure if Pop or Ma scared me more. Suddenly, I wanted to get as far away from the island as possible. It was as if the island had sprouted a fungus in the heat and humidity and rotted down the middle. I felt contaminated, like the decay was close around me. I wondered if Paddy had seen the decay in our family, too, and had fled from it. *What had become of him?* I wondered.

Suddenly, though, I knew it was time for me to go, too. I thanked God that I had Steven to lean on.

Unraveling

Chicago: May 1994

LESS THAN AN hour after calling Steven to let him know I had returned early, I opened the door to the apartment in Chicago quietly and slipped inside. I fought down the urge to slip out again
and run back across the street, to the hotel, or back to the airport: to just run away and keep running. But I knew that would
solve nothing, so I closed the door silently behind me and set
my luggage on the floor as I gathered my strength. I could hear
Steven in the bedroom.

The sun filled the living room, as bright now as it had been
dark last night. I walked down the same hallway and paused before stepping into the bedroom where, just hours before, my life
lurched so suddenly.

Oblivious to my presence, Steven bent over the dresser
drawer, putting something away. I watched him silently for a
moment. He had disrobed down to a pair of black, cotton boxers, and the sunlight glinted off the red flecks in the hair on his
muscled thighs. Despite my anger and hurt, and the certainty
that he had undressed to manipulate me, I still found him beautiful. I wanted to pull him onto the bed and make love to him, to

pretend last night hadn't happened. But I knew it *had* happened. And now, everything felt different.

As if sensing my presence, Steven stood suddenly and turned to face me. A brief look of worry vanished, replaced quickly by smug confidence when he realized I had been staring at his ass. He strolled brazenly up to me.

"Hi, baby," he said sweetly, hugging me.

"What are you doing home?" I asked. "I thought you were working today?"

"I was," he said. "But I rushed back here so I could welcome you in person. I've missed you."

"Have you?" I asked, returning a perfunctory hug. "I hope I didn't shock you too much by coming back early. You sounded so startled on the phone."

"Not startled," he corrected, "pleasantly surprised. You know how lonely I get when you're not around. I hate being alone."

I fought down the desire to slap him, to call him a slut and tell him what I had seen the night before. I suddenly felt supremely tired, exhausted, incapable of battling with him just now. So, I said nothing about last night's discovery, only listened as he told me how boring the last two days had been without me, how he had mostly worked, how he had slept so poorly without me in the bed beside him. I wanted to retch at the unending stream of lies—lies that slipped so effortlessly from his faithless lips.

What a fool I was to have given my love and trust to a man like him! Yet, like it or not, I loved him. Even now, I had no idea what I should do next.

"Well," he said at last, "I better get back to work. I told them I'd be back before the dinner rush. I just wanted to be here to surprise you when you got home." He rubbed his hand across the hair on his chest and stretched sinuously, then slowly pulled his clothes from where they were piled on the bed and dressed.

I watched him clinically from the doorway and he seemed a little uncertain how to respond.

After a moment, he said, "I'm glad you're home," and slipped past me.

"I guess I'll see you tonight, then?" I asked, following him to the door.

"Yeah, but don't wait up," he said, kissing my cheek as he opened the door and headed to the elevator. "That's why I came home now. I work until closing tonight, so I won't be home until late."

"Mmmm," I replied. "That's okay. I'm pretty worn out from my visit."

"Oh," he said, turning back toward me from the hallway, suddenly remembering, "how did everything go in Florida? How's your father?"

"Fine," I lied, remembering our huge blow-out. "Everything's fine. Pop was doing so well I just decided to come back early."

"Good," he said, checking his watch. The elevator bell rang and the doors opened. "I better go," he said as he stepped inside. "I'll see you later."

I watched the doors close. Then, he was gone, and the hall-way seemed lifeless and empty. I slipped back into our apart-ment, picking up my luggage from the entry and carrying it to the bedroom. I unpacked, and thought about how fucked up my life had become. When I finished unpacking, I called my boss at the newspaper office to let him know I would be back the next day: I didn't want to sit around feeling sorry for myself. I wanted to stay busy until I sorted out my feelings and decided what I should do next.

The week after my homecoming passed slowly, and I avoided Steven as much as possible. At night, I went to bed before Steven got home from the restaurant. But I couldn't sleep—I flopped over and back like a netted fish.

A hundred times a day I considered a hundred different ways to confront Steven about his infidelity. Each time, I dissuaded myself by deciding Steven had simply given in to temporary lust while I was away. Surely he would be completely faithful again now that I was home. Although I never convinced myself, I refrained from grabbing him by the collar, slapping him and demanding that he confess to everything because I didn't want to hear his confession. I feared what he'd say; feared what would come after; feared how it would hurt; feared opening a wound that might never heal.

While I was at work, I constantly wondered where Steven was and what he was doing. I would sit at my computer and feel my mind drift for minutes at a time. Was his new trick back in our apartment? Were they trysting even now? Or, had that been just a one-night stand? Surely that was it, I lied to myself, trying to cling to some vestige of self-respect.

Once, when I came out of such a trance, I found the department secretary staring at me, awaiting an answer to some unheard question. I blinked at her awkwardly and asked: "What?" as if I had been concentrating on something in my reporter's notebook.

"Where were you just then, Anthony?" she asked.

"Nowhere," I said hurriedly. "Just thinking."

"About what?" She touched my shoulder to show her concern.

"Things," I said, pulling away. "I've got a lot on my mind these days. You know, my Pop's been sick." I felt guilty about using Pop's illness to cover for my "breakdown," even though it was certainly contributing to my stress level.

"Oh, I'm sorry. I hope he gets better soon." I soon learned to use this "illness" excuse because it was so effective at disarming those who noticed my increasingly frequent lapses of concentration. They would hurriedly slip away with that discomforted facial expression that said: "Please don't tell me any more because I really don't know how to respond."

I found myself alone even more than usual, the way people in distress usually do. I wondered if I was emitting unconscious vibrations that kept others at bay. I would lose my place during news interviews, forget what I was asking—sometimes in the middle of asking it—and found myself apologizing for my embarrassing confusion. Like a sponge that had absorbed as much water as it could hold and now shed every additional drop, I was shedding all stimuli thrown at me. I could no longer manage even the most routine tasks: conducting a simple interview, writing an article from my notes, driving my car, remembering an appointment. Everything seemed effort- and stress-laden. I was wading through deep water, watching others move freely on shore.

Just after lunch on Friday, my boss called me in to ask what was wrong.

"What do you mean, what's wrong?" I turned his question back on him.

"I don't know," he said, rubbing his bristly chin. "You seem a bit"—he searched for the right word—"detached. Is something wrong?"

I began to panic that I would never shake this malaise that had settled over me. Steven's infidelity, Pop's heart attack, my feelings of inadequacy, work stress—it all seemed too much. I felt suffocated and claustrophobic.

"I'm fine. Really." I lied. When I could see he wasn't buying my story, I added, "Okay. I guess I'm still a little shell-shocked over my father's heart attack."

"How *is* your father?" he asked, looking genuinely concerned.

"Better," I said. "Still not out of the woods, but improving every day. I guess I haven't managed to leave it at home as well as I thought I had."

"That's understandable," he said. "Don't push it. Is there anything I can do? Do you need a few more days?"

"No, no, I'll be fine," I said. "Thanks for everything already. I appreciate the support."

Tarantella

He nodded and I took it as my cue to leave. As I reached the doorway, he called after me, "Why don't you knock off for the day at least? You're not working on anything that can't wait, are you?"

"I guess not," I said.

"Then, get out of here." He dismissed me with a wave of his hand. "That's an order."

I thanked him and returned to my desk. It was nearly three o'clock—Steven would already be at work. I decided to pick up some Chinese carryout on my way home. I could certainly use a quiet evening to sort out my feelings. I knew it was time—past time—to make some hard decisions and get on with my life. I couldn't delay any longer if others were starting to notice.

When I opened the apartment door, I immediately smelled the musky, woodsy scent of Jovan Musk—Steven's favorite cologne—like poisonous fumes. I grimaced involuntarily, as if I had been slapped. Steven never wore cologne to work. Cologne meant one thing: Steven had gone out cruising. I felt the blood race from my head, leaving me dizzy with tears pricking suddenly at my eyes.

I shut the door behind me and stood in the foyer for a moment to collect my composure. The apartment seemed unnaturally still. The living room looked more like twilight than midday since Steven had forgotten to open the blinds. I walked into the room, dropping my dinner and briefcase on the dining table before heading over to the windows. I looked around the peaceful living room: the olive-colored sofa with overstuffed cushions we bought together shortly after we moved into this apartment, the landscape of the Italian coastline we bought at a gallery in River North, the coffee table and floor lamp Steven had bought with my credit card while I was at work one day, the television and stereo I brought with me from Florida. How could it all seem so normal, so peaceful when my life felt so upended?

. I drew open the blinds and looked down at the Amoco Building's manicured plaza gardens nearly thirty floors below. People and cars looked like playthings, moving easily and smoothly along an invisible track. Although the sun blazed over Centennial Park to the south and east, the shade of the Amoco Building engulfed my apartment.

Returning to the dining table, I noticed the mail Steven had left there for me, especially the letter from Ma that lay on top of the pile. I popped open the containers of Kung Pao chicken and rice from my carryout dinner, then opened up Ma's letter. I read her words as I began eating with the plastic carryout fork.

Dear Anthony,

Just a short note.

I swear you and your father will be the death of me. I don't know what to do with the two of you sometimes. Everything I try is wrong. Now, I have you both mad at me, and I'm at the end of my rope. I think you're both acting like children. I know you love each other, but neither one of you will admit it. You're like two peas in a pod. Neither of you will take the first step.

Tarantella

When I saw you at the hospital, I was so happy. I really thought you were there to make a fresh start. And then, the two of you started fighting again. I wish you'd both stop.

You know how your father is. Maybe he's too old to change. But you're still young. Maybe you could try again.

I wish you hadn't rushed back to Chicago. Maybe you and your father just need to spend a little more time together. I know he was glad you came, even if he won't admit it.

Anyhow, he should be home in another day or two. I'm glad. I'm sick of the hospital myself. Maybe you could call and talk to him after he gets home. Me and Rosalia think it might help.

Well, got to go.

Ma and Pop

Ma always signed both of their names to her letters. I slid her note back in its envelope while I thought about her words. How could she think Pop and me were "like two peas in a pod?" Jesus! I'd spent my whole life trying to get away from him, trying to be as unlike him as possible. Now, Ma's words confirmed my worst fears that what Rosalia had said was true—Pop and I shared many— and mostly undesirable—traits. But where had she gotten the idea Pop loved me? I saw no evidence of that. Our interactions were uniformly negative: fighting, arguing, disagreeing, complaining. Pop was more concerned with my lifestyle than with my life.

I knew Ma was right about one thing: Pop could never admit his feelings. It was one of the traits we did share. I always felt panicky at the thought of sharing my feelings. Telling Steven I loved him had taken enormous effort, and granted him a power over me; look how badly that had turned out. How could I grant Pop that same power?

I knew I was running out of time to reach resolution with Pop. Rosalia said Pop's heart muscle had been weakened, leaving him at high risk for another heart attack that—next time—he might not survive. I wondered if our hearts really were the center— physical, spiritual, and emotional—of our lives. Perhaps Pop's inability to open up had caused emotional pressures to build, un- relieved and unvented, until his heart gave out. I was on the same path. We *were* two peas in one pod.

I got up from the table with the empty carryout containers, and dropped them in the kitchen trash can. That's when I noticed Steven's note taped to the refrigerator door. I instinctively hesi- tated before picking it up.

I felt my pulse quicken with nervousness as I ran my fingers over its slick white surface tentatively, as if it were covered with Braille imprints and I could glean its contents by touch. Then, I carried it into the bathroom and closed the door behind me, feeling somehow safer and more secure in the smallness of this familiar space. Looking in the mirror, I was shocked by the pale, worn-out face looking back at me.

I sat on the commode and picked up the note. My heart thudded against my ribs, the way it always does when you know something awful is coming. I unfolded the note crisply and rested my shaking hands on my thighs to read the sleek handwriting— Steven had beautiful penmanship, although his words were rife with spelling errors, incorrect punctuation, and missing words and letters. Reading his notes was a little like deciphering hieroglyphs.

> *Tony,*
>
> *Somethings up with you I know it only Im not shure what it is. Did I say or do something wrong cuz if I did I sorry. I never want to hurt you if I can. I guess you need time to work it out so Ill give you a little space tonite. Im going to work a double so I wont be home till very late probably after 4 a.m. at least. But Im off tomorow so maybe we can talk then. I think we need talk about whatevers wrong cuz I dont like fighting with you.*
>
> *I hope you know I love you,*
>
> *Steven*

Mostly it seemed innocent enough. But my eye kept going back to the "I won't be home till very late, probably after 4 a.m." line. I dropped the note to the floor and leaned back on the commode to think. The restaurant closed at 1 a.m., so why wouldn't he be home until after 4? He said he loved me, but I suspected he was meeting his trick tonight—and then, coming back here to me. I felt nauseous. Angry. Insulted. Violated. But Steven was right about our needing to talk. I couldn't go on like this much longer, either. I had to figure out what I wanted to do. If I stayed with Steven in light of everything, what did that say about me? Why was I even hesitating? Didn't I deserve better? And yet, I knew I still loved Steven. In spite of everything, every time I saw him, my heart raced and I wanted to be with him. I hated the thought of failing at another relationship, but how long could I go on like this—wondering where he was, doubting him, torturing myself?

I retrieved Steven's note from the floor. I tore it in half and in half again and tossed it into the toilet. Then, I flushed it and headed down the hall to the living room. The late afternoon sun reflected off the glass of the Amoco Building, throwing intense golden light deep into the heart of our apartment, illuminating spidery bolls of dust and hair along the baseboards, and revealing mars and chips in the paint like a pox on the walls of our home.

I turned on the stereo and searched through my CD collection for my most melancholy album. I placed the disc, "Diva," by Annie Lennox, on the player and punched up the volume. Plopping down in a big patch of sun on the floor in the center of the room, I cupped my hands behind my head and let myself drift in the current of the music. The sun felt warm and reassuring.

I recalled the day I asked Steven to move in with me. It was a Saturday, and I had only been back in Chicago a week. After making love, I had told Steven about my feelings for him. He said he felt the same way and suggested he move in with me.

"Isn't it a little quick to live together?" I asked.

"You already told me how much you want me," he said, caressing my arm. "Don't you want me here?"

"I do, but I just don't want to get ahead of ourselves," I said. "We really haven't known each other very long. I don't want to mess things up."

"If you think it's too soon, I understand," he said. "You've got your shit together: a good job at the newspaper and this apartment. But I'm still working on it. I don't want to pressure you, but I can't stay in that pit I live in much longer. A friend of mine said I could live at his place in San Francisco for a while, and I might go."

I remember feeling my stomach plunge at the thought of him leaving. I flashed on how my hesitation had triggered the end of my relationship with Cliff, and felt an uncomfortable sense of *deja vu*. I knew how this story ended, unless I did something different this time.

"Okay," I said. "Let's do it. Move in with me."

"Really? Are you sure?" he asked.

"Yeah. Let's go for it," I said. "Besides, I just got back to Chicago. I don't want you to move away now."

We made love again, and I felt satisfied and happy afterwards, certain I had made the right decision. All I had to do was look at him naked beside me and I knew how much I wanted him to stay there. I didn't care if it had only been a week: I only knew how much I wanted him at that moment.

The next day, Steven moved in, and we began our life together.

Feeling suddenly chilled, I realized the CD had ended and the sun had set. I hit the replay button on the remote beside me on the floor, advancing to the seventh song: "Little Bird." I felt like that little bird at the moment, wanting to fly far away from here. Steven had robbed me of my sense of self-esteem and security. Our apartment seemed more like a hotel room, a place for temporary assignations, a place to leave.

The clock read 4:12 am when I awoke with a start, my neck and back aching from sleeping on the cold, hard floor. Steven was still out, I realized as I stumbled my way into the bedroom and sprawled on the bed. Seeing that he still wasn't home felt like the final straw. Drawing the blanket tight around me as I drifted back to sleep, I decided, at last, that I needed to put Steven's infidelity behind me once and for all, and get on with my life.

When I awakened again, the sun was pouring in through the east-facing bedroom windows. I sat up, disoriented momentarily, glanced at the bedside clock—8:17—then, at the opposite side of the bed. Steven still wasn't there. I got up, still dressed from the night before, and wandered down the hallway to the living room. The stereo was still in the "play" mode, though the CD had long-since ended. I switched it off and went into the kitchen, where I poured myself a glass of water. I looked into the second bedroom, which we had set up as an office. No Steven. He had not come home yet. I felt my stomach lurch at the reality. I poured my water into the plant on the desk and returned to the bedroom where I pulled out fresh clothes and climbed into the shower.

I let the hot water stream over me for a long time before moving. The heat revived me a little and slowly relieved some of the tightness in the pit of my belly. I stepped directly under the shower, letting the hot water wash the tears down my face. After a while, I felt like I had no tears left—like I would never cry again. I scrubbed my skin furiously, as if I would find a new me somewhere underneath the old flesh.

At the sound of the toilet flushing, I jumped in spite of myself. A moment later, the shower curtains flew apart and Steven's face appeared in the gap. I prayed he couldn't tell I'd been crying.

"I'm home," he said, stifling back a yawn. He looked exhausted, like he'd been up all night. "It was a helluva night at work. We were busy as shit."

"Apparently," I said. "Where've you been?"

"We didn't get the place all closed up till nearly four, and then a bunch of us went out to breakfast and shot the shit. We just sorta lost track of time, you know. Besides, I didn't wanna wake you in the middle of the night."

"Well, that was considerate of you," I said, shutting off the shower and reaching around Steven for the towel bar. He moved aside and handed me a green bath towel. "Thanks," I said.

"So are you ready to talk yet?"

"I guess I am—if you let me get dressed first," I said, stepping from the shower stall and pulling on the pair of boxer shorts I had set on the bathroom counter.

"Why don't we talk over breakfast?" he asked. "I'm starved. I'll let you buy."

"I thought you were at breakfast for the past four hours?" I watched his face for a reaction.

"I didn't have any money," he said, without so much as a flicker of hesitation. "I just drank coffee."

"I see," I said. He was good, I thought. I took the blow dryer off the hook on the back of the bathroom door, plugged it in, and said, "Why don't you wait for me in the living room? I'll just be a minute."

"Okay," he said. "But hurry up. I'm hungry." He backed out of the bathroom and I closed the door after him before plopping down on the toilet seat. I didn't know if I could put his infidelity behind me, after all. Did he really expect me to believe he'd been out drinking coffee for the last four hours? I stood in front of the mirror and began blow-drying my hair. I felt like I had been swallowed whole by a snake and my body was slowly passing through as it digested me, the same way Steven's infidelity was consuming me. It was time I freed myself. I finished getting dressed—powder blue shirt with jeans and deck shoes—took a deep breath, and headed into the living room.

Steven lounged on the sofa, inhaling deeply on a cigarette. A cloud of smoke coiled around his head. I suddenly felt as if I'd never gotten a clear look at him. As if the smoke was an integral part of him: as if there wasn't anything real about him at all.

"All set," I said and he looked up, as if surprised to see me. He looked pleased and smiled at me.

"Great." He stood and walked over to me.

"Let's go," I said, opening the door and pretending I didn't notice he was about to put his arms around me. I could still smell the faint scent of cologne clinging to him, hidden under the smoke.

We headed to a little greasy spoon a couple blocks away on Wabash. Uncharacteristically for downtown, the streets were desolate and silent, the way they are sometimes on early spring mornings. As we crossed the bridge over the Chicago River, I noticed the mist hadn't quite burned off completely yet. It swirled over the water's greenish surface like some parasitic organism sucking life from the river. I understood how the river must feel.

At the restaurant, I ordered only a bagel and orange juice while Steven requested his favorite—pigs in a blanket—with coffee. While we waited, he lit a cigarette and said, "So, what's on your mind?"

I blanched, realizing how much I hated his little cloud of smoke, watching it engulf him again and coil across the table around me as well. I thought about the way the smoke could mask the truth. I thought about Steven's smoke, about Ma's smoke: about how we were all obscured by our little clouds in ways none of us understood.

"I've got a lot on my mind, Steven," I said finally, as the waitress delivered our food. "Jesus, you know Pop's just had a heart attack. The two of us had a horrible fight while I was there, and I don't really know how things will be if—when—he gets better. Maybe I'll never hear from him again. I don't know exactly; I've just had so much on my mind that I feel like I'll lose it if I have to deal with even one more thing right now. Can you understand that?"

"Is that all it's been?" Steven's face relaxed visibly. "I mean, I'm not saying that's nothing—it's just, well, I thought it was something about me. I mean about us. You know, about our relationship." He exhaled a long stream of smoke that seemed to reach straight across the table and down my throat. I had to wash the acrid residue away with a swig of orange juice.

"Well, it's not, so you can relax about that. Nothing for you to worry about," I snapped, aware that my hurt remained. "My family and I have been ripped apart. Nothing important, really."

"That's not what I meant." He stubbed out his cigarette and leaned across the table, ignoring the venom in my words. "I'm just glad I'm not the problem."

"Why would you think that? You got a guilty conscience?" I asked, striving to look innocent as I gave him rope.

"No, of course not," he said a little too quickly and lit another cigarette. "But I've felt like you've been avoiding me since you got back, so what was I supposed to think?"

"Well, like I said, don't worry," I said. "No reason you should feel bad since you haven't done anything wrong. Besides, I'm sure I'll get over it soon."

"I know. I just wish I could do something to help us get back to normal quicker." He looked out the window at the street. Suddenly, he turned back with a look of real excitement on his face, a look I hadn't seen in a long time. "I've got it!" he exclaimed. "Why don't we take a vacation to get away from everyone and everything for a few days? We could maybe go to the Caribbean— just us two—and sort of start over again." He flashed his bright eyes at me. "Sound good?"

"Sounds expensive," I said, shocked at Steven's gall. "How can you afford a vacation when you couldn't even afford breakfast?"

"I can't," he said, flashing a broad smile at me. "But *you* can. Aren't I worth it?"

"I just got back from Florida last week," I protested. "How can I ask my boss for more time off?"

"Well, we could we just go for a long weekend. That way, you'd only need to take a day or two." He watched for my reaction.

A man in black jeans, western shirt, and boots passed our table. Steven's eyes followed him until he disappeared into the restroom. He smacked his lips and said: "Ooh, Daddy!" I felt myself tense up and I wanted to smash the tight-lipped leer off his face.

"You never change, do you?" I snapped, my hurt welling up again.

"Oh, come on, Tony," he said, turning back to face me. "Lighten up. I'm married, not dead."

"Yeah, right," I said. "Well, if you're finished leering at him, let's head back. I need to leave for work soon."

"What about our trip?" Steven asked.

"I don't know," I said as I left money for our bill on the table. "I'll have to see if I can afford the time off and the money right now."

I rose and headed back to our apartment with Steven lagging slightly behind me.

At home, Steven headed into the bedroom as I collected my briefcase and car keys. When I went back to tell him I was leaving, Steven was stretched out naked on the bed.

"Why don't you go in a little late today?" he suggested, grabbing my hand and placing it on his crotch.

"I can't," I said, pulling my hand away and taking a step back.

"Your loss," he said as I grabbed my briefcase and headed back outside.

In the parking garage, I tossed my briefcase on the passenger seat, then started the engine and pulled out of the parking garage. I decided I needed to calm down before going into the office. I stopped at a metered space just off Michigan Avenue and walked across the street. The stifling heat rippled over the wildflower garden, filled with early summer clover and other blooms that Pop used to call weeds as he wrenched them from his garden. On foot, I continued east past the wildflower garden, past the checkerboard tables where street people and retirees played checkers in the shade, past the tennis courts empty in the heat of the day, past the grassy expanse and oak trees, across Lake Shore Drive. I sat in the cool grass that sloped down from the Drive to Lake Michigan at Monroe Harbor, letting the sun bake its heat into my skin. I watched a sailboat skim over the surface of the ocean-sized lake. I remembered driving down to the beach in Florida after my high school graduation ceremony, watching the waves angle in to shore, thinking about walking into the waves until they covered me and washed me away. Here I was again at the shore, again feeling like I didn't understand anything, again wondering what it all meant, again floundering.

Steven's infidelity had left me feeling adrift. Even if I could put it behind me, I wasn't so sure I could learn to trust him again. Hell, he couldn't stop himself from ogling other guys when I was with him. How could I believe he could control himself when I wasn't around? I needed to repair damage that had occurred over the last several years, not just the last week.

If I didn't do something fast, I might fall apart. I needed to break the pattern: Instead of running away like I usually did, this time I needed to stay put. It was Steven who needed to go. But how could I ask him to leave? What kind of monster would that make me?

I remembered a cool day in May 1989, when Steven had showed up unexpectedly at my office and asked if I could take an early lunch with him.

"Of course," I agreed. Clearly, something was wrong. Steven was fidgeting and avoiding eye contact, but I didn't smell anything on his breath. As I grabbed my jacket, I was, nonetheless, immediately on my guard. "Let's go," I said. "Where to?"

"Anywhere." He led the way outside, head down, staring at the ground immediately in front of his feet. He wore dark sunglasses, a denim jacket, and snug, worn jeans that emphasized the roundness of his ass. I felt my penis tingle, despite my concern. When we reached the car, Steven unlocked the passenger door and handed me the keys.

"You drive," he said and slipped into the passenger seat. I watched as he latched his seat belt. All my instincts warned me that something was wrong. Steven always insisted on driving. I went around to the driver's side and climbed inside. Steven stared silently out the window as I started the engine and drove out of the parking lot. Traffic was lighter than I expected. I remembered a little, family-style Greek restaurant called The Bacchanalian just up the street and decided to head there. When we arrived, Steven unlatched his seat belt and headed in without saying a word as soon as I shut off the engine.

Inside, an overpowering aroma of bread baking brought back memories of the hot bread Doughna always had waiting for me because she knew how much I loved it. The hostess seated us at a table in the furthest corner. Steven slipped his jacket over the back of the booth and lit a cigarette before taking off his sunglasses and looking up at me. He had been crying. His green eyes were glassy and red-ringed.

"What's wrong?" I asked, suddenly concerned. I reached out with my hand, but pulled it back before making contact with his short, erect, prickly looking hair. When he had arrived from the hair stylist with his new cut last week, I jokingly told him he looked like a hamster, and he had stomped into the bedroom, slamming the door behind him. It had taken me nearly an hour and profuse apologies to coax him back out.

Steven rolled the salt shaker between his palms for a moment. Then, he pushed it away and glanced up, directly into my eyes. I wanted to look away, but the tautness in his face held my gaze. One blood vessel pulsed angrily under the skin of his left temple.

"I went to the clinic last week," he said, and started crying. He quickly composed himself by grasping his left hand with his right. My stomach muscles contracted reflexively, and I felt sweat beading up on my temples. After a moment, he turned his hands palms up, like he was weighing some invisible object. He started sobbing and looked away.

I felt tears running down my own cheeks, and I brushed them away impatiently. I knew the rest without his saying it. I gripped the edge of our booth with both hands, watching this man in front of me: big, masculine, and unemotional under normal circumstances. He wept openly, and he seemed so small, like a child left by his mother for the first time: inconsolable. I wanted to take his hands, clasp them in mine, soothe him, and brush away the tears on his cheeks, but I couldn't seem to let go of the table.

As Steven continued sobbing, I signaled to the waitress, watching curiously from a distance, to give us a few minutes. Suddenly, it was like three of us were sitting together in that booth: me, Steven, and Steven's virus, all inexorably linked together.

I had noticed Steven's swollen glands shortly after we first got together and had nagged him to get tested ever since, but he had always refused, saying he felt fine. I think I had intuited his infection and that it was the subconscious cause of our reduced intimacy over the years. Now, my worst fears were confirmed.

"Don't worry, Steven," I heard my voice before I knew I had spoken. "I'll take care of you."

"You should run away." He wept, and I could feel his torment. "I wouldn't blame you if you did."

"No," I said firmly. "I've done enough running away in my life. This time, I'm staying put. I won't ever leave you."

"Things are gonna get really ugly, eventually," he warned. "Why should you have to go through it? You should get away while you can."

"There's nothing that could ever make me leave you alone," I reassured him. "I'll be here for you. No matter what."

I heard the faint honk of a car horn in the distance from Lake Shore Drive behind me. I rose and walked along the lake path.

Steven's diagnosis changed us both. I had something to prove, and I refused to run away. I was determined to be there for Steven until the bitter end, whenever that might be.

After his diagnosis, Steven withdrew, no longer wanting to do anything or go anywhere. His only outside activity was his job. If I suggested we see a movie or go out to dinner, he'd decline while insisting I go on my own, saying, "No sense you staying home just because I don't feel like doing nothing."

"It's okay," I'd say, "I don't mind staying home with you." I was uncomfortable with this reversal in our behaviors. I used to be the one who had to be coaxed to go out; now, I was beginning to feel stir crazy.

"Go," he'd insist. "I can use the time alone to think. I just need some time to deal with everything."

So, reluctantly, I'd go. I found it difficult to enjoy myself while Steven fretted about his condition in solitude. The first few times, I came home quickly; but Steven seemed fine and genuinely upset that I had intruded on the time he needed to cope. So, I forced myself to give him space and time to adjust.

About a month after Steven's diagnosis, I went to the clinic myself. Although we practiced safe sex after Steven's diagnosis, we hadn't taken precautions before that time—I had disregarded my "Sicilian radars," the warning signs that had led me to suggest Steven be tested in the first place.

"Is there any particular reason you want to be tested?" the health department counselor asked when I sat down in the sterile, beige room decorated with a worn table and a warped, safe-sex poster.

"My lover tested positive recently," I admitted quietly.

"How long have the two of you been together?" he asked thumbing through the paperwork I had completed in the waiting room.

"More than seven years," I said, watching this nondescript nebbish of a man who had barely glanced up at me since I entered the room. I wondered if he busied himself with the paperwork to avoid having to face his clients' anguish.

"What result do you expect?" he asked.

"That I'm positive," I said with authority, causing him to look up at me at last. He looked me in the eyes and I noticed he had an unusually expressive, sensitive face and deep-set, brown eyes. I imagined he would display great sympathy when my test results came back.

"How do you think you'll react if your results are positive?"

"I don't know," I said. "I think I'm pretty much resigned to it. I can feel the virus inside of me, like a poison."

Looking to the west, I saw the plume from Buckingham Fountain shooting water high into the warm air. The sound of the falling water soothed me.

I remembered my return visit to the same sterile room three weeks later. I started to cry when the same counselor happily pronounced me HIV-negative. My reaction startled him.

"What's wrong?" he asked with genuine concern. "I said you're *not* infected. That's good news."

"You're right," I lied. "I'm just so happy."

"I understand," he said. "You should get tested again in about six months, but this is pretty conclusive, considering you said your last unsafe sex was more than a month ago."

Afterwards, I had decided to walk home along the lakeshore. It was the longest three miles I ever walked. I was deliriously happy about my results, more so because I had been so certain I was infected. I felt like I had won the grand prize in a lottery for life, and the warm sun—a day much like today—on my skin made me feel more alive than ever before. But, in another sense, my joy felt like a betrayal of Steven, a slap in his face: a new dividing line between our lives. And we didn't need any more dividing lines between us.

For more than seven years, Steven and I had stuck together despite obvious problems, both of us knowing that we didn't fit together, except for our mutual—and mutually screwed-up—obsessive need to be in a relationship. I wanted to have someone in my life to take care of, and Steven wanted to have someone in his life to take care of him. In a pathetic, pointless way it worked well enough to sputter on for seven years.

I watched the sunbathers on the beach tossing Frisbees and running on the sand. It seemed obscene. Didn't they realize people were suffering? How could they be so happy in the face of so much pain? I had to concentrate to remember that, only a couple months ago, I had been like them—blithely oblivious. I passed a group of young men playing volleyball. They looked so young, so virile, so carefree. I wondered if I would ever feel that way again.

I passed the mansions of the Gold Coast and thought about the last seven years in Chicago with Steven. Our relationship had devolved into simple companionship a long time ago. We shared a home, a bed, and our finances, but that was about it. I went by myself to see movies and plays, enrolled in a master's writing program and, several nights a month, Steven went country-western dancing or played poker with some of his dance buddies. I told myself this independence demonstrated the strength of our relationship, but now, I saw that it simply had allowed us to grow apart. We spent little time together, and created no new experiences together. In fact, beyond our apartment, we had little in common anymore.

Over the years, our sex life had fallen victim to numerous and significant sexual incompatibilities. I wanted to make love, and Steven wanted to fuck. I wanted romance, and Steven wanted heat. I found anal sex painful and degrading, and Steven felt it was the only "real" sex. So, our intimate moments became few and far between. That they happened at all was more the result of physical need than emotional desire. Steven's diagnosis accelerated the slide, eliminating all but the safest of safe sex: no oral sex, no bodily fluids, no deep kissing. In this safe and clinical way, the final passion trickled out of our relationship like blood from a wound.

As I walked the final steps down Michigan Avenue to our lobby that day, I knew Steven and I had never really fit together. Yet, here we were, seven years together. One life cycle behind us and another, darker one ahead of us. I took a deep breath and headed up to our apartment. Glancing at my watch, I felt relieved that Steven would be at work for several more hours.

I had reconfirmed my test results the following spring and thought about fate and luck. Why was only Steven infected? We had been together more than eight years by now. Why had I remained uninfected after eight years together? Luck had never been a friend of mine—until now, it seemed.

After getting my results, I spoke to Steven's doctor. He said it would be best to let Steven know that I had tested negative during his next regular visit, so the doctor could guide us on how to proceed. Near the end of the appointment, his doctor turned to Steven and said, "I believe Anthony has something to tell you." Steven looked over at me with a puzzled expression.

"Yes," I said nervously. "I, uh, wanted to let you know that I got tested, too, myself." Steven sat back in his seat, but said nothing. "Yes," I said again nervously. "I'm negative. Just to be sure, I even had them test me a second time." Steven remained stone-faced, motionless in his seat.

"So, Steven," his doctor interrupted at last, "That's good news, don't you think?"

"Yeah," Steven said at last. "Of course it's good news." He stood up and put on his jacket. "If that's all for today, I gotta get going. I have to work tonight."

"Yeah," his doctor said tentatively. "If you don't have anything else to discuss, I'm done. I'll see you next month?"

"Of course," Steven said heading out of the office. "Next month."

We left in silence and rode the El home. Back at our apartment, I finally couldn't control myself any longer. "I can't believe you don't have anything to say about my news," I said.

"What do you want me to say?" He asked hotly. "Congratulations. Is that what you wanted?"

"You seem upset," I said, confused. "I don't understand. I thought you'd be happy for me. Would you prefer I tested positive?"

"No, of course not," he snapped. "It's just.... Forget it!"

"Go ahead and say it," I insisted. "I'd like to hear what you have to say."

"I'm happy for you," he repeated. "It's just that it sort of leaves me alone. I assumed we were both positive and going through this together. But we're not: you're healthy. You have a life ahead of you. Why should you hang around? You should get away from me now, while you can."

"Jesus, Steven. We've been through this before. I'm not going anywhere," I said firmly. "We're going to beat this thing together."

"That's what I mean about being alone," he said. "You don't beat this thing. You die."

"Come on, Steven," I said. "You need to keep a good mental attitude."

"Don't tell me what I need to do," he snapped. "I'm doing fine by myself, thank you."

"Bullshit!" I snapped. "Do you think not taking medicine means none of this is real? Can't you see your T-cell count is going down, down, down?"

"And everyone I know who took AZT has died," he shouted. "But I'm still fucking here."

"When will you start taking something?" I shouted. "After you're dead? You've got AIDS, for Christ sake. When will you stop living in denial and do something about it?"

"I know what I've got, Goddammit," he yelled back at me. "And I don't need you—who doesn't have a clue about what it feels like to live with this...this...thing inside you—to tell me what I should do. Just leave me the fuck alone, okay?"

"Come on, Steven, don't get mad at me. I'm just trying to help."

"Fuck you and your self-righteous help," he shouted. "You're only being nice because you think I'm dying. I hate it, do you fucking hear me?" He flung his arms out in frustration and walked over to the window, looking out at the lake.

"Steven," I said, "I'm sorry. I didn't mean to upset you. I don't know what to say to you anymore."

"You make me feel like I'm already halfway in the grave," he said, turning back to face me. His voice broke and tears ran down his face. "I'm still fucking alive! Do you hear me? I'm more alive than you are. That's a goddamn fact."

I said nothing, and after a few seconds, he calmed down. "I don't mean to yell at you," he said at last. "I'm just confused and upset. I'm going to take a walk and then head into work." He grabbed his coat and left.

After the door closed, I held my head in my hands. It was so hard to deal with his outbursts. They seemed to be occurring with greater and greater frequency lately. His doctor had warned me irrational fears and anger were all part of the progression of his disease, and that I shouldn't let it bother me. He said it was Steven's way of venting his fear about what might be coming. So, I let him scream. I let him call me names and curse me. I tried to understand what it must be like to be only 28 and looking death in the face.

Now, all these years later, strolling along the lakeshore with the smell of grass and boat-engine fumes in my nostrils, I decided to make one, last attempt to salvage things. Perhaps Steven was right—maybe we *should* get away from here. Go somewhere we could either tie the frayed strings of our relationship back into place, or else untie ourselves. Maybe the fresh air, the ocean, the tranquility would work their restorative powers on us.

I still loved Steven, but realized we either had to work this out, or move on, even if that meant I ended up alone again; even if it meant admitting I had failed at another relationship and my family had been right about Steven. Steven's infidelity was *his* failure. It didn't mean *my* life was a failure, or that Pop was right about me.

I resolved to book a trip with Steven as soon as I got into the office. It felt good to have a plan, at last. As I headed back to my car, I noticed clouds gathering to the west and hoped the storm would wait until after I got home: It didn't.

CHAPTER 11

Departure

Merritt Island: March 1981

ONE DAY, WHILE still in Florida debating whether to move to Chicago to be with Steven, I stopped by Doughna's place. Doughna, Ma's mother, was my only surviving grandparent, and the gentlest, most accepting woman I knew. I often wondered how Ma could be her child. I had told Doughna I was gay the day before I graduated from high school, before I was completely sure myself. She barely reacted, saying only, "Antonio, what you cannot change, you must accept." She was the only person I could tell I was thinking about moving to Chicago. Instead of judging, she would listen and help me think it through.

Doughna lived in a tiny mobile home on the north end of the island. Stopping by after work, I found her fishing in the broad canal behind her house. Doughna was a small, round, brown, Sicilian woman, soft as the bread dough she was always baking. She wore a big, floral dress, floppy straw hat, and clumpy black nurse's shoes—the only shoes I had ever seen on Doughna's feet.

"Hey, Doughna," I called as I approached the dock, "you look like an old Italian washer woman. I know some homeless woman somewhere is missing her clothes."

Tarantella

"Antonio," Doughna replied in her Sicilian-accented English. She set down her fishing pole, then turned to greet me with a hug and a wet kiss. "This is my fishing outfit," she said, twirling around in a small circle so I could see it from all angles. "You like, huh?"

"I dunno, Doughna," I said dubiously, taking on a serious look. "Those must be the ugliest shoes I've ever seen. And that hat—washer-woman wear, for sure."

"These are the best shoes ever made," Doughna said, as she always did. "They improve your feet. And this hat brings me luck."

"If those shoes help so much, then how come you've always got back pain?" I asked. "And what luck has that hat brought you lately?"

"I hate to think what trouble I'd have if I *didn't* wear these shoes," she said. "As for luck," she proudly snapped the top off the bucket beside her on the dock, revealing an enormous, moss-covered, nasty-looking snapping turtle, "look at this beauty."

"Ugh," I said. "What are you going to do with that?"

"Eat it, of course," she said. "He'll make a fine soup. Why don't you stay for dinner, Antonio?"

"Ugh, no. That's okay, Doughna. I've got other plans."

She recovered the bucket, shaking her head. "Your loss," she said as she retrieved her fishing pole, quickly threaded part of a still-live shrimp on its curved hook, and cast the wriggling bait into the canal with a flip of her wrist. I watched her slowly turn the rod, keeping the pinkish shrimp in motion just under the surface of the opaque, gray-brown canal. Without looking up,

Doughna asked, "So, bambino, you don't visit your Doughna so often these days. Tell me why you're here."

Doughna knew me too well. She spoke slowly and carefully, and her English was quite good. (When she first arrived from Sicily, Doughna once told me some schoolmates teased and called her a "dirty Eye-talian," so she taught herself "proper English, to prove I was a good American, too.") But her accent never completely disappeared, and an occasional word or phrase or a Sicilian pronunciation would pepper her speech.

"You and your intuition," I said, shaking my head.

"That's my 'Sichilian' radar," she said.

Doughna always used the Italian pronunciation of Sicily (as if it were spelled "Sichilia") when she spoke. She believed Sicilians possessed enhanced powers of intuition, which she called 'Sichilian radar.'

"I may be eighty now, but I still *capisce* some things."

"I know that's true," I said, chuckling. I sat on the dock and dangled my feet over the water. I looked back at her. Her face was round and almond-brown, surrounded by the tousled grey hair that peeked out beneath her hat. Her soft brown eyes simultaneously watched me and her fishing line, which was slicing through the water with barely a ripple disturbing the surface.

"You know, I always thought I'd live out my life on Merritt Island," I began. "That's why I came back after graduating from college."

"When will you be moving, bambino?" Doughna asked and reeled in her line. I watched her check the bait and recast. A dog barked somewhere on the opposite shore of the canal. The sun hovered low on the horizon. Doughna eased herself onto one of the two green-and-white *chaise longue* chairs on the dock. I marveled at how her skin still looked as supple as a baby's, despite her eighty years. Her flesh was deeply olive, like Ma's skin. I glanced at my arm—the olive in my own skin was fainter and, like Pop, I burned in the sun.

"I'm not sure. Soon, I think," I answered. Doughna had a way of making things easier. "I'm thinking about moving back to Chicago. It might be good for me to be on my own, and Chicago has so much to offer." I removed my shoes and socks, placing them in a heap beside me, and dipped my feet in the water. It felt sickly warm, like bath water; not in the least refreshing.

"Yes, your parents told me you met someone in Chicago." I looked over at her and wondered if she could read my mind. "Are you sure about this?"

"No," I admitted. "I'm a little scared. It's such a big step, and I just met Steven—that's who I met in Chicago. I don't want to make a big mistake."

Doughna didn't move or react. The tight grey curls of her hair looked like hat fringe. I swished my feet in the brackish water before remembering alligators often found their way into this canal. I stood and sat beside Doughna on the second lounge chair. She reeled in the line again as she considered my words.

"So what if you make a mistake?" she asked, studying my face. "You're young. You will make many mistakes. That's life. You can't be afraid of mistakes, or you won't be able to live."

"I'd be too ashamed to come back here if it doesn't work out," I said. "Ma and Pop would never let me live it down." I cracked the knuckles of my left hand with the right.

"So what? They will say things no matter what you do," she said. "Should that determine how you live your life?"

"No. Of course not." I cracked the knuckles on my right hand.

"Then you need to do what you think best. You can't worry about what your mother or father or even your old-but-wise Doughna says. You've got to make your own decisions, and you can't blame others when you aren't sure what to do. You just make a decision. After all, it's your only life."

"I guess I'm just scared about moving so far away," I replied, knowing Doughna was right, of course. I *was* using Ma and Pop as an excuse to delay a difficult decision. "I wouldn't really know anyone there, except Steven. Most of the people I knew at college have moved away. If things don't work out, I'll be completely alone." I picked a bad shrimp out of the bait cup and tossed it into the water. It floated momentarily on the surface, then vanished in a sudden whirlpool and a splash to some hidden, hungry mouth under the surface.

"I know a little something about moving far away," she said, turning to face me. She reeled in her line, plucked the now-limp shrimp from the hook, tossed it into the water, and placed the fishing pole on the dock beside her chair. "Where would I be if my family hadn't moved to America? Don't you think my parents worried about making a mistake?"

"That was seventy years ago," I said. "Times were different then. Lots of people were coming to America. It wasn't like they were the only ones doing it."

"Times *were* different," she conceded. "You're right about that. But it was even *harder* back then, not *easier*. If you moved and didn't like it, you couldn't just go back. There was no money for that. Think about it: My parents gave up everything they had—their country, their family and friends, their language—everything. If they had been afraid to make a mistake, they never would have come."

"Do you ever miss Sicily, Doughna?" I asked. "Can you even remember what it was like there?"

"I remember only glimpses of Sichilia." Doughna was staring across the canal, remembering. "I was just four years old when we left, but I see it sometimes in my dreams. Mostly, I remember flowers—we always had flowers in our villa. That's probably why I still keep flowers around my house: they remind me of when I was a little girl. And I remember the big church on Monte Pellegrino surrounded by a beautiful garden where I first heard about the miracle of Sante Rosalia. Your sister is named for her."

"Wait a minute," I interrupted. "Rosalia is named after a saint? I don't remember hearing about that."

"Well, it's true," she said, nodding. "Sante Rosalia is the patron saint of Palermo because she saved the city from a plague. Long before the plague came, Sante Rosalia had forsaken the ways of the world. She lived alone and died in the hills outside the city. At the time of the plague, an old priest said the long-dead Rosalia had come to him in a vision. He told the townspeople how to find the cave where Rosalia's bones rested. He said the plague would spare Palermo if they carted her bones around the city three times. The people did as the priest directed, and the plague spared the city." She crossed herself. "In my memories," she continued after a moment, "Sichilia was a magical place.

"Did you know that my mother and father, your great Gramma and Grampa, were younger then than you are now when they decided to move away? And they already had a child—me—to worry about. Still, they knew that—to have a chance to be anything but poor—they must go to America. Imagine moving to a place you had never even seen. You spent four years at school in Chicago and, still, you hesitate."

"Were they scared?" I asked.

"I'm sure they were terrified," she said, "the same way you're frightened to leave Florida. Sichilia was the only home either of them had ever known. Both of their families had lived in Sichilia for generations. But Sichilia was terribly poor, and they knew they must go if they were ever to have a chance for a better life.

"You see, Antonio, a place can be beautiful and full of friends and family and still not be your *home*. We Sichilians believe very much in destiny, you know. Sometimes you just know it's time to leave. If you ignore your intuition—or worry about making a mistake—you may never discover the life you're intended to live.

"Mama and Papi heard about America and knew they had to go. Many Sichilians believed America was a promised land, like in the Bible. They believed there were enough jobs and wealth for everyone—even for poor Sichilian immigrants.

"Did you know our family owned a farm in Sichilia?" she asked, and I shook my head in response. "Well, it's true. My mother and father gave the farm to my uncle when they left. They sold everything we owned to pay for the passage to America. I was only a little girl then, but I still remember how happy my parents were as we boarded the ship that would deliver us to our new lives. Many of our neighbors were on the same ship with us."

Doughna paused and watched the water ripple in the gentle breeze. It was nearly dusk.

"Mama only saw America in her dreams. She died on the boat coming here." Doughna's voice trailed off and she stopped speaking.

"I didn't know your mother died on the boat," I said at last. I had never really paid attention to family history before. I knew almost nothing about either side of the family, except that I was half Irish and half Sicilian. "What happened?"

"Mama dreamed we should go to America. If not for those dreams, I might still be living on our farm in Sichilia, and you might never have been born." She paused again, remembering.

"That first morning on the boat, Mama told me about America. 'America, she is green and beautiful,' Mama said. 'And the money is everywhere. It grows on the trees there. You will see Miriam: we will have a new home in America, the Beautiful.'

"At first, I was excited about America. I imagined we would live in a beautiful palace with flowers and palm trees all around it. Not at all like our little villa in Sichilia, with the paint peeling off the walls. But our little boat was horribly overcrowded and hot, and the voyage seemed never-ending. Many passengers fell sick. They vomited and suffered from diarrhea. Some collapsed and even died in the heat. The terrifying smell of sickness and death was everywhere. I will never forget that smell: like a thousand toilets. We were all filthy and smelly, and the crew treated us like animals. It's amazing what you can endure when you must.

"The women slept below deck on thin pads, covered with little, dirty blankets. We kept all our belongings on the bed with us because there was nowhere else to put them. I felt hungry all the time and complained continuously to Mama, who always seemed to find a little something extra for me to eat. She must've been sharing her meager portion."

A smile flashed across her face like a shadow, then vanished. In the dusk, she removed her hat and placed it on her lap. I closed my eyes and listened to the sing-song music of her voice, trying to envision what it must have been like for her as a four-year old on that ship.

"The only possession Mama brought with us, besides our clothes, was a small painting called 'Adorazione,' the Adoration. Mama loved it. She worried someone might steal it, so she kept it with her all the time—when she slept, when she went above deck, everywhere." She picked her hat off her lap, turned it around, then set it back down. "After Mama died, I kept the painting. It's on my dresser now."

"Can I see it?" I asked.

"Yes. Of course," she said. "Why don't you go look at it while I put away my fishing gear?"

I walked back to the house and into Doughna's bedroom. Her dresser was covered with personal items: two rosaries— one green and one white; pictures of her grandchildren tucked along the outer edge of the dresser mirror; a lilac-colored cameo with an engraved white image of Jesus; an odd triangular ceramic piece depicting three arms with hands clasped; and a small picture with a brass tag at the bottom engraved with the word "*Adorazione.*" The picture showed the baby Jesus in a glowing manger surrounded by Mary and Joseph, a collection of barnyard animals, the Magi, and numerous hovering angels—all with bowed heads. It looked like something you'd pick up in a country craft shop for a dollar. I picked it up and examined the tarnished tag, marveling that, other than Doughna herself, this object was probably the only direct connection to my Sicilian roots. Before heading back to the dock, I draped the white rosary over and around the picture.

"That's all I have left of Mama," Doughna said quietly when I returned. "But it's a beautiful way to remember her, no?" She sat back for a moment, and I was sure she was remembering her mother. Then, she leaned forward and continued her story.

"Just a few days before we reached America," she said, "we ran into a storm. While Papa was off talking to someone, Mama tried to distract me so I wouldn't get scared. She and I rolled our eyes and made faces at each other, and we were both laughing and laughing. Mama's voice, I remember, sounded like tinkling pieces of glass.

"The deck was crowded and, as the boat pitched back and forth, we kept stumbling into other passengers as we tried to keep our balance. Big, dark waves continuously splashed salty sea spray over the deck, like icy rain. A woman near us shouted,

'Jesus, Mary, and Joseph! It's a death sky.' I looked up at the ee-rie, white sky above us and asked Mama what a 'death sky' was. Mama said superstitious people believed a white sky meant God was calling someone to join Him in heaven. I asked her why and she said that only God, in His wisdom, knew why.

"The ship lurched again, and I panicked and ran towards the center of the ship, darting between the legs of passengers along the way. When I reached one of the tall, wooden masts, I clasped my arms around it for balance. The mast felt solid and comforting. Mama stumbled after me, urging me to wait for her. The other passengers surrounded me like trees in a forest, their voices sounded like rustling leaves.

"When Mama caught up with me, she stooped down and held out her hands in front of her, motioning to me and saying, 'Come, Miriam.' But, with the ship pitching strongly, I refused to let go of the mast. 'Do as your mother says,' a former neighbor woman named Louisa shouted to me from the crowd. 'If I were you, Teresa, I'd give her a spanking when I caught her.'

"'Hush, Louisa,' Mama said, "you're frightening her more.'

"'You shouldn't baby her so much,' she replied. 'She needs to grow up.'

"'She's only four,' Mama said as she walked up to me. She ran her hands across my face, pulling my hair back in place as she called back to the other woman, 'Let her be a child while she still can.'

"Behind us, I heard a woman shriek, 'Sante Maria,' followed by a rushing sound like gusting wind. When I turned, I saw this silver hunk of metal attached to a long cable swoop towards us from across the deck. As Mama stood and turned to see what was happening, it struck the side of her head with a crack, lifting her into the air. She fell backwards on the deck and didn't move.

"I waited, still clinging to the mast, for Mama to get back up. I even stomped my foot and said, 'Mama, stop playing.' Then, I heard startled, anguished voices behind me and felt the crowd surging toward me; I felt trapped and suddenly terrified. Mama was lying on the deck with her legs apart and her dress up over her head. She looked like a shattered porcelain doll. I started crying, 'Mama! Mama!' Young as I was, I instinctively knew something was horribly wrong.

"Louisa, who was a large woman with silver hair, came forward and knelt beside Mama, straightening her dress to cover her legs. Around us, the crowd suddenly hushed. I let go of the mast and took a step toward Mama. She looked like she was laughing, but her head was broken down the middle, broken in two like an eggshell, with red and pink things spilling from it. Her red, red blood was everywhere. Louisa must have noticed the horrified look on my face because, like a slow-motion movie, she stood up and covered Mama's head with her shawl. Then, she scooped me up in her strong, dark arms and whispered, 'Poor bambina. Poor bambina.' She turned me away from Mama and said, 'Let's find your Papa, Miriam. Where do you suppose he is?'

"'I don't know,' I said, twisting to see Mama, still not quite sure what had happened.

"'Let's go find him,' she said. I struggled to free myself, but her arms were too strong. 'It's okay, Miriam,' she said. 'You'll be okay. Let's find your Papa.'

"'Mama!' I screamed. 'I want Mama!'

"'Your Mama can't come right now, Miriam,' Louisa said gently. 'Let's find your Papa.' Her shaky voice told me something very bad had happened to Mama.

"I wriggled around to see Mama but the crowd had thronged around her, and I could see only her legs. A few feet away, where it had been knocked when was struck, Mama's painting lay on the deck. 'Mama's picture!' I cried. 'Mama's picture!'

"Louisa turned and called out, 'Luigi! Get that picture for Miriam.' From the time Luigi handed it to me until we moved into our new home in America, I never let that picture out of my sight."

Doughna fell silent. Her lips kept moving but no words came out. She seemed like she had dozed off, only her eyes were open, the way people look in church sometimes. She stared across the canal. The sky had turned purple-black with nightfall.

"We got to America soon after that, but I never saw Mama again after Louisa took me to Papi," Doughna sighed deeply. I watched her belly rise and fall. "I'm sure they had a funeral, but I wasn't included. Everyone was so busy protecting me that I didn't get a chance to say goodbye. Papi told me the angels took Mama. But I knew better. I knew what angels looked like from Mama's painting, and I knew angels hadn't taken Mama. God took Mama away from me with a big metal cleat He swung down from the white death sky."

Doughna traced a soft finger across my face. "You see, Antonio, you don't have to leave to lose people: you can lose them when they're right in front of you. And mistakes are not always what they seem. Mama died coming here. Do you think we made a mistake leaving Sichilia?"

"Of course not. I think you were very brave," I said, trying to imagine the horror of seeing your mother killed before your eyes at four years old. "I guess you're telling me I should go to Chicago."

"No," she said. "I'm saying you should listen to your Sichilian radar. What's your radar telling you?"

"It's telling me I should go," I said. "I mean, I love it here, but I feel like my future is waiting for me up in Chicago."

"Then, I think you already know what you must do," Doughna said quietly. "And I know we should go inside. The mosquitoes are starting to bite. Help your Doughna up, will you Antonio?"

I grasped both her hands in mine and pulled her to her feet. Her skin felt soft and loose around the small bones of her fingers. After I let go of her hands, she turned them over in front of her, as if surprised to see them.

"A couple years after we arrived in America, Papi remarried. My new mother had hands like pieces of wood and a voice that sounded like it had a scratch in it. Nothing like Mama's voice. And my new mother told me always to call her Andrea. She had dark, black eyes that sparkled and flashed, but they never laughed. Not like Mama's eyes," Doughna looked old as she patted my head and led me across the backyard to the house like I was a little boy again. She pulled the screen door open and said, "Let's go inside. We'll have a piece of bread before you go."

Inside, she cut a slice of bread for each of us and carefully spread each with a swath of butter. She handed one to me. It tasted heavenly. No one made bread like Doughna.

"I still miss Mama terribly," she said. "But I've never been sorry we came to America. In Sichilia, we had a saying: '*Chi lascia la via vecchia per la nuova, sa quella che lascia ma non sa quella che trava.*' It means, 'He who leaves the old way for the new knows what he leaves, but not what he will find.' That doesn't mean we shouldn't try new things. Life is a mystery, and the only mistake is not living it. Sometimes you have to leave to find yourself."

As I drove home that night, I knew I would go to Chicago, knew I needed to leave Ma and Pop behind. I thought about Paddy. Had he felt like this when he ran away? Had he wavered indecisively over whether to stay or go? What had decided it for him? On the surface, I was going to be with Steven, but I knew, as I suspect Paddy before me must have known, I was going partly to hurt Pop. Pop would never admit it hurt him, of course; but I think Paddy and I knew it would. I told myself I was leaving for other reasons—sensible reasons—and that the pain it caused Pop was merely an unavoidable, albeit not unpleasant, side-effect. Inside, I sensed that causing Pop pain had been part of Paddy's reason for leaving, just as inevitably as it was part of mine. As I drove home that night, I hoped it wasn't the primary reason. What I failed to consider was that I would also be leaving Doughna Mira behind, one of many unforeseen and unintended side effects.

I decided to leave after Rosalia's wedding the next month. That would give me time to make arrangements and give notice at work. If I was lucky, I might even be able to land a job in

Tarantella

Chicago before I left Florida. Excited by my decision, I called Steven to let him know, but he wasn't home. I left a message on his answering machine. I decided to tell Ma and Pop over our next Sunday dinner; I would tell Rosalia separately afterwards.

That night, dreams permeated my sleep. Because I so rarely remember my dreams, I attach great significance to the few that linger. That night, my dreams scared the hell out of me. Around 3 a.m., I snapped awake, bolt upright and panic-filled in the darkness, struggling to recall every detail. I had been hiking through dense undergrowth, thick with scrub palms and vines, feeling both happy and a little anxious. Every now and then, I thought I heard someone following me, but when I looked back, I saw only the thick vegetation. I slowed my pace, picking my way carefully, stopping in places to look for signs of whomever or whatever was following me. Nervous sweat prickled my back, and I started moving more quickly, hoping to put some distance between me and whatever was stalking me.

Suddenly, I emerged from the dark, shadowy undergrowth into a vast expanse of waist-high, sabre-sharp sawgrass and a few scattered palmettos and live oaks. Despite the blinding sun, the ground was swampy, and smelled of mildew. To my left, I heard a rustling. As I turned to look, I saw a shadowy figure emerge from the wood about a hundred yards away and head in my direction.

Seized by sudden terror, I scrambled to get away. The shadow-figure chased after me as I plunged into the sawgrass, wincing as the stiff, sharp blades sliced into my legs and arms, but I was too terrified to stop. Glancing over my shoulder, I saw the shadow-figure closing on me rapidly and effortlessly, apparently unaffected by the sawgrass or the uneven ground.

A few dozen yards ahead, Steven suddenly appeared in the distance and beckoned to me. Relief and surprise flooded through me, and I ran towards him. Steven hugged and groped me, then stepped back and pulled a gun out of his waistband. He put the gun in my hands and pointed at something behind me. I wheeled around, catching a glimpse of the shadow-figure racing towards us. I thrust the gun in front of me and shot frantically as I slipped in the mud and careened into the sawgrass. I tumbled over, ending up flat on my back, coated with mud and grass and my own blood.

I heard the sucking sound of Steven's feet in the mud as he approached.

"Are you okay?" he asked, reaching down to help me to my feet. He was golden and beautiful, like some sleek panther.

"I'm fine," I said, glancing at myself. Blood and muck coated me from head to toe. "Did I get it?" I asked, motioning towards where the shadow-figure had been and brushing the filth from me.

"I think you hit it. It fell in the grass over there," he pointed and started heading to our right. I followed him. Suddenly, he stopped short and I felt my pulse quicken.

"Whatever it is, it's right over there," Steven whispered. He took a final, cautious step forward, then gasped.

"What?" I asked, stepping around him to see for myself. "What is it?"

Tarantella

Before me, sprawled in the grass with a gaping wound in his chest lay Pop. His white hair practically glowed under the bright sun. As I bent over him to see if he was breathing, his eyes opened suddenly. He grabbed my collar and snarled, "You think you can run away, but you're wrong! You'll never escape me. Never."

I lay in the dark thinking about my dream. Surely it was a sign, I thought. While I was replaying the details, the sound of the phone shattered the silence. I picked up the receiver, glancing at my bedside clock—5:18 a.m.—who could be calling me at this hour?

"Hello?" I said.

"Tony?" It was Steven's voice. "Did I get you up?"

"Actually, I'm awake," I said.

"You been out at the bars, too, eh?" he said.

"What?" I asked, not following him. "No. Bad dream."

"Oh," he said. "Too bad I'm not there. I'd make you forget all about it." He was slurring his words.

"What are you doing up at this hour?" I asked.

"I just got your message and I wanted to call you." He paused for a moment and I could hear him taking a drag on a cigarette. "I can't wait till you get up here. I knew when I met you that I'd found me a keeper."

"Mmmm," I said, feeling drowsy. "I can't wait to get up there, either."

"So, what was your dream about?" he asked.

I told him, and I could hear him puffing on his cigarette while he considered it.

"That's some freaky shit, huh? My dreams are mostly about sex," he said at last. "Seems like a sure sign that you need to get away from your old man. Jesus, now he's hunting your ass down."

"Yeah," I said. "Seems like someone's telling me I should go. I wish I could be there with you right now."

"Me too," he said. "I'm horny as hell, and you know how bad I'm aching to pop that cherry of yours." I winced at his raw language. "I'd take real good care of you."

"Soon enough," I said, changing the subject. "I'll be there next month."

"I wish it was sooner," he said.

"Me too," I said, "but I'll be there before you know it." In the background, I heard someone's voice, and there was a pause before Steven spoke again.

"Well, I should get some shut-eye," he said at last. "Well, you get back to sleep, and don't let no bedbugs bite." Before I could reply, the phone went dead.

As I hung up the receiver, my thoughts returned to my dream. Perhaps Steven *was* my white knight. Perhaps he would rescue me from Pop's influence. I accepted the dream as a sign that I needed to get away from the island, that my move to Chicago was the right decision.

Heading to dinner at Ma and Pop's that Sunday, I felt a little nostalgic because I knew I would be leaving soon. I drove across the

island, feeling its pull on me like the sun pulling at the ocean.
Yet, I knew I had to go, or I'd always find myself battered against
Ma and Pop's craggy shoreline.

When I arrived at Ma and Pop's, I lingered in my car in
their driveway for a few minutes, bracing myself, and looking
at this house where I had grown up. My senses tingled, the way
they do on brisk winter mornings up north when you first step
out into the cold from the warmth of your house. On this day,
when I had come to take my leave, the air should be cold—
bitter—I thought. The ground should be frozen and white, like
tundra. But I was still in Florida. The sun blazed overhead, and
it was nearly ninety degrees: hot, even for Florida in March.
Heat rolled from the car's interior like a broiler pan and rippled
in front of the aquamarine coquina house.

Even inside the car, I could smell the intoxicating scent of
orange blossoms from the tree out back. They smelled overly
sweet, almost sickly. The house looked dark and still inside, despite the bright day. The windows reflected the sunlight like mirrors. No hint of life disturbed the stillness. The house reminded
me of Pop: dark, imposing, inscrutable.

For a moment, I considered leaving for Chicago right then,
without saying a word; just driving away and calling them after it
was too late for them to try to stop me. Instead, I climbed out of
my car and went inside.

Ma and Pop were seated just inside the front door on the living room sofa, a floor fan directed toward them, with the television blaring. An eerie white light filtered into the room through
the sheers, and the air was so thick with smoke, it made me gag.

Ma and Pop looked up at the sound of my entry, and Pop clicked off the volume with the remote.

"Well, well. Lookit who's come to visit us," Pop said belligerently. "To what do we owe the honor of this visit? You here to whip up more trouble? If that's it, you can just walk your ass right back out, same as you came in."

"Don't start, Pop, okay?" I said barely acknowledging him. "I don't have the energy for it today. It's too hot."

"Both of you stop," Ma said, already nervously fumbling with her cigarettes. She plucked one out, slipped it between her lips, and lit it with a match as she spoke. The cigarette bobbed up and down with each syllable like a tiny, impotent conductor's wand. She looked right at me and said, "Can we shoot for a little peace in this family for a change?" She glanced in Pop's direction. "Both of you."

"It ain't me," Pop said, pointing in my direction. "All he's gotta do is quit disrupting the family."

"Pretend I'm not gay, you mean." I waved my hands for a time-out, regretting instantly that I'd let myself get provoked so swiftly again. "It doesn't matter, Pop. I'm not here to talk about any of that." I took a deep breath and blurted out my news: "I'm here to tell you I'm moving back to Chicago after Rosalia's wedding."

"Chicago?" Ma pulled the cigarette from her mouth, shocked, looking first at Pop and then back at me. "Why? Does this have anything to do with your friend, Steven?"

"Yes and no," I said. "I mean, I hope things work out with Steven, but I would be moving even if he weren't in Chicago."

Even as I said it, I wasn't sure it was true: if Steven weren't in Chicago, I wasn't sure I'd be going back there. But Steven *was* in Chicago, so what I *might* have done if he weren't there wasn't really relevant.

"Sounds more like yes than no," Ma said, as if reading my mind. "Don't let him talk you into something you might regret, Anthony. After all, you hardly know the boy."

"He's a man, Ma, not a boy," I said. "And I'm a grown man. No one talked me into anything. This is my decision. I need a fresh start."

"You call it a fresh start," Pop interjected. "I call it running away."

"Bullshit," I retorted. "I'm not *running* away from anything." I hated when he could see right through me like that. It was like he had an unfair advantage. We never agreed on anything and yet, we were so much alike we could see right through one another's bullshit. It was infuriating, especially when—most of all—you were lying to yourself.

"You're just like Paddy," he said.

"I'm *not* like Paddy," I shouted, angry now. "I'm twenty-three years old, for Christ's sake. Paddy ran away when he was sixteen."

"Don't matter how old you are," Pop said, standing and pointing at me. "You can run away when you's fifty. You ain't going *to* Chicago so much as you's running *away* from here. You can't stay and fight your battles like a man, so you's running away from them like a scared, little sissy. But that's the way you been all your life. You and Paddy, both: two of a kind. Botha yous would rather run away than deal with a thing."

Hadn't I known it would play out this way when I arrived? I knew they'd be angry about my decision; knew they'd know my real reason for leaving; knew we'd end up fighting; knew I'd end up storming out of the house. In fact, we *all* knew all of these things. I also knew I needed to go through it all to work up my righteous indignation. This way, I could feel justified—both about going...and about hurting them.

"You're a son of a bitch," I said. "You got some nerve calling me a sissy. Hell, I can't even talk about my life in your goddamned house. You make all the rules and you make life hell if I don't obey them. Well, I'm not five years old anymore, Pop. You can't make me bend over and touch my toes while you paddle my ass."

Then, unexpectedly, I turned toward Ma at the table just beside the front door and said, "And you might be worse than him."

She looked up, startled by the rage in my voice.

"He's always at me about something," I continued, words pouring from me before I knew what I was saying, "but at least from him I know what to expect." I took a step forward and waved my index finger in her face. "But you're my mother and you *let* him. When I was little, you let him hit me, and now that I'm older, you're still letting him. Why don't you ever stand up for me? Why didn't you ever protect me? I was five years old, and you let him ruin me."

Pop jumped up and lunged toward me. "Don't you talk that way to your mother, you little bastard."

"Don't I wish that was true," I said coldly, letting my irony register. "Don't worry, I'm going. Maybe I *am* running away—running away from the two of you. And, don't worry Pop, after I go, I'll never be back under your roof again. You won't have to hear anything ever again from your fag son, since you're so fucking ashamed of me." I pulled the door open and stepped outside.

As I angrily backed out of the driveway, I saw Ma come running from the house. She was yelling something at me, but I didn't want to hear anything more from either of them. I looked her square in the face as I defiantly waved my middle finger at her. I instantly regretted my juvenile action as I put the car in gear and roared down the street, leaving a swirling cloud of smoke and dust in my wake. As I passed the house, Pop was silhouetted in the window, like a shadow watching me go.

That night, my own screaming woke me from my sleep. In my dream, I was standing before a mirror. My mouth was bloody and I was missing all of my teeth. I screamed at the reflection in shock.

After waking, the dream triggered a memory of how, every night, for more than a week when I was nine, Ma had screamed herself awake in the middle of the night. She would begin by moaning, and build to a wailing, shrieking crescendo. At the time, Paddy still shared a room with me. He would slip into my bed, cradling me in his arms, telling me to go back to sleep, and that everything was okay. I remember lying awake most of those nights, feeling simultaneously safe in Paddy's arms and too terrified to close my eyes until I saw the sun pouring in through the curtains.

Ma said she dreamed she was on a street corner with an empty tin can, begging for coins. But when she peeled off the plastic lid to look inside, the can was full of teeth—black, rotten, and smelling like dead fish. Panicking, she put her fingers in her own mouth and discovered her gums were bare. That's when she started screaming.

I hadn't understood, so Ma explained that Sicilians believe losing your teeth in a dream foretells you're about to lose someone in real life. At the time, I laughed and told her she was just being superstitious and silly.

Sitting up in my bed now, realization struck. I felt suddenly light-headed, my breath coming in short gasps. Fifteen years ago, back in New York, Ma's nightmares had stopped when Paddy ran away. Now, I was about to leave.

The next day, I met Rosalia for lunch to tell her I was moving. Of course, she would already have heard about it from Ma and Pop. After we ordered, Rosalia, direct as usual, cut to the chase.

"Okay," she said. "I already know you're moving to Chicago."

"I figured you would," I said. "Ma and Pop probably called you before I made it off their block."

"Sounds like you had a pretty big blow-out," she said.

"What else?" I said. "Is there any other way to tell Ma and Pop something they don't want to hear? Why can't they ever just support my choices?"

"Maybe they feel like your choices seem targeted at them," she said.

"Oh, come on, Rose," I protested. "I'm moving to Chicago because it has better jobs, better opportunities—Ma and Pop have nothing to do with it."

"Oh, really?" she asked coolly. "So, you didn't realize it would hurt them? Yesterday's scene wasn't part of that plan?"

"Of course not," I lied. "I mean, I knew they wouldn't like it. But that's not why I'm leaving." Rosalia usually backed me: I hadn't expected her to take their side.

"Right," she said. "If you want to believe that, fine." She forked at her salad for a moment in silence. "Look, Anthony, it's your decision and, of course, I'll support you. I just don't think you should lie to yourself about it. We all know part of this is about sticking it to Pop...even if all those other reasons are also true. And having a big fight with them yesterday is part of it—maybe the most important part. We all know that, too."

"Let's just say, I knew it'd turn out the way it did," I admitted. "I don't know that it's what I wanted. Just once, I'd like to tell them something and have them say, 'Great!'"

"Would you, really?" she asked. "I swear, you and Pop love the battle too much to ever get along. I don't think either of you could ever just agree with the other one." She signaled to the waiter to take the remainder of her salad. "Anyhow," she continued, "you know I'm gonna miss you like hell. I hate the thought of you moving so far away."

"I know," I said. "I'll miss you, too. But I'll come back to visit you and you can come to Chicago."

"It's not the same," she said, "but I suppose it'll have to do. Anyhow, I'm glad you're waiting until after my wedding to leave. Just promise me you won't fight with Ma and Pop at my wedding."

"I promise I won't *start* anything," I said. "But you know how Pop is."

"But nothing!" she said sternly. "I swear I'll never speak to you again if you ruin my wedding, Anthony. I don't care what Pop says to provoke you, you better not fight with him. Can't you just, for once, ignore him?"

"I'll try," I said. "If you'd rather I didn't come, I'll understand."

"I didn't say that!" she said. "Jesus, you're so quick to play the martyr. I just want you to behave. This day isn't about you, so please try to get along and enjoy yourself. It'll be the last time we'll see each other for a long time, so let's make the most of it. Okay?"

Rosalia got married on a beautiful Saturday afternoon in April 1981, in the gold pyramid of Divine Mercy. I arrived at the church shortly before the ceremony, and took my seat in the pew behind Ma and Pop, who watched me walk in, and turned away without acknowledging me. This was going to be difficult. I felt like a naughty school boy who was being observed closely for any hints of unruliness.

The ceremony was a full mass, led by Father James, whom I had not seen since I stopped coming to church because of my feelings for him. He was still a beautiful man, and all my long-forgotten feelings for him resurfaced. I decided to go up for the wine and wafer, despite never having made my First Communion, and I felt a surge of excitement as I took them from Father James' hands. As I returned to my seat, I noticed Ma and Pop scowling at my violation of the sacraments, and I looked away.

After the wedding, we headed to the Cocoa Beach Hotel ballroom for the reception. I planned to stay only a couple hours since I was leaving the next day for Chicago. But the party kicked into high gear after a meal of lasagna was served. The band began playing, and couples started to dance. I sat at the table with Doughna and watched.

Doughna wished me luck in my new life in Chicago. "And you better write to me," she added, laughing, "or I'll put a Sicilian curse on you. You don't want to mess with that."

Ma and Pop stayed at the head table. Every now and then, they got up to dance; they never said a word to me.

I lost track of time and suddenly, the band announced it would play two final songs: first, a traditional Italian wedding song for the new couple and their parents, and finally, a traditional tarantella for the rest of us. As Rosalia, Trap, Ma, Pop, and Trap's parents made their way to the floor, the band began playing the slow, sweet strains, and Doughna leaned close to my ear.

"Antonio," she said, "will you dance the tarantella with me?"

"Of course," I said, surprised by her request. I never recalled seeing Doughna dance before. "Are you sure?"

"Are you surprised to find out that I still dance at my age?" she asked, smiling with self-satisfaction at me.

"A little, I guess. I don't think I ever saw you dance before."

"I don't dance very often these days," she said. "But the tarantella is a very special dance. Do you know the story?"

"I don't think so," I replied.

"It's a very old Italian legend," she began. "If a tarantula bites you, the poison slowly works its way into you. The pain and fever increase gradually, until you're seized by a delirium that causes you to jump up from your sick bed and begin leaping and twirling around, as if you're dancing. The pain makes you move and spin faster and faster and faster."

The strains of the Italian wedding song slowed to a stop, and everyone applauded. As the first notes of the tarantella were struck, Doughna and I stood and headed for the dance floor. At the edge of the floor, Doughna pulled up short.

"What is it, Doughna?" I asked. "Have you changed your mind?"

"No," she said. "But I have to finish my story first." She reached out and touched my cheek. "Then, you will understand why I wanted to dance with you."

"What is it?" I asked, leaning down toward her.

"You see, Antonio, the poison and the pain bring on the frenzy. But if you whirl about fast enough, you can work the poison out of your system and live on."

"And if you don't?" I asked.

"Then, the poison kills you," she said. "Unlike you, when I was young, I had no choices. My parents married me to a man from the old country when I was only 13. By the time I was old enough to know my mind, I had responsibilities to my own children and to a husband I had promised to honor. My husband was very unhappy. His danced his tarantella for years, but the poison finally took him. After that, my life changed. Becoming a nurse was my best decision, but my path in life was already set. Don't let that happen to you! You are still young and you can do whatever you want. You must dance your own tarantella!"

She took my hand and drew me onto the dance floor. The rhythm gradually grew faster and faster and those of us on the dance floor whirled and spun around and around. The dancers clasped hands and moved across the floor in undulating formations. The music and the dancing became frenzied, and I imagined this was what the phrase "whirling dervish" meant. We were laughing and throwing back our heads, letting our hair flow free. Sweat poured off me, and I wondered how Doughna could move so frenetically at her age. She was holding her hair over her head with her hands and swaying with her hips. Near the end of the dance, Doughna grasped Pop's hand. Doughna linked me to Pop, and Pop was linked to Ma and Trap and Rosalia and all the other dancers. We spun and spiraled until the room itself seemed to vanish in a blur of colors—red and green and white—and only the pulsing music remained.

Then, abruptly, the music ended, and on the floor, we pulled up short. I could hear the wheezing of labored breath and scattered laughter. Doughna pressed her hand on her chest as she caught her breath. When the lights came up, I was standing directly in front of Ma and Pop. They blinked at me in surprise, still dabbing sweat from their foreheads. Neither they nor I knew what to say, so we said nothing, only nodded at each other as I turned to collect my things and headed for the door.

I spotted Doughna standing in the doorway, watching. I went to her and kissed her goodbye, hugging her tightly against me.

"Do you think it worked?" I asked.

She shook her head. "No way to know. Sichilian magic is mysterious and takes time. We'll just have to wait and see."

"Thank you," I said.

"You're welcome, *bambino*," she whispered. "I know you will work it out. This I am sure of."

"I hope you're right, Doughna, but I have never felt so uncertain," I said, then turned and headed toward my car.

After I got inside, I sat for a moment with my hands braced against the dashboard and exhaled deeply. In the silent darkness, I heard the whisk-whisk of the blood scuttling through my veins, as if trying to purify itself.

CHAPTER 12

Losses

Chicago: August 1994

RELUCTANTLY, I DECIDED to try one last time with Steven. Maybe by going away somewhere—just the two of us—we could honestly examine our relationship and fix it, or end it amicably. I booked us on a flight to the Bahamas. Before I knew it and could reconsider, we were on our way.

I pushed back in my seat to recline. Maybe if I could just close my eyes for a little while, I'd feel rested by the time the plane landed in the Bahamas. I looked over at Steven in the window seat beside me. He leaned up against the window, trying to glimpse the ground below. A thick layer of dense white clouds floated around and below us, frustrating his efforts.

"Why is it always so fucking cloudy whenever we fly somewhere?" he asked without looking at me. "I swear, I've never seen a thing in all the times I've flown."

"Uh-huh," I mumbled drowsily.

Steven turned toward me, quickly undoing his seatbelt. "Oh, no you don't," he said. "You let me out before you even think about going to sleep. I ain't getting trapped in this little space for the whole flight."

I roused myself and shot him an annoyed glance, then stood to let him pass. "Where you gonna go?" I asked.

"Nowhere," he said. "I'll just stand or go talk to the stewardesses. You can stay here, but don't even think about taking the window seat, cuz I'll be back."

"Fine." I resettled myself into my seat and closed my eyes. "See you later."

"Right," he said and I squinted one eye open, watching him trot down the aisle. I was still trying to convince myself that this trip would be just the thing to bring about a resolution: either to bring Steven and me back together again, or to end things once and for all. Yet, my insides quivered like gelatin, and something told me not to expect easy clarity or acceptance.

Steven, of course, looked on it all as a great adventure, apparently oblivious to the changes I felt so tangibly. I thought about the last week-and-a-half, waiting for this trip. Steven had suddenly become solicitous of me, returning home promptly after work each day, making dinner not once, but on three separate occasions, surprising me with a flowers-and-candlelight evening, moderating his drinking, and courteously not smoking around me. All of these changes, sudden and dramatic, created a rising panic in me, rather than what I'm certain was the hoped-for-response—increased generosity and softening towards him. Instead, I reacted with suspicion. The change was too fast, too easy, and too uncharacteristic to be sincere—a temporary, Bahamian-trip-induced transformation: I felt like I was being set up for something. Steven was playing the fiddle but, for once, I was demurring on the perimeter of the dance floor before agreeing to dance.

I started in my seat, aware I had been dreaming again. My back ached from my awkward position in the seat. A young, red-haired woman across the aisle glanced over and smiled at me briefly. Fighting to overcome the drowsiness instilled by the droning plane engine, I wondered where Steven was. I struggled to my feet, stretching to wring the cramp out of my spine.

Thinking back to when we first met, I now saw that Steven had been seeking someone to take care of him. He was in a bad place then, living one step away from the street in a lousy one-room in a bad part of town. Although he'd never admitted it, I suspect he was being evicted, and that's why he was in such a hurry to move in with me. Steven saw a soft-touch in me—someone who'd take care of him: house him, clothe him, feed him—and, in return, all he had to do was say the right lines and sleep with me. Those were two things at which Steven had become very accomplished by the time we met. Naïve and lonely as I was, I never questioned his motives.

I was not really blameless or unaware either. Hadn't I needed someone to take care of? Someone to raise and lavish things on; someone to reassure me that I was nothing like Pop; someone who would say all the things Pop had never said to me: things like how smart I was, and how good I was. I needed a man to hold me at night and still be there in the morning when I woke.

I had gotten just what I had bargained for: Steven had obediently said the right things, and had done what he had to do so he could feel safe and protected.

Christ, I thought, *I was as guilty of deceit as Steven.* We had used each other to satisfy our own needs. How could I now condemn him when I had done the same thing? Was I turning into Pop? Was it myself I was trying to run away from all this time? Had I deliberately sought out another man incapable of showing his feelings, so I could rebel against him the way I had rebelled against Pop? Did I think I could avoid the truth about myself by attacking Steven for not loving me and, if so, why did Steven put up with it too? What was he getting out of our relationship?

I felt like I might be sick, and headed to the restroom at the back of the plane. As I came down the aisle, I heard Steven laughing. I glanced down: Steven was seated with a curly, dark-haired man who looked about thirty. The man was tan and muscular and balding at the top of his head. He and Steven were so engrossed in conversation, I felt embarrassed seeing them together, as if I were invading their privacy. I slipped into a vacant restroom, bolting the door behind me.

I sat on the commode, shutting my eyes and cradling my head in my hands as a bout of nausea swept over me. I gagged and my throat convulsed, but nothing came up. Blackness swirled around me. I wished I could just vomit out all the sickness I felt inside. Spasms gripped my belly, but the sickness remained inside of me. Gradually, the blackness lifted, my spasms eased, and

Tarantella

I opened my eyes and gingerly raised my head. I stood at the sink, splashing water on my face, then wiping it dry with a paper towel.

Jesus, I thought, *why in hell did I guilt myself into this trip?* It was already a disaster and we hadn't even landed yet. What I really needed was private time to think and sort things out. Taking a deep breath, I opened the door and headed quickly past Steven and the curly-haired man. I got back to my seat just as the captain announced he had turned the seatbelt sign on for landing. A moment later, Steven reappeared.

"Have you been asleep this whole time?" he asked as he slid past me into his seat.

"Mostly," I said. "What've you been up to?"

"Nothing," he lied expertly, leaning forward to peer out the window. "Just stood around and talked with the stewardesses."

After we got to our hotel on Paradise Island, Steven decided to shower while I unpacked. He stripped off his clothes, piled them on the bed, and headed into the bathroom. I unpacked my bag, then decided to lay down and rest my eyes until Steven finished up. As I moved Steven's clothes to the chair beside the desk, a wrinkled scrap of paper fluttered from the pile. I caught it midair and uncrumpled it. In neat handwriting, it read: "Jim Ritts, Paradise Hotel." I felt stricken. Blood drained from my body, and I angrily recrumpled the note, dropping it like poison onto the pile of Steven's clothes. I slumped onto the bed, cursing Steven and cursing myself for being stupid enough to get sucked into coming here with him. I was hurt and angry and sad all at once. One second, I wanted to run away from here, to get as far away from Steven and his infidelities as I could. The next second, I wanted to storm into the bathroom and fling the dirty evidence at him in the shower and demand an explanation. Only, I didn't need an explanation. I could only too clearly visualize the curly-haired man I had seen on the plane—handsome and masculine. Obviously, they planned to meet. I wanted to cry. Or puke. I felt terrified and expectant, like I had while Ma and Mrs. Williams searched for me as a child on the cliff top in New York. Something was about to happen, but the outcome was still uncertain.

I heard the shower stop and Steven whistling as he toweled off in the bathroom. I imagined him thinking about Jim Ritts. I got up hurriedly, slipped off my Topsiders, and climbed into the bed fully dressed. Steven emerged from the bathroom freshly washed and refreshed. He put his hands on his hips and shrugged when he noticed me in the bed.

"What's wrong?" he asked.

I looked up at him. "What do you mean? Nothing's wrong," I said. "I just feel a little worn out, that's all. I think I'll take a little nap."

"Now?" he asked, as if I'd suggested the most ridiculous thing in the world. "I thought we were here to have a good time? Why don't we go check things out?"

"Go ahead," I said. "Why don't you come back here in about an hour and we can decide what to do next? By then, I should be rested."

"Fine," he said, clearly perturbed. He pulled on a fresh pair of white walking shorts and a salmon-colored polo shirt, headed back into the bathroom, and then I heard him blow-drying his hair. He reemerged and said, "See you later" as he headed out the door. I pulled the covers up around me and closed my eyes. The elevator chimed in the hallway as the scent of Jovan Musk drifted out of the bathroom. I wished I could fall asleep and never wake up again.

When I did wake, the light in the room had vanished. I sat up in the dark and checked the LED display on the alarm clock beside the bed: 8:12 p.m. I had been asleep for over five hours. I slipped out of the bed and turned on the light, wondering where Steven was. I noticed the message light blinking on the phone and called down to the front desk. Steven had left a message saying he was heading to the beach and would see me later tonight.

I hung up the phone, angry enough to spit. I picked up the receiver again and dialed the front desk a second time.

"Do you have a number for the Paradise Hotel?" I asked. I wrote the number on the notepad beside the phone, immediately dialed it, and asked for Jim Ritts' room. The room phone began ringing—once, twice, three times, and I nearly hung up. On the fourth ring, someone picked up and, after a short pause, a man's voice said, "Hello." I panicked and hung up, trying to decide if the voice had been Steven's. I couldn't tell for sure, and I felt stupid for calling. *What the hell was I thinking? What had I planned to say?*—"*Hello, Steven, get your dick out of that man and come back to me?*"

I didn't want to be around when Steven got back, so I quickly changed into clean clothes and brushed my hair. Looking at myself in the mirror, I decided I looked passable and headed out.

The night was humid and warm. Stars filled the sky, and I could hear voices of people talking and laughing around me. I decided to go to a restaurant in one of the hotels down the road. I sat alone at a table for two and ordered myself a glass of wine and jerk chicken, lingering over my meal, delaying my return while considering how I could make it through the next two days until our return flight to Chicago. I had no idea how to handle the situation, and gave up trying to figure it out. What would it help to worry about it now, anyhow? I would simply deal with it for two days. Then, we'd be back in Chicago. Steven would leave, and I would get on with my life without him.

I looked out the window beside my table and watched the light twinkling off the waters of the bay. The water looked dark, and a long, high bridge spanned the darkness west to the main city of Nassau, resembling the expanse of the Indian River between Merritt Island and Cocoa. I wondered what Ma and Pop were doing just then. Pop had returned home about a week ago. Rosalia had called to tell me when he left the hospital.

"You should call him," she'd said timidly.

"Right," I said sarcastically, "and Martin should call Lewis, and the Pope should call the Ayatollah."

"Come on," she said, "you know he's not gonna live forever. What'll you do if he dies? Do want that on your conscience?"

"If he dies, he dies," I snapped. "Not everything that happens to Pop is my responsibility."

Tarantella

"That's not what I meant," she said.

"I know," I said. "But I'm not calling him. Every time we talk, we fight. There's just no point. He'll never accept me, and I'll never accept his not accepting me."

"You know," she said, "sometimes people can agree to disagree. The point is," she continued, "we're down here dealing with this, and we need you."

"No one needs me, Rosalia," I said.

"Ma could use your support," she shot back. "And so could I."

"You just want us all to make lovey-dovey, and I wish I could. I really do," I said. "But it's not going to happen. The only thing that would happen if I flew down there is me and Pop would end up in another big fight. It's what we do."

"It could change if you wanted it to change," she said, frustrated. "I just don't understand how you can head off on a vacation at a time like this. Doesn't Pop mean anything to you?"

"What the hell should he mean to me, Rose? I'm not so sure I know anymore. There was a time when I would've been there before you could hang up the phone. Not anymore. It's all broken now, all screwed up. We're like two strangers to each other. In fact, two strangers probably treat each other better. I don't know what he is to me anymore."

"Your *father*," she said coldly. "He's your *father*, Anthony. And he's dying."

"I know who he is," I said, resolute. "He's nothing to me. And I'm nothing to him."

After I hung up, I wondered how the waters could twinkle so romantically while an old man was dying in Merritt Island and my lover was cheating on me at the Paradise Hotel, which I could see lit up in white lights at the end of the road.

I headed back to our hotel room, slowing my pace as I drew closer, reluctant to face Steven, and unsure of what I could say to him. When I unlocked the door and stepped inside, the room was dark and empty. Again, the message light was blinking. This time, his message said he had called to meet me for dinner but, since I wasn't there, he would just head over to a casino for a while and he'd be home later. I erased the message, wondering if Steven had been with Jim Ritts all day. I headed in to wash up for bed, wondering why Steven had even suggested this trip if he hadn't intended to make the slightest attempt to reconnect with me. Why go to such lengths? Was it simply to get one last trip out of me? He must know things had soured between us. I wondered how this trip would end. Would I have the courage to break things off when, in spite of everything, I still felt terrified at the prospect of being alone? Could I face the end of my relationship at the same time I was dealing with all the turmoil in my family? I tossed and turned for a long while before drifting off.

When I awoke the next morning, sunlight was streaming into the room and Steven was in the bed, naked, beside me. When had he gotten in? I sat upright and checked the time: 11:10 a.m. I looked at him sleeping beside me: his strawberry blond hair shimmered against the white pillow, and he inhaled and exhaled deeply and rhythmically. His skin looked soft and inviting, and his face was creaseless: full of innocence. I could still smell a residue of Jovan musk on his skin, and the sweet scent of alcohol on his breath. Despite myself, I felt my penis stirring in response.

Ignoring it, I reminded myself of Steven's infidelity. I considered how easy it would be to smother him in his sleep with my pillow, pressing it down on him until the sound of his breathing ceased and he stopped struggling. Or perhaps he would smother peacefully, crossing gently from sleep to death, like a cloud passing in front of the sun. Perhaps I would strangle him instead, wrapping my fingers tightly around his golden throat, squeezing for all my worth, crushing his throat and his breath and his life out of him. Why shouldn't I wring the life from him as he was doing to me?

I went into the bathroom and showered, letting the hot water cascade over me until steam filled the room and I felt life in my limbs once again. When I came out of the bathroom, Steven was still asleep. I kicked the bed roughly. Steven snapped awake.

"What? What?" he stammered uncertainly.

"When did you get in?" I asked, standing naked in front of him.

"I dunno," he said, letting his eyes drift across my body. "I played black jack for a long time."

"Right," I said, "black jack." I dropped into the desk chair and faced him.

"What about it?"

"Who'd you fuck?" I surprised myself by asking, and flinched at how coarse it sounded, even to me. I hadn't intended to ask, but I had, and now I watched Steven's reaction. He didn't flinch, didn't even seem surprised, only slid out of the bed and stood there in front of me scratching his balls enticingly.

"I told you where I was," he said evenly. "I left you two messages. Where were *you* when I called?"

"Don't give me that crap," I said. "And don't answer my questions with questions. I was asleep the first time, and right next door having dinner the second time. Where were you all goddamned day and night?"

"I already told you." He sauntered into the bathroom. I could hear him pissing in the toilet. "I went to the beach and to the casino." He flushed the toilet.

"Right," I said as he stepped back through the doorway, "and who's Jim Ritts?"

He only missed a half-beat, but I knew I had struck home. He recovered quickly, feigning nonchalance. "I don't know. Why don't you tell me?"

"His name was on a slip of paper that fell out of your pocket yesterday. I saw you with him on the plane."

"First off," he said, opening his suitcase and pulling out a pair of boxer shorts, "why are you going through my clothes? And, secondly, I was just BS-ing with that guy on the plane. Why didn't you stop and say hello if you saw us? I would've introduced you."

"No, thanks," I said, marveling at how smooth he was. "I don't need to meet any of your——." I stopped, pissed that I had let him see my pain.

"Any of my what?" he asked, stepping into the boxers and coming forward to confront me. "Go ahead," he said smugly, chin up. "What were you going to say?"

"Your fuck-buddies," I snapped crudely, looking him square in the eye.

"Fuck you," he shouted indignantly, turning away. "You don't know what you're talking about. I don't have to listen to your crazy accusations. Besides, if that's how you feel, what'd you come here with me for?"

"Obviously not for the same thing *you* came here for," I said venomously. "Of course, why should I expect you to behave any differently here than you do back home?"

"You're such an asshole." He pulled on a pair of walking shorts angrily. "I came here to try to work things out. To start over. I thought it was what you wanted, too, but obviously, I was wrong." He sat on the edge of the bed to put on his sneakers.

"How can we work things out when you can't control your dick?" I asked, walking over to him, and shaking my cock directly in front of his smug little, tanned face. "All someone's gotta do is shake one of these in front of you; your fucking hormones take over, and you can't remember who you're supposed to be with. You're a fucking pig. You don't deserve me."

"Fuck you!" he raged, pushing me back and heading for the door. "I don't have to stick around and listen to this bullshit."

"Where are you gonna go?" I shouted. "You better watch out or I'll leave your ass in the Bahamas. You think Jim Ritts will buy a plane ticket for a slut like you?"

"Why not?" he replied coolly, stepping into the hallway. "*You* did." He slammed the door shut.

I stood there naked and sputtering, furious and hurt, absurdly worried about where he'd go, and wondering who he'd wind up spending his day with. When I noticed his suitcase still on the floor beside the dresser, I felt a wicked satisfaction. To hell with him, I thought, I'm not going to wait around for him. I put on my swim trunks and headed down to the beach where I could be alone. On the way, I stopped by the beachside bar and ordered a martini, telling the waiter to keep them coming. I spread my towel across the white sand, downed my drink, then lay back and let the heat bake into me.

The waiter periodically brought me a fresh drink. Gradually, the heat and liquor sapped my energy and I dropped off to sleep, worrying whether I was destined to be alone the rest of my life. I dozed on and off as the sun blazed overhead in the hazy white sky. The other beachgoers flounced in the surf and sipped on mai-tais delivered by scantily clad young beachboys in white shorts with shimmering, sweaty chests. I closed my eyes to it all, smelling the salty air and hearing only the wash of the waves.

When I awoke, my skin felt hot and tight. Sitting up was painful, and when I pulled my sunglasses off, I could see my skin was scarlet. The sun had baked me like a piece of meat on a spit. I struggled back to the hotel and rummaged through my bag for the only thing I could think of to ease the burn, some aloe-and-cocoa-butter moisturizer I had brought with me. I brought it into the bathroom, turned on the cold shower spigot, and carefully—gingerly—peeled off my bathing trunks and sandals, stepping under the spray. Steam rose from my hot flesh, stinging slightly, but the cold shower gradually cooled my skin until I felt the pain fade to a tolerable level. I turned off the water, stepped dripping from the shower, and felt a towel drop gently over my shoulders.

"You look like a red pepper," Steven's voice said. "Make that a hairy, red pepper."

"A hairy, drunk, red pepper," I slurred, surprised by the relief I felt upon hearing his voice. The fight was out of me—my skin burned on my back, shoulders, arms, and legs. Even my feet were burned. Steven picked up the moisturizer from the edge of the sink and squeezed some into his palm.

"Come over here and I'll slip something more comfortable on you." He grinned slyly and motioned for me to stand in front of him.

Obediently, I stepped in front of him and waited. His hands gently smoothed the cool lotion across my back. His fingers worked down my back to my waistline, up again to my arms, wrists, and the backs of my hands, caressing and coating each finger, one at a time. Next, he moved to my thighs and calves and down to my feet, manipulating each toe. Although my skin still felt aflame, I felt my body buzzing with sexual stirrings. He finished by massaging the lotion into my chest, and I felt my nipples and my penis stiffening.

Steven placed his hands on his hips, appraising me. He shook his head and grinned, "I let you alone for one afternoon and look what happens: You've incinerated yourself. Let's put you to bed."

I let him lead me naked by the hand to the bed. He drew back the sheets and I climbed into the cool sheets, watching as

Steven unbuckled his shorts and pulled off his tee-shirt. He stood in front of me for a moment like a peacock displaying himself. I didn't protest, even when the heat of his body against mine burned my tortured flesh like flame. He slid gingerly on top of me, straddling my chest, and I reached up and touched his cheek.

"You came back," I said, ignoring the pain that engulfed my body. All I knew was that I needed Steven more than he needed me at that inebriated moment.

"Of course, I came back," he said, kissing me. "I love you. I was just pissed off."

"Me too," I mumbled as I slid my hand down to his ass, drawing him forward on my chest until I took him into my mouth.

"Are you sure you want to do this?" he asked, not attempting to pull out.

"Yes," I slurred, drunkenly. "I want to taste you." My brain flashed momentarily on Steven's HIV, but in my heated intoxication, nothing mattered as much as my immediate desire. Afterwards, Steven slid under the sheets beside me, and we both drifted off to the sound of the air conditioner humming and the white sunlight on the window blinds.

In my sleep, I felt water dripping onto my face—drip, drip, drip. I blinked my eyes open, expecting to find Steven leaning over me playfully. But the room was dark, and I could hear Steven snoring on the far side of the queen-size bed, sheets tossed aside and legs splayed apart, flat on his back. His genitals, silvery in the half-light, looked soft and tender as a newborn bunny.

Mystified, I slipped out of the bed and into the bathroom, closing the door behind me and looking at myself in the mirror. My hair was flattened against one side of my head and, when I leaned forward I could see blisters on my face and nose, dripping fluids that bubbled like poison welling up from my flesh. I gasped involuntarily, touched a finger to one of the blisters, and gasped again—loudly—at the intensity of the pain that shot through me. Tears prickled, and when I looked back in the mirror, I saw Steven's reflection.

"Jesus," he said. "We better get you to a doctor. You're a mess."

While Steven dressed and called the lobby to find out where he could take me, I gingerly pulled on a pair of shorts. Steven escorted me down the stairs and into a waiting taxi that quickly drove us to a clinic where a doctor took one look at me and nodded knowingly.

"Mon, what part of the States you from?"

"Chicago," I said.

"Yes," he said. "Always from up north. You forget how hot the sun is this close to the Equator. I should check you into the hospital, mon."

"No," I said, too embarrassed to admit I grew up in Florida and should have known better. "I have to go home tomorrow." I slowly sobered up—slowly remembered what I had done the previous night. I felt lost.

"Okay," the doctor said. "But you check with your doctor when you get home. You be okay in a few days, mon, but don't take no chances cuz you're cooked medium-well. I give you some creme that will help. But you must stay away from the sun until you go home."

By the time we got back to our room, it was after ten and we were exhausted. Steven rubbed the doctor's salve on my burn and we went back to bed. Before I drifted off, I wondered how I could have been so stupid the night before to let myself end up back in bed with Steven, how I could have risked my own health.

In the morning, we were awakened by the sound of rain on our window. I felt chilled, although my skin burned like fire. I shivered in bed, pulled the comforter off the floor, and covered myself with it. Steven volunteered to get me some breakfast as soon as he got cleaned up. He returned in a few minutes with juice and bagels. I gulped down the juice, surprised at my thirst, and nibbled at a bagel. Steven finished his food, then stood up.

"I guess I better get us packed up," he said. "You think you'll be ready for our flight this afternoon?"

"Yeah," I said, "I'll manage. I'd rather be home suffering than here."

"Well, why don't you stay in bed and I'll get everything together? Then, I might take a last walk around the island before we have to go—if you don't mind." He looked over at me expectantly.

"You want to walk in the rain?" I asked.

"It's not raining that hard anymore," he said. "Besides, I've barely seen anything around here." He tossed our belongings back into our suitcases and stacked them by the door. "I'll see you in a little while. Do ya' need anything while I'm out?"

I shook my head, and he came over and kissed me before leaving. I wanted to believe he was just going for a walk, but somehow I sensed otherwise. Then again, perhaps Steven was actually being kind, allowing me to rest, giving me as much time as I needed. When he returned, a little over an hour later, he awakened me, and we checked out and headed for the airport. He seemed subdued as he helped me carry my things. He remained beside me on the plane, even relinquishing the window seat, for once.

Back in Chicago, the blisters on my nose first turned black, and then sloughed off. The rest of my skin peeled off in sheets, and I felt like a snake shedding its old skin.

Nothing felt the same anymore. Steven seemed oddly passive, almost listless. Our lovemaking, when it happened at all, was perfunctory, safe, and mostly passionless.

I went back to work, and life seemed eerily normal. Even the news from Merritt Island seemed relatively positive. I hadn't spoken to Ma and Pop since my trip down there three months before, but Rosalia said Pop was gradually improving.

"He's stubborn as hell," she said. "I think he's gonna live to be a hundred, and I'll be the one in my grave. He won't do anything the doctors say. He insists they're all quacks who just want his money, but don't know nothing. He's gonna give Ma a nervous breakdown, I swear."

"If he wants to kill himself, no one's gonna stop him. Especially not me."

"Why don't you call him, Anthony?" It sounded like a plea, but I couldn't grant it. "Maybe if you'd just talk to him…"

"Why doesn't he call *me*?" I snapped, interrupting her before she could finish. "Seriously, Rose, why do you bring this up every time we talk? He doesn't want to hear from me—he made that very clear when I was down. And I don't want to put myself through it again."

"I still think you'll be sorry if something happens to him," she said, sounding sad and tired. "I keep thinking you'll realize it, too. I just hope you realize it before it's too late."

"You just said he's getting better."

"I know, but he's almost seventy years old, for God's sake. How long do you think he's got? For that matter, how long do you think Ma has got? Life might not wait for you to come around, Anthony. Jesus Christ, I just wish you could see how little it takes to make the two of them happy."

"Yeah, I know what it takes," I said. "All I have to do is give up my self-respect."

That Thanksgiving, I decided to surprise Steven with a big traditional dinner and a pair of tickets to see "Hamlet" at the

Tarantella

Goodman Theatre on the following night. Steven had to work until six on Thanksgiving Day, so I timed the meal for seven. Everything was ready by six-thirty, and I began carving the turkey and fixing the potatoes and gravy. Seven came and went, but Steven still had not appeared. I picked up the phone and dialed the restaurant, but got no answer. He must be on his way home, I figured.

By seven-thirty, I was convinced that Steven either had gotten into an accident and was lying in an Emergency Room, or had picked up a trick and was lying in another man's bed. At eight, I sat down and ate, gorging on the food and telling myself I wasn't going to let Steven ruin my holiday meal. I'd go out and maybe pick up someone myself to show Steven he wasn't the only one who could play that game. I put on my jacket and headed for the piano bar up the street.

When I got there, the pianist was playing old standards like "Over the River and Through the Woods." I sat at the back of the room and ordered a screaming orgasm. I'd never had one before, but I was in the mood to be outrageous. When it came, I took a swig and discovered it tasted like a milkshake with a kick. I gulped it down and ordered another. Glancing around the room, I noticed only three other desperate-looking men—all considerably older than me—were here tonight. Everyone else must be with their families; I felt a pang in my chest. I felt like we were four losers: the four least desirable old queens in all of Chicago, sitting here singing show tunes and old standards. I ordered another drink and checked my watch. It was after eleven and I decided I needed to get the hell out of this place and go home. At least there I could cry if I felt like it. I chugged the drink and pulled on my coat. When I stood, a wave of dizziness told me the drinks had been stronger than they tasted. I steadied myself and headed out the door.

The cold air outside snapped me sober and I headed home. Traffic was light on Michigan Avenue, which was bedecked with white lights for Christmas the following month. The cheery brightness only drove home how truly alone and miserable I felt. I looked up the street and saw a taxi approaching me, racing up the vacant street. I watched its headlights bob up and down over pavement and, as it neared, I stepped into the street directly in front of it and closed my eyes.

I heard the screech of brakes and a thump as the car hit something, and then everything was still again. I felt nothing. Then, I heard a car door creak open and a voice boom out, "What the fuck man! You trying to get yourself killed?"

I opened my eyes and turned in the direction of the voice. The taxi had come to a stop on the sidewalk and the driver, a black man about my age, was staring at me. I blinked at him, but said nothing.

"Are you drunk or something?" he asked twisting his head to look in my face. "Where do you live, man?"

I pointed at my building a little more than a block ahead. He closed his door and backed into the roadway, pulling alongside me. "Climb in, buddy. I'll drop you there before you fall down in the street and hurt someone." I slumped into the seat and he delivered me to my building, wished me a happy Thanksgiving, and drove away. I watched the red tail lights for a moment before heading inside and up to my apartment.

It was mid-afternoon the next day when I snapped awake to the sound of a key in the door. I was still dressed in my clothes from the night before, and stretched out across our sofa in the living room. I quickly sat upright and combed my fingers through my hair as the door swung open and Steven appeared in the entry hall. He looked at me for a second, then turned to close the door behind him. Through the window, I heard the sounds of traffic from the street below.

"It's snowing like a sonuvabitch out," Steven announced as he stepped into the living room and leaned up against the wall opposite me. He wore a tight grey tee-shirt and black jeans with a pair of cowboy boots. In spite of my anger at him, he looked like a sexy young boy as he shook the snow and wetness from his strawberry mop.

"So," I asked, "where were you last night? I made a turkey dinner for us, you know."

"I know," he said, lifting his head and leaning back against the wall. "I just couldn't deal with it, you know?"

"You could've called."

"I thought about it." He tucked his shirt in the front of his pants. "But I knew we'd just end up arguing, and I didn't feel like getting into it."

"So you just left me here alone cooking for you and worrying that something had happened to you?" I tried to control my anger, but I could hear my voice shaking, which pissed me off even more. "Jesus Christ. It's Thanksgiving, for God's sake."

"It doesn't matter what day it is," he said. "Every day is about what *you* want. Always about Anthony, and what *you* decide." He stabbed his chest angrily with his index finger. "This time, *I* decided. I can't keep going along to get along. This just isn't working."

I stood and took a step toward him, but he pushed off the wall and moved away from me. "I know," I said, shaking my head and sitting down again. "I know it's not working. Don't you think I realize that, too? I think we should talk about this."

"I can't talk with you." He squatted on his haunches. "You're the writer. You've got all the fucking words, and I can't compete with you. *You* do all the talking. *You* set all the rules. I feel like a little kid around you. If I don't behave, you get pissed, and there's hell to pay. Well, I'm tired of it: I won't do it no more."

"Oh, come off it," I said. "I can't make you do anything. You're about as independent as they come. I don't think you ever stop to consider how I'll feel before you make your stupid, unilateral decisions. Jesus Christ. I thought we were a couple? I thought you loved me?"

"I did," he said, then looked up at me and added quickly, "I do. You don't make it easy, though. You're just like your fucking father. You lay down the law: no drinking, no smoking in the apartment," he ticked off each item on his fingers, "don't eat in the bedroom, don't go out after work. Don't, don't, don't."

Tarantella

"Jesus Christ," I said. "We agreed on all of those things. They're not my rules."

"Sure they are," he said standing up again and pointing at me. "*You* set the rules. *You* tell me how I should act."

"As if you don't have a voice," I scoffed. "Since when can't you disagree? Since when are you too shy to fight back? Like now."

"Every time I argue, you threaten me." He turned away and stormed down the hallway. "But I don't give a fuck anymore," he shouted as he walked away.

"I've never threatened you," I shouted back at him and followed him down the hallway. He darted into the bathroom, closing and bolting the door behind him. "Don't run and hide when we're in the middle of this, you fucking coward," I said, yelling each word at the door.

The door flew open and Steven stepped into the doorway, red-faced and fuming, holding up his fists in front of him like a boxer. "Fine," he shouted. "I'm not hiding. So, what the fuck do you want?"

"I want you to take back your bullshit," I shouted back at him. "I never threatened you and you know it."

"You sure as shit *did* threaten me," he repeated. "Every time I wouldn't go along with you, every fucking time you didn't get your way, you threatened that if I didn't like it, I could leave." His anger filled the doorway threateningly.

I took a step backward, felt the words hit like a strike to my face.

His tone softened and he continued: "You never said it, of course, but you always made it clear that you were Number One in this relationship because you earned more than me. I'm just a goddamned dumb-ass waiter, isn't that right? And if I wanna live like this—" he gestured around the apartment, "then I goddamn well better play by your rules." He looked me square in the face. "Well, I don't fucking care anymore. Throw me out if you want, cuz I ain't playing by your rules anymore. You can go fuck yourself." He wheeled around and slammed and locked the bathroom door behind him.

I stumbled to the bed and heaved myself across it. My head pounded from the previous night's liquor. Steven's words— "You're just like your fucking father"—kept echoing in my head. "Don't. Don't. Don't." Jesus Christ, I thought. I really *had* turned into Pop.

I wondered if Steven had ever really felt stable living with me. Or, if he ever truly loved me. I felt a terrible emptiness in my gut. I wished my hangover would make me vomit. I wanted to retch the last ten years out of myself so I might be freed of them.

Steven reemerged from the bathroom and sat on the edge of the bed beside me. I turned toward him. He was watching the snow blowing outside our window. In the dim room, he looked like a silhouette, hardly real, like a piece of art.

"So, where were you last night?" I whispered. "And that last night in the Bahamas?"

He took my hands in his and held them against his chest. "I was just walking, mostly," he said, "thinking."

"No more lies," I said. "I thought we were being straight with each other tonight."

"I'm never straight," he said, deflecting.

"No jokes now, please," I said, sitting up and turning his face toward mine. "Just tell me the truth, okay?"

"Okay."

"Do you sleep with other men?"

"Of course not," he said, and started to pull away. I refused to let go of his hand and he reluctantly sat down again.

"I *saw* you," I whispered and felt the tears flow again.

"What?" he asked fearfully.

"Remember how I came back early after Pop had his heart attack?" I asked, and he nodded. "Well, I actually got home the night before I called you and snuck in to surprise you. Except I was the one who got surprised."

"Shit," he said.

"Shit is right. I thought I would die right there," I said. "Now, *please* stop lying to me. It's time for a little honesty."

"Why didn't you say something?" he asked quietly.

"Say what? I just wanted to get away. So, I stayed in a hotel that night and called you the next day." I let go of his hand and wiped the tears off my cheeks. The room was perfectly silent except for the sound of our breathing. I could smell the soap Steven had used in the bathroom. We were both sitting stock-still on the bed, not moving or speaking, but Steven and I were still dancing around the truth. I heard the tiny motor on the alarm clock beside the bed turning, slowly turning the numbers as time passed.

After a minute, I started laughing.

"What?" Steven asked, mystified by my behavior. "What's so funny?"

"I almost forgot," I said reining in my laughter. "I bought tickets to see 'Hamlet' tonight. It was a surprise."

He looked at me and said, "I can't."

I stopped laughing and answered, "I know." I climbed off the bed and walked to my dresser. "I'll go alone. We need some time apart to figure out the next step." I turned back toward him. "Obviously, we can't stay together like this."

"No," he said quietly. The wan light from the window caught his face, turning it silver and shadowy. "Of course not."

"I'm going to clean up now," I said. "It's already after five. I'll catch dinner on the way. I pulled my underclothes out of the drawer and glanced in the mirror over the dresser but saw only shadows in its dark reflection. "Have there been a lot of others?" I asked suddenly.

"Yes," he replied resignedly.

I felt hollowed out.

"Tony?" Steven's voice sounded disembodied, small.

"What?"

"What do we do now?"

"Now?" I asked, as if I didn't comprehend. "Now, I'm going to take a shower."

I gathered my clothes and headed into the bathroom. As I closed the door behind me, I waited for Steven to say something—anything.

He said nothing.

CHAPTER 13

Transitions

Chicago: May 1989

SEVEN YEARS HAD passed since Rosalia's wedding and my decision to leave Florida. I read somewhere how the phases of our lives last seven years. For me, this was the phase where I lost focus. The phase where I worked all day while Steven worked all night: the phase where I pretended I had no family. Rosalia became my sole link to family and home, but even she metamorphosed from a person with shape and mass into a voice—a voice I could avoid by simply not answering my phone. Emboldened by the distance, I refused to kowtow to Ma and Pop. Of course, my bravery reached only as far as Rosalia's phone line.

At night, while Steven was at work, I would sit alone in the window of our high-rise apartment until bedtime. After a passionate start, our relationship had turned into a series of brief, routine encounters—getting together for dinner or a show, a quick kiss before I left for work, a phone call to remind the other to pick up groceries. Sometimes I felt like I was back at college again—sharing a dorm room with a roommate. Intimacy was occasional and brief, but every morning, I woke up beside Steven and it still felt good. It felt like enough.

One beautiful spring night, while I was sitting on our sofa looking out at the yellow glow of the Chicago streetlights, my reverie was broken by the sound of the phone ringing. Noticing the late hour, I began formulating my reasons for denying tonight's request for money to buy something "essential." It was our nightly ritual—Steven asking for money and me denying his request. While my income had increased threefold in seven years, Steven couldn't seem to hold a job and, as a result, barely made enough to cover his incidentals. To me, it seemed that Steven devised ways to generate bills, and I paid them.

"The answer is no," I said as I picked up the phone.

"Anthony?" Rosalia's voice asked tentatively.

"Oh, sorry, Rose. It's me—I thought you were Steven," I apologized. "What's new, pussycat?"

"I've got some bad news. Are you sitting down?" I could hear the strain in her voice.

"Actually, I am," I said. "So, what'd Pop do now?"

"It's not Pop this time," she said. "It's Doughna Mira."

I sat upright. "Shit. What's wrong?"

"She's in the hospital..."

"Is she okay?"

"No, Anthony," she said, then added quietly: "She's dying. They don't expect her to survive the night."

"Jesus!" I gasped, disbelieving. "What happened?"

"Her liver has shut down," Rosalia said simply. "There's nothing they can do for her at this point except give her morphine for the pain."

Tarantella

I felt hot tears streaming down my cheeks. "I'll book a flight," I stammered. "I'll be there in the morning. I want to talk to her before she's gone," I said. "I've got some things to tell her."

"You're too late, Anthony," Rosalia said. "She's already out of it. She won't even know it if you come."

"I've gotta come down, Rose. I've gotta," I insisted. "I've hardly talked to Doughna since I left—just a stupid card or quick call here or there. Oh, Jesus!" I started to cry. "I've been so focused on getting away from Florida and Ma and Pop that I forgot about Doughna." I leaned against the back of the sofa. "I wasn't thinking she might...Jesus! I'm so stupid." I choked back a sob. "Doughna's always been there for me. I mean, she's like Sicily—this big, solid rock, you know? I never considered she might be gone one day."

"Yeah," Rosalia agreed quietly. "I know. But she's not immortal, Anthony." She paused for a moment, then added, "None of us are."

I ignored her pointed message, focusing instead on Doughna. "What if she dies and I never get to tell her how I feel about her? That I'm sorry for not staying in better touch these last few years? That I love her?"

"She knows all that Anthony. She knows why you left. She knows why you've stayed away. I'm sure she understands. Besides," she added, "it's already too late to tell her anything. If you want to come home for her funeral, fine. But get the deathbed confession out of your mind. It's not going to happen."

"I gotta try," I insisted again.

"Look, Anthony," she said, her voice taking on a sterner tone. "I wasn't going to go into this, but it's really awful. Doughna's down to ninety pounds. Her face is all emaciated. Her skin is gray. She's in terrible pain, in and out of consciousness. And when she *is* conscious, she's still out of it—either hallucinating or shrieking the whole time. She doesn't recognize any of us anymore. It's horrible." She paused before adding, "I'm actually *glad* you're not down here to see her like this. I don't think you could handle it."

"I hate this," I said. "I hate the thought of Doughna suffering. She's the gentlest, best person I've ever known."

"She's the best person any of us have ever known, and she doesn't deserve this," Rosalia agreed. "The only positive is that she won't have to suffer much longer now."

"I can't believe this," I said. "I need more time. How could I have been so stupid?"

"Don't do this now," Rosalia said, cutting me off. "I'll call you in the morning and let you know what's happening. Then, you can decide what to do next."

"Okay," I agreed reluctantly. "If something changes, though, don't wait until morning. Call me right away."

"I will," she said. "I promise. Now, get some sleep and I'll call you in the morning."

"Okay," I said. "Thanks, Rosalia."

I tossed and turned all night until the windows began brightening with daybreak. Steven, oblivious and snoring, was asleep beside me. I got up, pulled on my robe, and shuffled into the kitchen. I stood in the window to watch the day arrive. It was beautiful: the sun emerging from the lake, illuminating the city skyline in pink and yellow hues. It was May Day and, in Florida, Doughna was dying. A beautiful spring day was dawning that Doughna would never see or know about. She'd never again feel the warm sun on her skin, never again tell me about her Sichilian radar, never again bake a loaf of bread.

I remembered the last time I saw her, at Rosalia's wedding, the day before I left Florida. I remembered dancing with her, remembered the room spinning around us as we whirled to the frenzied strains of the tarantella. What had it all been for? I had run away to Chicago. We had barely spoken for the last seven years. Now, Doughna was dying.

As the sun continued to rise and brighten, I knew there was no reason to rush back to Florida if I couldn't talk to Doughna Mira. I didn't want to see her in a casket. And I didn't want to risk a scene with Ma and Pop at her funeral. No, it was time to assert myself and begin running my own life again, instead of letting life happen around me. Doughna understood why I had to move to Chicago, and she would understand why I needed to stay here now.

When Rosalia called around mid-morning, I knew without asking that Doughna was gone. "She's gone, isn't she?" I said. "I can feel it."

"Yes, Anthony," she said somberly. "Just a few minutes ago. It was quite peaceful, actually. At the very end, Doughna looked like she was dreaming. She let out a big sigh, and then she was gone."

"Jesus," I said, tears streaming down my cheeks. "I can't believe it. I miss her already."

"We all do," Rose said. "Look, Anthony, I can't stay on this phone long. I'm at the hospital with Ma and Pop. I'm sure the funeral will be over the weekend. Can you come down? You can stay at my place."

"I can't, Rose," I said flatly. "Much as I'd like to say goodbye to Doughna, I don't think it would be a good idea to come down there."

"Come on, Anthony," she said. "You know Doughna would want you to be here. I want you here, too."

"I know. And I thank you for that," I said. "I thought this through all morning. I'll help with anything I can—making arrangements, sending money, whatever—but I don't think I should be there. I don't think Ma and Pop would want me there right now. If I see them, I'll know we'll end up fighting, and I don't want to fight at Doughna's funeral."

"Ma and Pop *do* want you here," she interrupted. "Especially now. Maybe this is just the thing to help us put the past behind us. Maybe this will help us get back to being a family again." She sounded so hopeful; but I knew better.

"If they want me there, then how come they didn't call?" I asked. "Anyhow, it doesn't matter: it would be a disaster. When you have a minute to really think about it, you'll agree with me. If I come down, we'll end up fighting. It's the immutable, unalterable truth in our lives."

"So, don't fight, Anthony," she pleaded. "All you've gotta do is *not* fight. It's not that hard. You can do it."

Tarantella

"That's where you're wrong, Rose," I said. "I *can't* do it. I left seven years ago because I couldn't do it. I haven't talked to them for seven years because I can't do it. And I'm not coming to Doughna Mira's funeral because I can't do it."

I took a personal day from work. As I climbed into the shower, I thought about the beautiful sunrise I had watched while Doughna was dying. Was her soul already in heaven? Had she watched the same sunrise from a different vantage point? Did she really understand how much she meant to me?

Doughna's funeral would, of course, be held at Divine Mercy in the golden pyramid. I imagined the golden Florida sun streaming down through the skylight atop the pyramid onto Doughna's casket on the alter. I imagined her beatific face, her hands clasping a spray of flowers on her stomach, wearing her best Sunday dress. I imagined she knew how much I loved her and understood why I had been so distant these last seven years. Yet, I wasn't sure I understood it myself.

I dressed quickly and quietly, slipping out of the apartment without waking Steven. I wanted to be outside, to be by myself, to feel alive.

A light breeze blew across Centennial Park as I walked into the wildflower garden. Even though it was only May, the wildflowers were already filling out again, and the garden was filled with singing birds and squirrels. It always amazed me to find so much wildlife in the middle of such a big city.

Scot T. O'Hara

I always felt happy and rejuvenated here. I sat on a bench and took in the whole scene around me: the shell of the city visible over the oaks and ash trees; the pathways interlacing the green grass; the occasional jogger running by; the small group of men playing chess on the stone chess tables behind me; the warm sun on my skin; the red-winged blackbirds swooping over the wildflowers; a man and woman playing tennis on the courts beside me.

Doughna's passing was unnoticed by the rest of the world. I wanted to cry. I wanted to scream. Did Doughna's life matter in the larger sense? Were all of our lives—our struggles and deaths—non-events in the big picture? What was all the struggling for?

I thought about Ma and Pop, about the seven years gone by without a word. I wondered if they regretted it, too. Did they, like me, ever pick up the phone and start to dial, before letting their pride and their stupidity talk them out of it again?

Was I being stupid with them, too? Rosalia thought so. But I kept thinking about the way they had rejected my life, about the way they had insisted I live the life they approved of, about the way they belittled my lifestyle and my choices. I still heard Pop's voice calling me a faggot with Ma beside him in silent accord, and I felt unforgiving and angry all over again. Remembering, I felt justified. At other times, I wasn't so sure. Doughna hated it when Pop and I argued. She always tried to keep peace in the family, but we were beyond her control. At Rosalia's wedding, she had insisted we dance to exorcise the poison in our blood. Unsure afterwards whether it had worked, she had said, "We'll have to wait and see."

If Doughna couldn't bring us together, I wondered, what could? Sitting here in Chicago, I thought about Ma and Pop and Rosalia. We were all living our separate lives. We were like the scorpion in the story of the scorpion and the frog. As the frog was swimming the scorpion safely across the river, the scorpion stung him. "Why did you do that?" the frog asked. "Now, we'll both die." To which the scorpion replied, "I couldn't help it. It's my nature." Were we, all of us, trapped by our natures, scorpion-stung and doomed, dancing furiously to our separate, self-centered rhythms, and unable to change?

I could almost see Doughna shaking her head sadly at our foolishness.

On St. Patrick's Day, 1994, Steven left for his latest new job as a waiter at a nearby restaurant. I remember leaning on the door and watching him walk to the elevator. He was still so sexy. You'd never know that I had more t-cells in my little finger than he had in his entire body. His diagnosis more than five years behind him, the only visible effects of his infection were the permanently swollen glands behind his ears. He hadn't been sick a single day since his diagnosis, and even I began to treat him as if he were healthy again.

We had been together eleven years and little had changed, except that Steven had slowly come to consider his diagnosis like background music, something he knew was there, but paid little attention to. In many ways, he was back to his old self. He was again flirting shamelessly and commenting about every good-looking guy he saw. When I complained, he'd laugh and say glibly, "I may not be able to touch, but I can still look."

I, too, found myself looking at other men more and more lately. In fact, after my writing class the week before, an attractive classmate, Dean, asked if I wanted to get coffee with him. Although I had never socialized with any of my classmates before, I heard myself accept, and we walked over to a nearby coffee shop on State Street.

"I really like your writing," Dean said after we were served. He blew on his coffee. "Why did you decide to go for your master's if you're already working at a newspaper?"

"I don't know," I said. "I suppose partly to move ahead, and partly to fill my empty time." Without thinking, I added, "I have a lot of empty time."

"I see," he said smiling at me. "Then, you must not be married or anything."

"Mmmm, not exactly," I said. "I'm gay, actually. I hope that doesn't change your mind about having coffee with me." I watched for the usual reaction of disappointed surprise, but Dean started grinning from ear to ear, and two deep dimples creased his cheeks.

"Actually," he said, "so am I. I was sort of hoping you were, too."

I looked at him, and he suddenly, shyly, looked down at his coffee. He was strikingly beautiful: dark hair with a little silver around the edges, big, blue-green eyes and thick eyebrows under wire-frame glasses. I felt the old nervousness flutter up inside me, the feeling I always got when I met a man I found attractive. Dean blew on his coffee to cool it, obviously aware that I was staring at him. His face reddened into a broad blush, and I wanted to touch his face right there in the middle of the coffee shop—wanted to feel the heat of his blushing skin against my fingertips.

"So," he said, looking up at me again, "does that bother *you*?"

"No," I said, starting to blush myself. "I'm flattered, actually."

His smile broadened and I could see his white teeth. He lifted his coffee with both hands and sipped on it, keeping his eyes on me as he did. He had beautiful fingers—porcelain white and perfectly tapered.

"So," he asked still holding his cup between his hands, "are you seeing anyone at the moment?"

Oh, Jesus—what the hell was I doing here leading this guy on? I looked at Dean and wondered why I couldn't have found a relationship with someone like him *before* I met Steven, before it was too late. I was unhappy, but how could I leave Steven when I had promised to stay? He may not always act it, but he was still very sick. How could I live with myself if I broke my commitment to him? And, yet, here was Dean in front of me, looking interested and excited to be with me. God knows, it had been years since I last experienced this sensation.

"I, uh, well, actually, I *do* have a lover," I stumbled out reluctantly, and Dean looked embarrassed. I felt stupid. *What was I doing here with him if I had a lover?*

"I'm sorry," Dean said. "I didn't mean to put you in an awkward position."

"You didn't," I said quickly, touching his warm shoulder gently. "My relationship is just, uh, very awkward."

"I don't understand," he said, looking puzzled.

"I'm sorry," I said, "I'm being vague and stupid, and I don't mean to be. You seem like a nice guy, and I could really use a friend. But I'd understand if you'd rather call it a night." I felt very conflicted. Half of me wanted him to stay, and half of me hoped he'd stand up and say he'd see me around.

Dean stared at his coffee a moment, then looked up and said, "Friends would be nice."

"Good," I said. "I don't have many friends here in Chicago." I sipped my coffee, letting its warmth flow through me and relaxing again, pleased that Dean had not run off the minute I told him I had a lover. "So, tell me a little about yourself."

"Well," he said leaning back in his seat and placing his forearms on the table and drumming his fingers while he thought for a moment. He leaned forward again and said, "I'm 31—well, I will be in about two months. I work as a technical writer at a bank. And I really hate my job." He laughed—a rolling, solid laugh. "I guess I shouldn't say that because they're paying for this class. I'm supposed to be very grateful."

"And what would you rather do?" I asked, nodding.

"Well, if I had my druthers," he said, "I'd rather write plays. I love going to plays. And movies."

"Me, too!" I said. "I love theater and movies. I go all the time."

"With your lover?" he asked.

"No, mostly by myself," I said. "Steven doesn't like them much."

Dean took another sip of his coffee, then asked, "Do you think we could go to a play or a movie sometime? As friends? If Steven doesn't mind, of course."

"I think I'd really like that," I said. "In fact, that would be really wonderful."

About a week later, Dean and I went to a movie together on a Saturday afternoon while Steven was at work. I had mentioned Dean incidentally to Steven, telling him Dean was a classmate who shared my interest in plays and movies, and that we'd talked about maybe going to a movie together sometime. Steven shrugged and said I should do it and take him off the hook. As much as I tried to convince myself that Dean was just a friend, I knew my interest was deeper; but I wouldn't admit it to myself.

That day, after the show, we grabbed a quick dinner at an Italian restaurant near the theater. Over cannelloni, I told him, "You know, I'm half Sicilian myself, and half Irish."

"You must have a real temper, huh?" he said, cringing in mock fear.

"I have my moments. Especially with my father."

"Oh, Jesus, another father-son thing," he said. "Are there any fathers and sons who actually get along?"

"You, too?" I asked. "You seem like you could get along with anyone."

"Except Dad," he said, shaking his head. "I swear, no one could piss me off—excuse my language—the way Dad could."

"Could," I interrupted. "Has he reformed?"

"I guess you could say that. Sort of," he said, looking at me and grinning strangely. "Dad died about three years ago."

"Oh, I'm sorry," I said automatically.

"Don't be," he said. "People always say that and I think, 'You wouldn't be sorry if you'd known him.'" He looked through the window in front of our table. The sun was still out, though fading, and people thronged the sidewalk. Today had been the first springlike day of the year, and people were determined to make the most of it. "Dad was an alcoholic. When they called to tell me he had died, I felt relieved." He turned and looked right at me. "Does that sound really awful? I was glad he was gone."

"No," I said, wishing I had the nerve to squeeze his arm, and wondering how I'd feel if something happened to Pop. "Actually, I think I understand."

"I suppose," he said. "But sometimes, I wonder if I should have tried harder. After all, alcoholism is a disease. Maybe he couldn't help the way he acted."

"Everyone controls the way they act," I said. "I always say that, once you're eighteen, you're in control of what you do: it's time to stop looking for anyone else to blame."

Tarantella

"I used to feel that way, too," he said.

"Used to?" I asked.

"Yeah. Now, I'm not so sure," he said. "I've thought a lot about it over the last three years, you know. I've sort of come to the conclusion that someone can become so conditioned to behaving and thinking in a particular way that they're no longer even aware of other ways to behave and think. It's like they can get trapped into a pattern they're unable to break out of on their own. I mean, I don't want to excuse anyone from responsibility for his own behavior, but I've come to the conclusion that a person can become trapped by his own life. And that makes me wonder about Dad: I don't feel as sure as I used to that I was always fair to him. Maybe that's the thing about growing up—we end up *less* sure of ourselves."

"Don't beat yourself up," I said. "You shouldn't second-guess what's past. What good will it do, since you can't change it?"

"Yeah, I guess," he said, resuming eating. "But it's really hard not to. What's your dad like?"

"Oh, Pop," I said with a sigh. "Where to start! He's very distant, I guess. You know, sort of cold and emotionless. I mean, he's never once kissed or hugged me; I think he'd rather die first. And if he ever told me he loved me, *I'd* die."

We both laughed.

"Seriously, he's really up-tight about things, and pretty homophobic. It's weird—we've barely spoken to each other in years. It's like we're in some kind of sick contest—seeing who can outlast the other. I keep thinking he'll wake up and realize what a jerk he's been all these years. I mean, my older brother ran away when he was seventeen. No one has seen or heard from him since, and it's been almost twenty-five years. And now, I've been away for twelve years. What more does he need to realize he's doing something wrong?"

"Most of us are really good at fooling ourselves," Dean said. "Some never get it."

"My sister, Rosalia, still tries to convince me I should forgive and forget," I said. "But that would be like saying he was right about everything, and I can't accept that. I don't believe being gay is wrong. I don't believe standing up for yourself is wrong. I don't believe having your own opinion is wrong. Pop seems to think there's only one right way: his way."

"Well, I'll tell you what," Dean said. "You should try to make peace with him if you can. It can really eat you up after it's too late, if you know what I mean."

"Not really," I said and shook my head, "although Rosalia says so all the time, too."

"You have to deal with all the imaginary what-ifs, and that's really hell," he explained. "You wind up second-guessing yourself about everything, and what seemed so clear at the time seems less clear afterwards."

I nodded again, but I couldn't imagine "making peace" with Pop. He'd probably hang up on me if I called.

The next time we met for a movie, about two weeks later, Dean asked me to tell him about Steven. We were sitting in the semi-dark theater waiting for the movie to begin. I took a long swig of my Diet Coke before answering him.

Tarantella

"What do you want to know?" I asked, turning to look at him. The silver in his dark hair glistened in the semi-darkness. It looked so shiny and soft, I wanted to touch it with my fingers.

"Anything," he said. "What's he like? How'd you meet? If you don't mind talking about him with me, of course."

"No, of course not," I said. "I'm just not sure what to say." I paused and looked around our seats to see if anyone was eavesdropping, but no one was seated nearby. "He's a few years younger than me—he's only 32. He waits tables and he's got strawberry-blond hair and he's a little taller than I am."

"Sounds cute," Dean said.

"He was," I said, "I mean *is*." I looked up at the blank white screen before me. "I mean—I don't know what I mean."

"It's okay," Dean said, tapping my thigh gently, sending little dancing blue jolts arcing through my body. "You don't have to explain to me. I shouldn't have asked. I'm sorry."

I shook my head and exhaled deeply. "I'm just so conflicted," I said.

"Am I creating a problem for you?" he asked.

"No," I said quickly. "Not you. Jesus, you give me a minute of real life every now and then. You see—I haven't told this to anyone else—Steven tested HIV-positive a few years ago."

"Oh, I'm so sorry, Anthony," he said.

"He's doing fine," I added hurriedly. "His T-cells are down, but he hasn't been sick at all really."

"How are *you*?" he asked.

"Me?" I asked. "I'm fine." I turned and saw him looking at me with a pitiful and amazingly sad look, made all the more tragic by

389

the deep shadows in the theater. I suddenly realized what he was asking and added, "I'm fine. *Really*. I've been tested over and over and I'm negative. I'm very careful."

"Good," he said. "I was afraid. . ."

"No, don't worry about me. I'm fine," I said, and squeezed his shoulder reassuringly. I felt exhilarated by his concern about my health. "But Steven's T-cell counts keep going down. He won't take any drugs, and he won't talk about it at all. When we do, we always end up in a fight, shouting at each other. It's such a mess, I don't know what to do. I really don't know how I feel," I admitted. "There are times—too many times, I'm ashamed to admit—that I find myself wishing Steven *would* die so I could get on with *my* life. Sometimes I think Steven might be right—maybe I have filled our apartment with negative vibes. But, I have never—not even once—considered walking out on him. I may secretly imagine life without him, but I could never leave him as long as he still needs me. I couldn't live with the guilt."

"To paraphrase something someone once told me," he said, "'Don't beat yourself up about things you can't change.'"

I looked at him and grinned as I recognized my own words to him. He smiled back at me and took my hand.

"Using my own words against me?" I asked.

"Why not?" he said. "You were right. Steven is responsible for himself. You can't make him do anything he doesn't want to do. And you'll just make yourself sick trying. You have to take care of yourself, too, you know."

Tarantella

"I know," I said. "I just feel like I owe Steven something, you know? I mean, it's not like everything's hunky-dory between us. We've grown so far apart since his diagnosis. We hardly do anything together anymore. Hell, we barely have anything in common."

"Then, how come you're still with him?"

"I told you," I said without thinking. "Steven's sick."

"So, it's a martyr thing?" he asked.

"No," I said defensively. "We've been together twelve years. Don't you think I owe him something?"

"I see," he nodded, "it's a loyalty thing."

"No, I—"

"A pity thing, then?"

"I—"

He took my hand between his and said, "I'm sorry. I've got no right to say that to you. I don't know you that well."

"It's okay," I said.

"I just think you're a pretty terrific person yourself, and you shouldn't stop living. How does that help either of you?"

"I know what you're saying makes sense," I said, "but how do you walk out on someone you care about who's dying?"

"He needs to take care of himself," he said. "You can't do it for him. Believe me, I went through it with my Dad. I know how hard it is."

The lights dimmed suddenly and the sound kicked on with an advertisement for the theater. It urged us to "Sit back. Relax. Enjoy the show." I sat there in front of the flickering screen, seeing nothing. I kept hearing Dean's words: "So, it's a martyr thing?" *Is that really what it was?*

Suddenly, I could see Steven and Pop as two parts of a single entity, making me feel guilty for wanting my own happiness, telling me how selfish I was to think of myself. Was Dean right?

When I headed home that evening, my head was still spinning from our conversation. I stopped in the hallway, took a deep breath, and exhaled slowly as I pulled the key from my pocket and slipped it into the lock. I remember thinking how tarnished the brass door knob looked and making a mental note to call the maintenance desk in the morning. When I heard the phone start to ring, I flung open the door and gashed my finger on the jagged edge of the key.

I picked up the phone as I noticed my blood smeared on the door, and heard Rosalia's voice telling me that Pop had suffered a heart attack.

CHAPTER 14

Consequences

Chicago: November 1994

So it was that, in November of 1994, after finally confronting Steven about his infidelities, I emerged dripping wet from the shower and—for the first time in months—felt a sense of peace. Not a peace borne of happiness, but a sense that the storm had blown itself out, and I had somehow survived: a peaceful, leaden exhaustion following strenuous exertion. Steven left without a word while I was in the shower, as I had expected he would, in light of our fight. What did we have left to say to each other, now that every wound had been opened, every scab exposed? I felt like I was wading in neck-deep water, slowed to near immobility. Our relationship had irretrievably broken down, but where did we, each of us on his own, go from here? How the hell would I face everything alone? And what the hell was wrong with me anyhow, that I couldn't seem to connect with anyone? I wondered if Pop felt as remote and isolated as I did at this moment.

I toweled off and stood in front of the steamy bathroom mirror. I looked the same as before our fight and yet, I felt changed. My hair had gotten long, I realized suddenly. I had been so distracted by my misery lately that I had neglected everything. I pulled a pair of scissors from the bathroom cabinet and started clipping away at my hair. I felt the weight of it falling away as I carefully dropped each severed lock into the trash can beside the toilet. My hair was still wet, and it squeaked when my fingers slipped over it. Finally satisfied, I wiped the loose hair from the scissors and set them back in the cabinet. I snatched the brush from the counter and ran it through my hair. Then, I took a step back and looked up in the mirror. I felt less encumbered, lighter.

I switched off the bathroom light and headed into the bedroom to dress. I opened the window and felt the cool November air on my skin. With the window open, the bedroom, too, seemed suddenly lighter, the way it did in spring when I opened the windows for the first time in months. Ma always said you should open a window now and then, even when it was cold outside, to blow the stink off. I inhaled deeply. The air smelled like fall: crisp and invigorating. I pulled on a pair of jeans, a white banded-collar shirt, and looked at myself again in the mirror. I looked comfortable and relaxed. *Why don't we look like who we really are? If we did, Steven and I would never have connected. He would have looked like a slut and I would have looked like a loser. We would have walked right past each other, without even a second glance.*

I glimpsed the pictures on the dresser. In one, Steven and I stood in our kitchen on a New Year's Eve several years ago. Steven looked so happy in the picture and yet, I remembered how angry I had been that Steven had gotten plastered, puked, and gone to bed before midnight arrived. In another, Steven wore a suit and tie, looking so young and handsome I wanted to cry. The picture had been taken shortly after we had moved in together, and Steven had put on one of my suits. Another photo was of me standing on the beach in Waikiki nearly a dozen years ago. I wore a blue-and-black Speedo, and the hair on my chest looked dark and full in the photo. But the expression on my face, I noticed now for the first time, seemed distant and sad. Steven always complained that I never smiled in any of my pictures. I insisted that I just wasn't photogenic, but now I could see the camera had revealed what I didn't even know myself, at the time: I was unhappy, and it showed. *Why had it taken me so long to see it?*

I finished dressing and walked out into our living room and looked around the room. It looked beautiful: peaceful, and everything in its place. Even our super-clean, neat-as-a-pin apartment was a disguise, completely obscuring the deep gashes and cracks in our relationship. I walked over to the coffee table and pushed the stacked magazines onto the floor. *I need a little less organization in my life*, I thought. I fought off the absurd urge to pick them back up, grabbed my jacket, and hurried outside.

The day looked the way I felt: overcast, grey, and a little blustery. I flung out my arms and reveled in it. My head throbbed, a hangover from the drinking I had done the night before. But it was good to be alive, good to know I could, and would, survive without Steven—good to have taken a step, even if I didn't know toward what. I suddenly flashed on a childhood image from "Wild Kingdom." Jim and Marlon had just released an antelope back into the wild. Instead of bolting away, the animal took several timid steps, as if it was a little afraid to go. Suddenly seeming to awaken fully, it blinked and briefly gauged its new surroundings, then darted into the brush. I felt the hesitation of leaving the false security I'd known for the last dozen years, but I was excited about the possibilities ahead of me.

I pulled my collar up against the wind as I walked past the wildflower garden, now filled with dead stalks and dried flowers. The birds and squirrels had moved on, too. I was the only visitor on this forbidding autumn day. I felt like I was always going against the grain, always taking the most difficult path. I didn't understand the first thing about myself. Steven was right last night: I *was* just like Pop. Whenever Steven upset me, I had threatened to break up with him, implicitly threatening to take away his lifestyle, his home, and his stability. I wondered if Steven had ever really felt stable with me, or if he'd ever truly loved me. Probably not. I felt empty, and alone.

I reached the far end of the park and headed east, crossing Lake Shore Drive and walking the path along the lakefront. I trudged up the incline that curved around Monroe Harbor and sat on the brown grass, looking at the quiet, cold harbor in front of me. The wind whipped up waves and spray on the dark water. Even though the road was just a few yards behind me, the street noises were shielded from this protected valley around the harbor. The only sound was from a single seagull standing on the boat deck nearby. His cry was as lonely and empty as I felt.

I remembered coming here nearly six months ago with Dean. That was the last time we saw each other. *Jesus*, I thought, *had it really been six months already?* It had been spring then. The harbor had been filled with sailboats, children running, and beautiful

men throwing Frisbees. I recalled the invigorating smell of freshly cut grass in my nostrils and the hurt on Dean's face.

"I'm dropping out of the program," I said.

"What?" he had asked, clearly surprised by my sudden decision. "Why?"

"I have to," I said, watching a sailboat in the harbor. "I just
have to."

"But you love the program," he protested. "You're the best
writer in the class. Why would you want to drop out now?
What's going on?"

"It's not the program," I admitted, the tears starting despite
my attempts to stop them. "I feel like I'm using the program to
cheat on Steven."

"Are you talking about us?" he asked, and I nodded. "But
we're just friends. I thought you said you could use a friend?"

"I did," I said, starting to weep. "I could."

"Then, why do this?" he asked, putting his arms around me.
I could see tears in his eyes, too, and I felt sickened at the thought
that I was the one causing him pain.

"Because," I sobbed, "I can't *just* be your friend. It's too hard."

"What are you saying?" he asked, leaning back to look me
straight in the face. I could feel his sweet breath on my face. I
hardly noticed all the activity and people around us.

"I mean I'm falling in love with you," I blurted in between
sobs. "How couldn't I? You're the best man I've ever met." I
wiped my tears on the back of my hand. "But I have a lover already. I can't do this to him. Or to you."

Dean, looking stunned, sat back on the grass.

"I'm really sorry," I continued before he could say anything. "I just can't cope with everything. Remember, I told you my father had a massive heart attack last month and I flew down there to see him?"

He nodded.

"Well, when I got there, we had a horrible fight. Now, it's worse than ever between us. I just can't deal with him and Steven and you, too. Please, tell me you understand and don't hate me."

"I could never hate you," he said.

"Then, don't fight me on this, Dean," I said urgently. "I swear, I'll have a breakdown or something if I have to cope with all of this right now. I can't do it." I burst into loud sobbing in spite of myself and continued repeating: "I can't do it. I just can't do it."

"Anthony?" Dean said quietly, after a short pause.

"What?" I asked, looking over at him. He looked so beautiful; I wanted nothing more than to take him in my arms and stay here with him forever.

"I think I'm in love with you, too."

I leapt to my feet when he said it and started crying again. Before he could stand up, I turned and raced away on the path, not looking back again.

Now, sitting in the same spot where I had left him that day, I felt the strong need to contact Dean again. He was my only real friend in Chicago, and I desperately needed someone to talk to. I rose quickly and headed home.

I held my breath as I dialed Dean's number. I was reaching out from deep water, reaching for Dean like a lifeline, exposing my-self completely.

"Hello," came his voice over the line, and I exhaled at last, suddenly unsure of what I should say. "Hello?" he repeated.

"Dean?" I managed timidly. What right did I have calling him after all this time?

"Yes," his voice said tentatively. "Who's this?"

"It's Anthony," I said, "from class. Uhhh, formerly from class."

"Anthony?" I detected surprise in his voice.

"Please don't hang up on me," I said quickly.

"I wouldn't hang up on you," he said evenly. "It's been a long time, and I'm a little surprised to hear from you."

"I'm a little surprised to be calling," I said, nervous sweat prickling my forehead. "How have you been?"

"I'm fine," he said, then bluntly asked, "Anthony, I don't mean to be rude, but what are you calling about?"

"Well, I wondered if—" I began and stopped. *What was I call-ing for? Why did I think he'd want to hear from me again, after that day by the harbor?*

"Yes?" he prompted. "What did you wonder?"

"I mean, I'd really like to talk to you. If you're willing to talk to me, that is." I blurted out rapid-fire, then waited for his response.

"I thought we couldn't be friends?" he asked after a long de-lay. "I'm a little hesitant to start down that path again, if you know what I mean."

"Of course," I said, realizing that I had missed my oppor-tunity with Dean. I began rambling. "I would understand com-pletely. But...."

"But what?" he demanded.

"But," I fumbled for words, flustered, "but things are...different now. Would you be willing to give me some time to explain it to you in person?"

"Maybe," he said, and I felt elated, then he took on a more serious tone. "Maybe not. It depends."

"On what?" I asked, hopes dashed and nervous again.

"On whether you're planning to run away again," he said, "cuz I just sent my track shoes to the cleaners and I can't be chasing after you in pumps."

"Jesus," I sighed happily. "You really had me scared."

"Good," he said. "Payback, you know: it's really hell."

"Yes, I know," I said. "And I deserve it, too. But, let's save that until I see you. How about dinner? And I've got two tickets to 'Hamlet' tonight. I know it's short notice but—"

"What time?" he asked.

I fidgeted impatiently as I waited for Dean to arrive. I had suggested the Italian restaurant we ate in the first time we went out to a movie together, not so long ago. Finally, I saw his dark hair and gentle face in the doorway. I waved at him, and a smile dimpled his cheeks as he made his way to the table. He wore blue Dockers and a red, cotton shirt under a brown suede jacket and looked full of life; I felt like a battery in need of recharging.

Tarantella

I stood and hugged him, hard, when he reached me. He hugged me back, smiled again and sat down, shrugging off his jacket without looking away.

"So what gives?" he asked, watching my face. "I've been wondering all day."

"I hardly know where to begin," I said.

"Start with what changed your mind about finally calling me," he said.

"I really needed someone I could talk to," I said, and he looked crestfallen. I started again, "I mean, I really needed to talk to you." He brightened and I continued, "I feel like my whole life has unspooled since the last time I saw you. Pop and I still aren't speaking. My sister is mad at me. My job has been stressful...."

"And Steven?" he interrupted.

"The shit's all hit the fan," I said crudely. "Steven and I are over, except for the details." He nodded solemnly and I continued, "I confronted him this morning."

"Confronted him about what?" he asked.

"About cheating on me," I said, and he looked stunned. "I caught him the day I came back from seeing Pop after his heart attack. Only he didn't know I saw him. Until this morning."

"Whoa!" he said. "How did that go?"

"Surprisingly maturely," I said. "Jesus, it's funny how things work out, isn't it? After I confronted him, he basically just accepted it and the fact that our relationship wasn't working— hasn't worked for a very long time. Maybe it never worked. I don't know."

"So what are you going to do now?" he asked.

I smiled and gestured at him, "I hope reconnecting with a friend is what I'm going to do now." He smiled and I felt happy. "How about you? What have you been up to?"

"Well," he said, "I'm still working on my master's. I hate my job more than ever. I've started writing my first play and, I'm afraid to say this, but I think it's turning out pretty good."

"That's great," I said. "Really great." What I really wanted to know was if he was dating anyone, but the waitress interrupted and I decided not to push. After all, I had pushed him away six months ago and had only just broken up with Steven. No sense getting ahead of myself, I decided.

During the play, I glanced at Dean beside me. I felt a strength in knowing that he wanted to be with me. Unlike my past relationships, I felt energized being with him, not depleted. Could the *right* relationship counteract the poison? Was it possible to know someone's weak spots and vulnerabilities, and love them anyhow? Was it possible to be stronger together? Dean looked up at me, and, just then, I believed it was possible.

After the play, Dean walked me back to my building. I thanked him for agreeing to come and reached out to shake his hand. He pushed my hand aside, leaned forward, and kissed me on the lips. Then, he backed away and started to leave. I watched him hail a cab, and he turned around suddenly.

Tarantella

"By the way," he called to me, "I'm *not* seeing anyone." He smiled broadly and climbed into the cab. Rolling down the window, he leaned out and shouted as the cab pulled away, "In case you were wondering."

The apartment was dark and silent when I got home. I switched on the light in the front hall and called Steven's name tentatively. When I got no answer, I roamed through the apartment, but Steven wasn't inside. I pulled off my coat and shoes and headed into the kitchen to make myself a cup of tea. Recalling the fight with Steven, my light mood drained away, and I quickly felt as dark as the air in the apartment. I turned the burner knob to high, filled the tea kettle with hot water, and set it on the burner. I grabbed my cup from the cabinet and turned to get a teabag out of the canister atop the refrigerator when I saw the note taped to the refrigerator door. Not ready to deal with any more from Steven just yet, I decided to wait until my tea was ready before reading it.

I opened and dropped a teabag into my cup, then twined the string and tag around the cup handle so it wouldn't fall in when I poured the water. I ripped open a pink packet of Sweet 'n Low and poured it into the cup as well. Finally, I leaned against the counter, facing into the kitchen. Even from across the room, I recognized Steven's unmistakable scrawl on the note. I drummed my fingers on the simulated wood counter until the tea kettle began whistling behind me. I turned and switched off the burner before pouring the boiling water into my cup. I leaned over and let the steam envelop my face like smoke. My glasses steamed over, and the room vanished in a damp haze that cleared again as soon as I leaned back. I untwined the string and dipped the teabag a few times before tossing it into the trash under the sink. I stirred the brew and took a first sip and let the heat warm me inside.

Finally, I reached for the note. It was very brief.

> *Anthony:*
> *You sister called. They rushed your father back to the hospital. Call her back asap.*
> *S.*
> *P.S. I got called into work. Be home late.*

Jesus, I thought, it's never what you're prepared for. I felt like I was ready for anything Steven threw at me, but I wasn't ready for Pop—not now. I couldn't take another round with him at the moment.

I carried my teacup into the living room and dialed Rosalia's number. She answered on the first ring.

"Hello," she said, her voice full of uncharacteristic tension.

"It's Anthony," I said. "What's up with Pop?"

"Can you get down here right away?" she asked.

"Jesus, Rosalia," I said, "Are we back on that track again? You know my feelings on this subject."

"Anthony. Stop!" she snapped. "I'm not back on any track." She took a long breath. "Pop's had another heart attack. It's bad. *Really* bad."

"How bad, Rose?" I felt my pulse quicken. *Had the day really come?*

Before she could answer, she started crying. I had never heard Rosalia cry. Even as kids, she was the strongest person I ever knew. When she spoke again, her voice quavered and caught after every couple of words.

"I think this might be it," she said between sobs. "He had a massive heart attack around ten tonight. They rushed him to Wuesthoff Hospital, and he had two more heart attacks in the Emergency Room."

"Jesus," I said. I should have been grief-stricken at confronting my own father's mortality, but I felt stone cold, devoid of emotion. It was like I needed someone to tell me how to feel.

"Ma's a wreck," she continued, regaining her composure. "She hasn't left his side since they brought him in, and they won't let her smoke, so you know she's going nuts. She's afraid he'll wake up and she won't be there." She blew her nose, then added, "I was there until after midnight. I called you as soon as I could."

"I just got in," I said. "I went out to dinner and a play—"

"You need to come right away," she interrupted.

"I don't know, Rose." *Jesus*, I thought, *the last thing I need right now is to go down and fight with Pop again.* Between the mess with

Steven and trying to reconnect with Dean, this was just what I didn't need. "Last time was a disaster."

"Christ, Anthony," she said, "aren't you listening? Pop's *dying*. This is it. You don't get another chance."

"I heard you," I said. "I've gotta think first. We haven't even spoken to each other in twelve years. Christ, what would I say to him?"

"Fuck you, Anthony," she snapped angrily. "Why are you such a selfish bastard? Why's it always all about *you*? Did it even occur to you that *I* might need you here? Or Ma?"

"I didn't mean..." I started. I had never heard Rosalia so angry.

"You never mean anything," she interrupted. "I don't give a fuck what you say to Pop. Just get down here. Now! And not just for Pop. For *you*. And for the family. We should all be together right now."

"It's too late to do anything tonight," I said finally. "But I'll check on flights and call you back in the morning."

"You do that, Anthony," she said. "I'll be waiting. Don't let Pop go without saying goodbye." The line went dead in my hand.

I walked back to the kitchen and leaned against the counter, cradling my tea cup—still warm—in both hands. The apartment seemed so peaceful. It was hard to imagine that Pop was dying at this very moment. It felt like a scene in a book: a fiction, an untruth that you can read and imagine and disregard because it's not real. But this was real, and I knew I should feel something. Anything. Instead, I just felt numb.

Jesus, I thought, *what am I going to do? If I go home, Pop will have won—I'll be the one who cracked first. And, if I don't go and Pop dies, would Rosalia ever forgive me? Or Ma? How could I live with myself?* I felt like I was between Scylla and Charybdis.

I poured the rest of my tea down the sink and loaded the cup into the dishwasher. The clock on the wall over the stove read nearly 1 a.m., and I decided to leave my decision to the morning. I turned out the light and picked my way carefully to the bedroom.

While I brushed my teeth, I replayed the call with Rosalia. Why was she so pissed at me? Pop's heart attack wasn't my fault. Was she taking Pop's side? Had she forgotten what he was like and what he had done in the past? I refused to absolve him of everything simply because he was sick. The past had happened; I would never be able to forget it. Even Pop's death couldn't make it go away. Pop had destroyed my self-confidence, my hope for a healthy relationship, my ability to forgive. He refused to accept me or my lifestyle. Even if he was dying, how could I just forgive and forget now? Steven had shown me that sickness excused nothing: even the sick should be held accountable for the bad things they do. Making allowances and letting things slide only made things worse. It had been true with Steven; it was true now with Pop. I couldn't simply disregard everything Pop had said and done for the last thirty-five years—all the hurt and damage he'd inflicted; all the slights and slurs he'd flung at me; all the venom he'd spewed. I hated to disappoint Rosalia, but I didn't see how I could go home now. How could I accede to this new tyranny of Pop's illness?

I returned to the bedroom and peeled off my clothes, dropping them in a heap beside the bed. I drew the blinds open and let the soft, halogen-yellow glow of the streetlights below seep up into the room. A gentle snow fell outside and, after I set my glasses on the night stand beside the bed, I rolled onto my belly, crossing my arms over my pillow and resting my chin on top of my arms. Without my glasses, the night became a vast, yellow-white blur swaying gently before me. Memories of Pop flooded back, swirling through my head like the snow falling outside. I thought I had locked them all away, but now they came flooding back.

I remembered the day Pop caught me watching television and sucking my thumb. He had yanked my thumb from my mouth.

"You're too old to suck your goddamned thumb," he'd said, his voice flat and even. I was seven at the time. I could still visualize his ink-spotted, white hand—speckled and almost translucent, like a bird's egg—clasping my wrist and holding my hand away from my mouth, holding it so my thumb seemed suspended in space, isolated, as if it might infect us both. I tried to escape his grip, but couldn't.

Pop merely squeezed tighter and his fingernails cut into my wrist like four crescent moons that turned red with blood. I remember my shock at the sight of my blood. I struggled, begging him to let me go. Pop saw the blood, too, and looked surprised. He flung my wrist from his grip like he was pitching manure.

Tarantella

"Don't be a sissy," he said. It was the first time he called me a sissy. There would be many more times after that. "Only sissy-boys suck their thumbs. It's time you grow up."

In bed, nearly thirty years later, I rubbed my wrist reflexively. The four crescent moons from Pop's fingernails had long-since scarred over, leaving behind four raised white arcs like little Braille hieroglyphs on my wrist. Were we, all of us, so marked by our histories?

The sun was streaming onto the bed when I awoke the next morning. I felt warm and cozy, but outside, it was still late-November and cold. The events of the last day rattled through my brain, and I felt overloaded and immobilized. I was alone: Steven hadn't come home last night. Dean must be lying in his own bed—I wished he was here beside me right now. Wishes mean nothing, I thought. Actions counted. Actions.

Pop was in a hospital bed in Florida right now. Maybe he was feeling the same sun on his skin—his translucent, white skin. Maybe he was sorry for what he had done to me, to Paddy, to Rosalia. Maybe he didn't know how to fix the past any more than I did. Maybe he didn't know how to take away the pain. Maybe he didn't know his impact on me. Maybe he didn't mean to cause pain and damage. Maybe it was all just the fallout of a foolish, insensitive man. Maybe he meant well—I had continued to suck my thumb for another year until I got caught by a classmate and became the object of ridicule all over school ("Here comes Thumbsucker, now!"). Pop didn't know shit about tact, but he understood a few things. Much as I hated to admit it, he'd been right about a great many things. Only, he had tackled them so tactlessly that he caused needless pain and suffering. Even when I knew he was right, I resisted because it felt like I was losing at something.

How could I rush back to Florida? Now, when I was finally starting to pull the pieces together and take command of my own life? This thing between me and Pop was not over. If I plunged back in with Pop now, I might never again find my way back to myself. No, surely: now—just when I felt like I was finally beginning to heal—was not the time to run back to Florida. Wasn't now the time to keep my distance?

I sat up and braced myself when the phone rang again. I knew it would be Rosalia. I let the phone ring twice more as I steeled myself for the argument I knew was coming.

"Hello?" I said tentatively.

"Anthony," Rosalia said impatiently.

"Yes, Rose. It's me." I replied.

"I had a feeling you'd still be in Chicago," she said matter-of-factly.

"I just can't do it, Rose," I said. "But that doesn't mean I'm not thinking about him. Will you please tell Pop something for me?"

"I won't be telling Pop anything, Anthony," she snapped, and began weeping. "Pop died a few minutes ago."

"Jesus," I gasped and leaned against the kitchen counter. My mind reeled and dizziness swept over me. "Oh, Jesus."

"His heart just stopped, and he was gone. Me and Ma were with him."

"I don't know what to say, Rosalia," I managed, surprised by the tears that were flowing down my cheeks. "I'm sorry you had to deal with Ma and Pop by yourself."

"Anthony," Rosalia said after a minute, "we still need you down here, Ma and me. Pop's gone, so, *please*, come down now. It's time you came home. Tell me you will." "Okay, Rose," I consented finally. "I'll be there as soon as I can."

I sat in the middle of my living room after I hung up the phone. Pop was dead: the unimaginable had happened and now, I had agreed to fly back to Florida to help bury this man, this stranger whom I had never really understood, but whom I resembled as closely as a reflection in a mirror. After managing to book an afternoon flight, I threw some clothes in a suitcase and called my office to let them know.

Next, I left a note for Steven.

Steven—My father died this morning. I'm flying down for his funeral and won't be back for a few days. I want you to know that I still love you, but I think we both know it's time for us to move on and get our own places. Think about what you want, and we can resolve things when I get back....Anthony

Then, I called Dean. He wasn't home, so I left a message on his voicemail.

"Dean. It's Anthony," I began. "Thank you for last night. You can't imagine how much it meant to me. I am leaving for Florida in a few minutes. My father died this morning, and I'm flying down for his funeral. I'll call you when I get a chance. I'll count the hours until I get back. I'd really like to see you again."

On the plane, heading to Florida, I could hear the strains of "Danny Boy" playing over and over in my head. Pop had been a stubborn, old Irishman. He rarely talked about his own family, and I knew little about them. Pop had been an only son, and his mother and father had passed away before I was born. Pop said his family had been "black Irish," apparently the dregs of Irish society. I knew Pop enlisted in the Navy and served in the Pacific near the end of World War II. Unlike the vets who came back and relived their war glories for the rest of their lives, Pop came home and never spoke about his naval experiences. He put himself through accounting school on the VA Bill. A year later, he and Ma married. Paddy wasn't born until six years later. I was born seven years after that, followed by Rosalia two years after me.

By the time he died, Pop had lost both of his sons and had turned into a bitter, angry, old Irishman. He never did anything quietly. He refused to be ignored. He demanded what he wanted and took no shit from anyone. Yet, Pop lived with one woman for nearly fifty years, and I had no doubt in my mind that he was faithful to Ma every day of those fifty years. Why, then, was Pop so unable to express his feelings? Why had he been so closed off from his own children?

What was the lesson I could learn from Pop? I considered my own life. I had lived my life in Pop's shadow. I had made the most important decisions of my life based on what would aggravate Pop the most. My anger and hurt had cost me the very thing I fought hardest for: my independence. I had let my rebellion against Pop consume me. Now, Pop was gone, but I still felt the pain and rejection. To heal, I knew I had to change the past somehow. Without the villain in my life, I felt empty and lost; purposeless. I needed to find a new, *productive* goal. I was still behaving like a petulant child. It was time to grow up.

My anger and pain weren't serving me anymore. As a child, they had shielded me and given me purpose. As an adult, they were holding me back. It was time to stop meeting the expectations of my parents, or my lover. I had to stop trying to do what others wanted of me—or rebelling against them.

Had that been the lesson Pop had been trying to teach me? All this time, had he been trying to goad me into being my own person? Into carving out a life of my own? Jesus! I had been so consumed by despising the man that I had missed it. Pop had not rejected me because I was gay, but because I was so unsure of myself. Pop had always seen through the bullshit, and my entire life had been bullshit. Time and again, I had run away from my life, instead of running toward the things I wanted. How had I let my life get so screwed up?

I looked out of the plane window and saw the lights of Orlando starting to appear below me. I was nearly home again, but this time, for the first time, Pop was not there. Home had changed irrevocably; something had snapped in me. I thought about Dean's words, cautioning me to change my relationship with Pop before it was too late. I had not understood. How could I change our relationship, if Pop wouldn't change? Except, *I* was the one who had been unable to change. I controlled the dynamics of my relationship with Pop—just as I controlled the dynamics of my relationship with Steven—just as I would control the dynamics of any future relationship with Dean. Pop was Pop. I could never control Pop. Or Steven. Or Dean. Only Anthony. In fact, even though I was the only one I *could* control, I had never done it.

The villain in my life was *me!* I had prevented myself from seeing things as they really were and getting on with my life. With sudden clarity, I understood that Pop and Ma were just two people trying to find their way through life, too. They were harsh and blunt and, sometimes, mean. And, just maybe, they *had* actually loved me, too.

As the plane rumbled to a landing and Florida loomed up around me, I did not dread the thought of going back to the island. In fact, I felt it beckoning to me. This was exactly where I needed to be right now. The tarantella I had begun dancing with Doughna Mira all those years ago was finally reaching its end.

CHAPTER 15

Homecoming

Merritt Island: November 1994

TODAY, I KNOW that burying your past isn't as simple as burying your father. Which is not to say that burying a father is nearly as simple as you imagine it will be before you're faced with the reality of actually doing it. I feel bruised—even my skin hurts. I want to cry; in fact, I keep *trying* to cry, but I can't. I feel completely empty.

Now, here I am, back where I vowed never again to set foot, back on Merritt Island, waiting for Ma and Rosalia to finish getting dressed, while seated in Pop's green sofa chair in the house where I grew up. So much shit happened inside these four walls. I wonder how in the hell any of us got through it? And then, of course, I remember that none of us has really gotten through it. Ma is alone for the first time in nearly fifty years. Paddy is still lost in the oak forest. I'm dealing with the mess I made of my life. Rosalia is trying to keep it all together. And Pop is dead.

A gray light seeps in through the sheers that still hang on the windows. Sounds are muted until I get up and tug open a window to move the musty air. I am an intruder here, where I once lived in fear of being swallowed up. Every shadow and fall of light jiggles loose another carefully stowed and almost-forgotten memory.

I run my hands across the green cushion on Pop's chair, rough and timeworn, and glance around the room. The objects in the house look like museum artifacts. I wonder how Ma will manage alone. How will Pop's death affect Rosalia? How will it affect me?

Perhaps we hold on to the residue of our lives because we're afraid to move from the known to the unknown, even if the known is filled with unhappiness. Perhaps we must first immerse ourselves in the absence before we can move on. Perhaps it is this hole in the fabric of our selves that finally enables us to heal, the way the hole in my chest finally did.

I feel strangely reluctant to let go of this childhood home, despite all the negative memories. I wonder if my strange attraction to this house echoes the feelings a soldier develops towards the battlefield on which he once fought: I am surprised to discover a warmth, a nostalgia toward this place I thought I hated so bitterly.

I smell orange blossoms in the air, their sweetly intoxicating scent drifting in through the open window, along with the sound of a lawn mower humming somewhere up the block. I think back to my beginnings in New York. It's like a block of ice in my memory: cold and white and gray. I remember forsythia bushes and stately oak trees, but the memories are tinged with dark shadows and pain. Mostly, I remember the pervasive cold that crawled beneath my skin and chilled me from the inside. It's how I feel now—like my insides are frozen; like my blood has turned as icy as the winter waters of Lake Ontario. My organs feel like stones at the bottom of the lake's green-black water, heavy and cold.

I remember when we first arrived in Florida. I rejoiced at the prospect of living in this paradise where it was never cold, where it was always beautiful and bright and warm. I remember the shock I felt when a cold front struck the Deep South with a hard freeze. I remember lying in my bed, listening to the terrifying sound of orange trees dying as their trunks froze and exploded like bombs. Pop's death was like that, too.

Rosalia enters, and even from across the room, I can see her eyes are red from crying. Yet she looks lovely, clad in a black dress with her brunette hair pulled back.

"Ma should be ready in a minute," she says and sits beside me on Pop's chair. She reaches out and brushes my hair back. "You look like him, you know."

"I know," I say, and I *do* know: I have known for a long time. I remember how startled I had been when, as a teenager, I found a photo of Pop as a teen. We were like twins born thirty-four years apart.

"He'd been failing for a long time," she says, looking into the distance. "He failed a little every day, and he knew it, too. One day, I realized that he was terrified by it all."

"Of dying?" I ask. It is hard to imagine Pop being afraid of anything.

"No. Not of dying," she says, shaking her head and turning to face me. "Of people. Of his family. Of us."

"Of *us?*" I ask, not understanding. "How could *we* terrify him?" Pop had always been self-assured, certain he was right about everything.

"Because he didn't understand us," she says. "And he knew we didn't understand him. That was the cause of his problems with all of us, you know."

"I'm not following you, Rose," I say.

"He tried to force us to be like him," she explains, "and the more like him we got, the more we frustrated him because we still didn't understand him. I think that's why you upset him the most."

"Me?" I pull my legs up under me. "Why me?"

"Because," she says, "he knew you were the *most* like him." She puts her arm around me. "That's why he fought with you so much. I've thought about this a lot, and it's the only explanation that makes sense."

"What explanation?" I ask, looking up at her. "I still don't understand what you're trying to tell me."

"Out of all of us, Pop expected *you* to understand him. When you didn't, he didn't know what to do. You threw him a curve when you told him you were gay and insisted he accept it immediately. How could you two be so much alike if you were gay? You confused him, and when he didn't accept it immediately, you pulled away, then moved away." She pauses and touches my cheek. "After that, he didn't know how to get you back."

"How'd you get to be such an expert on Pop? I thought you didn't understand him either?" But I know she's right.

"I didn't," she says. "I've just been trying to piece things together. It's like putting together a puzzle."

"Pop was definitely a puzzle," I agree and smile at her.

"I'm serious, Anthony," she says. "You weren't here. You didn't see him. After his first heart attack, he changed. I mean, not everything. A lot of little things. But big for Pop."

"Such as?" I ask.

"Like greeting me with a hug when I would stop over," she says. "And saying he loved me before ending a phone call." She pats my hand. "It's like that first heart attack took the orneriness outta him. He turned into this mellow, little, white-haired man who looked and sounded like Pop, only the 'George Bush version' of Pop. You know—kinder and gentler."

"Well, I'd have to see that to believe it," I say, smiling at her, but unable to imagine a kinder, gentler Pop. To me, the concept was an oxymoron.

"That's why I kept trying to get you to come down," she says. "I really believe you two finally could have made peace. And I felt like it was important to you both—to all of us—that there finally be peace in this family."

"Maybe so," I say. "But I can't help picturing the opposite scenario—you know, the ugly scene at the deathbed: Pop dying while cursing me, and me cursing him back." I stand and pull her to her feet and embrace her with a big bear hug. "Don't you see? I just couldn't chance it?"

"I *do* understand," she says. "But I think Pop would have surprised you this time. I think he was ready to make peace. I think he *wanted* you here. I really do."

A confusion of feelings sweep over me. "I can't picture Pop *wanting* me around. It's kind of hard to imagine." I had steeled myself against feeling guilty about not coming down before Pop died; now, Rosalia's words had me questioning myself.

"At the very end," she says, "he couldn't talk, but his eyes kept circling around the room. Like he was looking for something."

"Come on," I say, "I wasn't his only missing son."

"But that's the thing, Anthony," she says, taking me by the shoulders and holding me at arm's length. "You *were*. Paddy was there."

"Paddy came?" I'm incredulous. Stunned. "How did he even know?"

"Ma called him," she says and I wrinkle my brow dubiously. "Apparently, Ma and Pop have always known how to get in touch with Paddy, but never did. They hoped he'd contact *them* someday. When all this happened, Ma called Paddy to tell him Pop was dying. He showed up the morning Pop died."

"Wait a minute," I protest. "Paddy shows up after more than twenty years away, and you're just telling me now? And Ma and Pop knew where he was all this time and never told us? Is it just me, or does this all sound more than a little crazy? I'm sorry, Rose," I say. "I don't mean to jump on you. But you gotta admit this is a big shocker on top of everything else. I need a moment to absorb it."

I pause and consider that Paddy, my long-lost brother, has reemerged finally from the dark oak forest. "Will Paddy be at the funeral?" I ask at last.

"He said he'd be there. He's joining us for dinner afterward, too."

"What's he look like? What did he say?"

"He looks kind of like you, only older," she says. "And he didn't talk much. He was mostly silent. I'm hoping we get a chance to talk more today, after the funeral." She looked at the silver watch on her wrist. "I better go get Ma moving or we'll be late." She kisses me on the cheek and hugs me again. "You okay?"

I nod and she nods back, smiles, and heads down the hall to Ma's bedroom. I sit back down in Pop's chair as I mull over what she has just told me. My head is spinning, and I feel as dizzy as that day I danced the tarantella with Doughna Mira. If Paddy has really reemerged from the oak forest, that means I am the last of Pop's children who is still lost.

I hear Ma and Rosalia coming down the hall. Pop's funeral is barely an hour away. I press deep into Pop's chair, feeling the softness of the cushion under me. I feel like I'm intruding some-how in this place that once was my home. All the knick-knacks above the bar remain exactly as I remember them, as I conjured them hundreds of times in my mind in Chicago. The room smells faintly of the musty odor of stale cigarette smoke. The scent has long since worked its way into the walls and settled on the furniture and the carpeting like a glaze.

Ma breezes into the room. She's dressed all in black, and her auburn hair blazes down her back. Rosalia, beside her, looks like her younger sister. I think about all the generations that have come before us, each a twin of the one before. Yet, not identical twins. We may look alike or sound alike or even act alike, but something is new, something is different in each of us. We are each our own unique being, composed of pieces from those around us, but adding unique characteristics of our own that make us individuals. I think about how families are strange, fluid things—bringing out the best and the worst in all of us. I'm surprised how contented I feel sitting here, in Pop's chair, just now, with my family around me.

"Anthony," Ma says. "I knew you'd come." She embraces and kisses me on both cheeks warmly, sadly. She crosses the room and seats herself at the large, wood organ in the corner. Rosalia stands behind her, resting her hands on Ma's shoulders. I'm startled when Ma begins to play the opening bars of "Ave Maria" and surprised to hear how good she is. Never in all my life did Ma ever indicate an interest in music. When, I now wonder, did she learn to play the organ? I can see the yellow nicotine stains on her fingernails and on the flesh between her index and forefinger. I cross the room to stand beside Rosalia, behind Ma. I think I can smell the faint odor of bread-yeast on Ma's skin and feel a rush of warmth. I swear I feel Doughna in the room with us.

Ma's tiny, olive fingers hover over the organ keys and, with each touch, the gentle tones of "Ave Maria" wash over the room.

Tarantella

She looks so frail, barely a hundred pounds of her, feet barely touching the pedals. She sways back and forth as she plays and she begins to sing the words in Italian. Her cheeks swell with each intake of breath, and her expression shifts as fluidly as the music. Unlike the mellifluous organ tones, her voice sounds gravelly and pained, as if scraping her throat on the way out. She seems happy and, in fact, I feel certain she *is* happy playing the organ.

The music stops suddenly and Ma walks over to Pop's chair. She clasps her hands in front of her and turns to look at Rosalia and me with her big brown eyes. "Oh, Jesus, Mary, and Joseph!" she exclaims. "I can't believe he's really gone. I wish I had died first." She looks frantically around the room. "Where in the hell did I leave my goddamned cigarettes?" Then, spying them atop the organ, she crosses the room again and taps a cigarette out of the pack and inserts it between her pursed lips. From her tiny silver purse, she pulls a silver lighter with a clear plastic base and what look like little minnows swimming in the lighter fluid inside it, flips back its cover, and snaps up a flame. She lights her cigarette and sets the lighter atop the cigarette pack. Then, she sits back on the bench, crosses her legs, and turns to face me.

"I knew you'd come home," she says firmly, inhaling deeply on her cigarette.

I look at Rosalia and say, "I'm not sure how you knew, Ma, because I didn't know myself. But here I am."

"Yes," she agrees, nodding. "Here you are." She flicks the ashes from her cigarette.

Rosalia looks at me and says, "I'm gonna go call the church to make sure everything's on schedule." I make a face at her for abandoning me. She grins at me and scuttles out of the room.

"We should probably get going, Ma," I try. "We don't want to be late."

"In a minute, Anthony," Ma says, not moving. "I have something to say to you first."

I feel like a child about to be scolded. I can't imagine what Ma will say, but I feel nervous nevertheless.

"I keep expecting your father to walk into the room," she says suddenly, crushing her cigarette into the ashtray. "I can't believe he's really gone."

"Me either," I admit. "I guess I never believed he'd be gone one day." I walk over and sit beside her on the bench. "Who will I have to fight with now?" I grin at her.

"I won't miss *that*," Ma says looking up at me. "Jesus, sometimes I just wanted to knock *both* your heads together. I never saw two such stubborn men in my whole life."

"That we were," I agree, nodding. "I guess I just wanted him to say—once—that he was proud of me, that I did something well."

"Oh, Jesus," Ma says. "He was *so* proud of you! He used to tell everyone, 'Anthony's gonna be somebody someday.'"

I'm so startled by her words, I don't know what to say. "Then, why was he always such a bastard to me?" I ask, incredulous.

"You don't even know what a bastard is, Anthony," she says. "You could have had a father who drank every day and screamed at you. Or a father who greeted you at the front door with a smack and said, 'That's for doing nothing. Imagine what you'll get if you *do* something!' Or, a father who pulled you out of school just months before graduation to work on a farm. That's the kind of bastard *I* grew up with.

"But *your* father was never a bastard, Anthony," she insists. "Your father thought you needed to be tougher. I know he overdid it. A lot of times, he was just kidding with you, but you'd get all upset and start fighting with him. You were *so* sensitive that, sometimes, it was hard to know the right thing to do around you."

"I was sensitive because he was always picking on me," I say. "It was a little hard to distinguish when he was joking from when he was serious because they felt the same to me." I refuse to accept anything that excuses Pop's inexcusable behavior. "Seems a bit clichéd to say Pop was a bastard for my own good. After I got older and it was obvious that it was driving us apart, why didn't he stop?"

"I don't know," she admits, resignedly. "I think, by that time, he didn't know how to change. Besides, by then, you were always ready to argue with him, so he never got a chance."

"No, Ma," I say, emphatically. "I don't accept that. I won't. Pop was a grown man and I was just a stupid kid. What Pop did amounted to abuse. Pop abused me."

"Let's not exaggerate now, Anthony," Ma says, scolding me. "He was a good father."

"He was a shitty father," I snap at her. "Maybe he was a good husband. Only you can answer that one. But he was definitely a shitty father. And, I'm sorry to say, I'm not gonna cry or get sentimental now about him being gone."

"Don't say that, Anthony," she pleads. "Your father always loved you."

"Yeah? Maybe, but I never knew it. What good did it do me? I always thought Pop despised me. That he considered me a total failure." I am surprised by my sense of outrage at the prospect that Pop loved me: believing Pop hated me seems preferable to thinking he might have loved me, but never expressed it.

"He was proud of you," she insists. "He loved you. Of course, he loved you. We *both* did."

"I'm sorry, Ma, but this is something I may never accept," I say finally.

"Why can't you just let it go?" she asks in frustration. "Why must you hold onto so much anger? Today is your father's funeral, for God's sake. You should be there out of love and respect for him."

"You're a fine one to lecture me about forgiveness, Ma," I say. "You spat on *your* father at his funeral. You *still* hate him. Isn't it a little hypocritical for you to tell me I should let it go where Pop is concerned when you've never let it go for your own father?"

"That was very different," she insists. "That bastard beat me. He was cruel and heartless."

"My father beat me with *words*," I say. "And he was cruel and heartless."

"If that's true," she asks, "then why *are* you here?"

"I'm here for Rosalia," I say. "And for you, and for Paddy. And for myself. But I'm *not* here for Pop—it's too late for him."

"How about me, Anthony?" she asks, looking me right in the eyes. "Is it too late for me?"

"I don't know, Ma," I say honestly. "I suppose as long as we're both still here and breathing, anything's possible. But, just now, I don't really know."

A long minute ticks by and we say nothing further to each other.

"Well, then," Ma says at last, slipping the pack of cigarettes into her tiny silver purse. She stands and turns around in front of me as if the last exchange never occurred and asks, "How do I look?"

I look her up and down and smile, setting aside my hurt feelings. For a moment, she's my beautiful mother: tiny as a doll dressed all in black with her auburn hair cascading down her back. Her soft brown eyes look a little swollen and red from crying. I can't ever recall Ma crying before. I have no memories of anyone in my family ever crying. Only me. Always me. But, today, *I* have no tears.

"You look beautiful," I say in all sincerity, and Ma smiles and smooths the fabric of her dress.

"I better go get Rosalia, so we can head to the church," she says at last, and walks slowly towards the kitchen.

I sit there, rocking slightly in place.

As we climb into my rental car, I scan Pop's yard. The palms he planted when I was a boy tower over the little aquamarine house, dwarfing it. It's the most beautiful yard on the street—a palm oasis, really. Unexpectedly, I feel proud. I back out of the driveway, pausing to look again briefly before pulling away.

"Jesus," Ma shrieks and points. "What's that?"

On the driveway, there's a dark shape and a smear of brilliant red blood. I shift the car into "park" and climb out to look. When I get closer, I recognize the crushed shape of a snake. Somewhere in my head I remember a voice saying that snake blood turns black and stains in the heat. I figure I better clean it up, so I hold up two fingers to indicate to Ma and Rosalia that I'll just be two minutes.

I head to Pop's shed and return with his shovel, scooping up the limp form and carrying it to the curb, where I drop it into the sewer drain. Despite my fear of snakes, it seems small and harmless in death. I wonder if it was poisonous as I wipe the blood from the shovel before putting it away. When I return, Rosalia is sitting on the hood and Ma is hunched in the front seat, window rolled open, smoking a cigarette.

"Jesus," Ma says, peering nervously from the window to twitch the ash from her cigarette. "Where in the hell did that come from?"

"Must've been hiding in the shade under the car," I say, calmly unwinding the hose and washing the blood off the drive. Another minute, and I'm turning off the water and rewinding the hose on the reel.

Glancing back as we finally get underway, I notice how the morning sun strikes Pop's rock garden. It's ablaze with light. I glance over at Ma and Rosalia and, although I know we're headed to Pop's funeral, I feel a little lighter somehow. It may be November but, suddenly, it feels like spring.

Heading into Divine Mercy, I walk between Rosalia and Ma and, again, notice their uncanny resemblance. I spot a man already seated in the first pew. He looks like a younger version of Pop, or a slightly older version of me: Paddy.

I feel goose bumps rise on my legs and arms as I, at last, face this specter that has haunted my entire life. I reach the pew, and Paddy stands and greets Ma and Rosalia with a kiss. As they sit, Paddy turns to regard me for a moment before reaching out to shake my hand tentatively.

"Anthony?" he asks in a voice that sounds like Pop's. "I'm your brother, Patrick."

I extend my hand automatically and shake his, all the while gaping at him. Silver-gray hair frames his very Irish features, and laugh lines crease his cheeks when he smiles.

"I'm Anthony," I say stupidly and redundantly, just as the organist plays the opening notes of Pop's funeral music. Paddy and I turn in unison as the rest of the congregation noisily rises to attention as the priest enters. To one side of the altar, the casket rests, square and dark and impassive. The lid is open, and I can see Pop lying there, impossibly still, his skin nearly as white as his hair. I catch my breath and expect him to sit up at any moment. But he doesn't move. Relatives and family friends, who have been filing past Pop's casket, return to their seats and fall silent, waiting expectantly.

The priest begins the service, and the whole scene drops away as I flash back again on the tarantella I danced with Doughna Mira before leaving the island twelve years ago. I watch the faces around me as the High Mass unfolds like a strange and studied dance. At one point, everyone turns to greet his or her neighbors. I shake hands with Rosalia on my left and the stranger on my right—the stranger who is my brother, Patrick. I smile, nod, kneel, and stand, as appropriate. I do all the steps to this dance, but comprehend none of it.

Then, I find myself following Paddy from our pew.

At the altar, I mouth the words, "Bless me, Father" automatically. The priest, who I suddenly recognize as Father James, responds by placing a communion wafer on my tongue and tipping the chalice against my lips. His hair is now white and wrinkles line his face, but he is still strikingly handsome. Yet, today, I see him only as a kindly pastor. I swallow the wine and wafer, but taste nothing.

I follow Paddy past Pop's casket to pay our final respects. I again recall how Ma spat on her father at his funeral. I know I can't follow her example. Six months ago, after Pop's first heart attack, I had imagined this day. Yet, nothing is as I imagined it. I see Paddy kneel in front of Pop's casket and I swear he has tears in his eyes.

Suddenly, I am standing in front of the casket, too. All I can do is stare. Unlike in life, Pop looks peaceful, lying with his hands clasped across his stomach, his glasses perched uselessly on his nose. He seems small and harmless, like a puppet with no hand to animate him. *Is this the man I feared so much? When did he become so small? So frail? When did he transform from the monster I remember into just a man?*

Again, I flash back on Rosalia's wedding and the way Doughna laughed as she swayed and dipped to the tarantella with me. I see Ma and Pop dancing beside us, and they're also laughing. Without meaning to, or even realizing it, I'm laughing too.

I've been waiting my whole life for the resolution to that dance. Suddenly, I understand that the poison never really goes away; if we're lucky, life teaches us to channel and neutralize it. The resolution is something we must each find for ourselves. This is the lesson Doughna Mira had been trying to teach me: the true message of the Tarantella. The mysterious Sichilian magic is finally working.

Unexpectedly, my laughter stops and I burst into tears. My sobs echo around and up the pyramid. I am surprised by the sadness I feel; yet, I am not sorrowful. Rosalia grasps my shoulders from behind and steers me back to our pew.

Finally, we stand as the casket wheels past our pew, and follow it down the aisle and out of the church. I feel like I'm in a dream, moving without thinking, hearing without understanding.

When I step outside, the November air feels cool. If I were still in Chicago, the rumpled, overcast sky would presage snow. But I'm in Florida again, watching as Pop's casket is loaded into a steel-gray hearse. Ma, Rosalia, Paddy, and I are escorted to a limousine and we follow the hearse to Graceland Cemetery.

The ceremony at the cemetery is brief and the casket is closed now: Pop is nowhere in sight. There is only a big, square, reddish-brown, shiny, walnut box that I touch with my hand before laying a white rose atop it. One by one, everyone present places a rose atop the casket and slowly walks away again, glancing back repeatedly.

I stare back at Pop's casket as our limo pulls away, watching until the shrubs that line the cemetery block it from sight. I wonder why we've created traditions that leave us with final memories of our loved ones in boxes.

But, hadn't I always put Pop in a box? The more I turned him into a monster, the more easily I could dismiss him. In turn, Pop kept me in a box of my own, which I have not yet escaped. The more we both stayed in our boxes, the safer we felt. We could both smugly write the other off and get on with our own lives.

Ironically, Pop's death has forced open our boxes. I am starting to question my memories, to see Pop in new ways, to recognize the box I have put myself into has *not* made me safer; it has held me back. I must release Pop from his box. I must also escape the box I have put myself into.

CHAPTER 16

Family

Merritt Island: November 1994

THAT EVENING, AFTER the relatives leave, the four of us sit down together for the first time and eat pasta dropped off by friends and family. In death, I muse, Pop has pulled his family together as he never could in life. I think about the ornery man who raised me, demanded the impossible from me, and never let up on me. I suspect Rosalia and Paddy are reliving their own, similar memories.

I wonder how different our recollections are. We all grew up together. Do we still have anything in common after all these years? Rosalia passes a pasta bowl splashed with a ribbon of scarlet sauce to me. I wonder if there will be anything to hold this family together after today.

"I remember I used to love funerals when I was a kid," I say, and Paddy looks at me like a ghost from my past. "I loved feeling surrounded by family and food and conversation." I shake my head. "Tonight, I couldn't wait for everyone to leave. I guess kids can overlook the sadness."

"Or maybe they just accept it," Paddy says. "As we grow up, I think we feel like we have to try to change things, even when we can't. I tried to change things by running away. But nothing ever really changed for me."

"How are things in Chicago?" Rosalia asks.

"Good and bad," I say. "Steven and I have broken up."

"I'm sorry," Rosalia says quickly. She looks startled. "I didn't know..."

"No," I say, touching her hand lightly. "Of course you didn't. It's okay. I'm fine. It's something I should've done years ago. It's been a long time coming, but it'll be better for both of us, I think."

"Well," Rosalia says, "it's still a tough thing to go through. I know. I'm still working through my own divorce."

"So," I say, turning to Paddy, "how about you? Have you done any better than us in the relationship department?"

"Guess not," he says quietly. "I'm divorced. Five years." He looks up, and I notice he has blue eyes like Pop. But Paddy's eyes are soft and pacific, not at all like Pop's icy, blue eyes.

"Do you still live in New York?" I ask.

"No," he says. "I've lived in Florida for years now. I moved to Daytona Beach only a few months after you moved to Merritt Island."

"You've been living only fifty miles away all these years?" I ask. I feel stunned and a little angry to think of Paddy living just around the corner all these years. From Rosalia's face, I can see that she's already been through this conversation and waits patiently as I catch up.

"Yup," he says, between mouthfuls of pasta. "Ironic, isn't it?"

"I'll say," I say. "What happened to you after you left?"

"I moved in with one of my friends and his family," he says. "They sort of adopted me for a while."

"I never told anyone I saw you leave, you know."

"I knew you wouldn't," he says, looking up at me.

"How come you never contacted me?" I ask. It's a question I've wondered about for twenty years. Why not contact the brother who watched you go, and kept your secret like a death-bed promise?

"I don't know," he says, poking at his pasta, looking uncomfortably at all three of us. "I guess I just didn't know what to say. I know that sounds lame, but it was, like, after I left, I couldn't figure out how to get back again." He sets his fork on the table and pauses for a moment, considering. "But then, it's not like any of you were beating down my door either."

"But we didn't know where you were," I protest.

"Ma and Pop knew. Most of the relatives knew," he says firmly. "People would have told you, if you had asked them." He turns toward Ma and asks, "Why didn't you try to bring me back home after I ran away?"

Ma looks reflective. "That was a long time ago," she dodges. "A lifetime ago."

"That's no answer, Ma," I say, refusing to let her off so easily. "How long have you known where Paddy was?"

"We always knew," she admits quietly. She looks straight at Paddy and says, "Your father said you'd come back when you were ready."

"Jesus," Paddy curses. "When you never tried to get in touch with me, I figured you really didn't *want* me around. After a while, I couldn't come up with an excuse for coming back. It just got harder and harder to find a reason to return."

"I know exactly what you mean," I interrupt. "After I moved to Chicago, I decided to try a simple test." I look right at Ma. "It was a stupid, childish test: I stopped calling and waited to see how long it would be before *you* called me. But the joke was on me because you *never* called. And the longer I waited, the harder it was to pick up that phone again."

"How could I call?" Ma asks. "How could I choose between my husband and my children? Seamus said you both had to live your own lives and, when you were ready, you would come back."

"Jesus, Ma," I say. "Pop was your husband, not your master. Pop was...a stubborn, old bastard; but I never understood your part in this."

"You just don't understand," she says.

"Then, explain it to us," I say.

Ma sets down her silverware and looks at all of us for a moment. She seems so frail. A walker rests behind her chair. "A wife stands by her husband," she says at last, "No matter what. That's what my mother did. And that's what I did."

"You are *not* Doughna Mira, Ma," I say flatly. "Times have changed, thank God. Today, you don't stand by a husband who abuses your children, Ma," I say. "You speak up. You tell him you won't put up with it. You tell him to go to hell."

"I didn't grow up today, Anthony," she says. "I grew up seventy years ago. When women *did* stand by their husbands. No matter what. And your father never hurt any of you. Ever. He was a good man. He just didn't understand you."

"Or how to be treat his children with respect and love," I add.

"Are all families this fucked up?" Rosalia asks.

"I guess you get the good-son prize," I say, turning to Paddy. "At least you got to say goodbye."

"I only came back because Pop was dying. It wasn't for love or any other noble reason," Paddy admits, and looks away. He looks back at us, and I can see the guilt on his face. "I'm embarrassed to admit that's why I came. But once I got here, I felt like I had to stay. I mean, Pop never said a word, but I couldn't leave." He looks over at me and adds, "I'm sorry you couldn't make it in time. Rosalia told us you couldn't find a flight out in time."

Rosalia looks at me. She covered for me, despite her own anger over my actions.

"Rosalia was protecting me," I say. It's time we all stop blowing smoke and running from the truth. "I *could* have come home when Rosalia called me," I admit. "But I was still pissed at Pop and chose *not* to."

"But you're here now," Rosalia interjects brightly.

"Yes," I say, turning to face her. "I *am* here now. But there's a lot of water under the bridge. I think we will all need some time to figure out where to go from here—I know *I* will."

"Try not to take *too* much time," Ma says, looking at me.

"It will take as long as it takes, Ma," I say. "I have thirty-five years to work through, so you need to give me time." I am not ready for Ma to make demands. Thirty-five years of poison has left behind a great deal of residue.

We are starting to feel more comfortable together, but it's a comfortable feeling that's hollow in the middle. At the end of the evening, as Paddy leaves, I wonder if I will see him again. Soon after, Rosalia heads home, too. I have decided to stay the night with Ma before catching my return flight in the morning. I kiss Rose's cheek and tell her, "It's time you come to see me in Chicago" and she agrees to come in the spring.

Ma and I sit down on the living room sofa: neither of us is ready to say goodnight yet. Ma drinks a late-night cup of coffee, while I sip hot tea. I will have to decide, soon, how Ma fits in my life. At the moment, I'm still unsure.

"I'm very glad you came back home," Ma says, then turns her head, as if looking for something.

"Are you looking for your cigarettes?" I ask. "I think I saw them in the kitchen."

"No," she says. "I was looking for your father. I find myself wondering where he is every now and then, until it comes back to me."

"It's gonna take a while, Ma," I say. "What will you do now?"

"I suppose I'll be following after your father before too long," she says wearily.

"Come on, Ma," I say. "Don't rush things."

She smiles at me and announces suddenly, "Well, here's one thing—I've decided to quit smoking."

"Since when?" I ask, stunned. I can't even picture Ma without a cigarette in her hand.

"Since today," she says. "Your father always wanted me to quit, but I never would. Just as stubborn as the rest of you, I guess. It was the one thing I had complete control over."

"So, why quit now?" I ask.

"I think it's time I make a few changes," she says. "Don't you?"

I nod, saying nothing. Ma eases back, scooping up her hair and dropping it across the back of the sofa like an auburn halo around her face. She sips on her coffee slowly and smiles quietly between sips. I pull my legs up in front of me and massage them absent-mindedly with my hands. Steam rises from my mug on the end table, beside me.

"Rosalia never mentioned your walker," I say. "When did you start using it?"

"It's only been a couple of weeks now," she says. "Rosalia didn't know until today either. I really only need it for balance. I hate relying on it, so I only use it when I'm home."

"Don't let your pride stop you from using it if you need it, Ma," I say. "The last thing you need is to lose your balance and fall and get hurt."

"I know," she admits, "But I need time to adjust, too. It's hard to admit you're getting old, Anthony."

"It's hard for this family to admit *anything*," I tease, then add: "But, I'm glad Rosalia will be staying with you for a while. That should be a big help. I'm sure it'll be hard adjusting to being alone in this house after so many years."

"You know, I don't really miss him yet. Is that wrong to say?" she asks. "It's just that it still feels like he's going to walk in that door any minute now."

"I understand, but he's not coming home again, Ma," I say. "Hard as it is, you need to get used to it. Pop's gone."

"I know that," Ma says. "But it just doesn't seem real yet."

"It doesn't seem real to me, either," I admit. "Pop has always been here: when I was born; when Paddy ran away; when we moved to Florida; when I went to college; when Rosalia got married; when I moved to Chicago. Pop was here every day of my life. Until now."

"None of us lasts forever, Anthony," Ma says. "We're just human, after all. Sometimes, we forget that."

"I hate to admit it," I say after a short pause, "but Pop and you were right about something."

"What's that?" Ma asks.

"Pop used to say Steven was all wrong for me. He was right about that." Even now, it's difficult for me to admit this.

"Your father was just angry because you moved away," Ma says.

"Yes, I remember," I say. "I also remember the first time I left the island to go to college. Do you remember that day, Ma?"

"Of course," she says. "Why?"

"As I was boarding the plane that day, I heard Pop say something to you about 'that dumb boy.' I have never forgotten it, even after all these years," I say, turning to watch her face.

"I remember it, too," Ma says, "only that's *not* what he said. He said, 'That's *some* boy!' You misunderstood him. He was so proud of you: the first of his kids to go off to college."

As soon as I hear her words, I recognize the truth of them. Replaying the scene in my head, I now see pride in Pop's face as he says the words. Once again, my memory has failed me. Once again, I spent years reacting to what was never said. I have much to work through to find my way to the life I want to live. For the second time today, I start weeping.

Ma pulls herself up with her walker and comes over to me. She gently places her brown, soft hand on my cheek and asks hopefully, "Do you think you'll ever move back to Florida?"

I fight back the tears and say, "No, Ma. My life is in Chicago now. I need to go back."

"Of course," she says. "You're right. You must live your own life."

"I'm working on it, Ma," I say, thinking—for the first time—how much she reminds me of Doughna Mira. "I'm done with running away. It's time I stay put and make my *own* place in this world, at last. I think it's the only way I'll ever be able to be happy."

She smiles at me and says, "Well, I'm beat. I think I'll head to bed now." She leans down and kisses my cheek. "Don't stay up too late, *mi precioso bambino*. I'll see you in the morning."

"See you in the morning, Ma," I say. I watch her shuffle to her room as I sip the last of my hot tea slowly. The heat feels good as it goes down, like it's cauterizing something.

Time is marching forward. The house is quiet. I think about how Ma must feel, losing her partner of fifty years; I can't imagine such loss. I think about Steven and Dean in Chicago: my past and—possibly—my future.

At last, I put my cup in the sink before turning out the dining room light. I stand there in the darkness for a moment, waiting for my eyes to adjust.

Where are you now, Pop? I wonder. Somehow, in our own ways, we have all reached the same destination. Some of our paths seemed enviably direct and easy, while other paths, like my own, seemed tortuous. I had to leave to find my way back. But our paths have converged again somehow.

I cautiously trace my way down the hallway to my child-hood bedroom. In the darkness of the hallway, I pause to listen again—straining, straining to discern the frenetic cadence of the tarantella.

But there is only silence.

Acknowledgements

SO MANY PEOPLE contributed so much to this book, I hardly know how to express my gratitude. You have all enrichened this book and my life immensely. Your support and constant encouragement have enabled me to get off my butt and finish this story, which has been idling in a state of near-completion for years.

First, I must thank my own family, who will likely recognize some of the events in this book, but not the characters or the details, which sprang from my imagination. Heartfelt thanks to the extended O'Hara and LaRocca family members who cheered me on over the years. Hugs and love to my siblings who never stopped pressuring me to get the book done: Connie, Brett, Ann, Norita, Gary, and Debbie. While my Mom and Dad have both passed on, they always believed I would one day publish my book. I know they are smiling in heaven to see it happen at last!

To the members of my Writers group and to the other writers who have read or attended readings and commented on earlier versions of this manuscript, you have helped me shape and find my voice. You have my undying appreciation: Judy Handschuh, Bobbi Ischinger, Denise Leveron, Brian Treglown, and Corney Wormely. Thanks also for the feedback and support from the fellow writers I met at the Iowa Summer Writing Festivals where I workshopped scenes from this book, especially: Denise Blomberg, Dawn Leger, Andrea Viggiano, and Terri Weston Willits Wiebenga.

To the published authors who agreed to read and provide comments about my book, I thank you for your positive encouragement and kind words: Michael Kiesow Moore (*What to Pray For*) and Rachel Hyde (*More Than We Know*).

To all of my instructors in the Fiction Writing MFA program at Columbia College Chicago, thank you for helping me listen for my voice and pay attention to the details that make scenes come alive. Special thanks to some especially instrumental influences: Randy Albers, Andy Allegretti, Ann Hemenway, D.R. Heineger, Shawn Shiflett, and John Schultz.

Thanks to Philip Dembinski for the terrific author photo.

Most importantly, thank you to Dale Boyer, my husband and partner in both life and creativity. You are my Dean, and you have made every day since we've been together special and loving. Thanks for supporting my work with your comments, edits, and encouragement since the day I met you!